a murder of
magpies

Sarah Bromley

Month9Books

Month9Books

For Tim. You don't scare easily. Thank God for you.

a murder of magpies

Sarah Bromley

One for sorrow, two for joy
Three for a girl, four for a boy
Five for silver, six for gold
And seven for a secret never to be told...
—"Magpie" English Nursery Rhyme

Glossary of Romani Terms

Bapo: grandfather

Baro: big man; the Romani tribal leader who is of great esteem

Dati: a term of endearment for one's father. *Dad* and *Dat* are commonly used for Father.

Drabarni: a Romani female herbalist, healer, and fortuneteller

Gadje: non-Romani; outsider (*Gadji* for female; *Gadjo* for male)

Hokano: trick; most often used as *hokano baro*, "the great trick"

Kris: Romani law court presided over by tribal elders

Melalo: dirty, usually from work

Rom: the all-encompassing description of Romani people, an ethnic group widely spread across parts of Europe and North America. Some call them "gypsies," which is considered a racial slur because it is thought to stem from the idea of them "gypping" people.

Vardo: a horse-drawn covered wagon for living.

Vitsa: the extended families that make up a Romani clan.

Chapter One

Vayda

Disaster came as a boy in a Catholic school uniform. That boy was my brother, Jonah.

We'd seen disaster, somehow crawled out from the ruins, and lived. It didn't just happen, all explosive and bombastic so we knew everything changed. A real disaster began with a spark of fire that rose in the air and snuffed out. When the ash landed, it was still hot enough to burn, and from that ember, everything we knew went up in flames.

It happened before. I had reason to fear it would happen again.

My fingers drummed on the time-scarred armrest of a chair in Monsignor Judd's office. Someone had etched a cross into the wood five, ten, maybe twenty years ago. A saint's stare bore down on me from the stained-glass window; no comfort lay in his face, only my guilt for not knowing the saint's name. Outside the office, Monsignor stood, fingers steepled, while the heating vent blew the draping of his cassock. His ear angled to the young nun whispering with him over the manila folder of Jonah's permanent record. Curls snaked from her nun's habit, and her eyes slid to watch me. Dull, dark. Nearly dead.

My hands grew warmer. I forced my breathing to slow. *Calm down, Vayda girl. Nothing to get worked up over yet.*

Not easy when I was a human magnet for emotion.

Slouching in his chair, Jonah fidgeted with a hole in his blue trousers. I always thought he'd blow our cover someday, but that didn't mean I was ready for it. A bruise purpled his cheekbone. His heat, a mix of emotion and energy, radiated to further prickle my hands until they were scorching. I needed to cool down, put everything on ice to stabilize Jonah and myself. I exhaled in hope of a cold breath. My twin's fury was more than I could absorb.

You outdid yourself this time. I pointed the thought to his mind like a laser. *Do you honestly think fighting with Marty Pifkin is worth all this trouble?*

He avoided eye contact, naturally. That didn't mean he didn't listen. Silent to all but me, he answered, Dati's *already gonna read me the riot act. Don't give me any grief, especially since I was defending* you.

Defending me from Marty Pifkin *of all people. Let it go. What's done is done.* I didn't know whether to give my brother a good wallop upside the head like our mom would have or pray we'd skate on by. *Keep at it, Jonah, and people will notice what you can do. Throwing a desk without using your hands isn't exactly wisdom for the ages.*

Why don't you keep that in mind the next time you lose it and break all the light bulbs in the science lab? He swiped a rogue strand of long, dark hair from his face. *You lack subtlety and finesse, Sis.*

Subtlety. Finesse. Words sixteen-year-old boys knew oh-so-much about. I choked on a laugh and lowered my eyes to the ratty, blue Chucks I paired with my Catholic school plaid, wool skirt, and tights. Even if it wasn't my school uniform, I wore dresses most days. I could move my legs and didn't feel so caged in.

Brushing away the glass dust on my thighs, I ignored the blood drying on my hands and clasped them together. They were less dangerous that way.

The door to the office lobby opened. The new nun resembled a black dandelion seed as she glided into Monsignor's office. She was followed by the head priest and my father. The scent of wood dust clung to him. Most parents visiting St. Anthony of Padua High School rolled in wearing suits or golf attire, and then there was Dad with his Fat Tire shirt and varnish-splattered jeans—evidence he'd been working on a restoration when called to the school. Even if the fight between my brother and Marty hadn't already strained my mental barriers, I still would've noticed Dad's disappointment.

Dad lived by so-called cardinal rules. Looking at Jonah, there was only one rule I thought: There's a devil on every man's shoulder, whispering in his ear. Only he decides if he'll throw salt at the devil or feed him his soul.

"What happened, Magpie?" Dad asked, a Georgia-born drawl buttering his voice as he checked out the cuts on my hand.

"Broken glass, *Dati*," I answered.

"You ought to be more mindful, don't you think?"

His question had nothing and everything to do with breaking glass.

Monsignor cleared his throat. "Sorry to have you back in my office so soon, Mr. Silver."

"Twice in one week is overkill." Dad stood behind Jonah and me, a hand on each of our shoulders.

"I've spoken with our new staff psychologist, Sister Polly Tremblay." Monsignor introduced the new nun. "She was hired this year after Dr. Fernandez took a position in Madison. Our newest Sister is a licensed practitioner, educator, and bride of Christ."

Dad raised an eyebrow. "Is she now? That's all so very impressive, Sister. Do you go by Sister Polly or Sister Tremblay?"

The nun blinked twice, no emotion registering on her face. "Sister Tremblay. Polly is from my past life."

Monsignor grabbed the manila folder from the nun's hands and hurried through his words. "Sister Tremblay has acquainted herself with Jonah's file and feels he may benefit from some sessions with her. If I may be frank, Mr. Silver, your family came to Wisconsin two years ago, but of the people I've spoken with, no one really knows you. Certain appearances are important, especially for an institution such as St. Anthony's. I'm sorry to have to say anything in front of your children, but you must all be aware of the situation I'm in while I'm deciding Jonah's punishment."

"You're a widower running an antiques business," Sister Tremblay added.

"What's that got to do with anything?" Dad snapped.

"The adjustment period after moving, especially when grieving, can be prolonged. In that regard, two years isn't very long at all," Sister Tremblay answered. "Teenagers often cope by acting out. If you're as busy as I suspect—"

"I've got time for my kids," Dad argued. "Always."

The heating vent blasted more hot air into the office. My brother burned with frustration, and my shoulders tightened. I cracked my knuckles, all too aware of how the lights dimmed. Monsignor Judd let out a sigh. "Sister Tremblay is only suggesting that talking to someone away from family could be good for Jonah."

There was no "outside the family." There never was. Hard to make friends and get past the New Kid stigma when we were either cooped up at home or at Dad's shop under his watch. No wonder our classmates thought we were weird—we were.

The hairs on the back of my neck stiffened. I shifted in my chair for a better view into the lobby where another boy waited to talk with Monsignor. The hair curling near his jaw was the color of liquid cinnamon dashed with espresso, and a wire tethered an iPod to his ears as he held an icepack to his bottom lip.

Jonah's sort-of friend, Ward.

He averted his eyes from mine.

My hands grew hot while the overhead lights flickered, drawing everyone's attention to the ceiling. Dad's grip pumped my shoulder.

Jonah stretched his legs. "I'm not hanging out with no damn shrink. Marty Pifkin's got everyone wrapped around his finger."

"Here we go again," I muttered. "Jonah, stop it."

"That guy is a creeper, and—"

I glanced to Dad for sympathy. "Marty asked to compare answers on our homework and Jonah lost it."

"—he was bothering Vayda," my brother talked over me. "Guys like that shouldn't be talking to her. He's *gadje*. I didn't throw the first punch, didn't ask for Ward's help. I barely know the kid."

Monsignor waited until Jonah and I both quieted down. "What's *gadje*?"

Jonah gave Dad a pleading stare. We never let others know the meaning of words we'd grown up with, but Dad confessed, "To some, it means outsider, though you could say we're the outsiders here."

Monsignor gave a reluctant nod. "Marty claims Jonah threw a desk. That's not behavior that will go unpunished."

"And the physics lab? Every light was broken." Sister Tremblay crossed her arms.

I sank into my chair and hid behind my hair. No one could avoid those dull eyes. I wanted out of the office. Now.

The flickering of the lights grew faster. I shuddered, not cold, but burning up. The poster of a kitten clinging to a clothesline while cheering "Hang in there!" obviously didn't relate to how fragile my grip was when so many emotions flooded a room. Usually I kept it together with mental barriers to deflect the constant flow of others' feelings, but so much tension…

"You're seriously suggesting a couple of kids broke every light bulb just like that?" Dad's voice rose. He gestured to the palsied lights. "Y'all would be better off hiring an electrician before the school burns down."

The room skewed left, and my vision blurred, head dizzied. Too hot, cluttered. My hands aching—I shut my eyes. Monsignor and Sister Tremblay had to be staring, but I couldn't worry about them.

Energy. Rising.

Crack!

A fracture drove down the length of the fluorescent light above the desk. Sister Tremblay yelped and snatched Jonah's folder to her chest.

"Hell of a power surge." Jonah's black eyes searched for a way into my mind. *Not gonna let him in, not this time.* He was worried, but nothing was wrong, nothing at all, except that I felt like I could pass out.

"Vayda, go get some fresh air," Dad ordered. "You're flushed."

Monsignor dismissed me, and with the expected curtsey before hoisting my backpack onto my shoulder, I cracked my knuckles one last time to diffuse the energy swelling in my hands. I stepped out of the office, out of the glow of the stained-glass window, and paced near the chairs where Ward waited. Jonah started this whole mess. Marty had done nothing to me—this time. Marty never listened until Jonah made him. Ever since that first fight, Jonah had his anger centered on Marty. Anything Jonah felt, I felt ten times worse. When he was happy, he was very happy, but when he was angry, he was furious.

Mom had been the same way.

"I promise you won't go belly-up if you hold still." Ward's voice was deep, raw honey. His head rested against his chair, his left eye cracked open, watching me.

I gave him a weak smile. I liked his voice.

Ward had been at our school only since Monday, and already the social boneyard where Jonah and I roamed had claimed him. After we transferred in following Christmas break nearly two years ago, we tried blending with the nameless, faceless uniforms, but it wasn't so simple. The other students never warmed to us, and we hadn't to them. We weren't from here, didn't look or act like them. We were among the Avoided, but, as of yesterday, we had a shadow. A *gadje* shadow.

"How's your hand?" Ward asked.

I glanced to my brother and father talking to Monsignor. That Jonah hadn't chased off Ward was a tacit tolerance of him. "A few cuts. I'll live." I twisted my black hair, skimming my hips. "You hardly needed to play the white knight. Marty's not much of a dragon, more like a salamander."

"Maybe I like fighting salamanders."

Chipped, gray polish colored his nails. Artsy in an I-don't-give-a-damn-I'll-wear-it-if-it's-clean way. If Monsignor noticed, that'd earn Ward a detention or two.

"Listen, *gadjo*." He didn't deserve social devastation all because of my cavalier brother. He needed to back off from us. While he still could. "Marty won't bother you if you don't bother him. Tangling with him will never be forgotten."

His mouth twitched, neither a grin nor a frown. "I don't scare easily."

He slipped on his headphones once more. Must be nice to be so untouched, unfazed. Must be peaceful.

"Hey," I called. He lifted one side of his headphones. "What are you listening to?"

"Music."

Smart ass.

Thud!

A chair had overturned in Monsignor's office and rocked ever so slightly. A chair no one had been sitting in. Dad's muffled voice came fast as he pulled Jonah by the arm. From the dark expression on his face, we were in for a major talking to.

"We need to leave. Now," Dad said as he steered Jonah out of the office.

He whisked us past the sanctuary where our footfalls echoed on wood floors polished by nuns until glistening. The school was a dour extension off a century-old Catholic parish. The walls in the language arts wing were painted rich blue, the Virgin's color. Hung between classrooms were carvings from the Stations of the Cross, thick with dust except for Christ's gaze, which followed us and knew my family's secrets and sins.

Outside was better. Riding in the car, the windows lowered to allow in the fire-musk smell of October, but there was something else, an odor of things buried deep in the black earth. Dad steered into a parking lot by a grocery store. The heavy silence in the car made it impossible to push back the memory of the last time we pulled over like this. Instead of a parking lot, it'd been off a highway in a forest in northern Georgia and, with the haze of morning fog guarding the Chevy we'd escaped in, Dad had vowed we were going straight to Black Orchard, a town in Wisconsin near Canada. There, we would start over.

Find somewhere new. Claim different names.

Dad pushed his fingers through his black hair, streaked with silver, and set his eyes, the same green as mine, on my reflection in the rearview mirror. "This stops now. Your mama might've called what y'all do Mind Games. But I won't play."

"Yes, sir," Jonah and I answered.

"Mind Games, if you must work them, are private. Working them in public is how your mama found trouble." He twisted his wedding band. "We can't risk a repeat of Georgia."

I jerked my head to the view out the window. Black Orchard, Wisconsin. Easter egg-colored Victorian homes lined the streets, and people spoke with northern accents, which sounded friendly no matter what they said. But pretty towns and nice people could betray you.

Last time that happened, we escaped with nothing but our lives.

If it happened again, would we even have those?

Chapter Two

Vayda

E vergreens formed a thick barrier along the road until we came to a driveway that serpentined to a house. With flagstone walls under a soaring slate roof, it bore no resemblance to the small Spanish bungalow we had left as a smoldering pile of ashes in Georgia. The home contrasted oddly against the ramshackle barn some fifty-odd feet away. That barn always creaked against the wind.

The phone was already ringing when I walked inside. I set down Dad's canvas grocery bag of coffee beans and nicotine gum and checked the phone. The Caller ID read HEMLOCK, GA. My breath hitched.

"Stop it," I muttered to myself. "You're fine."

No one from Georgia ever called but Rain Killian—my godfather. Mom had always insisted we be careful about who we let into our lives. Though we didn't have a *vitsa*, a clan of all the families we knew, Rain was close, despite that he was *gadje*.

"Hey, darlin', how's the weather?" Rain asked. "You taking care of that summer house of mine?"

"The house is gloomy and haunted by ghosts of blackbirds once trapped in the attic, but—"

"I get it, Vayda dear, you hate the house."

"It's always cold, even in summer."

"You're thirty minutes from Canada. You can't expect the tropics. How's the boy half of you?"

"Acting like he's the dim one of the litter." I paused as Rain muffled a laugh. "He got in a fight."

"Do I need to give him a talking to?"

So very Rain, like a second dad. I teased, "That's *Dati's* job, don't you think?"

"Okay, not gonna step on old Em's toes." He backed off, and I felt the warmth of his hug from over a thousand miles away. "Speaking of that devil, is your daddy about the house? There's trouble with your mama's grave down here."

My smile broke. "What about her grave?"

"Since the headstone went in, vandals have been desecrating the grounds. People here ain't forgetting what Lorna did."

A sick kick jolted my stomach, and the canisters on the counter rumbled. A rainbow of dry beans bounced inside their jar. My eyes scrunched shut. *Breathe. Calm down.*

Within hours of knowing my mom was dead, Rain entrusted Dad with the keys to a vacation house he owned in Black Orchard. I'd never seen Mom's grave. Her burial occurred after we ran, and as such, we never properly mourned.

My voice came out terse. "I'm gonna hand you over to *Dati.*"

"Vayda, I don't mean to upset you. Just giving you the facts," Rain said.

I didn't want to hear anymore. As I entered Dad's study, he snapped away from reviewing an auction catalog to take Rain's call. I had a hunch this wouldn't be one of their typical talks about what was new on the museum scene.

With time to kill before I needed to begin supper, I wrapped an apron at my waist and pulled together flour, salt, and several fat, brown-shelled eggs. Next, milk, butter, and sugar warmed on the stove before I added yeast from an amber glass jar. Boredom, distraction, whatever the reason, I enjoyed making bread, diving my fingers through the powdery flour, using the strength in my hands to knead dough. Creating instead of breaking.

Jonah poked his head into the kitchen. He'd changed out of his school uniform, opting for a thrift store T-shirt. He laid a yellowed Henry James biography on the table and tied back his hair. Glossy and one shade removed from black, we both wore our hair long. Like Mom.

Picking up the sharp knife lying on the pine table, he ran the blade through sprigs of fresh rosemary and thyme before dumping the herbs into the dry mix I sifted with my fingers. "*Dati's* still pissed."

"And the Wonder Brain prevails again." I dusted the table with flour, ready to knead the dough. "We messed up. *I* messed up. I let down my barriers, took in too much energy. It released, and the lights broke. A sideshow for all."

The doorbell chimed. Jonah and I stared at each other. No one ever came to the house. I wiped my hands on my apron and reached the entrance before my brother, and then I opened the hinged speakeasy in the door. A delivery truck idled in the driveway. All deliveries went to Fire Sales, Dad's antiques shop downtown.

I opened the door to the man holding a flat box. "Package for Emory Murdock."

"Let me handle this," Dad said, suddenly beside me.

Cold spiraled to my limbs. I balled my hands so they couldn't do anything unwieldy. Dad took care of the deliveryman before fastening the chain and twisting the key in the speakeasy. More clicks and spins down multiple locks as he barricaded us inside. Wariness pinched his face, his back pressed to the door. Jonah and I shared a glance. Going into Dad's mind to gather what he was thinking was off-limits. Cardinal rule. If he was riled up enough, Dad broke that rule on his own, and Jonah and I'd get more than intended.

We didn't need to know Dad's thoughts. We all heard the name: *Murdock*.

Someone knew.

Someone *knew*.

The nervousness careening from Dad to my hands crackled. He waited until Jonah loosened the drapes and shut out the world before he withdrew his pocketknife and sliced the tape sealing the box. I yanked shut one sliver where the curtains weren't sealed. It didn't matter that the woods around the house had grown murky with the half-light of sunset. Anyone could be out there.

Dad fished through the packing peanuts to find a large envelope, opened it enough to peer inside, and smacked it against the coffee table with a hiss. "Isn't that nice?"

Cussing under his breath, he slammed the door to his study. I flinched, though not from the noise. That wasn't anger coming off Dad. It was fear.

Jonah's breathing was loud, amplified by the sudden quiet in the house. He removed a newspaper from the envelope. *The Hemlock Herald*, dated the Sunday after Thanksgiving two years ago. "Local Woman Dies in House Fire, Family Disappears." Below, a photo culled from our parish directory pictured my mother. A metal clip pinned up her black hair, and her mouth spread in her scarlet smile. Marker scrawled one word across the picture.

Gypsy.

Chapter Three

Ward

Underneath the night sky by the backside of an evergreen forest, I set up shop on the driveway of the rehabbed Victorian I now called home. With just a T-shirt under a flannel one, I didn't feel the cold.

Everything I needed was right there: a metal sawhorse dragged out of the garage, plenty of sharp tools, and a gallon of orange juice. A pair of extension cords snaked out from the garage's open blackness. I switched on a work lamp and studied the sheet of copper. Nothing to interrupt me.

The blowtorch's blue flame hissed loudly despite my welding mask, so I kicked up the volume on the cheap stereo stored in the garage. So old it had slots for cassettes. The speakers worked, and my foot found the demented carnival bass of Wolf Parade's "You Are a Runner, and I Am My Father's Son." Already stenciled on the copper were a handful of circles. The blowtorch was the easiest way to carve out the shapes. After they were loose, I'd hammer them into small cups and attach them to the wind sculpture I was building. Finding an old lightning rod with long arrows and a purple glass ball in the center had been a nice bit of luck.

The kitchen window over the driveway slid open, and Heidi gave me an impatient scowl. "Turn it down!"

I dialed back the volume a skosh and lowered the welding mask. Copper wasn't always the easiest metal to shape, but the rust patterns made it the most interesting. Didn't come cheap.

The snaggle-toothed guy at the recycling plant told me a bunch was stolen 'cause the resale price was better. I didn't much care as long as I could bend it, burn it, hammer it, whatever.

Amid a shower of glittery sparks, the circles took shape. I killed the blowtorch and slung it over my shoulder before punching out the metal. A scalding edge bit my index finger, slashing and stinging in one swoop.

"Shit!" Blood dripped onto the rusted copper. Should've worn gloves. One lesson I'd learned at least a dozen times.

With my hand wadded in my shirt, I let myself inside and bypassed Heidi, buried in the walk-in pantry, on my way to the bathroom. The cut gushed blood, and rinsing the wound with cold water felt about as good as jabbing in an icicle. My hand quaked as I dug through the cabinet for bandages.

"Did I tell you he got in a fight at school?" Heidi's voice came through the heat register. Old house. Everything echoed. Everything.

Chris, her husband, scoffed. "Actually, I talked to him. He said some friends were in trouble. He probably wanted to fit in, prove himself. Weren't you ever the new kid?"

No Band-Aids, but there was a tube of Krazy Glue. Meh. It'd work. I squeezed a line of glue along the cut and pressed the edges together. *Don't glue your fingers together, okay, dumbass?*

Heidi's voice kept traveling through the vent. "Oh, so you're saying he should have friends that get him in trouble? Jesus, Chris. If this is just the beginning—"

"You'll what? Kick him out?"

"No…"

"Then it's an empty threat. Everybody's getting used to each other, Heidi. He's been here only a week. You said he couldn't stay at that apartment."

"There were rats!" Heidi sounded like rats were the worst sin of that place, but she had no idea. "He's lucky he doesn't have tuberculosis."

"So what are going you to do?" Chris asked.

My sight trained on the shiny blood seeping where I glued

the cut. Heidi's pause was long.

After a while, she sighed. "I don't know what to do with Ward. There's no one else to take him. Believe me, I checked."

Not this again.

Toenails scratched at the door until Bernadette, a geriatric salt-and-pepper schnauzer, poked her ragged beard inside. That dog followed me everywhere and snored like an amplifier in need of rewiring. If I weren't already an insomniac, she'd cause some wicked sleep deprivation.

Standing behind Bernadette, Chris raised an eyebrow at my bloodied shirt. "Do I even want to know?"

"Art is pain," I quipped.

"Dinner's almost ready. Heidi wants you. While you're at it, change out of that bloody shirt. It's gross."

"Already ate."

A microwave eggroll and coffee were astonishingly nutritious. Or not. Orange juice might give me the vitamin C needed to kill a dry cough.

Chris didn't leave the bathroom, inciting the devil on my shoulder to prod me with his pitchfork. I asked, "You want fries with that? Or you got more orders for me?"

Bernadette rolled on her back, silently guffawing.

"That dog is a traitor," Chris said. "So what are you building out on the driveway? I saw the tools you brought from Minnesota."

"It's nothing," I replied with a cough. "I'll clean up afterward. Blood and all."

Chris examined my hand despite my first instinct to pull back. "Metal, huh? A pencil probably won't land you in the ER in need of stitches."

"You should see the other guy. I flattened him, seared him with a blowtorch, and left him hammered."

"You know, if you joked like this with Heidi—"

"She'd still think I was fucked up."

Chris didn't argue. I picked up the old dog at my feet and scratched behind her ears with my uninjured hand. Bernadette blinked her liquid-brown gaze and apologetically licked my hand as she traveled with me into the kitchen to learn what hell Heidi planned to dole out.

Heidi was my half-sister from my father's first marriage. I doubted she was thrilled when the child welfare department of the fine state of Minnesota tracked down my one responsible family member. Most Ravenscrofts had trouble staying out of jail. Heidi spooned some putrid homemade baby food into her son's mouth. At six months old, Oliver knew goose shit was more palatable. Heidi wiped a green streak from her hair and motioned for me to sit.

"St. Anthony's is a good school. You cannot get off on a bad foot. The Pifkins have some clout, so..."

Her silence implied everything I needed to know.

"Which kids got you in a fight?" she asked.

I set Bernadette in her dog bed and studied the cobweb-strung chandelier over the table. "Nobody got me in a fight. I did it to myself."

"I know this is different from what you're used to."

Oliver emitted a banshee-wail, and his sippy-cup nailed me in the shin before splashing in Bernadette's water bowl. I offered the cup to Heidi who paled as if handed raw chicken.

"Wash it off!"

I tried to be helpful, but...This family charade was jacked.

I started toward the living room. "I wasn't done talking to you," Heidi called.

"Later," I grunted and retrieved the backpack I'd dumped at the foot of the creaky staircase. I found my sketchpad for my metal sculpting and came across a line drawing I'd done during Lit class. The girl's hair in my sketch was black and bled into her skirt.

The phone on the end table by the couch rang. I should've known better than to answer a Minnesota area code. Nobody good was up there.

"What?" I growled into the phone.

Drake's low voice slurred, "Just checking on you, kid."

A hiss escaped between my teeth. I'd heard this line before and lied, "I have homework."

"I might get out soon."

"And? What home will you go to? You fucked up. Again."

Drake staggered to keep me on the line. "I suppose you're living with your sister."

"Obviously, since you called her number and I answered."

My cough reared up. I couldn't talk to that bastard. Without hanging up, I set the phone on the table and tromped up the steep and shadowed stairs to my room on the second floor. Bernadette tailed a few steps behind, and as I flopped on my bed, I scooped her into my arms. Her fur was coarse and her breath reeked, but she was what she was. No bullshit. Only something warm for my lap.

I didn't miss Drake. I never missed him. So why did I have a bag in my closet with enough cash and clothes to get me back to Minnesota if the whim struck? Minnesota meant sickness and solitude, but as awful as they were, those things were familiar.

Black Orchard was a mystery. I didn't trust the unknown, didn't like it, didn't want any part of it, and it'd be so easy for me bail. Except whatever kept me in Black Orchard had strong hands and didn't dare let go.

Chapter Four

Vayda

The pine forest crowded in closer. Steam rose from my breath against the chill. I squinted past the evergreens, through the blue hour of dusk. Every rustle in the underbrush, every shift in the wind prickled my skin. Maybe I wasn't just over-alert. Maybe I wasn't alone.

"Who's out there?" I called.

A squirrel chattered while it pawed the frost. The stoic, black trees kept their watch, but my body refused to let go of the certainty someone was out there. The fabric of my nightgown was stiff as I slid my hands to my legs, shivering. I wasn't like my brother—I didn't push myself out there to find other peoples' energy, it was drawn toward me, and my feelers vibrated in my fingers and ached to dispatch into the woods in search of a second beating heart. *Do something. I know you're there.*

Without warning, hands with scars twisting across the skin hovered over my waist behind me. I reached for them.

Light.

Hesitant.

A smell—mineral with a metallic edge—grounded me as he held me. I liked being close to him, whoever he was.

"Why are you here?" I asked and tried to see him, but he stopped me with his cheek. "Who are you?"

"I'm around." His mouth brushed the side of mine. "And I know what you can do."

***

I lurched upright. My shoulders trembled from ghostly fingers following me out of my dream, and I clutched my blanket to my chest. The sun streaked outside my window, breaking the sky. The boy's words, so softly whispered, made me uneasy. It was only a dream, and yet the newspaper sent to my house proved it wasn't my imagination running amok.

Someone knew.

After everything Dad had done to wipe away any traces of our former lives, someone knew the truth. I didn't want to run again.

In the attic, something *thumped*. We didn't use the attic, but on occasion, birds became trapped, pinned inside with no room to fly. I lay still, waiting for more flapping, yet the silence thickened and left me with the unsettling sense of something else inside the house.

"Just birds, Vayda," I muttered and climbed out of bed. "Some damn birds."

After dressing, I found Jonah with his feet propped on the kitchen table. A new book rested on the placemat, a biography of Edgar Allan Poe. Mom wasn't well-read, my *bapo* said his daughter hadn't needed to read to be a good wife, but Dad wasn't like him and insisted we read as much as we could on whatever caught our interest. Biographies were my brother's quirk. As he reached for his morning coffee, he grinned. "Good dreams, sleepyhead?"

I cringed. Why must he know *everything*? I picked up his book and tossed it at his forehead, but it froze mid-air.

He teased. "You can try all you like, Sis, but you won't get me."

"Show off."

He dropped his hand, and the book thudded on the table. "You're jealous 'cause you can't push like I can."

Every Mind Game he worked was a push. In the way he forced energy and emotion out and away, I drew them. He sought out thoughts. Thoughts came to me. He charged up on his own feelings and released it as heat. I pulled everyone else's and numbed myself with cold to avoid becoming overwhelmed. He moved solid things with a thought. If I concentrated hard enough, I felt the emotion attached to them. Twins, yes, but hardly the same in the Games we played.

And I know what you can do.

The words from my dream snapped like pieces of brushwood, and my mouth tightened. My brother tipped his head. "What are you fretting over?"

"You oughta know. My dream," I answered.

"Those dreams mess up my head. Sister Tremblay will never be hot, even in dreamland, but she does crack a mean ruler. And whip. You should see what's under her nun's habit."

"Pervert. I'd rather not."

"Eh, you're right. Any dream with Tremblay is a nightmare."

Most mornings, I'd laugh, but I was too shuddery as the coffee splashed against the white bottom of my mug. My memory had jagged holes like torn fabric where the boy's face in my dream frayed. And as I rubbed away the tension in my arms, I wiped clean the transparent handprints of a *gadje* boy I couldn't quite recall.

***

Dad parked the Chevy in front of Chloe Halvorsen's house, student ambassador extraordinaire and Jonah's girlfriend for four months once upon a time. Mom had said our heritage insisted we be with others like us, but there weren't any others. Not empaths—I'd never met any—but other *Rom*. We were Romani. Jonah wasn't bothered that Chloe was *gadje*. He dated her when she wasn't working her way from lowly ballot counter to obvious Homecoming court nominee. The second she came back from our last spring break with a Key West tan and a plan for social hierarchy domination, she ditched the tall boy who kept to himself. No matter what movies and rock stars showed, quiet guys with black hair weren't cool or mysterious. People mocked them, and if Chloe wanted the tin-and-rhinestone crown during senior year, she couldn't be with someone who was a joke.

I sat in the Chevy, fingers splayed on the foggy window. The clouds rippled with every shade of gray and blue like God scooped the ocean's froth and threw it skyward for a change. A storm was brewing.

"We can't trust her. She wants something, *Dati*," I said as he reached across my lap and muttered something about how doors of old beater cars sometimes stuck. The Chevy's doors never stuck. "Stop it. I won't leave until you tell me why you insist we dump our low-profile shtick."

"It's not a shtick," he replied. "It's who we are, and who we are doesn't work here, Magpie. Monsignor's right. We need to fit in better. I'm going to some heinous Chamber of Commerce meeting, so you're not the only one suffering."

"But hanging out with Chloe?" I argued.

"She's a teenage girl, not the devil."

"We can be one in the same."

He snorted. "Don't I know."

I climbed out of the car with a canvas bag on my arm, and before I could change my mind, Dad was gone. I trudged up the leaf-strewn sidewalk where I fingered the cutesy garland of candy corn and pumpkin lights strung across the Halvorsens' porch. An inflatable pink octopus wearing a witch's hat decorated the lawn for Halloween. "The Dunwich Horror," this was not. Lovecraft would shudder at this tentacled abomination.

Maybe Jonah and I hadn't exactly been approachable, but since coming to Wisconsin, the times classmates asked me to hang out numbered less than five. Keep saying no, and eventually people stop asking. Even when Jonah dated Chloe, she and I were nothing more than passing hellos. Then that morning she sent an email begging me to come over.

Maybe it was Find-the-Loneliest-Loser Day, and she decided I was her pet charity case. Her usual method was to give the underlings enough attention to ensure they'd wear a button with her smile plastered across it around student election time and that the nuns and priests noticed her saintliness, but really, never count on Chloe to be less artificial than the fruit flavors in a pack of Gummy Bears.

"Vayda!" she called while bounding down the steps, dressed in a purple plaid skirt with coordinating tights and turtleneck. "I'm so glad you came! I half-expected Jonah to be with you. It's like you can't do anything without him."

"Oh, you know. Protective brother. You wanted me to scrapbook with you?"

Ushered into a home that smelled of cinnamon buns, I followed Chloe through a kitchen that couldn't squeeze any more beige into the design. *Act like everything's normal, that you hang out with her all the time,* I reminded myself. Dad hadn't asked much of me, and I tried to keep that in mind as she led me downstairs. My jaw dropped. Dad had no idea that nothing was normal about scrapmania in the Halvorsens' basement.

Ribbons cascaded off a shelf in a neatly organized waterfall by a lagoon of papers arranged by color, theme, and thematic colors. Packages were labeled "punch-outs" and "die-cutters." Who knew scrapbooking was so violent? A bookcase was loaded with scrapbooks marked "SCHOOL." I'd long been convinced Chloe remembered the name, favorite color, and zodiac sign of every classmate. Now I suspected she made scrapbook pages with that information.

She fluffed her Nordic-blond hair. "Jonah said you have tons of scrapbooks."

Jonah, of course. His fight with Marty made him interesting again.

Seizing my bag, she dove into the pages of my scrapbook and creased her forehead at the seedpods and leaves pressed in wax paper. "This is unusual. I might be able to brighten up this…layout."

Perhaps the buttons I scrounged from Dad's shop and blue jay feathers found in the woods weren't what Chloe expected.

She gathered an armload of glittery embellishments.

"You aren't putting that junk in my book," I blurted.

"You need help. Your style's *natural*. Like *organic*."

Organic? Was this Chloe-code for creepy-girl-who-collects-dead-things? I wasn't surprised. She leaned in closer, enough to release a wave of fizzy currents. Even if I wanted to be offended, I couldn't—her cheerfulness was emotional cotton candy. Yet when I picked up a pack of her shimmering stickers, that giggle, which left my barriers on a sugar-high, died away, insecure and tense. She'd left emotional residue on the package, a touch of the real Chloe, not the one I avoided every day at school. The change was enough of a jolt that I gawked at her; the way her glossed lips pressed together in thought, how her eyelashes batted—she had a few false ones glued in. She probably hoped no one ever looked at her so closely.

"What?" she asked.

"Nothing," I muttered.

"You are so bizarre."

For a while, we worked separately. She didn't touch my extra supplies, but I spied a spool of leather cord similar to a magenta choker Mom wore and snatched it, flipping to a pencil doodle of Mom that Dad scribbled on a Thai menu outside Memphis. I wove the cord through some holes at the paper's edge.

"Is there a method to your madness?" Chloe teased as she stacked some homemade cards.

Ignoring her, I asked, "So what do you want to know about Jonah? I know he's why you invited me. Why don't you ask him yourself? He'd like it if you called."

Her cheeks blushed, but she said, "Is he suspended?"

"For all of next week," I confirmed. "He'll be in the class for deviants."

"Jonah's a deviant all right." She gave a husky giggle. "I overheard Monsignor say Jonah should be expelled. Sister Tremblay said no, and no one messes with her. She's a…"

"Megabitch?" I asked.

"You said it, not me."

Such thoughts about a nun should send me to the Confessional, but there was something off about that woman. From her dull eyes to the way she floated. I was used to plump, chatty nuns who got chalk on the backs of their black skirts. One of them, Sister Mary Elena, fell in the parking lot last winter and looked like a penguin sliding on ice. Sister Tremblay wasn't like them. She wasn't like anybody in Black Orchard, and that made her like us. Untrustworthy.

"In all the time Jonah and I dated, I didn't realize he has such a temper," Chloe interrupted my thoughts. "Granted, he and Marty haven't gotten along since, well, you know."

I cracked my knuckles. My hands were hot again. "Jonah doesn't forgive easily, and he doesn't forget the past. Especially not when it comes to Marty."

"I guess not." Her stare held me a second too long. "Anyway, he should be careful. People talk about him. About both of you, really."

Great. Exactly what we needed.

Chloe rose from the scrapbooking table and motioned me to follow her upstairs to her bedroom. An ornate wooden bed swallowed much of the room, and some pungent smell—the wet rot of mildew—emanated from between the cracks in the floorboards. The clouds had whipped into a dark swarm, and I could hardly tell where I was going. She grabbed some matches from her nightstand, scratched one across the flint and paper, and brought the flame to a candle's wick on her dresser. The fire guttered and rose in a smoky point.

Thunder grumbled as Chloe brought out a junky white box. "You ever see one of these?"

The box read OUIJA and contained a board painted with letters, numbers, and a YES in one corner, a NO in the other. GOODBYE dead center in the top. Spirits talked through a plastic triangle, a planchette. Fortunetelling was nothing new to me. Mom read tarot cards and taught me palmistry. She'd also believed spirit boards were the devil's playthings.

"This is a bad idea," I said.

Chloe pulled me to the floor and giggled. "Are you scared?"

"No. Just—" I had to be careful how I answered. "I come from a superstitious family."

"It won't hurt you," Chloe insisted. She opened the box, tossed the lid on her quilt, and dumped out the board. "You're doing this, and what happens stays between us. I swear to God."

Her eyes flicked to the silver cross hanging above her bed. She vowed her honesty on that cross. Promises made on a cross, if broken, brought upon a curse.

The board sat between us, and the planchette was a celluloid triangle, once white but jaundiced with age. Chloe placed her index and middle fingers on one side.

"Come on, Vayda," she coaxed. "You're not afraid of a little game, are you?"

I wasn't about to be called chicken, but Chloe had no idea what she asked of me. I was wedged between fitting in like Dad wanted and my superstitions, but I ultimately had to live with my father, not my ancestors and their beliefs. My barriers rose, steeling against any residue left behind by past hands, and I placed my fingers on the game piece.

The planchette bounced.

"No way," Chloe whispered. "You feel that?"

"Shut up." I teased and tried to sound dismissive. "It was the wind."

But there wasn't a draft.

Rain plinked off the windows. In the storm-darkened room, the hollows in her cheeks were sickly. I'd never seen her so unwell. It was the bad light, nothing more. Wasn't it?

"Spirits," she began, talking to the board as she tried not to laugh from nerves, maybe from the ridiculousness of hoping the Ouija board had power, "tell me a secret about Vayda."

"What? Why me?"

"Quiet!" She noticed my fingers lifting off the planchette. "Don't you dare let go!"

I choked on a reply when the celluloid triangle moved in a lazy circle across the board. Chloe was moving it. She *had* to be moving it. Yet emotions never lied, and she felt spooked.

The planchette spiraled inward on the alphabet before coming to rest on the M. From there, it skated to U. A chill shot down my veins to my hands.

"M-U-R-D-" Chloe read aloud as the triangle dashed from letter to letter.

Shit. I didn't like how this felt, and the planchette moved too fast for either of us to control it. I could tell Chloe that Murdock was a family name. She didn't have to know. It could be a coincidence—

M-U-R-D-E-

That wasn't how to spell Murdock.

Lightning cracked close outside, and a blue-white flash reflected off the board's sheen. I ran my tongue along my lips, and the nervousness streaming from Chloe soared until the flutter of energy in my fingertips grew so strong the planchette vibrated. An acrid smell, something burning, hit my nose. The legs of the triangle began to melt. I yanked my fingers away but not before the planchette settled on one last letter.

M-U-R-D-E-R.

***

We didn't speak during the drive home. Leeriness squeezed Chloe's expression, and the evergreens jammed the road's shoulders, growing wilder away from her safe suburbia. After the Ouija board incident, she decided to take me home. She hadn't asked if I was ready to leave. Before we left, she let me wash my hands, observing as I murmured the prayers my mother swore would remove bad spirits. The storm passed by the time she placed the board under her bed and blew out the candle, but the afternoon sky remained tinged by fireplace smoke and threats of sleet if the wind grew colder.

"I forgot how crazy isolated it is by your house. Do you like living out here?"

"It's home," I replied and hugged my bag of scrapbooks.

"Well, I guess you can't complain about nosy neighbors."

Just because you can't see them doesn't mean no one's there. The evergreens melded into a blur of dark green and shadow. Plenty of places someone could hide between the trees.

"Vayda?" Chloe said my name as if she'd called me a couple of times.

"Sorry."

She slowed and swerved into my driveway. "What happened at my house—" I didn't know if she would finish, but I waited. Being Chloe, that didn't take long. "I think we both shouldn't talk about it."

"Don't worry," I said. "I won't tell anyone who matters you were with the likes of me."

"That's not what I mean."

"I'm giving you grief." I cracked a half-smile. "It was the storm, right?"

"Right."

As she steered up the drive, the trees hunched over the road. Above, a gray sunbeam pierced the clouds. Someone was crouched on the front steps. My hand gripped the car door. No one but Jonah should be home, and that boy wasn't Jonah. He had a vagabond-poet air, dark trousers and shirt, scuffed combat boots, his fingers laced in the pages of a paperback. Messy, auburn hair hung over his forehead as his head bobbed in time with music from his headphones.

Ward.

Chloe shut off the car and waved me ahead, begging off to call her mom, and I approached the steps where I cast a shadow over Ward. He squinted as he peeled off his headphones.

"You're blocking my light."

"There is no light, *gadjo*. Too many clouds." I pointed to the open book. "What are you reading?"

"Tennessee Williams."

I pushed my hair over my shoulder and peeked into his script. Pencil underlined sections of the play's text, scrunched writing in the margins. "Williams, huh? You reading it for school?"

"Nope," he answered. "I have nothing better to do."

He wasn't being sarcastic.

"Everybody knows about 'The Glass Menagerie,'" I rambled, checking the windows for any sign of Jonah. Ward didn't turn away from his book, but I kept on because not talking about Williams meant asking him why he was here. "'Cat on a Hot Tin Roof' is good, though I'm partial to 'Sweet—'"

"—Bird of Youth.'" He showed me the book cover and offered it to me. My barriers rose, and I examined the binding. Old, worn from many readings. Ward tilted his head. "What are you doing?"

"My family works with antiques. Jonah likes old books, so it's habit. Whoever wrote in it hurt the value but makes it interesting."

He took back the book. "I wrote in it."

I hadn't yet stopped cringing when Chloe joined us and held out her hand, which he regarded as though offered a poison apple. She asked, "You're new, right?"

"Well, I'm not old," he muttered.

Her perpetual grin faltered before she reached for the door. "I'm gonna see what Jonah's up to. God help you, Vayda."

She let herself into my house, leaving me with Ward who slipped on his headphones and snickered as she disappeared. "That girl ditched you."

"She couldn't handle your cheery disposition. Not the best way to make friends."

"What if I don't want friends?"

"I get it. You don't play well with others. But everyone wants friends, especially guys who need to be cool by saying they don't."

Ward smiled. His teeth were straight but for one too-sharp canine. "If that were true, you'd have friends other than your brother."

Touché.

"What are you doing here?" I finally asked. "You're outside reading when it could storm again any second."

"I had some time to kill."

"And if another thunderstorm came along?" I asked.

"I'd knock on the door, or, you know, become a human lightning rod."

Ward studied the house with the oddly angled roof and copper awnings. It wasn't the homiest place. Drafty on the inside while the flagstone exterior needed more maintenance than Dad had time to work on. Some rocks had broken away, mortar crumbling against the blustery wind. Cracks marred the slate roof; the gutters rusted. Water from the earlier rain gushed down the drain and pooled near our feet in a black soup. Across the yard, the weathervane atop the barn groaned, and Ward glanced over both shoulders. "Where are the gargoyles?"

"Since it's daytime, they're on the north side in the shade," I answered. He laughed—score one for Vayda—and I pushed open the front door. "Don't worry. It's not haunted."

He reached for my hand to help him stand. I backed away from his outstretched fingers, but he grabbed my hand anyway, discharging a zap of electricity. The surprise jolt hiccupped in my throat as he rose. Maybe six inches taller than my five-foot frame, he stood close enough for his knee to bump against my long skirt. My pulse struggled to calm down. No boy ever got this close, near enough to smell skin that was clean but metallic. His skinny wrists opened into wide palms, his fingers long with knuckles like knots of burled wood. Scars new and old mangled his skin. They were hands that had worked. I knew these hands.

I'm around. And I know what you can do.

An anxious undercurrent needled the air between our palms. Pulling. Repelling.

"You okay?" he asked. "It's the scars, isn't it? They're ugly."

"They're not ugly," I answered, "only unexpected. What happened?"

"Nothing happened. I work with metal. Sometimes it bites."

If he was at all self-conscious about the mess of his hands, it didn't show, nor could I sense it, and that was a relief. I pointed him inside. The door clicked behind me. We had a guest in the house, two if Chloe counted.

No matter where we'd lived, my parents mixed their traditions with southern hospitality. Southern hospitality got my mother killed. I was in the north now, but southern habits lingered like gray tendrils of Spanish moss hanging off cypress trees.

I prepared glasses of iced tea for our guests and brought them to the living room. Jonah perched on the couch with Chloe taking the seat closest to him. She angled toward him, and I sensed his barriers. Yet through his wall, a need to impress poked through. Hope. "I reckon your mama's gonna be griping tonight. Something about babysitting her friend's holy terror?"

She beamed and inched closer. "You guessed again! I've never known how you played that game. I must be giving it away."

"You're not. It's magic." He patted her thigh.

Real nice tom-catting. My brother better guard himself.

As Chloe bid Jonah goodbye, she bent over and pecked his cheek. I pursed my lips, my gaze meeting his silently mocking one. It seemed to be okay for Princess Perky to get herself dirty with an outcast like Jonah as long as no one from school was around to see, and I was sure she didn't think of Ward as anyone important. As she pranced down the steps to her car, a sly curl spread on Jonah's mouth. *I'm so gonna hit that again.*

Sometimes I fantasize about hitting Chloe, too. Over her head, I joked. *I know you don't care that she's* gadje, *but you do remember she chose her social life over being with you, right?*

Jonah ignored me. "Ward, I told you this place was a walk through the woods, but I'm kinda surprised nothing snuck out and grabbed you off the path. Those woods are dark, and no one really knows what's out there. So do you not have anything better to do or are you *killing time?*"

Jonah. Pushing his way into places he didn't belong. I conjured the image of my palm slapping his head. He raised his face, and a new picture awakened in my mind. Me in my nightgown in the forest with Ward's hands running up my body.

My dream.

You're dead, I promised, stifling the heat pouring into my cheeks.

Snickering, Jonah took Ward's Tennessee Williams book and scanned the back cover before handing it over. "I read in a biography this guy choked to death on the cap of a bottle of eye drops."

"Only you would remember something morbid like that." I snorted.

"I'm saying weird shit happens. Surely, Ward here has seen something out of the ordinary once or twice."

What are you thinking? Are you out of your damn gourd? That gadjo *is gonna ask questions about us.*

Jonah didn't balk while he spoke in my mind. *Take a deep breath, Sis. Everything's golden.*

"Lots of things are strange." Ward glanced from my brother to me, his gaze so intense that I retreated until my back met the cold wall. Every muscle in my body went tighter the longer he watched me. "So what's strange about you two? I mean, there's gotta be something."

The rumble of the Chevy's engine announced Dad was home. I let out my breath and relaxed. The knob on the front door jiggled, and Ward's glance went to the fortress of locks on the door then peered over his shoulder to where Jonah now waited at my side.

As Dad entered the house, his attention went right to our visitor. "Are you going to introduce yourself, son?"

"I'm nobody," Ward replied.

"Ward recently moved here," Jonah intervened.

My father's appraisal was studious, if not suspicious. "One of your parents find a new job or something?"

Ward rolled his book in his hands. "It wasn't a planned move."

Sort of like how we came here, though I doubted he was covered in ashes as we'd been.

Dad beckoned me to the kitchen. He couldn't be more conspicuous. A lecture was coming, about either fitting in or contradicting what he'd said earlier by saying we shouldn't allow outsiders into our home.

"Magpie, I gotta get back to Fire Sales. But I'll stay if you want."

"We're fine, *Dati*. Jonah invited him. You know, this goes along with fitting in," I assured him.

"But you just met him. He's an outsider and not a friend. Not yet." Then his face softened. "I assume there's a reason your brother invited him. Keep an eye on Jonah. He gets lax when we're home."

Did he think I didn't know my own brother? For as tired as Jonah was of hiding Mind Games, he'd never endanger us.

With Dad heading out and the murmur of Jonah and Ward talking in the living room, I set about creaming brown sugar and butter for cookie dough. My hand gripped the bowl, and I stirred in flour and vanilla before raiding the cabinets for Mom's secret ingredient for the chewiest cookies in the South—cornstarch. Worked like a charm, as she promised.

The hair on my neck tightened. Someone was watching me.

I whipped around to find Ward leaning against the gray granite counter with his thumbs hooked in his pockets. "Hey."

"Hey, yourself. I thought you were hanging out with Jonah."

He shrugged. "Jonah can wait."

I said nothing, returning to mixing the cookie dough. Normally, if I stared at someone too long, I was subjected to at least a whisper of their thoughts. Energy and emotions snarled so much in ours that Jonah and I learned to protect ourselves with barriers before we hit preschool. It was the only way to live a semi-normal life. Yet nothing in Ward caught me. Energy brewed but passed through like a hot knife in cold butter.

The tips of his fingers brushed mine as he checked out the cookie dough, and a flutter of electricity breezed over my hand, a current running a clear course. Ward was bitten by the shock and mouthed, "Ouch."

His hand cupped my forearm, but I pulled back. "What are you doing?"

"Wondering if there's another spark."

Ward had no idea.

Thousands of sparks flared off him and burned through me.

Chapter Five

Vayda

*S*hadows *blanket Jonah and me in the hallway while Rain's in the kitchen, lighting one cigarette off another. Mom's impish grin doesn't impress him, and he covers her hand with his. "Lorna, darlin', this ain't funny. These charges are real serious."*

She unfastens her hair from her French twist, setting a hair comb on the table. The comb is silver, inlaid with green stones for leaves beside hand-painted roses. Dad made it for her in art school years before. "I'm not worried. You and Em and I, we've seen hell worse than this."

My godfather puffs on his cigarette. "You don't get it. They've been after you, and this time, they might have gotten you."

"Then get her off, Rain." Dad swirls his scotch. "Lorna made your law career. You owe her."

Rain leans back in his chair. "I'd do anything to help y'all, but the town wants someone to pay."

The diamonds in Mom's wedding rings twinkle like Christmas lights as she streams her hand through Dad's black hair. He rubs his cheek against her fingers, and she whispers a hushed promise in Romani before speaking louder.

"We'll be fine, Em. We always are."

***

They weren't fine.

Not since Mom pitched a fit two years ago. Not since Dad, Jonah, and I showed up at Rain's with smoke in our lungs and hair gray from ash. Not since Dad's best friend helped us disappear.

The wind scraped my cheeks, driving off my memories. The day Mom died was cool and gray like this one, but this far north, the trees didn't hang on to their leaves. The branches were bare and spiked like church spires without crosses. My hands burrowed inside my sweater for warmth.

"Want my coat?" Ward offered, coughing into the crook of his elbow.

"I'm okay. Besides, you sound like you're coming down with something."

"I always have a cough. It's nothing."

For over a week, he'd come by after school to debate books with Jonah. Most days, I kept to the kitchen, either working on dinner or homework, eavesdropping on the boys, noticing how Ward often came to the doorway, offering me a smile. That Jonah had a friend, even a *gadjo*, was good, yet I still had no one. Chloe nodded at me in the hall, but she wasn't my friend. I didn't want to be alone anymore.

I wasn't alone, not right then. When Ward slid on his coat to leave, he'd tilted his head in a silent request that I join him for the walk to his house. I'd deferred to Jonah, expecting him to shake his head, not after the last time. Instead, he'd given me a wave of blessing. Maybe I was a trifle overeager to go along, so excited I forgot my coat.

While we walked, the wind blew hard from the north, and we listened to our shoes crunching the twigs.

"You have an accent," Ward remarked. "It's not real strong, sort of comes and goes."

"You can't make me believe you wanna talk accents." I nudged him. Seeing his pale cheeks burn made me smile. "I was born in Georgia. My parents took us to Montana when we were little, but we moved back to Georgia. Small town, bunch of busybodies. We thought about moving to Vermont, but we came here. We haven't been stable, honestly."

"You move around a lot, like you're gypsies or something."
A hiss passed my lips. Ward noticed my balled hands. "I said
something dumb, didn't I?"

"Gypsy isn't a nice word," I explained. "People say gypsies
are thieves, gyp people."

He stuck out his lower lip. "So I guess that's why you keep
to yourself, huh?"

"Kind of. You're *gadje*." I tried to unknot his brow by
adding, "Not Romani. There's no one like us in Black Orchard."
Really not like us, not with what Jonah and I could do.

Ward kicked a rock. "I'd never left Minnesota until I came
here."

Now it was my turn to ask questions. "Why'd you move?"

He wrinkled his nose. "'Cause I fucking hate junkies."

Well, that was a can of worms. We walked a ways, our feet
shuffling the quilt of fallen leaves, until we neared the remains
of a dried creek bed. I spotted a glittering geode broken open. I
grabbed it and tucked it in the pocket of my skirt. As I stood, an
odd frequency emanated from Ward, not emotion or tension,
but a drive to know more, more than I'd cared to know about
any boy before. "So you came here to get away?"

He crossed his arms, his leather coat jostling. "I didn't
have much choice. When you're dealing with addicts, you cut
them off or they get worse."

"So," I began, "the junkies, they friends you don't want
anymore?"

He chewed his lip and kicked another rock. "It's one junkie,
mostly. Drake—my father—is messed up."

I caught his eyes before he cast them down to his boots
again.

"It's a far cry from your charmed life, eh?" he said with a
snort.

"My life's hardly charmed," I muttered.

"Sure. It must be hard having a nice house, nice family.
You got everything you want."

"You don't know what I want, and if you're gonna act like

this, well, then maybe you're not it."

Miles away, thunder followed a glint of lightning. We glowered at each other, neither one of us willing to apologize. The sudden change in him reminded me of a time when I'd been five or six. I'd been running through a field of wheatgrass, dead in autumn. A single blackbird circled overhead and arced in graceful swoops until a gunshot cracked against the sky. The bird guttered mid-flight, stunned, and then jerked in a hideous, awkward fall, feathers spilling out around it. At the time, my barriers weren't so solid, and I chased the falling feathers until I found the bird in death spasms on the ground. I felt its terror and pain, and I felt its release from life. I didn't ever wish to feel those things again.

Something inside Ward at the mention of his father was like the blackbird torn apart by a bullet. I had to back away. The last thing I wanted was to get a hit of what went on inside him, what he felt.

"Vayda, I'm sorry. Please stop."

He jogged toward me and took my hand. A jolt *zinged* from his skin to mine, and I recoiled. It wasn't that he was *gadje* and touching me, but rather I wasn't ready for such a dose of energy. We were both too open and sore to stop my feelers from grabbing what they found in him. I'd never seen such sad eyes like Ward's. Mercury-gray with a paler ring around his pupils, breaking the darkness enough to assure me there was some warmth inside his cold soul of iron.

Everyone had barriers to cover the doorways in their minds. Jonah and I opened them. By touch, even by proximity. We also had to guard our own barriers. Ward was different, at least for me. His barriers were curtains, moth-eaten and fragile. Full of holes through which I could poke my fingers, and yet even with the burst of energy, his head didn't tangle me up. Maybe I could trickle in his thoughts if I tried pulling them, but it was nice to slip through in silence.

"I'm such a prick," he admitted.

He stood close enough that his breath condensed on my cheeks. The wind wheezed, and he wrapped his coat over my shoulders. The leather was heavy and smelled of sweat and rust, his scent that whispered of things elemental.

"I touched a nerve," I said.

"Sorta."

Like he was "sorta" an ass. I'd learned one truth: the boy couldn't lie worth a damn.

We kept walking, and he raised his face to the bleak October trees. "I was a jerk back there. Talking about Drake, there's a reason I don't. *If* he gets clean, it lasts maybe a month. It never takes."

"What about your mom?" I asked.

"Taos, New Mexico, in a hippie commune."

"That's different."

"Or she's a fishmonger in Seattle. Maybe she's back in jail in Arkansas." He jumped for a low-hanging branch, missing it. "She used to send postcards but stopped a long time ago."

I stopped myself from touching his shoulder. Sticking my finger in a light socket would do less damage. But I wanted to. I wanted to put my fingers on him and take away the hurt, swallow it into mine. I knew the hurt of losing a mother. When I wanted to bolt from him before, I'd been afraid of his anger, but it wasn't truly anger. It was grief. Even if he wasn't *Rom*, we had this thing in common, and it was pain. Pain was something I could take. As my hand caught his shoulder, a tic in the corner of his lips jumped.

I got it, and he knew it.

The woods thinned until we reached the main road into Black Orchard. Ward led me across the road to a cobblestone driveway I passed daily. On each side, conifers like sentinels guarded the driveway, threatening to collapse and suffocate any trespassers under their weight.

I ducked into Ward's coat and stayed close behind as he guided me down the driveway where we came to an inhospitable gate.

He grimaced as he wiped away a spider's gauzy web tacked between the metal bars, and he wedged the gate wide enough until he could slip inside and heave it open wider. "The button

in the car makes it appear so easy, but this thing weighs a ton."
He waved me forward. "After you, my lady."

I walked around him, stopping as I came to his bowed
head. His mischievous smile stretched wide, and warmth crept
into my cheeks; I had to glance away. A soft laugh echoed
behind me, not the mocking sounds that chased my mother,
chased Jonah and me in Montana and Hemlock. A gentle tease
that, because I'd blushed, knew he unraveled some tight part
of me. He was *gadje* and utterly frustrating.

I wanted to hear his laugh again.

I walked around the driveway's curve where his house
came into view. The Victorian restoration was deep lavender
with dormer windows and spindle-trim painted magenta and
white. Three stories high, the distance from the ground to the
tallest gable was intimidating. A lightning rod curly-cued off a
turret where a Velvet Underground poster covered a window,
Ward's room I guessed. Half-dead ivy devoured the house,
crawled up from the earth to reclaim the wraparound porch.
The ivy pulled as if wishing to snap off pieces and drag them
under the dirt after sunset.

A silver dog wandered off toward the evergreens, and Ward
trotted across the grass, tucking the dog under his arm, and met
me on the porch. "Bernadette wants to say hi."

My mother's *vitsa* never let her keep dogs or cats because
they weren't clean. Yet we had barn cats that my father fed
with cans of tuna in Montana. I offered the snuffling schnauzer
my hand. Her irises were milky, and the fat stump of her tail
convulsed. "She's cute. You bring her when you moved?"

"Like I've ever had a pet." He set the dog in a wicker basket
and patted her before standing. "Bernadette's my sister's dog,
but she likes me best."

In the fading sunlight, the waves of his hair gleamed
copper, which he pushed behind his left ear to reveal a steel-
ring cartilage piercing. As he rose from settling the dog, his
gaze locked on mine. I should've slipped away and waved
him goodbye, but I stayed. His chest swelled with breath. The
toes of his combat boots nudged against my blue Chucks, still

I didn't back away. Something held me because I needed to know what would happen if I stayed beside a boy I shouldn't be near. The tip of his tongue wetted his lip. Heat melted my cold as his face inched near mine. My fingers twitched. I wanted to touch him.

"Vayda," he whispered.

I turned my face. "I should probably go. Here's your coat."

"I think it's going to rain. I'll get it later."

I hopped down the steps.

"Vayda," he said again, louder.

I stalled, spying a funny twist on his mouth.

"You have the longest hair," he remarked.

"Thanks, I guess." Again, we said goodbye, but I pivoted to see him on the porch, arms crossing his chest. "Something working your mind, young man?"

He approached me. Our fingertips touched. A small *zing*, enough to make my fingers prickle. Again his mouth was close, his cheek not quite against mine. I lowered my barrier to touch him. The energy was easy and light, a tickle. I wanted more.

"It'd be cool to hang out. Without Jonah," he said.

I wanted to see him again, but so many complications made it hard to say okay. The memory of my dream—the pine trees, his hands. Why him?

I lifted my barrier, retreating. "I don't know if I can."

"I see." He trudged up the steps and held his dog, scratching her ears. I thought he was going inside with nothing to say until he swung around. "It's the whole Romani thing. Or maybe you want someone who isn't a wreck."

Before I could tell him it wasn't either of those things—I wouldn't have walked with him if I had a problem with him being *gadje*, and I didn't care what kind of background he had—he wrenched open the screen door and disappeared inside the towering house. The door clattered behind him with such force I covered my ears to drown the sound and his annoyance with me still echoing where we had stood.

Alone, I kicked the dirt. "Shit!"

My vision swam, all the sharp evergreens jarring right.

The woods were menacing as I faced them, the points of the branches like knives seeking to cut and bleed me. To open me. To Ward. My family kept the kinds of secrets we couldn't share. With anyone. I stayed away from everyone for fear that the truth might slip out. Hiding was exhausting, loneliness tiring.

As I walked home, I wrapped tighter in Ward's coat, but nothing stopped the chills.

***

A silver Toyota parked by the barn. Chloe's car. I supposed when she'd dropped me off and saw Jonah again some bit of remaining feeling for him rekindled. Neither Jonah nor Chloe were around when I let myself inside.

Yet I remained by the open door a moment. Energy swelled around me, the snarl of regret and want inside me. I tried to push out those feelings but only pulled them in deeper. The bleak sky swarmed with clouds as if my unrest could influence the weather. My hands vibrated, a smell of ozone touched my nose as sparks fractured around my fingertips. Seconds later, raindrops pinged on the copper awnings, falling so fast puddles spread on the gravel drive. Halloween was a few days off, and in another week, this rain could well be ice. I was beginning to like the cold.

I backed away, slamming the door. The paranoia of locks remained undone, but I removed the curtains from their hooks. Jonah always let in the light, and I closed it out. I could pretend to protect the antiques from the sun's glare. That was a fib Jonah could push past if he so chose.

I spotted an iPod on the coffee table, tagged by masking tape scrawled with Ward's name and number. I wound my hand into my skirt to keep a thin shield between any remnant of Ward and myself. Scanning his playlist, half the artists weren't anyone I recognized. Old Crow Medicine Show, Sun Kil Moon. My, what a strange boy Ward was.

I touched his coat and lowered my barriers for Ward. To

really let him through. I didn't practice the Mind Game often. Sometimes someone's possessions carried enough energy to let me inside their head, to see what they did. Knowing what emotions adhered to objects was unpredictable, and I didn't like using those objects to work minds.

I held the iPod, concentrating, seeking Ward, when a massive wave of melancholy rolled over me so strong my gut churned. The lights flickered, dimming for a beat before glowing far more brightly than the LED bulbs should've allowed. Dull-bright-dull-bright.

Then I saw him.

He washed his face in a bathroom with blue walls and white tiles. He was shirtless, defined muscles on thin arms. Freckles dotted his shoulders. A tattoo of a gray-scale raven began on his right shoulder and wound halfway down his bicep. It was an unkind bird, a broken bird, its head swiveled so it glared as if to say, "Back off." Trailing away from his arms, I moved to his abdomen, which was boyish despite a shadow of muscles. His unbuttoned jeans hung open below his hips and brought my curiosity lower.

My heart thumped faster as I lifted the telephone from its cradle and dialed the number on the iPod. On the second ring, I hung up and yanked myself from his mind. Not before I saw him scowl as he checked the Caller ID on his cell phone.

He didn't call back.

***

There was little chance anyone from school would see Chloe leave my house, but she crept out with her head ducked and face obscured by enormous sunglasses as she snuck out after spending an hour in Jonah's bedroom. I should've offered her a hooded cloak. It'd hide her better.

She didn't trust us. Didn't trust what we'd say. Didn't trust that she'd remain unseen.

Only certain souls deserved trust. Dad taught us that. Even if we hadn't been so superstitious, no one would've understood my family, how our minds worked. Not unless we counted Rain, but he'd known about Mind Games since before Mom met Dad. Mom trusted Rain and Dad with her secret, nobody else. She still wound up dead. Murdered.

Jonah plodded down the stairs in time with the rainfall. "What the hell were you doing?"

I took off Ward's jacket and hung it on the coat tree. "What do you mean?"

"The lights in my room kept dimming when I was with Chloe," he answered.

I lowered my face. Nothing got past him. "I was working a Mind Game."

He whipped his body off the last step and stood over me, his long shape stretched high over my head, burning. "You need to stop fucking around and get serious. Either work your Mind Games or don't, but this half-assed stuff needs to stop!"

Cold spread through my muscles, and I ducked out from under him. "It's not as if I don't ever use them. I just don't rely on them. What's wrong with that?"

"Because you aren't careful."

"Careful?" My jaw dropped. "Are you for real? You work Mind Games all the time! You can't tell me you didn't work one to get Chloe hanging around you again!"

He folded his arms and leaned against the wall. "You worry about you, Sis."

"Jonah, someone knows we're here. Someone's watching us. This is how things went bad in Hemlock. Mom wasn't—"

"I'm not Mom!" He slammed his palm against the wall. "My Mind Games are fine! When you use the Games only when they're convenient and deny them the rest of the time, you do things like screw up the lights! Why don't you hang a sign flashing 'Freak' above your head?"

I jerked my face as if he'd slapped me. My hands tingled with his anger, my panic.

Jonah's scowl shifted to the walnut coffee table. It was an enormous piece collected from one of Dad's first buying trips for antiques after we came to Black Orchard, back when he was stocking Fire Sales. The legs of the table were thicker than my calves and lavishly carved. The table could support both Jonah and me as we'd learned when swapping out Rain's contemporary chandeliers for ones to match the stone house's period, and yet now the heavy table hovered above the floor as if taking a deep breath before it careened toward me. I had no time to react except to scream and steel my body for the blow.

Nothing.

Less than an inch away, the table froze and waited for the next command from its master. My arms trembled.

"You should've seen that coming." Jonah tapped his temple. "Use your head like I use mine. Get the thoughts before they become an action. You could have this kind of control. This is what a Mind Game really is, Vayda."

The door swung open. Glancing between Jonah, the table, and me, Dad slammed the door behind him and hurled aside his wet raincoat. "Put it down!"

My brother lowered his hand. The table fell, and I slumped to my knees. *Why, Jonah?*

Furniture polish from Fire Sales clung to Dad's shirt as he placed his hand on my shoulder, guarding me from my brother.

"*Dati*," Jonah murmured.

"Quiet!" he spat. "What the hell were you thinking? Room! Now!"

Jonah slogged upstairs while I forced back tears I didn't want to cry. "I'm fine. Really."

"I know you're okay, Magpie." Dad's body droned with fear and papa bear-protectiveness. He pushed my hair from my forehead. "Didn't expect to walk in on such a scene."

I gulped down a few calming breaths. I knew my twin. At least, I thought I did. His temper, his anger because I didn't see Mind Games as the gift he did, what if he let that drive us apart?

My heart sped, and the lights buzzed, dimming a second or two. Jonah was right: I needed control of my Mind Games, but how could I when I'd only seen them used to hurt?

"You're thinking awfully hard there," Dad said, sitting beside me, one knee to his chest, the other leg stretched out. "This business with the lights didn't start up until last spring when that Pifkin boy—"

"I'm not talking about him. Nothing happened."

"Except the lights go wild whenever you're upset now." Dad took off his glasses and cleaned them on his shirt, carefully regarding me from under the black and silver hair falling over his forehead. "Don't get me wrong. Your brother's in a heap of trouble, but you also gotta get a grip, Magpie."

"Sometimes I wish we could be normal," I admitted.

"Yes, well, you are your mother's child, and that little fact altered what your normal could ever be."

He sounded so accepting of Mom and her Mind Games, of what her abilities had produced in Jonah and me. I didn't have that peace. She died before I knew how to handle the Mind Games, and I didn't want to be like Jonah, testing them on other people.

The phone rang. Dad sighed and rose to answer. He walked around the living room then the kitchen, listening, and popped a piece of nicotine gum in his mouth. "Sister Tremblay, we both know that Jonah won't speak to the likes of you. Give him some time to figure out his mess."

I doubted Jonah had told Dad how often the nun demanded he come to her office at school, and this was her third call this week. Even Dad's manners had worn thin. His jaw clenched tight on his gum, and he carried the phone and a pile of mail to his study.

My hands ached with tension, and I set to work on supper, beginning with dough for Spanish flatbread. From the time I was tiny, Mom propped me up on a chair by the counter. Every dish created by memory, she assured me I'd figure out the measurements by visualizing the pulse of the food.

Guessing had been Mom's way. Dad protected us. Sometimes that meant we damaged his mental walls. A slight slip of his barriers or mine was all it took to gather what rolled through his mind from where he sat in his study.

—no match for Jonah. Vayda's too weak. Damn it, Lorna, I wish you were here.

My throat tightened. Dad couldn't deal with us—he had no wife and was stuck raising abominations. No wonder he spent his time hiding in his study or at Fire Sales.

The light flickered. I pulled in calm, freezing in all the cracks forming inside me, and the lights regained their strength. *Vayda, I'm sorry.*

Jonah reached out to me from his bedroom, but I let my mind build a barrier, row upon row of stones with mortar caked between the layers. I wasn't ready to forgive.

After a half-hour, I had completed my physics homework, and only minutes remained before the flatbread with pesto and goat cheese finished baking. I entered Dad's study. Propping up his head with the heel of his palm, he slid a magazine my way. "Look."

I knew the respected antiques magazine. Dad's old shop in Hemlock was a frequent feature, and he'd occasionally worked as a fact-checker. A blurb in the "of interest" section lacerated me like a spear made from ice.

MAN WITHOUT A TRACE

Emory Murdock, a dealer of Civil War-era antiques and owner of Antiquaria, was at the top of his game. A workaholic known for poaching deals from rivals, his fortune was expected, and his expertise sought. "No one was as good as Em, and he knew it," says a friend.

Murdock owed some success to his wife, Lorna, a constant presence in Antiquaria. Yet criminal charges against Lorna and the subsequent legal battle crashed Murdock's idyllic life. Lorna died in a house fire thought to be arson. Murdock and the couples' children vanished. Two years later, the sign for Antiquaria remains, its showroom empty, and what happened to an influential name in southern antiques trading is unknown.

I handed over the magazine, not caring to touch it any longer. "Why are they writing about you now? It's been two years."

"A good mystery's always intriguing." Dad stuffed it in his desk drawer and rubbed his goatee and mustache. "This and the package last week, it's no coincidence."

I picked at the ends of my hair. We hadn't done anything wrong. Why would anyone want to scare us? "Do the police know we're here?"

"Nah. They'd have brought me in already. I gotta check with Rain, see if he knows of anyone snooping around."

"Sister Tremblay—"

"Don't go there. Magpie, you know better than anyone you don't go making accusations you can't back up. If someone in Black Orchard sees this article and has visited Fire Sales, we'll be in trouble."

"*Dati*, the picture with the article barely looks like you," I offered. And it didn't because he shaved then, but...

"We'll fit in here, but I gotta lie real low. You and Jonah do the same. We have to be less than invisible. We have to be ghosts."

***

After a silent dinner, Dad returned to Fire Sales to strip off the old varnish from some tables. Before he left, he gripped Jonah's shoulder, stern and eye-to-eye. "Careful, boy."

Jonah looked away first. Dad was the only person who could make him do that, but I feared the day when he couldn't.

Throughout the evening, gusting winds battered the glass chimes outside. The noises of the house sounded like footsteps going up the walls, walking overhead, none of which made me any less disturbed. A draft lingered above the hardwood floor and burrowed through flesh into my bones. Even with a blanket swathing my shoulders, I couldn't warm up. Setting aside my history book, I gathered newspaper and kindling to start a fire in the woodstove. No matches in the basket beside the stove, but I found a flint and steel in an old box. I whacked them together, producing nothing more than sparks.

"Want help?" Jonah asked, shutting off the television.

I set the flint and steel on the floor so I wouldn't have to touch him. He was already closer than I wanted. The ineptness, the hurt he created in me, I wanted to smack him, to shove him, but I wasn't that kind of person to lash out with my hands, not even hands like mine. A gnashing grief ripped through me. He had gone after me. To show me how powerful he was? I didn't care. What he did wasn't okay.

Jonah reconstructed my stick teepee among the shredded husks and hit the flint and steel, blowing on the spokes of fire. The cinders reignited, and flames spread until heat streamed from the stove.

"See? Boy Scouts *was* useful," he joked, though his good humor was forced. He pressed his lips together, whispering, "I'm sorry, Sis. For everything."

"You need to be," I said. "I don't believe you. And that hurts."

"You know acting like that isn't me. Read me if you have to."

He closed his mouth, and I felt his barrier drop, the iron door melt from his internal heat and liquefy around us until it disappeared. I lifted my fingers, unsure, but then I touched his cheek. He was warm and smoky. If his apology was anything but genuine, I couldn't feel it. "I don't like being afraid of you."

"I don't want you to be afraid of me." He curled in a ball and paused to tend the fire. "And you were right. I worked a Mind Game on Chloe."

"Jonah! Why?" I shook him. "Can't you let things be?"

"Don't worry, it's all taken care of. We're golden. I didn't do anything bad. I wanted to know why she dropped me after we hooked up before, so I got into her head, asked her some questions. Let's call it a chance for her to rethink things. If she then decided to give me another chance and bare all, so be it."

Sorry meant nothing to him. I jammed my fingers into my

hair to stop myself from strangling him. "You tricked her!"

"Now, listen to me, Vayda girl. I didn't hurt her. I'm giving her a choice. I asked her what she would do if she didn't worry so damn much about what other people thought. And you know what? She made a choice to hook up with me, the way she did before she decided she cared about her reputation more than me. It wasn't a trick. It wasn't forced. It was a question, and she answered it by going upstairs with me."

Could I believe that she'd have done that without Jonah's mental prodding? How'd he go from parlor tricks to mastering skills with which he wasn't born? He said I denied what I could do. If this was where Jonah's power led him, I didn't want it.

"I hear you loud and clear." Jonah lay out on the floor, arms stretched at his sides. "I've always moved shit with my mind. I send out my energy. Objects react."

"So you're moving thoughts in Chloe's head," I argued. "That isn't right."

He stared at his hands, palms wide, fingers long and thin. The flames through the glass door of the woodstove formed a wavering shadow on his face. "If you want to blame someone, blame Mom."

My stomach flipped. For all I thought about my mother, we didn't talk about her. When she was alive, she said we weren't to speak of our dead because they were with our ancestors. Now *she* was our dead, and I still had questions.

Mom, like so many *Rom*, read tarot cards. She taught Jonah and me as well, but she used telepathy to hear her clients' wishes and told them what they wanted. She had conversations with us without parting her lips. She used herbs, spells, and candles. She recited prayers and laid out charms. Most of what she did intended to remove negative energy and draw in positive.

Yet there was a dark side of my mother, the side that muttered curses and warned us. She'd said in a clan, she'd have been a *drabarni*, a medicine woman. Alone, she was Mrs. Murdock, the brownie-baking-classroom-mom whose best trick was tying a cherry stem in a knot with her teeth.

Jonah's smile was sad. "Do you remember when our house

was burning, how all those people stood outside yelling that Mom was a gypsy? A witch?"

Those voices rising above the fire haunted my dreams. No, I'd never forget.

"She had power." Jonah was off somewhere in his mind, marveling at the memory of our mother. How he wanted to remember her. I remembered someone different.

"She lost control of her powers," I said. "They would have destroyed her if she hadn't been murdered."

"She would have gotten control again. She taught me how to use mine, how to hold the reins tight."

So she groomed Jonah but not me. Why?

"I still hear you," he said. "Maybe Mom didn't teach you because you never wanted to learn more Mind Games. What a waste."

I stood and made my way to the base of the creaky stairs, observing my brother lying on the floor with only heat and the faint red glow from the fire surrounding him. "Not showing off Mind Games isn't a waste, Jonah, not if it keeps our family safe. You used to know that. You're exactly like Mom, and that means you're going to get someone killed."

Chapter Six

Vayda

"How's the weather on Planet Chloe?" I asked, closing my locker as she approached me. She wore pink glitter devil horns with matching platform heels to go with her school uniform. Leave it to Chloe to make Halloween cutesy. She scrutinized other students, a tight smile as people gaped at her standing with me, but she handed me several glittery ghost stickers. New cardinal rule: Be nice to everyone, even the class pariah.

"I brought you this," she said. "For your scrapbook. Right now it's weirdo-recluse-in-the-woods stuff, which is dead-on but scary."

I murmured my thanks, sliding the stickers through the slot in my locker. Perhaps I'd leave a token for the next student to take my locker.

"My mom hosted her book club last night and the subject of Heidi Brettenhoff came up," she announced.

My brow knotted. "That name matters why?"

"Heidi is Ward's sister. After Heidi came up, you did. Because you've been seen with Ward. Now I've heard rumors that Jonah and Ward are buddy-buddy, but you're not getting any ideas, are you? Ward shouldn't even be on your radar."

Chloe's checklist today: cute costume, perfect hair, and the complete guide to insulting classmates. Queen of the motor-mouth brigade, Kate Halvorsen delighted in sniping about whose baby was as ugly as a Muppet. Hardly a mystery where

Chloe inherited her penchant for gossip.

She pulled me into the bathroom while she slathered on a coat of before-school lipstick and said, "Vayda, you're a bookworm with potential because you're sort of pretty. But you wear too much eyeliner. It makes you look like a cat."

"I like my eyeliner."

Her mouth wrinkled. "I guess if you think you can pull off whatever look you're going for…Anyway, about Ward. If you're thinking about him, stop. He's trash. You don't want to be seen with him. Birds of a feather and all. Look at the guy."

This was the Chloe I recognized.

"Ward isn't trash," I argued. "Besides, why do you even care what I do? You don't want to be seen with me or my brother."

She jutted her chin. "Fine. Point made."

"Hey, you're the student ambassador," I added. "What happened to being charitable?"

"Shove it, weirdo." She cracked a wry grin. "I'll go out there and hold my head high while I elevate you off the low rung of the social totem pole. I have that kind of pull."

She had no idea what kind of pull my brother had on her.

Passing several nuns who waved at Chloe and me while whispering behind their Bibles, we made our way down the windowless halls of St. Anthony's, entering the wing where the walls were painted deep red. The color of Christ's blood. All the rooms in this wing were wider: gymnasium, band room, cafeteria. For as much as I hated the claustrophobic classrooms and tight hallways, the spacious ones were worse. They held more people, more emotions, and no matter where I stood, I couldn't be sure I saw everyone. Someone could always be hiding.

Yet I forced myself to go with Chloe to the cafeteria where Ward and Jonah parked at an isolated table in the back. Ward saw me coming and made a move to leave, but I tucked my hand into my sleeve and touched his shoulder before he could escape. "Stay, *gadjo*. I want your company."

The storm cleared from his face. I might've even seen a hint of a smile.

As Chloe took the seat next to Jonah, I settled in beside Ward, careful to keep several inches between us. Amid sprinkles from a Donut World breakfast, an Othello game was set up on the table. The board was one-sided in Jonah's favor.

"You best be waving that white flag, boy." He grinned, mischief dancing in the energy around him. "I never lose."

My brother hadn't won a game of Othello by honest means in years. Board games with telepaths weren't fun.

"I surrender," Ward admitted and cleared away the pieces. His hand brushed mine while packing away the Othello board. Static dashed from my fingertips to my elbow. He froze, staring hard at our hands, lips parting.

Jonah glanced between Ward and me before nudging Chloe. "Come on. I wanna show you something."

"What is it?" she asked skeptically.

"You're so sweet, thinking you've got something to be afraid of. I don't bite. Not hard. You should know that by now."

An energetic sheen that tasted of sugar surrounded Chloe. A few students gaped as she walked out of the cafeteria with my brother, hand-in-hand, and I doubted she cared. Maybe she was truly happier if she wasn't so worried about what everyone else thought. If she only stopped to wonder why she wasn't afraid anymore.

Alone, Ward swiveled to face me. "Why are you so quiet?"

"My mom liked to say that if a secret's revealed it's the fault of the person who confided it," I answered.

"You have secrets?"

As of right then, I wanted more than ever to tell him mine.

That would be foolish. Dad worked too hard to protect Jonah and me. My hands twirled the hair pooled in my lap. Ward ducked his shoulders and smiled when I lifted my head.

"What happened when you walked me home?" he asked.

"You won't understand. There are a lot complications and—"

"Try me. I don't scare easily."

His hands covered mine, fingers coiling around my wrists. His body mirrored mine, leg tucked up on the bench while the other hung limp. I dispatched my feelers to grab onto his energy, to find any trace of a lie. He wasn't afraid of the challenge of being with me.

He should have been.

He should have been terrified, and he wasn't, and I didn't know what to make of that.

"Chloe doesn't care that Jonah's Romani," he piped up.

"Chloe has other things working her mind," I said. "You won't leave me alone."

"Never."

I sighed. "You're a jackass, *gadjo*."

"I've been called worse, gypsy girl."

The skin on my neck pulled tight. The playfulness was gone, replaced by something cross. He knew I didn't like that word. He wouldn't forget now. I jabbed my finger into his chest where his uniform shirt was open to reveal a Califone one beneath. "You ever call me a gypsy again, and I'll curse you so your breath blows cold."

Ward enveloped my pointing finger with his scarred hand. His voice lowered. "Then I'll beg you to take it away."

"Your breath or the curse?"

He coughed and leaned in closer to me. "You figure out that one. If you go about cursing people, you're bringing them into your life instead of getting rid of them. I don't think you want to get rid of me at all."

I had no words. I had silence. His thoughts, his emotions, none of them skated into me despite the tightness of his hand on mine. He was a human barrier against all the scattered insanity around me.

Did I want to get rid of him? No. Because he made everything quiet.

I broke away, climbed off the bench, and slipped my backpack over my shoulder. Regarding his expectant face, I murmured, "You can stay."

***

In the language arts wing, the blue walls were like the gloaming, that time between sunset and nightfall, when hidden secrets showed yet remained unseen for what they were. Those windowless halls were an artificial dusk, and though the church grounds were consecrated, a black pall leached along the wood floor.

My pulse rose; my breath quickened. I couldn't see it, but even through my barrier and Ward's shield, I felt something malicious. My mouth grew metallic, sick. Around me, girls chattered at their lockers while my hands crackled with their radio static. Overpowering all was a sticky psychic tar.

I stopped, spinning in a circle in search of the source. At their classroom doors, Sister Mary Elena and Sister Hillary Lauren blessed the students entering their rooms. Though Sister Hillary Lauren got a certain giggle when lecturing Walt Whitman's "Song of Myself," neither she nor Sister Mary Elena created the vile energy slinking down the floorboards. Yet their pallid faces with rosy, apple cheeks weren't visages of flesh and blood but dolls' heads, painted and lifeless, sewed upon stuffed bodies. The vomitus sludge overwhelmed all, spilling down the floor over my feet.

Again, I whipped around. Where was it? Ward placed his arm around my shoulders. "What's wrong, Vayda? You okay?"

Sweat beaded above my upper lip, and I wiped it on my sleeve. "I have to go. Come with me."

Ward kept pace behind me, unquestioning as we pivoted from the language arts rooms. A rush of vertigo threatened to drop me to my knees. Instead of escaping the ooze of bad energy, I fell further into it. Ward steadied me, and as much as I wanted to wave him off and swear I was okay, I couldn't. The darkness circled up my legs. It brushed up beneath my skirt, and then it snaked around my waist and chest. Pressure. Pressure. Pressure. I couldn't pull it off because nothing was there.

"Vayda?" a girl's voice asked.

I didn't answer, but I knew Ward talked to Chloe. I was too focused on the sickness spreading over me. Ward's arm slid from my shoulder, and then his hand fastened with mine. "Chloe, get Jonah. Something's wrong."

Something was *very* wrong.

Something tainted was on church grounds, and if I told Ward or anyone other than my brother—who didn't have the purest of souls himself—what I sensed, I'd sound insane. The end of the hall beckoned my gaze where the walls arched over a pair of wood doors, the original church exit that separated the school from the sanctuary and Monsignor's office.

The doors were ajar, and I was certain the hem of a long, black skirt floated past the opening.

"Sister Tremblay," I whispered.

The doors shut.

The foulness lingered, the way over-ripened tomatoes still clung to their vines, pretty and glistening far away, stinking with rot up close.

"Vayda, hey!"

Marty Pifkin jogged toward me. He wore a dark blue, V-neck sweater embroidered with the St. Anthony's shield. I clutched Ward's hand harder, brought him closer so the length of my arm ran down the front of his body. I wanted silence.

Marty's eyes flicked from my face to Ward's then low to our joined hands. He motioned across the hall to his friend, Danny Milagro. As he waited for Danny, he made no secret of sizing up Ward's combat boots and loosened necktie, but then he smiled at me. "I wanted to thank you for your help with the physics homework. Too bad Jonah didn't get what was going on."

My body went rigid. Ward seemed to notice, stayed close, and rested his hand on the small of my back. He was observing, letting me handle Marty. This was something Jonah would never allow.

"Marty, that was a while ago," I said. "Apologize to Jonah, not me."

He shifted from one foot to the other, arms crossed over his wide chest. The different athletics' coaches had courted him as they had Jonah, but the only sport Marty was involved in was wrestling. More trouble with my brother could hurt his place on the team, if Monsignor actually followed the rules in the school handbook, and the mention of my brother's name made Marty's nose wrinkle.

"I'd rather be talking to you, Vayda."

"Marty, don't," I warned.

"Are you guys a thing? Really? *That* guy?" He backed off a step and addressed Ward. "Danny says you're the new go-to guy to get anything harder than a nickel or dime."

Puzzled for a moment, Ward's jaw then set and his nostrils flared. I sensed his pulse accelerate. "Get out of my face, man."

"Relax."

"I said go away. Get your fix somewhere else. I'm not the guy to get it from."

Marty scratched at his spiky, brown hair and chuckled. "No, but I see you're the one Vayda's finally getting it from, eh?"

A dam of pent-up anger cracked. I let go of Ward's hand to grip Marty's sweater, pulling him down close enough to slap his cheek with a loud smack. His head whipped to the side. The din of my classmates' chatter hushed. Everyone stared, all too eager to see what would happen next, and when Marty shook off the hit, his hazel eyes darted along the walls at the crowd before settling back on me.

"Go away, Marty," I said, struggling to keep my voice even.

He rubbed the reddening welt left by my palm. "I warn you, Vayda—"

"I wouldn't finish that threat."

Jonah glowered behind Marty. A smoky haze of rage radiated from him, so concentrated his energy burned. By then, the noise drew more spectators. I looked back for any nuns to break up the crowd, but there weren't any.

Danny circled Jonah, but Marty stayed him with his hand. "We're out of here."

Jonah's teeth bared, his fists clenched as Marty pushed past him and jabbed him hard in the ribs. A flare from my brother's temper was another blast of hot air. The heel of his palm popped the back of Marty's head. "Speak to my sister again, and I'll tear you in half."

Marty scoffed. "Bet she likes it when you talk rough. Maybe that's why you Silvers don't let anyone else in, 'cause you're riding each other."

"That's it!" Jonah swung around. Shouting in Romani, he cussed out Marty and thrust his fist into Marty's gut. Marty staggered back and crashed into the lockers with an echoing bang.

"Jonah, come on!" I grabbed my brother's arm, trying to pull him away. The dizziness from before still hadn't worn off, and the frenzied rush of the other students' excitement mixed with my panic until the walls and floor tilted. I needed rest and quiet and calm, but there was only noise in my head, static in my hands, everything in me too wild. The fluorescent lights blinked.

"Vayda, look out!"

Chloe's voice cut through as she yanked me away from my brother and Ward, tucking me inside the crowd where the madness of countless thoughts and instincts thrashed against my barriers.

Marty charged with his head down and rammed Jonah, lifting him up off the floor and slamming him into the lockers. Fists and black hair, neckties swinging and shoes squeaking on the floor, they locked with each other, and behind them, Danny pounded on my brother's back. Ward weaved into the middle and shouted for them to stop. Jonah pivoted away, shaking out his hands, dissipating the energy collecting in his palms. His power searched for a vent through which to escape. It nudged me, but I was already too full. Marty leapt onto his back.

Don't, Jonah! I shouted in his head. *Don't touch him!*

Too late. He reached back, enough that his fingers grazed Marty. Yet as effortlessly as passing a basketball, Marty hurtled over his head and soared until he thudded against the floor, skidding down the wood until he came to rest against the arched doors. A couple of girls screamed, but most of the hall fell into glassy silence.

My brother's hair hung loose as he panted, unbridled. Chloe whimpered, "Oh my God," over and over while I found my way inside my brother's mind. *What have you done?*

He said nothing. His temper wandered an invisible trail. So hot, I needed cold. I needed to shut out everything. The lights blinked off and on. Danny stumbled back from Ward and scurried to Marty, who groaned as he made his first movements to get up.

The bell signaling the start of school resounded. As the crowd dispersed, Jonah leaned against a locker and clutched his head. Blood ringed his nostril. Chloe separated from me and dug through her purse for some tissues. Instead of checking on my brother, I paced along the lockers, my fingers bouncing off each of the combination locks.

We couldn't run again.

I stood across from Jonah, cracking my knuckles to diffuse the energy cascading through me, any sparks smothered under my fingers. Ward came over, pressed his back to the locker, and lowered until he was my height.

"Remind me never to really piss you off. I'm delicate and you'd leave a mark."

I snorted and kept my hands where he couldn't see them. "You sure you want to hang around?"

"I've met my fair share of Marty Pifkins, and they're all the same," he answered. "I haven't met any Vayda Silvers before though."

He wasn't ready to know that Vayda Silver wasn't all who I said she was. Still, I gave him a tempered smile from behind my hair.

Jonah's nose had stopped bleeding, and he shuffled toward the trashcan, muttering, "I'm so finished."

I expected him to rejoin Chloe, Ward, and me, but he shuffled down the hall. If he thought he could grumble about how much trouble he was in and walk away, he had another thing coming. I stalked after him, a plume of steam scalding my palm as I grabbed his shoulder, and I yelped. Jonah winced as he pivoted.

I'm sorry, Sis. I'd never hurt you.

That was a lie.

I rubbed an unseen blister on my hand left by his heat. He could have hurt Marty when he threw him. Maybe that was his intention. My feelers scrounged his mind, searching for remorse, but they returned empty.

"You don't care," I said.

"He had it coming. That *gadjo* insulted you and threatened you," he growled. "What do you expect me to do?"

So you threw him down a crowded hallway with your Mind Games? That's your answer?

Seeing his destruction was like watching Mom again.

Ward nonchalantly approached us. "I'm ditching class. Join me?"

I'd skipped school a few times, mostly to sit with my brother until he calmed enough to get his act together, yet Ward was so blasé about it. Jonah couldn't afford to be caught cutting class. He was on fragile ground with Monsignor, and someone would talk about the fight this morning. Hell, maybe we *should* disappear. Chloe bobbed between all three of us before finally, not without cringing, nodded that she'd come.

We grabbed our coats, and a minute later, the double doors to the school flew open as we drew near. They weren't automatic. Ward paused, brow furrowed. "That was weird."

I elbowed Jonah. Not the right time for Mind Games, not that he cared.

As I stepped outside, I blew on my hands for warmth. Tall evergreens spiked the autumn sky, and snow flurries whipped around the air. Built directly off the church, St. Anthony's school was red brick covered in ivy. Rows of arched windows stood out like bared teeth, and at the center of the top row was a nook for a statue of St. Anthony of Padua. The church was also red brick with an imposing bell tower below a greened copper steeple. The cross atop the steeple could be seen above the dark forest surrounding all of Black Orchard, and the melancholy drone of its bell tolling Sunday mornings echoed for miles farther.

Ward bounced, rubbing his hands together. "We should go, get off campus before anyone sees us. Besides, I'm freezing my ass off."

"Coffee break, anyone?" Chloe asked and jingled her keys. She led us to the back row of the parking lot when Jonah stopped and scanned the next row, startled.

A familiar energy caught me. Constant, unwavering.

Fifty feet away, Dad leaned against the Chevy, a cigarette between his fingers. He'd quit smoking six years ago, mostly to stop Mom's nagging, and replaced his addiction with nicotine gum. Until that afternoon.

"Damn." Jonah steered me between two parked cars, ducking to hide his six-foot frame. Chloe and Ward crammed in beside us, but my vision was pinned on my father. I spied the black dress flutter as Sister Tremblay drifted across the lot. Dad's spine stiffened, matching the hardness of the nun's posture. She held out her hand, and he shook it like a good southern gentleman. Yet his stare was cold.

My jaw flexed, and I shoved my hands in my pockets to stop from spilling out chaotic energy. Nothing hollered, "Notice me" like breaking a row of headlights in a parking lot.

"Scandalous," Chloe clucked. "Sister Tremblay and your dad meeting in private. It's personal. Why else wouldn't they be in her office? You think nuns take a vow of celibacy?"

Ward shushed her. "Pipe down, Blondie. You'll get us busted."

Maybe it was Chloe. Maybe it was Ward. It could have been that we were all too nervous about ditching class and making loud mistakes, but Dad's head snapped up. "Polly, hold on a second."

Dad checked the aisle and between the cars. I curled in a ball, heart thundering in my ears, and I looked from Jonah to Ward, mouthing, "What do we do?"

Ward indicated to weave backward through the cars, but Dad was too fast and stood over us. His voice was stern. "Magpie."

Take me to the gallows now.

Sister Tremblay joined his side, and a dark gloom washed over me, the same sickly grime I felt inside the school. I steadied myself against a car. Sister Tremblay pursed her lips, which were dry and split, a drop of blood rising to the surface.

The closer she came, the less I could breathe. I had to get away, and I bolted, sprinting across the lot. The wind smacked my face until my cheeks were numb, but my hands burned. I wiped my palms on my skirt as if I could scrape off the skin. I had to get Sister Tremblay's smile off me.

Jonah caught up with me, and his arms were warm around my shoulders. "Calm down."

"That nun." I gasped. "There's something off with her."

A shadow formed on his cheeks. *What do you mean? You think she knows?*

Before I could answer, Dad reached the sidewalk. "Why'd you run from me?"

"Not you. Her." I pointed to Sister Tremblay. "Why are you meeting that woman?"

He retrieved his cigarettes, lighting a new one as he devised something to say. "Now don't go jumping off a cliff. The good sister and I are having ourselves a chat. Nothing more."

His answer sucked.

Cardinal rule: Some rules need to be broken. Especially if you're being jerked around.

I prodded Dad's mind. He blocked me by focusing on the glowing cinders on the end of his cigarette.

Something was up.

I persisted, "*Dati*, that woman isn't right."

He tipped his face skyward as he exhaled. "This is not how it looks. Sister Tremblay and I have some issues to work out, all right? Now get to class."

"*Dati!*"

That hard air about him again. "This isn't your business."

I whipped away, every muscle in my body cramped. He was never this short with me. Jonah? Yes, but never me.

I tossed my father a wary glance as Ward guided me back inside school and out of the cold morning. My father was smart. I trusted that he looked out for us. He warned us to be mindful of prying eyes.

Hopefully, he took his own advice.

Chapter Seven

Ward

Sometimes I missed the lights of Rochester, Minnesota. Nice city. I couldn't say the same for the people shouting in my old building. This house—hell, all of Black Orchard—was quieter than a church at midnight. Here, I lay awake because of the wind sighing in the attic.

At least living by the woods, I didn't have to deal with trick-or-treaters. No one came to the bleak house surrounded by the foreboding gate, but I still carved a half-dozen jack-o-lanterns and nestled them among the dead leaves on the front porch, their orange glow lonely against the night. At my old apartment, Drake only got tricks. Lots and lots of tricks. Some in stiletto heels, some in fur coats and probably not much else.

Oliver screamed over the baby monitor. I set aside my crossword puzzle and trudged upstairs to the nursery. My nephew sat in his crib, face red and tear-streaked, and I lifted him up, murmuring the words Heidi crooned during the night. "You're okay."

His fingers clawed my hair as I sank into the rocking chair beside his crib and patted his back. I caught my reflection in the window and coughed. A month ago, I'd have given them the crazy look if someone said I'd be babysitting. A month ago, I was still in Drake's apartment.

The studio unit where I'd lived with Drake was a matchbox, cluttered with takeout containers and overloaded ashtrays. The water in the pipes was glacier-cold in winter and lukewarm on sunny days. I remembered standing on the roof, my shirt sweat-adhered to me as I stared at the street. A metal sawhorse, shears, my blowtorch—all my tools scattered around me. The roof's door squeaked as it opened. Louis, this guy I palled around with after bumping into each other at an Arcade Fire show, squinted in the July sun and hollered, "Man, I trusted you! What are you doing with my girl?"

I'd lit a cigarette, sneering. "Giving her what you can't."

He'd come at me, throwing me to my back. The heat from the roof had scorched my skin as I tried to deflect his flailing punches.

It wasn't easy to forget all the hitting, the fighting, the anger at being stuck in a shitty life. The acceptance that things wouldn't get better. They had, even with Oliver's chubby hands batting my chin as I wrestled him into a cloth diaper, attempting to decipher Heidi's cryptic notes on folding and fastening the damn thing. Was I so dense I couldn't fold a piece of fabric? So it wasn't perfect. At least the kid had what he needed.

Food. Shelter. Parents. Lucky guy.

The day I fought with Louis was the same night I last saw Drake. I had to piss about midnight and found Drake passed out near the toilet with a syringe in his arm, mouth hanging slack like a rubber mask left out of a costume bin. I checked his pulse. Alive. Kind of. It wasn't an overdose this time, only his typical drug stupor. By morning, he'd disappeared.

After three weeks, his lawyer stopped by. Peeking through the peephole in the door, I zeroed in on the guy in the sweltering hall. He had a pig's button eyes, and his suit smelled like fish tacos. In five minutes, he stank up that apartment.

"I'm sure you guessed Drake was arrested again." He spoke flatly. No surprise. No apology. We were used to Drake's bullshit. "He was busted in an underground opium den. He pled out to get court-ordered rehab. You know the drill. Find someone to stay with."

Usually Mr. Lawyer Man was able to dig up Drake's Hooker of the Week. My father had some money socked away from his years as a singer, but he'd always been as famous for his love of opiates as he'd been for his gravel voice. That time was different. No one came. No ditz in a leopard print nightgown swung by to make pancakes while not getting cigarette ash in the batter. It took until September before one of my teachers noticed I was wraith-gaunt and coughing despite that I'd quit smoking. Sometimes you're so desperate, it doesn't matter what you say when someone asks if you're okay—they know you need help.

At some point, Drake's brain fired the synapse with Heidi's married name, and beckoned by a caseworker, she drove to Minnesota. Heidi had twelve years on me and sat across the table in a clean, blue dress, tapping her fingernails as we played twenty questions.

Was I on drugs? Uh, no. How many times was I arrested? Enough. For what? Stupidity since that's what got me caught.

Over diner coffee and scrambled eggs, she told me I was moving to Wisconsin. No choice. The court granted her emergency guardianship, and I packed my duffle bag. I doubted she liked it any more than I did.

Sleep didn't come easily in this house that whispered at night, but I could count on a few hours where my brain blacked out.

The front door slammed. Heidi's footsteps echoed off the woodwork. Babysitting detail complete. If she thought I'd guard her demon baby at her every whim, she could forget it. I bounced Oliver in my arms to soothe him before taking him to Heidi. He whined until my half-sister unbuttoned her top, at which point he became excited and I became very weirded out. She stroked his head and asked, "How'd it go?"

"The kid hates me," I said, rooting in my pocket for my iPod. Damn. Left it upstairs.

Bernadette tottered out from the kitchen and dropped at my feet. I hoisted her onto my lap. Her fur was grimy, but I was rather gross when we met. All was fair.

"I think you need to get used to him," Heidi said then cooed at Oliver, tapping his nose.

"So did I pass your test?" I asked. "I mean, Oliver's still alive and the house didn't burn down."

Heidi lifted her chin. "What test?"

"I'm shocked you trusted me to babysit."

My half-sister's lips narrowed. "I don't think you're a bad guy, Ward. I think you've been through some crap, and Lord knows Drake's good at messing up and hurting others."

I tsked. "I don't see how he hurt you, and if he did, you still turned out okay."

"I wasn't always this person, Ward."

The phone rang. I jumped, and Heidi's neck cracked as she whipped her head in the direction of the phone. Casual calls didn't come at ten on weeknights. Drake might've been a drunk-dialer, but he was an every-seven-days guy. Our last conversation went:

Drake: You doin' okay?

Me: Better than if I was with you.

Drake: I'm clean, buddy. We'll move to California, live the high life.

Me: Was that a pun? Shut up.

Drake: Now, hold up. You're no better than me. I'm your dad.

Click.

Chris appeared in the doorway with the phone, his face long. "It's about Drake."

Of course, it was.

Heidi took the phone and listened, promising to be in touch. Only one call made people's skin the color of raw potatoes. I sank into the couch, a cold moat winding through my stomach, and enfolded Bernadette in my lap. The dog snuggled close, and I ran my hand over her head and down her back again and again. I didn't want to know. I didn't want to care.

Heidi passed Oliver to her husband and touched my shoulder. "Ward, I'm sorry."

I patted Bernadette's bony sides. Her leg kicked as I hit her ticklish spot. I wouldn't cry for that son-of-a-bitch, instead, burrowing my face into the crook of my elbow and coughing.

Heidi rubbed my back. "You're okay."

If I could believe that, I would. God, I would.

Depositing Bernadette on the couch, I bolted upstairs and flung myself onto my bed with my pillow covering my head. I shoved my headphones in my ears and switched on my iPod. The drums were a frenetic backdrop as the singer screamed. Yelling wouldn't help. It was all noise.

Shut up.

I'm your dad.

Heidi opened the door. "Chris and I don't want you to be alone."

A skosh late, wasn't she?

I bit my lower lip. Hurt like a mother.

Chris took Heidi's place at my door, kissing the back of her head before he sent her away. He felt along the walls of my room, the sketches I'd drawn of the woods, line doodles of Bernadette's whiskers and shiny nose. It used to be his office, but he'd never said a word about giving up his workspace for me.

"We'll drive to Rochester tomorrow," he informed me.

"Have a blast."

"You don't have to decide right now if you're going to Drake's funeral," he said. "But you might want to grab some stuff from the apartment."

"Oh, great, and bring the plague here." I didn't want anything from my life there. "All his stuff can all be burned. I don't give a damn."

"Like I said. We'll leave in the morning," Chris said and shut my door.

A gooey tongue licked my fingers hanging over the edge of the bed. Bernadette was on her hind legs, wiggling her ass as she waited for help onto my bed. "Not now, girl."

Her ears drooped. Like I could resist hurt doggy kisses. I lifted her off the floor, and she circled several times before laying her head beside mine, her dog smell overpowering. I once asked Drake for a dog. He told me to make some money walking the beagle across the hall. Then he took the money and bought an eight-ball.

Don't think about Drake. Can't do anything for him. I believed in God, but didn't believe God wouldn't give people more than they could bear.

I got up from my bed and wandered around the room until the promise of distraction put me in front of the computer Chris let me use. If it weren't so late, I'd be outside, putting the finishing polish on the lightning rod wind sculpture. After a moment of mindless surfing, I noticed Jonah signed in to instant messenger.

WardofRavens: Up late, I see.

SilverTongue: Can't sleep.

Another message chimed to get my attention.

SilverTongue: I'm V.

Vayda. I smiled.

SilverTongue: Why are you still up?

WardofRavens: Bad night.

SilverTongue: Call me.

The clock read shortly before midnight. I dialed the number Jonah gave me for his house regardless.

"What's going on?" Vayda asked.

"Nothing good." I cleared my throat, shaking out the kinks. "Drake's dead."

Vayda was silent. Maybe she didn't know how to respond. Hell, *I* didn't know how to respond.

"Do you need to come over?" she asked.

I breathed out. Relief, release, something. I wouldn't have to be alone. "Yes."

Heidi was in bed with Oliver. Downstairs, Chris watched some singer warbling off-key on a late-night show. I leaned against the back of the couch and said, "I'm heading out."

He looked me over, seeming to wonder if I intended to get stoned, drunk, or any of a hundred ways I could get fucked up. "Where will you be?"

I wrote down the Silvers' number on a scrap paper. "Call in a half-hour if you want to check on me. That'll give me enough time to walk over there."

"You are not walking this late. There's already a hard frost, and that cough of yours isn't getting any better. We'll take the car."

This wasn't typical of Chris. Maybe he felt bad for me. Maybe he wanted out for a ride. I didn't know but slipped on my leather coat and followed him to his Jaguar. Nice, not terribly easy to break into. Chris tossed me the keys. He was gonna let me drive his baby? Seriously? I wasn't about to say no and held my breath as I settled in the driver's seat and negotiated the car down the driveway. *Don't mess up.*

"This car's meant to go fast," he told me as I pulled onto the street.

I could do fast. The Jag's engine kicked in, and we careened along a forested stretch of road on a pitch-black night. No other cars on the road. Chris and I might be the last people awake in Black Orchard. The only creatures out at midnight were spooks.

The Silvers lived so close the Jag barely had time to pick up any speed. As I parked between the gray stone house and the barn, Chris opened his door to switch to the driver's side and admitted, "You're not bad behind the wheel. Heard you can hotwire a car pretty fast, not that you should be proud of that."

I snickered and handed back the keys.

The porch light outside the Silvers' home was a welcoming lantern, but the hair on my neck rose as I stepped inside the house. The sole light was the fire in the woodstove and shadows shrouded the living room. Hard to tell where the walls ended. Vayda emerged from the kitchen, set down a steaming mug of hot chocolate on the coffee table, and hugged me. Her arms were icy, but her body was warm. She smelled like a blast of snow, cold but burning, and I hung on tight.

"How are you?" she asked.

"Shitty," I blurted.

"It must be a shock."

No, it really wasn't. Drake never cared enough to get clean. She must've seen something in my face and asked, "You truly think that?"

The unnerving tingle on my back intensified, and the firelight wavered. My head felt strange. Open. I didn't mind the feeling, actually, and wished it were stronger. Vayda angled her head, her big eyes the same green as century-old copper. They stood out against the darkness of the rest of her, and I could've—very willingly—let myself drown in their unsettled waters.

The front door opened, and Emory Silver set his briefcase on the floor. She backed away, folding her arms over her chest. Maybe to cover herself. Maybe because she was still miffed about seeing him with Sister Tremblay that morning. Whatever the reason, the hardwood floor might as well have been eggshells.

"Ward, it's a school night," Emory stated, tired but firm. "Get on home, boy."

"It's not a social call, *Dati*. His father died," Vayda murmured.

Emory stopped mid-yawn, taking note of my jacket and threadbare trousers. He didn't know me. Why should he let some stranger seek refuge in his home?

"I was a kid when my mother died. Rough times." He cleaned his glasses on his shirt. "You live with your sister, right? She knows you're here?"

"Her husband does," I answered.

"Give me the number to talk with the fellow, make sure he's okay with this. I'm sorry, Ward." He patted my shoulder. "Don't stay up too late, you two. You hear?"

Huh? He wasn't kicking me out?

After I gave him Chris's cell phone number, Emory walked over to his study. I lingered by the door a minute to watch while he shuffled some kind of art magazines and then took a picture frame in his hands. Vayda looped her pinky finger around mine and pulled me away before she shut her father's door.

"He's always up late," she said.

"Insomnia?" I asked.

"Of a kind." She slipped me a cup of hot chocolate. "Try

this. I made it from scratch. You'll like it, *gadjo*."

"We'll see about that, Betty Crocker."

She motioned for me to follow her upstairs, and I trailed behind her a step or two. The walls of her room were purple, and the furniture was distressed white as if dropped off a junk truck onto a cobblestone road. She tugged on the strap of her pale blue top, no bra, and I averted my gaze, hoping she didn't realize that I'd noticed. Her hand thumped her bed, encouraging me to sit. "Will you go to the funeral?"

"Hell no...I don't know." I drank the entire cup of hot chocolate without stopping to breathe. I liked the heat.

"You should say goodbye even if he wasn't good to you."

Pushing up the sleeve of my T-shirt, she ran her fingers over my raven. How did she know I had a tattoo? It wasn't something I showed off. She asked, "You draw that bird?"

I scoffed. "Drake's idea of a birthday present. He had the same tattoo, thought we could bond or some shit."

"Did it hurt?" she asked while inching down my sleeve.

"You get used to the pain after a while, forget it's there."

Our arms touched. Vayda's hand rested on my thigh. I liked her touch. A lot.

"You're tired," she said. "You should lie down."

I stretched out on the mattress. The girls I used to know would never have me in their rooms, nor would I have been there, without an ulterior motive. Vayda's fingers twirled my hair, and I sank into the pillow, blissed out.

The dream hit me abruptly.

The pine trees caged me in. Everything had a darkened blue cast, a shadow of nightfall before the sunset. Snow dusted the soil, and a smell of something burning was bitter on the wind.

I saw her, a pillar of cold fire, luring me closer.

Her back was to me, black hair cascading to her hips. I hesitated, but the magnet pull of her body was too forceful. I seized her waist from behind, hands moving over her nightgown and resting on her arms. She pushed aside her black hair to expose her neck, my lips swiping her skin.

The words swelled in my throat. I had to tell her I knew, but I had no idea what I was supposed to know.

Awake.

Vayda's bedroom was black. I lay under her blankets. Her body was firm under my arm, but pliable like a girl-shaped pillow. I drowsily slid my hand from her hip, along her soft stomach, and stopped short.

Go back to sleep, Vayda's voice echoed in my skull.

My eyes fluttered open. Was this a dream or something else? I couldn't tell where reality ended and the dream began. I only knew that I was with Vayda, and all at once, I never felt safer and more in danger.

Chapter Eight

Vayda

The glare of sunlight through the living room curtains awakened me. I blinked against the bright light before I sat up, rubbed my neck, and wondered what time I fell asleep on the couch, why Dad hadn't moved me up to my room.

Midnight.

Ward. His dad died.

I remembered now. How I stayed with him even after his exhaustion claimed him. I'd been too afraid to move and startle him, so for too long, I'd lain beside him with my fingertips wandering over his arm to the veins mapping his hand. No one saw us, but was a line crossed? Jonah had it easy compared to me—my family's traditions demanded chasteness of me. Yet last night, the weight of Ward's arm, his breath near my ear, felt good. A complacent current had dovetailed our bodies, like electricity tracing the copper filaments in an antique light bulb—from me to Ward and bouncing back. His mouth had grazed over my neck, and I wondered when he'd awaken, what his fingers, what his lips might do then. What I wanted them to do. I slipped away once he slept hard and began to dream.

My skin prickled, frozen. That dream. Did mine spill into his, or—I was getting ahead of myself. It was nothing. It didn't have to be something.

Cardinal rule: Wishes and dreams weren't childish things. They were the soul's secrets.

Something about Ward knew mine.

Twenty minutes later, I'd showered and descended the stairs, catching a reflection in a mirror in the landing. A burning chill unwound beneath my ribs, a power seeking release. Mom's smoky gaze reflected back from what should have been mine. I approached the mirror, my head hooked in the same angle as Mom's when she examined her tarot cards, and inched my fingers toward the glass. A bolt of blue-white light sizzled from my fingers when Jonah jerked me back from the mirror.

"What was that?" Dad called from the kitchen.

"Electrical glitch," Jonah fibbed and held my hands within his, smothering a fire. To me, he whispered, "And you say I'm the one like Mom."

I didn't want to be like her.

Dad and Ward sat in the kitchen, each cupping a coffee mug to absorb some heat in the chilly house. Ward stole a peek as I passed him. As I splashed my coffee with cream, I tuned in to Dad and him.

"You go around hunting down old furniture to sell?" Ward asked.

"You have to know what has potential, son." Dad rubbed the heel of his hand on the table, one he'd restored. "I can take something busted to hell, fill in the cracks, and sand its jagged spots. Shine it up real pretty and make it worth something. Takes skill and patience."

"How'd you learn what's good?"

"I'm self-taught, learned some in art school, though my father was pissed his only boy would rather draw than play football. I was kinda pissed my father was such a closed-minded bigot."

"Hmph." Ward circled the rim of his mug with his thumb. "Heidi thinks I should go to art school 'cause I work with metal."

Dad stood and grinned. "Don't take this wrong, but you're no quarterback. Come by Fire Sales once you're home from paying respects to your father, and I'll show you around."

He gathered his mug and newspaper, motioning me to follow into his study. Joy, here it came. "Awkward" redefined.

Dad sat at his desk where he removed his glasses, squeezed the bridge of his nose, and took a long time to inhale. "Vayda, is that boy being decent to you?"

"Nothing happened."

It would take me two seconds to get from his desk to the door. Three if I stumbled. This was worse than going clothes shopping and he got so flustered when I had to buy bras.

"Can I go?" I asked.

"Not yet." He played with the Chinese magic box on his desk. "I know you're friendly with Ward. Don't mistake your feelings for trust. Not yet." I crossed my arms over my chest, and he added, "He seems honest, and you and Jonah laugh an awful lot around him. Keep your head."

About to leave, I halted as my hand brushed a newspaper on the desk. The newspaper from Hemlock with Mom's photo. I unfolded it, tracing the curse written across the picture. I tried to seek out any emotion attached to the paper, any clue for where it came from, but I got nothing. Odd that whoever sent it had left it without any emotional imprint, especially with such a hateful word written across the paper. Maybe Jonah was right, and my abilities were unwieldy because I didn't use them.

"Any luck figuring out who sent this?" I asked.

"I have an idea," Dad replied.

"You gonna tell me?"

"You don't have any business fretting over it. Everything's taken care of."

"*Dati!*" The light bulb in his desktop lamp switched on and glowed brighter the longer I stared at him. "Why do you need to have so many secrets?"

"Vayda Lisette Murdock, I don't know what's gotten into you, why you're questioning me." Dad's drawl was clipped, his green eyes hot. "Everything I've done is for you and Jonah. If I say it's okay, believe me. Now get ready for school."

I stormed from Dad's office and tossed some blueberry waffles into the toaster in the kitchen. The plate of food clattered on the table as I set it before Ward.

His shoulders rode up around his neck. "Is he pissed because I stayed the night?"

"He's *Dati*." I melted the butter into the perfect crispiness of the waffles. My appetite was toast. "One of his cardinal rules is that you don't turn your back on a friend in need."

Ward's hand ran through his sleep-messy hair and touched my chin. Pinprick shocks stung my skin. I reached under the table to hold his hand. The few times I saw my grandpa Bengalo, he always claimed that *gadje* didn't understand *Rom*. *Bapo* said in the old lands, *gadje* treated *Rom* badly. It was different once their clan came to Georgia. They settled. They were accepted, though they still wouldn't trust *gadje*. That my parents were friends with Rain was an anomaly, but Dad said times had changed. Ward sat across from me, radiating warmth from his hand, the roughness of his scars against my fingers. He was *gadje*. He didn't know my world, and yet I wanted him to. That meant trusting him.

My mom's friends, our neighbors, they betrayed us before. Mom was rash, but none of us hurt anybody on purpose. That didn't mean people weren't killed. We were different. If Ward found out how different we were, could I be sure he wouldn't go Judas on me?

***

The afternoon was a gloomy Sunday, over a week into November, over a week since Ward returned to Minnesota. The sky was quilted with clouds, and the surrounding evergreens were dark, pointy, dense. I sat outside on the steps, working in my scrapbook.

Mom's frantic as she clings to Dad on the living room floor. His arms fold around her as she rocks back and forth. Someone else's blood sprayed in reddish dots on her forearms and neck, on her face. There's death all over her. Death she caused.

"Oh, God, Lorna!" Dad gathers her against him until she's in his lap. "What'd you do?"

When Mom died in the fire, all my tangible memories were lost with her—from the Snow White costume that she sewed for my third-grade play to the lipstick I stole from her vanity. A thousand snatches of her charred and lost. Six months ago, Rain sent some photos he found dating to when he, Mom, and Dad were in high school, a history of my parents' early days through Jonah's and my first birthday. I glued dried Spanish moss from a craft store to the page with a cutout of peaches from a can of pie filling. Two things I recalled best about Georgia. Next, I mounted one of Rain's photos on the page.

"I like that picture." Jonah pointed to our parents' wedding photo. They were so young, only nineteen. It was hard to believe they were only a few years older than I was now.

"Think *Dati* knew about her Mind Games by that point?" I asked.

Jonah shrugged. "I'm more curious if he knew we'd inherit her abilities."

Mom's father had worked Mind Games. So did his mother, my great-grandmother. Grandpa Bengalo had steel-gray hair smelling of chicory hanging to his belt. *Bapo* had lived in Hemlock and died when I was seven. When you're little, sometimes you overhear things and not know what they mean. *Bapo* always said he couldn't be seen with Mom, that his clan's *baro* might bring him to a *kris* for talking to her. *Kris* were for only terrible offenses. Mom said it was fuddy-duddies gassed up on cigar smoke and wine, casting judgment and telling people what they could and couldn't do. So what had she done that'd been so bad even her own father abandoned her?

We were alone with no clan. Because of Mom. Dad never discussed his *vitsa*, but Mom once let it slip after too much wine that his family disowned him. What had they done, and why did I feel like Jonah and I were paying for it?

Jonah's palm rested on my shoulder, and his voice slipped over my mind. *Ward wants you to meet him at Café du Chat Noir in an hour. I told him you'd be there.*

I elbowed him. *Got anything else to put on my calendar while you're at it?*

Truth was I hadn't seen Ward since the night he stayed, though we'd talked. He'd been too tired to talk much, but even his voice over the phone had brought a welcome hush. Still, my body hummed with electricity.

Try not to knock out the lights, Jonah wisecracked and sat beside me.

If it happens, I'll use your old standby: just a power surge.

He put his arm around me. The currents coming off him were relaxed. He tucked my scrapbook under his arm and gathered my supplies. *Sister Tremblay called.*

What'd she want? I wondered.

Dati *took the call, but I'm keeping my eye on her. We're golden, all right? Don't worry.*

Sister Tremblay stopped by Fire Sales twice. Each time, Dad leaned back and played with his glasses. Uneasiness swelled around him even if he didn't say anything. I felt it. They spoke in whispers, and Dad was too good at blocking Jonah and me from his head.

I touched Jonah's arm. *Mind what you say to that woman. And especially mind what you do.*

He mimicked my concerned face, the bunched forehead and penetrating stare, and snickered. "Vayda girl, come on. I'm not dense."

"No Mind Games around her. Period."

"If the lady of the manor insists."

Did he really think his Mind Games were immune from detection? I liked Black Orchard. I liked the conifers and isolated roads. I even liked the cold. All it took was the wrong person to spot him opening a door or retrieving a pencil with his mind, and we'd be gone.

"By the way, I'm hooking up with Chloe while you're away," Jonah announced. "Give me a signal when you're coming home so I can scoot her out of here."

"So are you two are really back together or fooling around? If you're messing with her head to make her be with you…"

"You gonna throw stones?" The sunset warmed his skin with its dying rays, but his eyes remained black. "I didn't think so. I helped Chloe. That girl was so wound up in doing what everybody else wanted that she was miserable. Is it that hard to believe she's happier forgetting about them?"

"It's not who Chloe is."

"I haven't forced her into doing anything. She hasn't been hurt. Actually, she has a damn good time with me, the way she used to. You really think what I'm doing is wrong?"

I wrapped my arms around myself while Jonah descended the steps and strolled past the barn to the woods, heading out for a walk. The boy was trifling with something he shouldn't, something twisted and, yes, wrong. All that energy he pushed onto others, some of it had to come back.

***

As I entered Café du Chat Noir, I snuck up on the table where Ward was lost in the beat from his headphones, his left hand working in a sketchpad. I drummed on the table, and he yanked off his headphones. Before either of us spoke, his arms wound around me, and my body snuggled close despite the shocks bursting between us.

"It's good seeing you," he said after a waitress came by to take my order.

"I missed you, too."

As the waitress set down his coffee and my hot tea, Ward handed me an iPod along with a makeshift booklet. The tracks he'd loaded on the iPod were an indie hodgepodge, and ink and pencil sketches filled the booklet. My house. Me from behind in the woods with wind tugging at a long, black skirt. Him sitting on stairs. Stacks of Tennessee Williams's work. Bernadette.

"Magpie's Mix," I read aloud. "What's this?"

"Some songs you can't live without," Ward said. "I thought about calling it 'A Flock of Magpies' or something like that, but I don't know what the name for a group of magpies is."

"It's called a murder." My fingers running over the booklet, I beamed. "This is incredible, *gadjo*."

He sipped his coffee. The currents from him whizzed through my hands. With his stormy eyes and skewed smile, he was distinctly Ward. Except for the clinks of the baristas washing coffee mugs and spoons and some old-time jazz on the speakers, the café was quietly comfortable—until I faced Ward. Energy arced between us. He licked his lip and leaned in toward me, his hand sliding across the table to cover mine. I shifted back. Then toward him.

"How was Minnesota?" I asked.

"Same as when I left." Ward paused while the barista brought him a second black coffee. "Drake, strangely, had friends. Even the ones he burned came, and not one spit on his grave." His mouth frowned, and he coughed a few times. "The obituary read that Drake died unexpectedly. What the fuck. He was a smackhead for years. It wasn't just heroin either, though that was the cheapest and easiest to get. He did laudanum, morphine, and opium when he could find them. He was a dope fiend through and through. That he died wasn't unexpected."

He ducked low, his leather coat too big on him, made for someone taller, broader. Cold ebbed out of me. If it relaxed me, maybe this wash going over him would do the same.

His voice grew firmer. "I don't miss the midnight barges into my room raiding my cash drawer for a score. I don't miss being careful of needles in the trash. My dad died years ago, but the body was still Drake's, you know?"

The bitterness of his words plunged into me. I couldn't imagine not missing Mom. Her voice singing harmony with the radio, the messes she left in the kitchen, and the mock-innocent look she gave Dad when he bemoaned her accounting mistakes. I hated living without those things.

Ward tilted his head. "Why so sad?"

Few people knew Mom was dead, and no one in Black Orchard knew how she died. Ward couldn't really know me unless he knew about Mom.

"My mom died two years ago," I admitted. "It changed everything."

"What happened?" he asked.

"She was murdered."

He almost didn't react but for a slight rise of his brow and a whispered, "Jesus."

There it was, out in the open.

For the first time since I'd come to Black Orchard, someone knew my mother's death wasn't an accident. It wasn't only a house fire. That Dad, Jonah, and I survived was a miracle, but some miracles had a blood price. My mother could've been saved. She deliberately wasn't.

"I sound like such a prick," Ward blurted. "I had no idea. I really thought your parents were divorced."

"To talk about the dead is to call back the spirit instead of letting it rest, *gadjo*. I let my mother rest." He cocked his head, but I cut him off. "Before you speak, no, what you're going through isn't the same. Doesn't mean it's any easier. It hurts. It hurts like no other pain."

After a while, his coffee was gone, and we left Café du Chat Noir for a walk in the November darkness. Trinket shops lined the street, and eccentric bistros interspersed with banks and offices. Surrounded by mock gaslights and cobblestone roads, walking there transported me to olden times. Tiny snowflakes rambled down from the clouds, and Ward eyed the rising moon. A brief smile etched on his lips before he swiped at the snow in my hair. Spheres of electricity swirled in my palms as he lowered his face. I wanted to let go and damn the consequences of blowing up every street lamp in downtown Black Orchard.

"You're strange," he said. "I'm calm when I'm with you, and I don't know why. You're doing something to me, Vayda."

"No, I'm not."

His cheek grazed against mine. "You are. I want it."

And I know what you can do. He reached for my hand, almost too polite, but when I laid my fingers in his palm, he tugged me against him. I wrapped my arms around his neck and stood on my tiptoes while his hands roamed down my sides to my hips. *And I know what you can do.* Perhaps the wind flared my skirt. Perhaps it was the charge of our energies feeding through me. His breath scalded my cheek as his mouth hovered over mine.

An inch apart.

A centimeter.

Less.

"You know what you can do?" I asked against his lips.

"I'm going to kiss you," he whispered.

The whirring in my chest became a blitz as his lips pushed into mine. A flick of his tongue deepened the kiss. His hand curled around my neck, and my fingers tugged on his coat's lapels for balance while my mind wound in a dizzying spin.

This was happening too fast. I was scared and wanted more and—He kissed me again, rough, fluid, far from timid or innocent. His fingers on my hips gripped harder, and his mouth found my neck. Snowflakes pirouetting from the clouds melted in my open eyes.

"Stop," I choked on the word and pushed off from him.

He winced. "Vayda, what the hell? What'd I do?"

"It's not you. I'm sorry," I hiccuped and dashed over the sidewalk as fast as my blue Chucks would take me. The soles of Ward's boots trampled the concrete behind me. My breath flooded the air with white smoke. I couldn't stop. If I stopped, he'd find out what I was.

Chapter Nine

Vayda

School the following day physically hurt. My head throbbed. Light stung. All because my barriers had shattered, and rebuilding the wall took more time than a single night.

Ward inspected the origami triangle I dropped in his lap while returning from the restroom. He maneuvered it between his fingers before flicking it into the recycling bin.

Damn. He even punted away my note.

I'd dreamt of kissing Ward, of his lips, rough and thrilling. Then his face, sand dollar-pale and equally fragile, broken. A snap, dust. Running away like that, what was I thinking? All he'd done was open up to me, and in return, I hurt him.

With a huff, Ward hunched down. He wouldn't look at me, listen to me, or read my words. There was no easy gliding through him today. There was nothing.

Sister Hillary Lauren scrawled a William Blake quote on the chalkboard. The walls were inscribed with lines from his poems. On her desk, she even had a picture of herself posing near Blake's grave. Vanity was clearly her sin. On the chalkboard, her cursive read, "'I was angry with my friend: I told my wrath, my wrath did end. I was angry with my foe: I told it not, my wrath did grow.'"

Satisfied her penmanship was legible, she said, "Time for a pop quiz."

The rip of paper torn from notebooks punctuated a

collective groan. Sister Hillary Lauren asked three questions to answer in three sentences. When finished, we exchanged quizzes. Ward took my paper, and I had his. His responses were:

1: This

2: Is

3: Bullshit.

The shaking in his shoulders turned to coughing. I reached into my backpack and slipped him a honey lozenge.

"Thanks," he grunted, his voice hoarser than usual.

I should've failed him, but when Sister asked for his score I murmured, "One hundred percent." Across the room, Jonah scoffed. During their Othello game that morning, they didn't speak, moving black-and-white discs over the green squares like chess grandmasters negotiating an endgame. For once, Ward won, and not because Jonah let him.

He whispered, "You shouldn't have done that."

"You know the answers," I told him. "In theory, they're on the paper. Invisible ink."

"I'm not talking about the quiz, Vayda."

If I were like Jonah, I could've rebounded and shoved my way into his mind, learned how to fix this, but that wasn't how I worked.

By the time lunch roared into the cafeteria, a headache squelched my appetite. As I picked the pith from my orange, I spied my brother's hand on Chloe's back across the cafeteria, oblivious to the whispers of the other students. Not long ago, she'd have gawked right along with them. Jonah gave her a long kiss, interrupted only when Ward approached them. The boys began to walk outside when Chloe darted to Jonah, kissed him once more, and giggled as she backed away. I felt like I could puke, and threw away the remnants of my lunch. That wasn't the same girl who begged me to keep quiet.

Chloe sidled up beside me with her neat paper sack. I'd come to know her fizzy energy well. She was all cherry soda, bubbly and sweet.

"Oh, man, I missed your brother," she exclaimed. "What

was I thinking when I broke up with him?"

"That if this school was a caste system, he'd be an untouchable," I grumbled. "Chloe, don't you care that everyone's talking about you two being together again?"

"Trust me. He's worth it. I'm so, here's a ten-cent vocab word, *uninhibited* with him."

I knew what an uninhibited Chloe did with Jonah.

She opened a bag of chips, offering me one. "Are you gonna tell me what happened between you and Ward?"

Nice to know Chloe was still active in the gossip mill even if she didn't care that she'd become one of its favorite subjects. I dismissed her with a limp wave. "I'm not discussing it."

"Please, for some mysterious reason, you like Prince Mood Swing. It's obvious you give that boy the worst hard-on, so how'd you piss him off?"

I opened my mouth but was distracted as Ward stopped by the vending machines. A cute sophomore pointed to the Modest Mouse shirt visible under his dress shirt and necktie. He didn't object when she fixed his hair. I blew on my hands, trying to cool down.

"Hey, Vayda," Marty leered and plopped down beside me.

He helped himself to a crunch from Chloe's bag of chips and leaned in close. I pushed him back with my elbow. Maybe some girls went for the devolved type.

"So," he began, "everyone's been talking about you and the Ravenscroft guy. I mean, a week ago, you two seemed tight, but something happened?"

I said nothing. One more spike of anger or smugness, and my head would blow.

Marty set down an unopened can of lime soda, a mocking twist to his mouth as Ward fed money into a machine with sandwiches and yogurt containers. "You know, guys like him, you can't trust them. He's all kinds of messed up, and I'm worried about you. I'm not saying that 'cause I think you'll listen. I already know what you think of me, but that guy's trouble, Vayda. As much as I freakin' hate Jonah, I hate guys like that more."

"Marty, you're wasting your breath," Chloe hissed. "You don't even know Ward."

He snorted. "I don't want to know him. I can't understand why Vayda would."

"I'm right here, Marty. You can talk to me, not about me." I shifted away until I hung halfway off the bench. The pounding in my head wanted him gone. I didn't like the energy coming off him. This wasn't concern—he was jealous, and it felt like a black slime leaching out and soaking the table.

"You wouldn't give me a chance because I'm not one of *your kind* of people, but you'll give it to him?"

I focused on Chloe, taking her hand and flipping it over to examine her palm. Mom had shown me how to read palms, and reading Chloe's would be a good distraction. I might get some idea of exactly how far my brother's influence had taken her off her life's true course. My feelers focused on hunting Chloe's energy, feathery and light.

"What, Vayda?" Marty snapped. "Am I not good enough to talk to? Frigid bitch."

Chloe yanked her hand from mine and sneered. "Oh, sure, the way to get a girl's interest is to call her a frigid bitch. Marty, get thee to the Confessional."

When even Little Miss Student Ambassador was fed up with you, perhaps the hour for self-reflection had dawned.

Marty ignored her and put his hand on my shoulder. I wasn't ready. My barriers couldn't take that great a shock. Beyond jealousy over Ward, something dark was in him, and it surged through me. I'd felt so many emotions from others, but this was worse than spite, worse than a grudge between him and Jonah, between him and me. He had hate in him, and it drenched me in a foul wash. I braced my hands on the table and felt like I might be sick when my little finger bumped his drink. Energy into electricity, from me into metal, the can ripped open and splattered radioactive green soda all over Marty's face and uniform.

"What the hell?" he bellowed, beads of syrupy soda dripping from his chin. He jumped up from the bench and thundered toward the restroom, stopping long enough to shove Ward into a candy machine, amid some chortling from the girls' basketball team.

Chloe's skin flushed maroon as she cackled, but even with Marty gone, I was nauseous and losing the battle with my gut. I got up from the table, head down as I fled, only to ram right into Ward.

I wanted to go around him and leave before I got sicker. Yet he stifled it. He stifled all of it.

He didn't move away. Steel. Unbending. His jaw contracted, and he coughed until I gave him another throat lozenge.

"I guess I got sick standing in the cold," he explained.

What could I say? *I'm sorry your immune system blows?* "*Gadjo—*"

"Stop." He put up his hands in defense and took a step back. "I don't know what you want from me. If you'd said, 'Hey, I don't like you that way' or you weren't ready, I'd be fine, but don't act like it's cool and then bolt if I make a move without telling me what happened. Stop it with the mind games."

What a choice of words.

I stammered, "I-it's complicated."

His voice rose sharply. "You think I won't understand complicated? Get the hell over yourself. Until then, I'm done."

He stormed past me, leaving me unguarded. My weakened barriers cracked against the force of so much emotion hitting them at once, as if every student in the cafeteria had picked up a stone and thrown it at me. Each stone was their joy, stress, fatigue, glee, and it all pelted me. I grabbed my head to block the static and whipped around to see Ward's back as he smacked his palm against the doorway before disappearing.

By study hall, Jonah zipped through Sister Hillary Lauren's copious notes on William Blake while tracing his finger over my palm. To anyone else, he appeared to be predicting my future as I had tried with Chloe. In truth, he basked in the heat of the energy I'd taken in, energy I couldn't handle, and left me with a chill that took the faintest edge off my headache.

I want to be normal. My words ran the psychic trail

between us. *I hate what I am. If I were normal, I wouldn't have to worry about scaring people. I wouldn't have to worry about winding up like Mom.*

My brother worked the currents through my palm. *You aren't normal, but you won't be like Mom 'cause she actually knew what she was doing with her Mind Games. What we do isn't a curse, you know.*

It isn't a blessing either, Jonah. What we do gets people killed.

He gave a loud sigh, though he couldn't argue. Mind Games killed people. Mom hadn't been innocent, and she paid with her life.

My brother opened his mouth to reply when a willowy figure materialized in the doorway. I felt drained, ill, and squirmed in the presence of Sister Tremblay. She rested her emotionless eyes on mine and curled her index finger. "Miss Silver, you are to come with me."

Jonah began to stand when Sister Tremblay whisked into the room and laid her hand down on his desk. As she planted a seed of darkness, a spiritual shadow mushroomed from her fingers, blooming across the desk to touch both of us. "Not you. *Her.*"

The other students distracted by their conversations and homework began looking up. I swallowed hard and grabbed my backpack. My legs quaked as I walked out of the classroom with the tall nun, Jonah's voice faint in my mind. *I'll be listening.* This time, I didn't mind letting him in.

Every breath reminded my heart to slow, and yet I searched the hallway for any place where I could escape from Sister Tremblay. As we walked, my footfalls echoed off the walls. She took me through the blue, lightless language arts wing, past the arched doors. Then, on the way to her office, we passed the sanctuary, and I glimpsed the altar. I'd never been inside a church so dark but for the flickering light of votive candles in red glasses. St. Anthony of Padua was the saint for missing things. No one going into that church would find what they sought.

Sister Tremblay shut her office door and gestured for me to sit on a stiff, wood chair. There would be no slouching on her clock. "We haven't had the pleasure of getting to know each other, Miss Silver."

"The pleasure is all yours," I muttered. "What do you want? If this is about Marty—"

"I have no interest in Marty Pifkin. Monsignor deals with him and all the other crude devils." She blinked, the only sign of life on her blank face. "Your father's concerned about your brother and you. I'm very familiar with what grief can do to the soul. Losing your mother, I imagine that's been very hard for you both. You must be lost without her. Maybe even out of control."

My lips buzzed, and worry swirled in my fingertips.

"We don't talk about my mother," I said.

"Yes, that's a Romani belief, right? Not to speak of the dead? I do know a little about your heritage, Miss Silver. It doesn't change that your father's worried about you."

"He wouldn't tell you that," I said. The worry in my fingers swelled to a sharp prickle. Overhead, the light hummed.

"In not so many words." Her hands sprawled like a daddy long-legs. "Your father's rather cagey. I don't suppose he's always been that way. Perhaps something's raised his guard."

With her spider fingers, she picked up a Bible from her desk. I spotted a coffee mug, white emblazoned with a black-and-red G, on the desk. University of Georgia. Rain had always kept a flag with that logo flapping on his front porch. Dad went there for a semester. I'd have known it anywhere.

Sister Tremblay noticed me studying the mug and plucked a tissue from a box on her desk, dabbing her nose. A single drop of blood stained it. "I was raised in Atlanta, but I also lived for a while in a town called Hemlock. Do you know it?"

The hair on my neck felt as if a spectral fist yanked it. In. Out. Breathing deep. I sat on my hands to mute the blitz in my fingers.

"Wh-wh-why would I know anything about that town?"

She sat forward, locking on me. "Your father has an

unmistakable southern accent. Jonah has traces of one, too, but yours is nearly imperceptible. Like you're hiding where you're from."

Energy ripped out of me. The computer screen on Sister Tremblay's desk glowed bright, near blinding, until it split amid a shower of sparks. Yowling, the nun leapt and opened a window to release the smoke and rancid stink of melting plastic.

"I have to go," I blurted and darted from my chair.

My shoes pounded the floor as I raced past the empty sanctuary and Stations of the Cross, past portraits of saints and rows of lockers to my study hall. Jonah waited by the door. His arms clenched my back as I tumbled into him.

"I heard everything. We're gonna be okay," he promised in a quiet voice. "Let me handle Sister Tremblay."

I nodded, though I wasn't reassured. That Sister Tremblay was from Hemlock and now in Black Orchard wasn't a coincidence, so what was she doing here? If she had been searching for us, then bully for her. Mission accomplished. Now that she had us in her sights, what did she plan to do?

Chapter Ten

Ward

The cursor at the end of the Google search box blinked too many times before I lost count. Two words were in the box: Vayda Silver. What could I find out about her with a little digging around? Something of her life before she came to Black Orchard? She didn't talk about her past. Neither did Jonah. Searching for her online? Wasn't that how people got to be stalkers and crazy shit? Besides, was it fair to judge people by their past? It wasn't as if I didn't have my own secrets I was tight-lipped about, and Vayda was obviously hiding something. Her mother was murdered, but she hadn't said how or why. She wouldn't talk about her.

I glanced once more at the cursor begging me to hit the Enter button. Instead, I struck Delete.

"Are you sure you won't stay for dinner, Jonah? I'm making goulash."

Heidi uncovered the piping cauldron of organic vegetables on the stove. Bubbles swelled and popped on the surface. I shook my head at Jonah. *Don't do it.* He looked a little sick as Heidi sank a wooden spoon into the goulash.

Jonah forced a grin and handed over a tin of some red spice. "Smells good, Ma'am, but *Dati*'s a stickler for us eating supper as a family. Something tells me Vayda's making supper right about now. She's good in the kitchen. It's one of her secret talents."

I shut my notebook beside the laptop. I never did have

much patience. "Hey, Jabber Jaws, shut up and help me write this speech."

He ducked his shoulders while he fidgeted with the chain hanging off his wallet. "Are you sure I can't hold up cue cards for you to read? Speaking in front of class gives me fits."

"Jonah Silver, are you shy? I'll never believe it," Heidi teased.

"Nah, I'm not all that shy." He grinned. "I'm better one-on-one."

I slapped the laptop closed. Jonah knew how to lay on the charm. Chloe had worn that same dim mask Heidi wore now. It was like observing a sculptor chiseling marble. A dash of his hand pushing Heidi's hair from her face, the polish of a flirty nudge, every move plotted and executed.

Heidi blushed and stirred the pot again. "Jonah, you're trouble. Parents should lock up their daughters from you."

This ended now. I shoved my chair away from the table and motioned him to follow me outside onto the porch where I tied Bernadette to her leash. She scratched the snow, her beard frosted. Jonah lagged behind and rummaged through his backpack. He handed me a Grateful Dead vinyl like some kind of a peace offering.

"Here, take this," he said. "It came in at Fire Sales, and I thought it'd be up your alley. You're so tense *I'm* getting a headache. Mellow out, *gadjo*."

My teeth clenched as he used his sister's word for me.

"What is this?" I asked, waving the album cover. "Peace, love, and smoke up? You do know how Drake died, right?"

"I'm not trying to push your buttons," he insisted.

"Funny, 'cause you had no problem pushing yourself on Heidi."

He nudged my shoulder. "Relax. Flattery don't mean no harm."

"Tell that to your arm candy."

He laughed, but the smile didn't meet his eyes, so black and piercing that I felt myself slip. I saw him and yet at the same time wandered inside a room with no doors in the frames and a rickety, wooden floor. I didn't know what was happening, but whatever it was, I couldn't fight it.

Then I was walking down the hall at St. Anthony's. Except I wasn't. Somehow I saw myself pushing through the parade of other kids yelling and tussling to get to my locker. Jonah stood near his locker with his hand on his forehead, like someone staving off a monster headache. I reached for my combination lock, ignoring him.

He followed and waited as I stooped down to tie the laces on my boot. Always a few steps behind, he regarded me with a curious intensity. I hadn't had any idea. We came to Sister Hillary Lauren's class where he moved around me and whispered something to a girl before taking a desk across the room. I wadded up a busted set of headphones, no idea where to sit, until I spotted the girl he'd talked to, one with black hair and sea-glass irises. She smiled and pointed to the desk in front of hers.

If it hadn't been for him, the desk in front of Vayda's wouldn't have been open.

"You know," he said. His voice brought me back from the strange view into my memory to his serious face. "Vayda's as closed off as you are. When people are that closed, one of two things is at play: their attic's empty—hardly your case— or they're hurting something fierce. They don't want to be nudged, and you can't push them. Did you mean it when you told my sister you're done with her?"

"I'm not talking about Vayda. Not with you," I said. "What happens between her and me is private."

He cracked his knuckles and folded his hands behind his head. "You tell yourself it's private if it makes you feel better."

I clomped down the steps and followed Bernadette's tracks in the light snow. Dog had gotten off her lead and wandered to the woods. Jonah whistled. A moment later, Bernadette poked out her head from some dead underbrush and trotted toward him. I jerked my head and gave him a what-the-hell look.

"What can I say? The dog likes me," he answered as he picked up Bernadette, scratching her head and handing her to me. "My sister's a nice girl."

"If she's so nice, why's she yanking my chain?" I asked.

He observed the clouds shifting across the night and took a long time exhaling. When he spoke again, his usual arrogance was gone. "You're *gadje*, but that doesn't bother me. It's not like we have a *vitsa* to answer to. It's harder for Vayda. There's a lot she hasn't accepted."

I scoffed and crossed my arms. "So it's all because I'm not one of you?"

"It's because you're not like us."

Something wasn't being said, and I was ready to grab him by his shirt collar and give him a good shake. If I was good enough to be their friend, then why wasn't it okay for me to be something more to Vayda? "Don't make excuses for her. If you want to meddle with my shit, do me a favor and tell your sister to make up her mind."

"Will do." Jonah stepped off the front porch, falling into the shadows away from the lamplight. "I'm telling you now, if you hurt her, I won't be so gentlemanly next time." The threat slipped from his mouth, and he laughed. "You have no idea what you're in for."

I followed him with my eyes as he walked down the gravel driveway toward the woods. Vayda, and, to a lesser extent, Jonah: I was drawn to them. They had something peculiar, a magnetism I couldn't ignore. No, I didn't know what I was in for with them.

But it'd be a hell of a trip.

Chapter Eleven

Vayda

T here was a kinship between antiques dealers and dumpster divers, but I'd never admit that to Dad. I combed through some papers, ruling out private auctions with no promise of a jewel amid the boxes of Bing Crosby records, but not even the prospect of a treasure hunt let me forget that this Saturday was two days after Thanksgiving. Two years ago, Dad sent us home while he stayed late tallying receipts from the Black Friday sale. He met Rain for drinks and darts while Mom, Jonah, and I wrapped the good china in tissue paper and put it in a box set aside for the move to Vermont Dad was scheming. Hours later, Mom died, and our lives were bits of char and a half-empty gas tank in a Chevy borrowed from my godfather.

To give Dad a hand, Jonah and I worked at Fire Sales every Saturday, a routine we'd practiced since we were small. Mom used to say she found Dad's first gray hair after he stammered to a Portuguese diplomat that the candleholders he'd paid an exorbitant price for had been used as hockey sticks. Our choice for a puck fared much worse.

"Magpie, have you found that Sotheby's preview guide?" Dad asked, sitting cross-legged on the floor by the sales counter.

Scads of auction catalogs surrounded him. Researching projects or organizing the backlog threatening to overtake the storeroom—wherever Dad was, catalogs were nearby. Instinct drew me to a booklet with an Ansel Adams photograph. I handed him the catalog. "Landscapes? Hardly your style."

The shop was empty, and I sat beside him. Dad sighed and touched a page of Adams' Montana shots, his grief palpable.

"I miss Mom, too," I said.

"That obvious she's on my mind?"

"I'm an empath, remember? Emotions are my vice, and even you can't keep everything from Jonah and me."

He pushed up his glasses. "Your mother wanted one of Adams' pieces. I'd negotiated for a signed photograph for our twentieth anniversary. Obviously, that deal fell apart."

I caught something, a memory of Dad as the man who draped his arm around Mom as she topped off the wine glasses in the smoky kitchen. Four nights a week, Rain came by with wine, playing cards, and a pack of cigarettes that lasted halfway to dawn. On weekends, Dad and Rain were in the same bowling league. "Gentleman time," Mom had called it. Now, without his wife and closest friend, Dad spent all his time wiping off the dust of other folks' lives.

"Vayda, there's a trinket box to go through." He pointed to a package by the register. "Came with a vanity. You might find something you like."

I dragged over the box. Hand-mirrors, vintage medicine bottles, whiskey flasks. Nothing for my scrapbook. I picked up a long string of faux pearls and felt the joy of dancing and flapper dresses only for a second before I let it go. Sometimes it was nice to bask in some tender waves of happiness no matter from how long ago and daydream about who once owned these things.

"Were you scared of Mom's Mind Games?" I asked.

He choked on his coffee. "That's a hell of a question."

"You've never told us. So what'd you think when you learned what she could do?"

He rolled his neck around and chuckled. "I thought my weed was laced with acid."

Dad never kept it secret that he was a stoner when he spotted Mom with Rain at a showing of his paintings. It wasn't long after that the three of them were inseparable.

He stretched his arms and pulled out his nicotine gum. "Mind Games kept life with Lorna interesting, I'll tell you that much. What gives?"

"Curiosity." I wrung my hands together. "Ward—"

"Say no more. I wish I had an answer. If Ward finds out what you can do, you can't predict how he'll react."

Words I didn't want. "So why'd you stay with Mom?"

"Your granddaddy had a way of instilling the fear of God in me, but I stayed with Lorna 'cause I loved her. Nothing more magical than that." He paged through a few catalogs. His thumb reached behind his pointer and middle fingers to twist the gold band on his ring finger. "It wasn't our choice to raise you and Jonah alone. Your mother had problems with the *vitsa* and we were better off to take you both away."

"What kind of problems?" I asked.

"Think about your mother. It's not that hard to guess. She got herself into trouble because she was impulsive. Her family really didn't like impulsive."

"And what about yours? There had to be somebody."

"There was Rain. He and your mother became my family after I lost mine. We made terrible mistakes when we were younger, and they followed us."

Maybe that gave Jonah and me an awareness of kin and country that was much scarcer in the north. After college, Dad worked with antiques dealers, learning restoration and how to get a bargain. It wasn't until we lived under Montana's endless skies that he opened a junk joint Mom named Baubles. What I remembered of Montana was sunsets and fields. Trouble decided to come for Mom when I was eight, and to spare her, Dad uprooted everything to Hemlock where he entered the antiques big leagues and became something of a legend— and not only because of his trading. Then trouble came to Hemlock, too.

The shop's bell chimed as Jonah sauntered into the showroom. Ward traveled close behind. He didn't move his focus from his boots. Great, not only was I a human mood ring, I was also invisible.

Dad called the boys to the storeroom, an area closed off from Fire Sales' showroom. Inventory from a buying trip to North Carolina had arrived. It meant Jonah and Ward would wind up with sweaty, sore backs from lifting, while I handled any walk-ins, not that we had many, at least no one from Black Orchard. Antiques tripped Dad's trigger, and Jonah and I both inherited his honed vision for value, but we each had our quirks. Jonah liked old books. Sometimes I felt like I was still figuring out what I liked. Never occurred to us we might one day help run his shop in Wisconsin of all places.

As I entered the storeroom, the phone rang. Dad answered the line at his desk. I lingered behind an armoire and sharpened my hearing to catch what I could.

"Where the hell have you been? I've been trying get a hold of you for days. I've got a feeling something's not right. Someone's watching us. We've been here long enough people are looking at us a little harder, and I don't have answers. Maybe it's time we stop this charade. I don't want to go to jail." Dad listened, jotting notes. "I'm tired of getting spooked... Rain, stop yapping and let me talk."

He laughed, but my feelers didn't detect humor. Anything he put out was frustration.

The logistics were sketchy. He and Rain had a deal where my godfather acquired Antiquaria the night Mom died. Rain was also the ghost-owner of Fire Sales and our house. He hooked Dad up with the retail space a few months after we left Hemlock, and I knew from press clippings the business earned a reputation over the past two years as a small but lucrative shop in the upper Midwest operated by the rarely seen E.J. Silver. All this to keep Dad off the grid, but it was tricky—for both Dad and Rain if caught. A person might not even risk that much for his blood family.

My father hung up the phone. "Come out, you little eavesdropper."

I skulked out from the armoire. "Are we gonna stop hiding?"

"I don't know, Magpie. We went into hiding to protect you and Jonah from the people back in Hemlock. We can't pop back up like, 'Oh, hey, here we are!'"

A wave of relief slid under my skin. Guilt followed right behind.

"Is it wrong that I'm used to calling myself Vayda Silver?"

"Not if you don't forget Vayda Murdock. Burying your past causes more harm than good."

***

By four o' clock, Jonah and Ward finished moving furniture. Playing hostess, I took them some water. Jonah collapsed on an Art Deco fainting couch while Ward overlooked the chairs and sat on the floor. Pinpointing someone unfamiliar with antiques was a game I played. They treated old things as far more fragile than necessary. Dust made sturdy chairs rickety and bone china as delicate as spun sugar. So they feared.

Jonah guzzled his water. "I'm heading outside to cool off. Coming, Ward?"

He watched Jonah stand but didn't move.

Alone with him, I took the seat on the couch. Everything I imagined saying sounded horrible in my head. I hadn't been able to get things right so far.

Ward fumbled with some papers in his pockets. "Emory hired me to work some hours."

I raised my brows. Dad never took outside employees. Not in Montana. Not in Georgia. A family operation kept it simple. So why hire Ward?

Again, silence. He moved from picking at his pockets to a loose thread on his T-shirt.

"Pretty cold weather, huh?" I searched for conversation.

"Sometimes it's so cold this fluffy shit called snow falls from the sky. Crazy, right?"

He was such an ass.

Without cracking a hint of amusement, he snorted, "Your small talk sucks."

"Gee, thanks." I crossed my arms over my dress. "You're hardly Mr. Congeniality."

"I never pretended to be. I don't lead people on."

I looked at his mouth. The mouth that kissed me and was now thin with flushed lips contrasting his pale skin. I wanted to touch his cheek, to rub the sandpaper of his stubble, which tinted more brown than red like the sweat-wet hair curling near his jaw. He would be scratchy and rough. Real. He wouldn't be the dream Ward whispering of things he knew about me. I wanted the real Ward.

I circled him, one finger tracing across from his left shoulder to his right. My skirt rippled near his boots, and then I stood over him.

"I don't know how to act around you," I confessed.

He raised his head but only enough to stare at my hand. He grabbed for it and placed it against his cheek. He placed it exactly the way I would have, and his skin was sharp and jagged, as I had imagined it would be. He was also soft and warm against the iciness in my fingers. His breath shuddered.

"Don't act. Just be Vayda."

I dropped my hand from his face and dragged myself over to the wall. I felt bare, so exposed to him, and slipped behind a dressing screen in need of repair. Ward's fingers crept around the screen's edge. We hid together, not speaking, and then he pushed my hair off my neck, sending shivers down my spine while he drew down the curve to my shoulder, my arm, before he very simply held my hand. A nest of quiet built around the two of us. I wanted that quiet. I wanted more.

"I thought about everything that happened that night," he said. "I wanted to know what I did wrong, but I don't know. It's not that I'm *gadje*, as you call it. But I know that's part of it."

I took a deep breath, nodding. "It's some of it, Ward. I'm trying to figure out things."

"Okay then. I have a hard time believing that's all it is, but I can be patient, if it's for you. You're not easy."

"You were hoping I'd be easy?"

"That came out wrong." He gave a true laugh and took my chin between his thumb and forefinger. "I like you, Vayda. I mean, *really* like you."

I liked him, my *gadjo*, too. Not only because of the quiet.

I listened to his breathing. Our noses touched, and I tilted my face to bring our mouths closer. There would be no running this time. His lips skimmed mine as if testing my temperature before his mouth opened the kiss wider. I draped my arms over his shoulders and slid my fingers through his hair. He leaned back against the wall and swung me in front of him so that I pinned him to the old brick. We kissed until our mouths ached and our lips were exhausted, but even then, we didn't stop.

***

By seven, the shop was closed. Ward hugged me goodnight as Chris arrived.

"You ever have something happen that you can't explain?" I asked.

His chin rested against the top of my head. "Not every little thing is meant to be explained."

Except what I hid from him wasn't some little thing, and I had no idea how to tell him. If I could ever tell him.

An hour later, my head ached from working too long at the computer, and my mind wandered away from editing photos for the shop's website. Cardinal rule: Idle hands do the devil's work, and Dad made sure that, if nothing else, we found ways to keep busy. I was starved, and we wouldn't eat until nine, though that didn't stop me from daydreaming about food. Fresh herbs. A tangy vinaigrette.

"Will you stop thinking about food?" Jonah asked as he checked off items on an inventory list. "I'm so hungry I could eat this paper."

"I'll give you five bucks if you actually do," I said.

"Got some salt?"

He sat in his favorite chair, a horseshoe-shaped number he and Mom restored. Together, they covered the cushions with a patchwork of reclaimed leather. Fate smiled when Jonah kept his chair at Antiquaria instead of home and again when Rain shipped it with the first load of inventory to Fire Sales.

He swiveled toward me. "Don't think I don't notice you eyeballing my chair. You best not put an evil eye on it."

"I don't care about your chair," I said. "It's yet another thing you and Mom did together."

He wrapped his hands around the back of his head. "Whatever you think Mom taught me about Mind Games, you're way off-base."

"Am I?"

My brother's lips were a grim line as he examined the inventory list, but I glared at him harder. He rubbed the back of his neck and pretended it didn't bother him. Except the pulse in his neck told me otherwise. *Tell me I'm wrong about Mom, that she didn't pick a favorite from the two of us.*

"Mom never excluded you," Jonah said. "You avoided her."

It was true. I couldn't change the past. Jonah missed what he had with Mom. I missed not only what I didn't have but also what could never be.

He combed his fingers through my hair. His big hands weren't quite dexterous enough to be relaxing, but he tried.

"Think what you want about Mom," he said. "It's not like she can prove you wrong. I don't know what else you want to hear."

I wanted to hear what Jonah remembered, how the night Mom died haunted him.

Because I remembered.

I remembered the frost nipping at my skin, the acidic smell of burning peach trees, and gravel digging into my bare feet as we staggered along the country road to Rain's house, the only safe place we knew. My godfather charged down the steps of his farmhouse, and with ashes stinging our noses, we gazed over the treetops in the direction of our house where the night glowed amber.

The heel of my palm blotted away tears before they slipped

down my cheeks. Mom was gone, and I was angry. Angry at her favoring Jonah, for recklessly using her Mind Games. Angry at her for dying.

"Ready to call it a night?" Dad asked before his final lock-up of the shop.

Jonah passed off the inventory list to Dad. He allowed our father's arm to wrap around his shoulder. Warmth filled my chest as they stood so close. Though Jonah still reveled in the attention from Chloe, whatever came over him unclenched him from its grip. That gave me hope.

Glass shattered in the showroom.

Before I could make sense of what happened, my chest smacked the ground. Jonah pushed me down and shielded me with his body. My breath rushed out in a single, hard punch. Dad crouched beside us. Dazed and numb, we held still while a hush fell over Fire Sales except our breathing and the soft tinkle of tiny glass shards raining on the floor.

Jonah rolled off me and whispered, "What the hell was that?"

Ignoring the cold dread stalking me, I sent out my feelers and stumbled through the panic trailing out of my father.

"Stay here," he ordered.

The hairs on my forearms prickled. I couldn't sit by doing nothing and snuck over to the door to the showroom, trying to glimpse between the furniture and darkness.

"You there, stop!" Dad yelled. The bells by the entrance jingled. "What the hell are you doing?"

I raced into the showroom, working on instinct instead of thought. Dad was gone. Glass shards scattered over the floor by the window. A hole smashed the glass, fissures cracking to the corners, and my gaze fell to a rock on the floor. This felt too vicious to be a prank.

Running, I made it outside seconds after Jonah. Dad was halfway down the block, chasing someone. Two storefronts were behind me when the heel on my right shoe snapped. Knee-first, I hit the sidewalk, concrete biting my palms. "Shit!"

Jonah whipped around. "You okay?"

My skirt was torn, and I hiked up the fabric to examine my bloody knee. Every beat from my pulse rattled my bones. Jonah put my arm around his waist and helped me walk a few steps toward the shop. Dad's footfalls slowed as he gave up the chase, retreating to join Jonah and me.

"I couldn't keep up," he panted.

"What are you gonna do?" I asked.

He shook his head, not ready to talk, and noticed the blood running in a hot trail along my shin. "Hang tight. I'll get the first-aid kit from the shop."

Unable to put much weight on my leg, I let go of Jonah and slouched with my back to the brick wall. The scrape wasn't deep, but my knee would swell something fierce. Dad halted in front of Fire Sales, one hand covering his mouth. Jonah went to his side, and a moment later, a frightened blast shot from him. I raised my barriers to hold off the anxiety and pushed through the pain to walk.

Dad clutched Jonah's shoulder. "Now, boy, we can't jump to conclusions."

"Someone knows about us!" Jonah shouted. "You swore you handled it!"

"Quiet!" Dad massaged his temples. His fear whizzed over my skin, flickering and sick. "Let's get your sister taken care of."

I edged closer, cringing from the fire in my knee, when more glass shattered. My arms covered my head as the window of some stranger's car parked curbside blasted apart. Blue fragments of glass glittered under the streetlight, and then the window of another car cracked into a spider web.

"Jonah, stop!" I screamed.

He shook his hands free of energy. I felt his anger. His terror. It crawled up me and burrowed into my veins. His face appeared gaunt and wary. "Why won't they leave us alone?"

"Because we don't know who 'they' are," Dad answered. He tried to sound firm, but his voice shook. "We'll figure it out. Calm down."

Dad scooped me into his arms and carried me down the

cobblestone toward Fire Sales. My lips parted, and I jerked my head from side to side, searching for someone in the shadows. Someone spray-painted bright red letters on the bricks below the broken window, the paint still wet and dripping like blood.

Freaks

Chapter Twelve

Vayda

*M*om slices cucumbers in the kitchen while Rain sips a beer and places his hand on the slope of her back. Her head swivels toward him, amused, and his fingers move to her shoulders for a one-armed hug.

From the vegetable garden, I can't make out much through the cloudy window over the sink, but I see enough. He says something that doubles her over with giggles. She peeks over her shoulder, and I drop a clump of basil leaves into my basket. A moment later, the backdoor clatters with Mom scurrying down the steps. She has the body of a retro pin-up girl, even dresses like one with her cigarette pants and kitten heels. With a flick of her wrist, the basket of herbs leaps from my hands to hers.

"Vayda, baby," she intones, "Rain don't mean no harm. That fella's buttering me up so I'll be in court tomorrow. I gotta put a feeler on the jury for him."

I yank a zucchini off the vine. "Dati said you were done meddling."

"It ain't meddling if you're opening up people to the truth. A freed mine is a sound mind."

***

"Not going out tonight?" I hollered over Frank Zappa's winding rock on Jonah's stereo.

He muted his music. His history textbook was open beside him, but a Wordsworth biography was in his hands.

"Chloe asked, but whatever. If she wants to come by Fire Sales after I close, well, I'm not gonna stop her." He broke into a lusty grin.

"She's not a game, Jonah."

"Sure, she is. Twister."

I crossed my arms over my black dress. "That's not funny. You shouldn't be playing her like that."

"I'm kidding. Geez." He glanced at the lamp on his nightstand, the bulb switching on by his will alone. "Lighten up."

"Chloe likes you. A lot."

"Yeah, so much she ditched me in front of our entire algebra class last year. She called me a loser. You know what it's like to have even the nuns laugh at you?" He smiled and shut his textbook. "It's in the past. She's done with letting other people control her. Right now, I'm having a good time with her. I won't hurt her."

The way he said it, he was promising. I hoped like hell he'd keep it.

His energy boiled under his skin as he stretched. He gestured to my black tea-dress with a plum-colored cardigan. I'd paired it with knee-high boots. "You look pretty, Sis. How's your knee?"

I'd nearly forgotten about the scrape and swelling. In two weeks, I'd healed pretty well. Still a little bruised on the outside. On the inside, I felt like I was still bleeding. At the shop, the window had been repaired, but Dad, Jonah, and I knew it wasn't the same. Real or not, the cracks remained.

"I'm okay," I replied.

Jonah cocked his head. "Vayda, did you try searching out whoever did it?"

I hadn't. I couldn't. Any time I even got close to where the bricks were painted, such fear came over me that I wanted to run away screaming.

Jonah understood even without me answering. "Then we

won't know who did it unless someone confesses. Dad said the police think it was someone screwing around."

"But we know it's not true."

"Believe it's true. At least for tonight."

The doorbell rang. I descended the stairs in time to find Dad fixing the collar of Ward's black oxford shirt. I'd noticed he didn't have many clothes, but I hadn't ever seen his dark trousers paired with this unbuttoned vest. With the sleeves rolled to his elbows, his scars were darker than usual, and, of course, he wore his boots—now artfully mended with electrical tape. He handed me a single green-white rose. "For you."

Like a gentleman, Ward led me outside to Chris's Jaguar and opened my door. The engine made hardly a sound as he started the motor. An acoustic ballad by Iron & Wine greeted my ears. Sparks crackling over my skin, he kissed me, teeth grazing my lip before he drew back.

"I like kissing you," I murmured.

He wet his lips. "I'd do more if you wanted to."

His words hung in the air, expecting a response.

And in a breath, the moment to say something passed, though his words lingered, ghostly and playing again and again in my mind.

After finding a parking space outside Café du Chat Noir, Ward killed the engine, and we made our way to the crowd standing on the sidewalk. December had brought more cold, and I wished I'd brought my coat. Ward wrapped his arms around my shoulders, his comforting warmth coursing down my arms and through my skin. In the weeks since he'd kissed me in Fire Sales, we spent a lot of time together, whether at the shop or him teaching me to play guitar on one he loaned me when he came to the stone house in the woods. We might slip away and kiss, protected by the quiet I had with him. That night was different. Expectation hung in the air. So much promise.

The doors to the coffee shop opened, and the crowd pushed inside.

The café smelled of flowery body-splash and espresso. A college student did a decent job of covering Billie Holiday and Etta James. Ward and I loitered at the edge of a makeshift dance floor and watched a few couples spin before he stopped hedging.

"I suppose you want to dance," he said.

"Actually, I thought we'd hold a séance." I gestured to the tables lit by candles and wiggled my brows. "How weird are you willing to get with me?"

He laughed until he coughed. Vayda scored again.

I led him into the crowd where his palms grew clammy. "I'm sorry," he blurted and clumsily wiped his hands on his trousers. His feet were glued in place as he swayed with his hands dusting my hips.

"I'll never make you dance again, *gadjo*," I promised.

"Not close enough to calling this even." He lifted his foot off mine and cringed. "You've got me so strung to agree to this."

I released my barriers, but the static of everyone's thoughts in the crowd was crushing. It must have been my rattled nerves, even with Ward there to hush everything. Chaotic babble, no words in the clutter. Cold and hot patches on my skin hurt as my stomach swam with too much energy.

Ward stopped dancing. "You don't look so hot."

I laid my cheek against his shoulder, our feet still, and his arms curled around me to hold me close. "Sometimes I feel like I'm going to fall."

"I won't let you fall."

"There are times it hits me so hard that I can't tell it's coming. Next thing I know, I'm going down."

He pushed my hair behind my ear, and I lifted my face. "Well, in that case, you can drag my sorry ass down with you."

Over the course of the next hour, we took to the floor only when the beat was slow enough that Ward could trot along. The closer he was to me, the less noise rattled in my head. When the singer's voice began to croak rather than croon, the stereo came on. Within a few measures, I recognized the lyrics of a man lamenting how he hurt his girl. Ward's expression darkened, and he stalked off the dance floor.

Giving him a minute to himself, I purchased two *coffees con panna* and joined him at a secluded table. I trailed my finger along his arm. I could pry him open, if I wanted, but that was Jonah's style. He sipped his coffee and fidgeted with a leather cord he wore looped around his wrist as a makeshift bracelet.

"Why so blue?" I asked when the song was over and the next song on the album began.

He replied, "This is Drake's music."

This band, the Unkindness of Ravens, was his dad's? My parents owned Drake's albums. All of them. Why didn't Ward tell me his dad was famous? He admitted one time that his father was a musician, and that was all he gave up. Yet it was obvious once I knew. Ward's voice—it twinned his dad's baritone. He took after Drake, too, more than I suspected he cared to admit. How did he deal with Drake popping up on the radio at any given time? I eased my hand inside his, drawing a current both reviled and sorrowful.

"Tell me about Drake."

Ward moved his face close to mine. Whatever he intended to say was only for me. "He was on the cover of *Rolling Stone*, which he was proud of. Had it in a frame on the wall. He spent a lot of time at his buddy's studio in Minneapolis. I'd be alone in Rochester for days. When he was around, he read a lot, liked old movies. During the last year, something changed. He slurred when he talked after one of his overdoses." A panicked expression crossed his face, and he gulped his coffee. "I can't talk about this, Vayda. Not tonight."

"When?" I asked.

"Ask me anything as long as it's not about him."

For all the time we spent together, he rarely spoke of his past. His life in Minnesota was a mystery. I wanted to know more. He wanted to pretend it never happened. The past wasn't like that. You couldn't hollow it out and discard it like an unwanted peach pit. Sometimes memories were so hard and stony they cracked your teeth when you bit down on them.

"What *do* you want to talk about?" I asked.

"You."

I cleared my throat and threw him a crumb. "My mom read tarot cards in *Dati*'s shop."

He drummed his thumb on the table. "So I suppose you've got psychic powers, too?"

My heart hitched. "No! Of course not."

"Why'd she do it?" he asked. "For fun? 'Cause she actually predicted the future?"

"Because she was my mother. That's what her *vitsa* raised her to be. That's all she knew how to do."

I reached over and took his left hand. My mother said the left hand was the one men were born with, while their right was all the life experience they'd gathered into them.

"*Melalo*, you have working hands, *gadjo*," I murmured. Such hardened skin, so many scars. He half-smiled as I ran my fingers up and down the length of his palm. Then I pointed to the creases in his hand. "The love line, life line, and head line. You also have a fate line. Not everyone does."

"What's that mean?" he asked.

"It's a line, Ward. Hands change, but they can tell you a lot about someone."

Drake's album continued playing, and a girl giggled close to our table. I glanced up from Ward's hand and spotted the girl with blond ringlets and a sky-blue dress tipping back her head as she drank from a Coke glass.

Chloe's hand was nearly attached to Marty's. She alternated leaning in close to talk to him and sipping from her glass, her pitch getting louder each time she pulled away. Her aura was hazy, but then she rubbed against Marty, not letting go of her drink.

A hot ember glimmered in my skull. Jonah. My fists clenched, and I snuffed him out with as much force as I could rally. *Stay out of my head. If you want to spy on Chloe, do it without my help.*

Enough of the "important" kids from school were here to play with Chloe, to praise her hair, her dancing, whatever compliments she could accept. They'd talk, and she'd ascend her throne again by Monday—without Jonah. His spell on her was broken. She was Chloe Halvorsen and had a reputation to uphold.

Marty parted from Chloe and moseyed over to where I sat with Ward. An overpowering smell of Coke mixed with liquor—some cheap, rat-piss excuse for bourbon—wafted from him. Ward put his foot on Marty's chair and scooted him back from the table. "Go get some coffee. Better yet, water. Your head's gonna be killing you come morning."

"I ain't worried. Danny's around somewhere, and he's driving. So bottoms up." He reached into his trousers and withdrew a small flask. He swiveled around and gave me a sloppy grin. "I was talking with Chloe. She said you read palms and shit. Here, let me try reading yours."

Before I could stop him, he snatched my hand, and grimy energy whooshed from his touch like opening the lid on a pot of stewed quail. I breathed deeply, trying to freeze out Marty, but the alcohol in his blood meant he wasn't thinking or feeling normally.

"So"—he swayed in his chair—"where's your love line? You can tell how many guys have been on your ride by the number of notches in it, right?"

"Marty, let go," I growled.

He elbowed Ward. "You know I had a crack at her first."

Ward's jaw flexed, and his nostrils flared. He reached for my other hand. The angry current inside me shifted, eased, though not much. All the anger I felt toward Marty streamed out of me in concentric circles, each ring more blustery than the previous. Ward squeezed my hand and motioned that we were leaving when he began coughing. After a solid minute of Ward struggling to get the kick from his throat, Marty rolled his eyes.

"That guy's a gutter rat," Marty declared. "I know who your dad was, and if you think you're something special, you're not. I wouldn't be surprised if you caught something from living with your old man. Whatever it is, you probably gave it to Vayda."

Ward quirked his lips. It wasn't the easy expression that let me slip through him unfettered. This was something harsh and bitter. His hand pumped in a fist at his side.

I didn't want a fistfight and angled myself between him and Marty. "Ward, stop," I said. "He's not worth it."

"Yeah, but you are." He glared at Marty. Didn't yell. Didn't lay a hand on him. His voice was low and steady. "You ever say shit about my girl or me again, and I'll break each of your fingers and won't give a damn. Don't test me."

Marty shrugged, and then he reached for me.

"Stop!" I shoved his chest.

The condensed anger shot into him. He tumbled backward in an oafish lurch, lolling on the floor before dusting off his pants. "You skank! You don't push me away when I'm talking to you!"

I had to get away before he made an even bigger scene. I snatched my purse off the table and bolted. Ward could handle Marty, even a drunk Marty ranting God-only-knew-what about me. I needed silence, and while I could have gone outside, I needed some place Ward wouldn't follow me. The girls' restroom was safe enough.

Damn Marty Pifkin. Nobody would listen to him because he was so clearly drunk. That was my hope. That was my prayer.

What if they did?

People already talked about us, and if Marty felt what I'd done in shoving him, that'd give people a reason to talk louder. I could have dodged or screamed or any of another dozen scenarios running through my mind that didn't involve my hands, fingers teeming with too much emotion. I didn't want to be like Jonah and use my hands. I didn't want to be like Mom.

The lights flickered and stall doors swung wild as I took some meditative breaths. Every word spoken, every touch from Marty spilled out of me. I had to let go of it. Throwing some cold water on my cheeks, I felt the currents of electricity spiraling through my fingers and rumbling out of my feet to course over the floor. The light switch by the door sparked. *Please, stop. I don't want this.*

The bathroom door opened. I bunched my fingers into fists, and the stall doors all slammed shut. Chloe entered the bathroom, pausing when she saw me. She looked me over from head to foot and positioned herself by the mirror where she checked her teeth. "Having fun?"

"Ward and I are heading out soon. I'm exhausted." I played nice and ran a brush through my hair. "What about you? Jonah told me he would visit you later."

She slid her hands down her sides, admiring her silhouette. "I'm having a good time right now."

"What are you doing with Marty?" I asked. "You can't stand him."

"No, Vayda, you and Jonah can't stand him. He's actually a lot of fun to party with."

Fire bore through my veins, Jonah's rage stoked to life. *You know her running around with Marty's wrong.*

Stop it. I'll handle her, I said from the base of my skull.

I didn't want to have this conversation with her, not when I knew my brother was lurking in my mind. "Chloe, you know why Jonah doesn't get along with Marty."

"Because of you. It's always you, Vayda." Her pupils darkened, and she zipped her purse closed with enough force I thought for sure she'd pull out the stitching. "I broke up with him before because I didn't want to compete with you for his attention."

"He cares about you, Chloe. He's not popular enough for you, is he?"

She wrinkled her nose, void of any of her sugary energy, replaced by something that burned. "I'm done talking about him. Right now, I'm on my own. End of story."

My throat constricted. Jonah's voice pushed down on me. I cleared my throat as if dislodging something, but Jonah wouldn't go. I sucked in a staggered breath, but he exhaled through my mouth and put his words on my tongue.

I couldn't stop him. Somehow he'd become that powerful

and I hadn't even known it.

"So are you gonna get on your knees for Marty tonight?"

I clamped my hands over my mouth. Shit, that wasn't me! *Jonah, get out!*

Chloe's mouth dropped into an indignant O. "Excuse me?"

"I-I—" My apology failed as Chloe's slap scalded my face.

"Bitch!" she spat. "Oh, your life's gonna be hell! Everyone will know about this! You wait!"

She barged out of the restroom and left me alone by the mirrors where my reflection held haunted eyes. A crimson welt formed on my cheekbone. What had Jonah done?

***

Ward waited in the hall, twirling his car keys around his finger. He frowned at the red badge on my cheek. "That looks sore."

"I deserved it," I mumbled. "I said something horrible to Chloe."

He stuck his hands in his pockets. "Well, why'd you do that?"

Shaking my head—I couldn't explain what happened, I held up my purse to veil the siren-red handprint. I didn't want him to see me messy and vicious. I wasn't that kind of person. Unless pushed. He lowered my purse, stroked the mark with his thumb. "My girlfriend the wallflower, traveler, and pugilist. Got any more secret identities?"

Neither one of us had to ask the other if it was time to go. A misty rain fell as Ward maneuvered the Jaguar away from downtown Black Orchard to the outskirts where the conifers grew steep. By the time we reached his house, the raindrops bounced off the windshield as chips of ice. He guided me up the porch steps and inside, which was empty but for Bernadette's toenails clicking on the floor.

Alone.

With Ward.

In a very dark room.

"Where is everyone?" I asked while he locked the front door.

"Visiting Chris's brother," he answered. "Which means we have the place to ourselves."

He stretched his fingers through the darkness until they found mine. His touch began light, fingertips winding with mine before he caressed my arms. My teeth chattered from a draft, from excitement singing in the air. I backed up, my fingers laced through his vest, until my hips pressed against a wall. I pulled him closer. Ward slipped off my cardigan and again chased the vibrations down my now-naked arms. In the darkness, his lips found mine and pressed hard against my mouth, none of those tentative kisses we shared before. He kissed me as if he could take everything and draw it far inside himself. His mouth burned while the plaster against my shoulders chilled, and in the middle, I was like fuel, combustible. I didn't close my eyes because it was too black to see.

"Come on," he whispered.

I followed him through the darkness, up the staircase with a twist so steep I felt like falling backward. The shadows blanketing the walls were thick, velvety things. I wasn't sure how far off the stairway we were when he made a sharp angle into his bedroom.

A match fizzed as it ignited, then a votive candle bathed the room in tranquil amber. I sat on the foot of the bed and unzipped my boots. Before me, Ward unbuttoned his shirt. My chest rose with measured breaths. The shadows folded into the muscles where his trousers rested below his waist.

"I want you so bad," he breathed, slinking onto the bed.

Something shivered in my body. "I want you—"

His mouth blocked me from speaking. The fingers against my skin weren't the same ones painted with chipped gray polish I'd noticed when I met him, more deft and eager. My palm numbed from a tremor of electricity as I placed my hand over his and broke from kissing him.

"I'm afraid we won't stop if we start."

In my ear, he whispered, "Would that be so terrible?"

I thought about it and answered, "No. It'd be perfect."

His fingers slid down my dress's zipper, coaxing the fabric to reveal more of my skin, and then tiptoed under my skirt. Even though I wanted him, what would happen if we did this? How would he look at me afterward? I focused on the candle on the dresser, how the flame danced on the wick, whipping and flitting. A sense of awe so strong I didn't know if it came from Ward or myself or both uncurled in my body, and I couldn't keep my eyes open through the wonder but heard Ward's hushed laugh.

Forcing myself not to heave him across the room, I pressed my hands to his chest. He smiled as I needed to catch my breath. The candle burned in a cup with arches like church windows cut in the metal. His hair shined like copper.

"You want to?" he murmured.

I managed to nod before he unfastened his pants and guided my hand inside. So muffled, the candleholder rattled on the dresser. I touched him. I was scared of what might come next, but I didn't want to stop. The candle's flame thrashed in circles, moved faster, and flickered brighter. He pushed up my dress, our bodies separated by less space than the distance between our mouths.

"Hang on," he said. "I need a condom."

A high-octane rush pumped into my veins. The corona of light around the candle widened until a plume of fire burst from the wick and torched the air.

"Shit!" He leapt off the bed and smothered the flames with a blanket from the floor.

My hands were quiet.

Ward switched on a lamp with a loud click. Molten, blue wax spilled on his dresser and dripped to the carpet. He grimaced at the gooey mess. With the lights on, I saw him, as he was— a damaged, lanky boy unsure of himself and bashful.

"What the hell happened?" He gave me a dubious glance and flopped down beside me.

"I've never seen anything like it," I answered. Which was true.

My finger outlined his hand on his thigh. A modest smile

twitched his mouth, and the push of energy was too loud, too tenuous for me not to hear his thoughts riding the current to my mind. *My girl.* My cheeks warmed, and I smoothed my rumpled dress. What might happen if the lights went out and we were in the dark again?

Vayda!

My brother's yell was sharp and echoed in my brain.

Leave me alone, Jonah.

I gathered the ash of my exploded barriers. So help me, God, Jonah better not have been near my head when a single candle lit the room.

Vayda, come now!

A spike of ice speared my mind, brutal in its pain. My face ached and jaw locked, teeth clenched from agony, and I grabbed the blanket to stop my fingernails from cutting into the heel of my hand. This wasn't Jonah reaching out because he got a rise out of invading my space. Something had happened. My chest tightened as though Jonah dropped his shields on top of me with a solid, reeling thud. Ward furrowed his brow, and though his mouth moved, I couldn't make out anything he said. A tang puckered my mouth. I darted to Ward's bathroom. "I'm gonna be sick."

Throwing up was impossible to stop once it started. Ward held my hair, not reacting to my sickness except with a steady, concerned regard. He filled a cup with water. I swished out my mouth. The sound of the water rushing through the faucet thundered in my ears. Sweat pooled in the divot above my upper lip.

"Take me to Fire Sales," I panted.

He grabbed a sweater for himself and covered my shoulders with his coat. "You're sick. You should go home."

"You don't understand! Jonah needs me!" I barked, ignoring his insulted expression.

Panic overruled any damn I gave about hurting his feelings. I slid on my boots and barreled down the stairs, outside. The sky should've been black with stars at nine o'clock, but clouds invaded the night. Covering the ground were pellets of ice, which crunched under my feet, transforming the walkway into a slick gauntlet. Ward caught my arm and stopped me from falling as I slipped.

"The roads are gonna be bad," he said.

I didn't care. "Get me there as fast as you can. Something's wrong."

He scraped off enough ice from the Jaguar's windows to drive, and once the engine was running, he steered the car toward the open gate. The tires spun in search of traction when the car hurtled into the street.

Vayda, help! My brother panicked in my head.

"I'm coming, Jonah. I promise," I murmured. Ward glanced at me. I didn't care what he heard.

Within fifteen minutes, we settled by the curb in front of Fire Sales, and I flung open the car door. All the lights in the shop shone on an otherwise dim block of the business district. The showroom should have closed an hour ago. Still two feet from the entrance, I raised my hands. Energy spurted from my fingers. The door threw itself open, the hinges sprung. My shoes clicked against the floor, faster and faster, while I scanned the racks and gaps between furniture.

"Where are you?" I whispered. "Come on, Jonah."

I shut my eyes, shut down the alarms raging in my head until all was silent, not even the crackle of a radiant coal of Jonah's heat. I needed to try again. I held still and searched for the center of the energy racing through me, the place where it would be quiet. I shut out all the chaos, and after a moment, muffled but detectable, my brother's heartbeat vibrated against my fingers.

"There."

I spread my arms as though slicing a field of wheat with a sickle. China cabinets, armoires, and every other piece of furniture skated to the sides to reveal a straight corridor to the storeroom. My twin's pulse signaled me. The overhead lights popped with a shower of electric sparks. No matter how fast I weaved through the furniture, no matter how forcefully I shoved, I couldn't breach Jonah's barriers. Why couldn't I find his mind? I reached the storeroom and again shoved open the door with the energy collected in my hands.

I found him.

Jonah's defeated body was sprawled on the floor by Dad's desk, surrounded by the strewn remnants of a splintered end table.

"Jonah!"

He lay on his stomach. Bruises marbled the left side of his face. Blood seeped from his nose and mouth to pool in a dark halo on the floor. A scream rattled the glass cases and antique mirrors.

"GOD, NO! JONAH!"

I ran my fingers through his hair soaked with blood. His skin was clammy, his cheekbone blackened with bruises spreading from under his widow's peak.

"—at Fire Sales downtown. We need an ambulance," Ward dictated to the phone mounted on the wall. Unruffled as if he'd had to call for help countless times before, he spoke in a calm tone despite that his skin faded to the same stark white as linen. He glanced at me, mouth falling open, and looked away. A second unconscious figure lay ten feet away. "Two ambulances...They're both unconscious. Bleeding...I'll stay on the line."

I scurried toward the showroom where the furniture stayed shoved to the sides. I clenched my fists, searching for energy. *Move, damn it!* If Jonah could do it on command, why couldn't I?

A kindling spark swelled over my fingers. Some chairs and an old bookcase spider-crept away from the rest of the furniture and disrupted the measured hallway I'd blasted through the shop. I checked Jonah once more before moving to the second body.

I knew Marty even before I saw his face. Lying on his back, a gash in his forehead, he still wore his clothing from the coffee shop. His shirt stained with blood, but he was breathing.

Ward set down the phone. As I moved toward him, he stepped back once. Then a second step back. His spine was inflexible, his chest swollen as though ready to strike or safeguard himself—whichever he needed.

He knew what I could do. He put his hands on me and now knew about the Mind Games.

Abruptly, the room swarmed with emergency help. A blond woman took Jonah's vitals and spoke into a walkie-talkie. A second paramedic slipped a stabilizing collar around his neck. I heard myself give my father's cell phone number to an officer, aware of his uniform and the sound of his pen scratching on his notepad, but my gaze didn't move from Ward and his didn't leave mine.

"We need statements from both of you," the officer declared as the paramedics wheeled out Marty on a stretcher.

After I lied that I'd found Jonah while checking on the shop, the officer allowed us to leave. I clipped my seatbelt and waited for Ward to steer the car away from the curb. He didn't drive anywhere. The car's engine hummed, the heat drying my eyes, and Ward's hands coiled around the steering wheel hard enough to whiten his knuckles. He stared at the dashboard, the grinding of his teeth audible.

"What the fuck are you?" he asked. I reached out, but he blocked me. "Don't touch me."

I flinched, and my face was wet with renewed tears. "Ward—I—"

There was nothing to say. I'd succeeded in what I'd dreaded since I met him and knew he was the *gadjo* in my dream. I terrified him by unleashing my Mind Games, and now I was strung up in this nest of unwound thread I'd spun.

Chapter Thirteen

Ward

"Hell of a night." Emory tapped an unlit cigarette against his hand. "You don't have to stick around."

"Where would I go?" I asked, sinking into my seat in the emergency room's waiting lounge.

"You'd go home. Heidi worries about you, Ward."

I coughed. "Because I live there doesn't mean it's home."

He slipped his cigarette behind his ear. "There's a saying that your home is wherever you seek shelter in a storm. Every kind of storm."

I was hardly in the mood for preaching, but Emory didn't push me further. The fluorescent lights in the waiting room made his skin greenish. Few people sought help tonight—bad weather keeping everyone inside, out of trouble. Vayda dozed on a loveseat. The black make-up smudged around her eyes had dried, and where she held Jonah's bleeding head left stains on her hands.

Hands that opened doors without touching them.

I smelled something sweet. Her scent, snowy and brisk, clung to my clothing and my skin. My stomach heaved. *I didn't—If I—*

Damn thinking straight.

Vayda stirred in her slumber. The light above her sizzled.

Tonight, I saw things that went against reality. The "shh" of the furniture drifting over the floor. My girlfriend with her arms stretched, a black-and-white bird with wings angled for flight.

I'd had nightmares like this, whipping around, blindfolded, in a forest maze with no idea how I got inside or which path would free me. When I awakened from those dreams, my skin was always cold and sweaty.

"Can I get you a Coke?" Emory asked.

I grunted a response, distracted by the television where a rapper in some hip-hop group flashed a gargantuan ring. He thrust his hips with about as much sexiness as the pair of boning lemurs I'd witnessed on a class field trip to the Minnesota Zoo. Hell, at least lemurs weren't pretentious about getting it on.

"Mr. Silver?" an attendant called. Emory didn't respond. The attendant called again, and he startled, realizing he'd been summoned. "We're ready for you."

With Vayda's dad gone and crap on the television, boredom came quick. Even an aquarium with one of those giant algae-eating fish couldn't hold my attention. My head was too noisy. Vayda shuddered in her sleep, and I picked up my coat from the chair to lay it across her hips.

In my room. The fire. Had she done that, too?

I reached for her, my hand aching to touch her cheek, but pulled back. I couldn't do this.

Her eyes opened. I'd never pictured irises so light green like chips of springtime. She sat up, rotating her neck. "How long was I out?"

"An hour."

Her voice raised a half-key. "You stayed?"

"Nothing better to do," I muttered. Yet that meant staying here. With her. I collapsed in the chair across from her. "I want to make sure Jonah's okay."

She took off her boots to rub her feet. "Are you mad at me?"

"I don't know," I said. She moved to the chair beside me, and I leaned away. "Stay back."

She flinched and hugged my coat to her chest. Hearing her sniff back tears, the bones protecting my chest crumbled. I never wanted to hurt her. More than having my nerves rattled, I felt something else: a dread, a fear. What else could she do?

"I don't understand what happened," I whispered. "Obviously, this isn't a Romani thing, right? Otherwise, there'd be a lot more people like you. So are you a witch?"

"Don't call me that." The begging note in her voice stung. "You can't know how much names hurt."

I wasn't hurt? Jesus. I took another gander at the aquarium where a silver angelfish hid in a plastic cave. It had the right idea. Did I ever truly know Vayda?

I knew nothing.

The door to the exam rooms creaked open, and Emory trudged into the waiting room. Furrows from his crow's feet drew shadows down his face. He straddled a chair, drained as he reached for his daughter's hand.

"How's Jonah?" I asked, drawn closer to them even if a ring of uncertainty surrounded them.

"He has a concussion, a dislocated shoulder. Some broken ribs," Emory explained and cleaned his glasses on his shirt. "And he needs surgery. The doctor said there's internal bleeding. Not much. He'll be okay." He frowned. "Am I speaking gibberish?"

Emory made more sense than most of what I'd witnessed that night. So much hurt for a body. When we'd arrived at the hospital, I'd overheard a couple of attendants saying Marty hadn't gotten nearly as jacked up as Jonah.

Vayda popped her knuckles and hid her hands in my coat. "Can I visit him?"

"Not now, Magpie." Emory twisted his wedding ring. "He's lucky you found him."

I scoffed. Luck had nothing to do with her finding him.

Emory cocked his head. "You got something to say?"

"I'm speechless," I replied dryly.

Vayda's voice hushed. "He knows, *Dati*."

Emory froze as he retrieved his cigarette from behind his ear. Something strange glinted in his glasses. That sentence could've meant a hundred things, but he seemed to know what she meant. "Son, we're going outside for a talk."

"But it's cold," I argued. Like hell I was going outside. He might fling shit around and break lights. I'd already seen what kind of destruction Vayda could unleash.

Emory stood over me. "We're going outside. Now."

I knew that stern look, saw it plenty of times from cops, and each time, it meant I was going along whether I liked it or not. I followed Emory through the entrance into the cold blast of night. As we stood in the bus shelter, better known as the smoker's hut, snow lingered on the wind. The cars in the lot gleamed as though preserved in glassy coffins of ice. I coughed and burrowed my hands inside my sweater to spare them from frostbite.

"What'd you see tonight?" Emory asked, drawing on his cigarette.

"Nothing." Head down, crushing some rock salt under my boot. "I saw nothing."

"Don't lie to me, boy. Something's fucked you up good."

I opened my mouth only to snap my jaw shut. He flicked ash to the sidewalk. The embers died the instant they reached the ice.

After a few minutes, I asked, "Are you like her?"

"No."

"Is Jonah?"

He nodded. "Unfortunately. Tonight's not the only time you saw something, only the first time you got slapped in the face with it. This can't be a total shock, else you would've been long gone by the time I got here. Something gave you pause before this. Could've been lights flickering or a case of the chills. Hell, maybe you've watched those two have a conversation without speaking aloud. You ignored it 'cause admitting anything sounds like you cracked your head and your wits spilled out."

No. I hadn't. Had I? What I saw inside Fire Sales seared my mind, branded it.

Emory watched a car spin its tires on the ice. "I've been where you are, Ward. I told you my mother died when I was a kid. I was fifteen. My family didn't want me around, so I had to go find one. I was trouble, and my life needed changing."

"Is that when you met Vayda's mom?" I asked.

He smiled. "A couple of years later. I'd say to Lorna, 'Tell me what's on my mind.' It was our game, you know. One day we were fighting, and she put the furniture in my room on the ceiling and kept it there until she decided to put it back. Scared me damn good. I didn't speak to her for seven days. Guess I cared too much to run away but needed time to wrap my mind around what she did. Lorna's father called them *hokano,* a trick. My wife called them 'Mind Games.' The name stuck."

"Mind Games," I repeated.

My fingers jammed into my hair, my lungs pushing out a heavy sigh. Bullshit.

"Can I go?" I asked.

Smoke billowed from Emory's clenched teeth. "Not until you get this through your head: Vayda isn't any different than she was yesterday. What's different is how you see her."

I crushed more salt. How could the girl I saw in Fire Sales be the one who played with my hair and picked up bird feathers when walking in the woods? She was made of flesh and bone, hair and blood, but now I'd uncovered some secret metal, an alloy unknown in most people.

"What I saw was crazy," I argued. "You sound like talking about this shit is simple and rational. It's not. It's fucking abnormal."

Emory ground out his cigarette. He spoke in a low register, the deepest his voice could manage. "Ward, I'm telling you what my late father-in-law said to me: People die over these abilities. I've spent over half my life protecting Lorna and my kids because they're different. You're now responsible for guarding Vayda's secret, and you're decent enough that I believe you will. You have no choice. Otherwise, she could be killed. You don't want that on your conscience."

The seriousness of his words was heavy and pushed down on my shoulders, but I didn't think he intended to scare me rather than give me the brutal truth. Maybe he took me out in the cold to make sure I was awake. Between the wind chafing my cheeks and the sights my mind replayed, I didn't know when I'd sleep again.

Vayda set aside a celebrity gossip magazine as her father and I reentered the waiting room. She didn't balk from me, but I wished she would. Listening to Emory tell me about the Mind Games was one thing, but being in the same room as her reheated the confusion firing in my gut.

"Magpie, you need to rest." Emory kissed her forehead. "Ward, get her home safely."

I blurted, "Okay."

What had I agreed to?

Vayda slid into my coat, and I tried not to cringe. Before all this, I gave her my coat dozens of times. I'd *liked* giving her my coat. Now? She was supposed to be the same, but it didn't matter what her father said. She wasn't. Not to me. Emory hugged his daughter and peered over her head to give me a firm nod.

The car slid on the ice as we left the hospital. Even after midnight, when the sky was its darkest, the snow tinted the streets and lawns blue. The bad roads allowed me to focus on driving and not succumb to the temptation to peek at the girl beside me, the one breathing too loud and tugging her skirt down over her knees. The awareness of her filled my head, and the only way to get rid of it was to keep going until I steered onto the driveway. The woods were black. Everything was black with shadow except for the Silvers' house patiently waiting with a single light by the front door. I parked the car and finally allowed myself to look at Vayda.

She wasn't different from before.

"So"—she paused—"what are you thinking?"

I twisted the different stereo dials, but I wasn't in the mood for music and let the car fill with silence.

"*Gadjo*, I can do more than what you saw at Fire Sales. I can read minds."

The hair of my neck stretched tight, and my hands froze despite the heater in the car. My head turned until I came to her watery eyes and her fists covering her mouth.

"Are you saying you've listened to my thoughts?" I asked.

"Not you. Not really. Sometimes I can't block what you're thinking. The thoughts are so strong they reach me by accident."

I leaned against the car's door and twisted, the leather seat squeaking beneath me. Acid rolled up my throat, burning my nose, but I swallowed it back down. I hated this trembling in my blood. Throwing open the car door, I stomped across the icy gravel. Vayda stepped out of the car and inched toward me, but I changed paths and slogged toward the barn.

She'd eavesdropped on my thoughts. How much had she heard? Christ, what if she knew what I was thinking when she was in my bed? If she read my mind, then she knew shit about Drake, things I stopped myself from thinking. If I wanted her to know something, I'd say it. She stripped that from me.

"Where are you going?" she called.

Her voice was a kick to my back, and I wheeled around to face her. "First, you spring on me that you're a fucking magician, and now you've invaded my mind?"

She reached for me but recoiled. "You're so mad I can't touch you. It hurts my hands."

I gritted my teeth and propped against the open barn door. The wind whistled through holes in the roof, and some unseen bird flapped over the hayloft.

"What do you mean your hands hurt?"

"I'm an empath," she said. "I feel peoples' emotion as energy. Sounds like bullshit, I know." Her voice wavered as she searched the sky.

"You're nuts," I barked.

"Let me talk."

I rested my head against the raw wood of the door.

Peeling away from the barn, she circled her wrists as though kneading invisible bread. "People's emotions emit energy. There's something in me pulling that energy. I shut it down as best I can unless someone reaches to me." She sounded as if she was dictating notes, not talking with me until she looked at me. "Most of the time, I don't know how or why, but it goes right through you. But then you reach to me. I responded to what you already wanted."

"You read my mind and then told me what I wanted to hear?" I choked on the words and tried to close my mouth, but I was wide open and afraid that the acid I swallowed before was about to come back up. I gestured between us. "You and me. Us. We're a lie! How much of us is real and not you playing me?"

"Don't do this to me, Ward."

"Don't do this to *you*? I'm not the one dicking around in your head!"

I'd told her things about growing up with Drake that no one knew. She wasn't frightened by my baggage, but this... Good God.

"I trusted you," I seethed.

"You still can," Vayda pleaded. "And my telling you about the Mind Games shows that I trust you, *gadjo*."

I didn't want her to call me *gadjo* right then. She'd used it before to set me apart from her, but it wound up pulling me closer. Scowling, I found a rock and threw it as far as I could into the woods. "You wouldn't have told me about this if tonight hadn't happened! You do *not* fucking trust me!" I threw another rock. "And, apparently, I can't trust you!"

She hugged herself as her eyes shined with tears. "Are you breaking up with me?"

"I don't know!" I punched the barn's door, cutting my knuckles. My hand throbbed as blood oozed into the scrapes. "Shit!"

"Here." Vayda scooped some snow and placed it against my torn knuckles. I gasped, the nerve endings overloaded by the cold. I didn't know what was worse, the pain or shock of ice.

She reached toward me, nearly running her fingers down my arm, but drew her hand back before we connected. Her voice thickened, her head dropping forward. "I'm sorry. I honestly am."

She walked away and paused on the steps of her stone house. Then she vanished inside.

The wind sliced clean through me as if I had no clothes on my body, no flesh over my bones. The cuts on my hand ached, bruises formed over my scars. I'd take care of the mess once I got home. Right then, I had to clear my head.

The Jaguar was a fast ride to Heidi's house where the living room glowed like a campfire. The dashboard clock read ten to one. Over ninety minutes past curfew. Shit. As I entered through the door off the kitchen, Bernadette was at my feet. Her tail bopped as she snuffled my shoes.

"How much trouble am I in?" I asked, rubbing her ears.

She spun several times, dog-speak for "a hell of a lot."

"That's what I figured."

I headed into the living room with my dog trotting behind. Heidi bolted up from the glider when she saw me. Her hair was knotted, her face puffy. She reached out to grab my arm, but I darted away from her stretching fingers. No more touching.

"Heidi, I'm not in the mood," I cut her off. "I've had a bad night."

She studied my black-and-bluing hand crusted with blood. "What happened? With the bad roads, I kept picturing you and Vayda in a car wreck or dead. You should have called!"

I slumped on the couch. "I'm home now, so you don't have to worry."

Her arms folded over her robe. "Ward, I can't let this slide. You showed up with a broken curfew and busted hand. This is the kind of crap Drake pulled."

Curses tipped my tongue, but I counted arcs of the pendulum swinging in the grandfather clock. *Calm down. Breathe. Be cold.*

Heidi snapped her fingers. "I've bent over backwards to give you a decent place to live. Without me, you'd be on smack or in jail. Like your dad."

Something in my mind splintered. "You love letting me know when I fuck up, don't you?"

Darting off the couch, I stomped up the stairs. I didn't have to listen to this crap. Life, as rotten as the days were in Minnesota, was simpler when left to fend for myself, and I didn't worry about people's emotions or my own. I could shut down and exist. That was that.

Bernadette scooted in behind me before I slammed the door to my room. Oliver screamed from the racket, and Chris called for Heidi's help. I picked up my shirt and vest from earlier. The only other time I wore the outfit was to Drake's funeral. Chris bought me the one suit off the rack that didn't need alterations. Dragging out my packed duffle bag from the closet, I unzipped it to reveal two extra sets of clothes and checked my wallet. Thirty-two dollars, my Minnesota driver's license, an emergency contact card still listing Drake. Bernadette flopped onto the bag and lowered her nose to her paws.

"Sorry, Dog," I told her. "This is a solo mission."

From my nightstand, I retrieved a few more items. The iPod I'd stolen off some kid at my last school, my self-annotated anthology of Tennessee Williams.

"Ward, open your door!" Chris called from the hall.

I unlocked it and resumed throwing in the shirts from my dresser. He let himself into my room, nudged my duffle bag, and I snapped, "Make it quick."

"Where do you think you're going?" He grabbed my arm. I set my jaw and shirked his hold on me. "You need to get a grip and take care of your hand before you do anything. If you leave, Heidi won't let you come back."

"Whatever happened to second chances?" I grumbled.

"You're on your second chance," he warned. "Think hard before you make up your mind."

He shut my door, didn't know I flipped him off on the way out before I slid to the floor, drawing my knees to my chest. My boots were ugly as sin. Shit kickers, Drake christened them. They belonged to him before they became mine. He quit wearing them around the time he stopped performing.

I reached into my nightstand. A stack of photos caught my fingers. Vayda and I took them with an old Polaroid camera I found at Fire Sales. Lousy quality and no chance to delete the goofy ones. We lay on my bed and held the camera above to photograph us. So many times in her room, she sat behind me, one of her arms wrapping around my chest as she blanketed me with her hair. Sometimes I'd take one of the guitars Drake hadn't pawned for rent to her house, and I'd play while she sang. Sometimes we sang together, old folk songs from the southern mountains, whatever made our voices sound good together. We'd talked about nothing and everything and kissed for more than an hour straight.

Was all that negated now?

The moments meant something at the time, but knowing, at any second, she listened to my thoughts and plotted what to say based upon those thoughts...How much of her was real and not what she thought I wanted her to be?

I flopped on the bed, rolled onto my side, and smelled traces of her on my pillow. Holding the fabric to my face, I inhaled. My gut ached. She made me laugh. Laughing hard didn't come naturally to me. Or without a price.

I wanted more than a notch in my belt.

I didn't scare easily.

That girl was a tinderbox. A bundle of kindling ready to ignite if given the right spark. Knowing how incendiary she could be was both horrifying and riveting.

Plodding downstairs, Heidi and Chris trailed me without getting up from the couch, silent, as I absconded from the kitchen with the phone. I went outside to the garage and sat atop the metal sawhorse, startled by my reflection in a sheet of polished copper. My face might've been distorted from the waves in the metal, but God, I had broken eyes.

No wind, no sleet. Only forest, snow on the ground, and moonlight. I opened my wallet and pulled out the gray business card, dialing the number handwritten on the back.

"Who is this?" a man's southern drawl asked through a yawn.

"Emory? It's Ward. Can we talk?"

Chapter Fourteen

Vayda

"The story is Jonah flipped his shit and got his ass locked in the psych ward."

"Only a matter of time before he went off the deep end."

"I give Vayda three days before she winds up rooming with him."

"Bitch is whacked. You hear what happened with her and Chloe?"

My head felt firebombed by the chatter. Barely nine in the morning, and this was how it'd be for the rest of the day. The comments behind my back, the pointing, would be better off as knives. They'd hurt less. Three nights ago, Marty beat Jonah. It wasn't right or fair that he roamed free on bond while my brother stayed awake for thirty-minute sprints before he was exhausted.

"Chin up, Magpie," Dad urged while he poured coffee this morning. "You're going to school. Cardinal rule: The only way to make life normal is to live and not let the whispers control you."

I'd live all right. Under a rock.

Deep within the library stacks, I found a secluded table and rifled through my backpack undisturbed. I had one of Jonah's books and Ward's music for me, some songs he'd been showing me how to strum on a guitar. I didn't switch on the music. All I wanted was quiet. Ward's quiet.

A crumpled paper snuck out of my backpack and plummeted to the floor. I picked up the note, which I searched over in hope of some hit of Ward's energy, his electricity. It wasn't easy to find, and what I felt as I unfolded it for the seven hundredth time was a muddled mess:

V, Still…thinkingupsetconfusedspookedlonelysilent.
Still you. Still me. Still we?
—WMR

The paper was smeared and wrinkled as though trashed and retrieved more than once before stuffed in my locker. At least it was some attempt to communicate. Even though we shared several classes, I hadn't seen him. He probably ditched school. The genteel thing would've been to ask if I wanted to come, too.

An abrupt blackness gripped behind my ears, raised every hair, and the force whipped my head over my shoulder. Sister Tremblay stood at the end of a row of books, not moving, with her sights fixed on me.

"It's not polite to stare," I grumbled.

"I'm curious how your brother's faring." Her voice was low, nectar-rich. "It's strange he would be taken by surprise. He always struck me as the type who enjoys control."

My hands buzzed as her darkness slid into my palms. No one else was in this part of the library, and there was no way for me to flee without going through her.

"It must be difficult not to have Jonah protecting you." She floated down the aisle and spread out her fingers on my tabletop. "It makes you more vulnerable, doesn't it? No wonder your father goes to such great length to secure your safety."

I gripped Jonah's book. "What do you want?"

She reached inside her robes for a handkerchief to dab her nose. "I believed Jonah was the wilder of you two. He's talented, strong, and willing. But you're out of control. It would be a shame if you lost your hold, fragile as it is. It wouldn't take much to send you over the edge."

"I'm fine," I argued.

"I'm sure that's what your mother thought as well."

I clutched Jonah's book tighter. With a wave of her hand, Sister Tremblay glided back down the aisle of books. The light above me buzzed.

A moment later, the fluorescent bulb broke and darkness veiled me.

***

It took a while, but I was finally hungry. I carried my paper sack into the cafeteria, bought some milk, and as I put the change into my pocket, I smacked right into Marty.

How could he be allowed in school after what happened? Despite the bruising on his face and knuckles and the healing gash on his forehead where my brother got him, he wore the same smug mask as usual. So much damage to Jonah, so little injury to him. It wasn't fair. The only reason he wasn't hurt worse was he'd hit Jonah first. His fingers reached for my cheek.

"Touch me and I'll scream," I hissed.

"All the good girls scream my name, and you're still a good girl, right?"

I batted away his hand. "Leave me alone."

Trying to step around him, I halted as his hand gripped my upper arm and pulled me close enough against him to rub the flesh under his shirt.

"You're in such a rush to go." He dropped his voice and moved his mouth close enough to my ear so that I felt the steam of his breath. "But if you think you can run away from what I know about your brother, think again."

My throat ached, mouth dry. He'd been drunk. That didn't mean he forgot what happened that night. I needed to talk to Jonah, find out exactly what went down in Fire Sales.

Marty released my arm and ran his hand over my hip before pushing me away. I yelled for him to stop, not caring if people gawked. Every step I took away from him, my shoulders tightened, waiting for him to say something. I couldn't take that risk.

I put down my head and claimed my seat at my usual table, so empty today. No Chloe. No Jonah. No Ward. Just some chive bread and me. At two in the morning, I'd begun baking. Dad woke and was awestruck by my flour-speckled apron and the counter overrun with poppy-seed muffins and fresh bread. The only question he managed was whether we needed a bigger breadbox.

Chloe unwrapped a pack of red licorice from her lunch and sneered at me. She was polished and well-planned from the headband that matched her plaid skirt to the diamond studs shimmering on her ears. Her mission was clear: stop at every table in the cafeteria.

"…wanted to know if I'd get on my knees for Marty." Her voice carried over the usual cafeteria noise. "Only a girl who knows about that kind of thing herself would think to say it."

My stomach grew queasy as she tittered. The energy coming off her was tense and edgy, not cheerful. To me, she felt like her teeth wanted to crack. She glanced my way and curled her lips, the girl she was talking with gaping at me.

After she finished her promenade from table to table, she sat across from me. "May I join you?"

"Is it safe?" I asked. The girl was a social piranha. I knew what happened if she smelled blood. "I've seen you ear-hustling everyone on your way over here. You tell them what a bitch I am?"

"Oh, they know." She giggled. "Everyone does. People listen to me, Vayda."

"Golly, Chloe, you're so humble. Why don't I call you 'Jonah?'"

Her self-satisfied giggle ceased, replaced by a rabbit-like twitchiness. "Don't say his name."

She gripped her lunch bag, and her hands trembled.

"He listens, Vayda." She drew her hands to her mouth, eyes too wide. "He's always listening. I've been getting chills and can't stop thinking that I need to make things right with you. Why the hell would I want to do that? After what you said, *I'm* supposed to apologize to *you*."

She whimpered, mouth pinched with pain. A distinct heat saturated her energy. Jonah had to be awake right now. That or his abilities rotated out of control like an askew gyroscope.

Defiantly, I said loud enough for Jonah to listen across the trail linking him to Chloe, "If you don't want to apologize, then don't."

"I can't help it." She gave a shrill cackle, and her hand smacked the table as she fought it. "I'm sorry. I said it. Can't take it back."

Something was very wrong with her. Twisted.

Jonah, do you even know what you did to her mind? I shot the thought to him and hoped he netted it.

He was silent.

***

After the final bell, I rummaged through my bag for the Chevy's keys. Dad had me drop him at his shop this morning and said he'd catch a bus to the hospital. Electricity *zinged* up my back, and I pivoted to face Ward. Violet streaked the hollows in his pale skin. Evidently, his insomnia won again. Maybe it was wrong to hope he was "off" without me, the way I felt without him.

"You weren't in class," I remarked.

He tugged his backpack higher onto his shoulder. "Heidi took me to a dentist. Not as if Drake ever took me."

"But your smile's so pretty."

"Pretty horrendous." He paged through Vonnegut's *Slaughterhouse-Five.* "Did you find my note?"

I dug out the smudged paper from my pocket. "You often string together random words and expect girls to understand them?" His cheeks reddened, and my fingertips ran over his, a test. Static churned between us. It was noisier now that he knew. "How are we, Ward?"

His voice was exact. "On life support but hanging on. Vayda, I—" He huffed and blew the auburn hair from his face. "I need to know where this goes."

"You've been working a lot at Fire Sales, helping out *Dati*," I said. "Thanks."

"I'm learning a lot from him."

We avoided looking at each other for fifteen seconds that felt like an hour. He glued his back to his locker, and he couldn't retreat but shifted, unsure if he wanted me any closer. If only he'd let me relax him. I could calm down myself. Why not help him? I'd made my Mind Games my enemy for years, but did it have to be that way? I wanted to fix things. I wanted to fix myself. If they were what broke, maybe in some insane way, Jonah was right and that I had to use them before I ruined everything with them.

My right palm filled with cool energy as I reached for his hand, pushing my fingers between his. He opened his mouth to protest when a valve in my hand opened and flooded him with a blast of cold over hot over numb. He yanked away his hand, breathless.

"What was that?" he demanded.

"I'm sorry!" I winced. "I didn't mean—"

"Don't be sorry. It felt like feathers. It wasn't bad. Actually, it was nice. Really nice."

The uncertainty ebbing from him mingled with alertness. Arousal.

"Come on, Vayda." He snatched up my backpack and led me toward the exit.

Outside, salt crystals melted the ice as slush puddled in the parking lot. Icicles hung from St. Anthony's gutters, ready to fall and pierce. All the trees were bare and black, sorrowful, and did nothing to hold back the wind sinking into my joints.

Ward kicked a chunk of ice before asking, "What the hell's going on? Emory told me to keep an eye on you, and the way he said it, he wasn't asking because you'd be upset about Jonah. He's acting like he thinks someone's going to hurt you. You guys are so jumpy, and the broken window at Fire Sales, the spray paint, what's going on? What are you hiding? No matter what you think, I'm not stupid."

"*Gadjo*, don't say that," I protested. "This was never about me thinking you were stupid. I thought you'd be afraid. You were. Are. I don't know."

"Tell me what's going on."

I couldn't. He didn't know about Hemlock, how everyone turned against my family. Even if Dad talked to him about the Mind Games, he would keep certain things hidden—our old names, what Mom did, the fire. Having all those secrets spoken aloud in one breath might drive away Ward for good.

White noise, the whooshing of blood, assaulted my ears, and static crackled in my palms. Ward reached for me only for me to stop him. Too much energy swelled in my fingers. I didn't want to shock him, so I placed my hand on a sidewalk lamp's post. My body relaxed as the current fled from my fingers and jumped into the metal. Standing some ten feet below the bulb, I heard the glass pop followed by a fizzle. I ducked my face as slivers of glass rained around me.

Ward glanced at the broken light. "You done yet?"

He walked me to the Chevy and placed my backpack in the front seat. By the driver's side, he cupped my face in his big hands. My barriers stretched to the sky, stretched so thin I quivered as my control threatened to let go, but I didn't feel or listen to anything. All the energy was quiet. Wonderfully quiet. I wanted him to say something. He ran his fingers over my cheekbones then drew his thumb across my lower lip. A stinging spark shocked both of us, and he backed away.

He wasn't ready.

Chapter Fifteen

Vayda

The coat bunched beneath my head crinkled every time I shifted. I tried to open my eyelids but couldn't. Still too heavy with my dream.

"You ain't got much time. People are gonna be coming here looking for y'all soon." Rain shoves some apples, the rest of a loaf of bread, and a jar of peanut butter into a bag, which he hands to Jonah.

Still in his sweatpants and T-shirt, my brother is as grimy with ash as I am. My lungs and throat throb as if I choked on acid. How is it only an hour ago we clambered out of a burning house, and now Dad and Rain are figuring out how to get us out of town before we can so much as clean up?

"I gave your daddy some money. After you're outta Hemlock, he'll stop and get you some decent clothes." Rain shakes his head, sadness tacking his blue eyes to mine. "I'm so sorry about your mama."

"Vayda."

My right eyelid cracked, but the light drove me back into the dream.

"Remember now. What's your name?" Rain asks.

Dad's chin trembles. "Emory Silver."

Silver because it's Mom's favorite metal. Was her favorite metal.

I slump in the front seat of Rain's old Chevy and wipe my face. Probably some grit, some char. I'm not crying. Right now, I've got too much to keep it together for. No time to cry.

Jonah's breathing doesn't sound too good as he tucks under a blanket in the backseat. How much smoke had he breathed in while he banged on my door screaming at me to get up? He saved Dad and me.

Rain and Dad hug, my godfather promising, "I'll get some new papers in order for you. Stay in touch, Em, and may the angels keep their watch."

Jonah's voice broke through my slumber.

"Vayda, wake the hell up."

Being in Jonah's hospital room, being with his energy, his skull hurt so badly that my own head brimmed with pain. The sound of my voice was like hail on a tin roof. "I'm sleeping."

"I mean it, Sis. Get up."

Something in his voice, stern but frightened, I opened my eyes. Chloe stood by Jonah's bed. She quaked with an uneven energy. The tension I'd sensed in her at lunch had spread into her every cell.

"You've been on my mind all day, Jonah," she said. "I can't get you out of my thoughts."

A gray haze around her was at odds with the soothing green walls of the hospital room. I gripped the armrests of my chair, ready to stand, and yet I stayed put. I couldn't be sure what would happen if I touched her or what she'd do if I moved.

Jonah's head dropped forward. His face was a patchwork of bruises and small cuts, one eye still too swollen to open. A sling harnessed his left arm. Veins pumped full of painkillers, all the injuries muddling his brain—how the hell could he work a Mind Game? Unless whatever he'd done spun out of his control.

I climbed out of the chair. Chloe took hold of Jonah's good hand, and he gasped. He felt something from her. I drew closer, lowering my mental walls for a better grasp. Her disjointed energy slinked over me. Chaotic, flashing. She needed to go, get away from my brother and whatever hold he had on her.

"Jonah can't have any visitors but family," I said. "You have to leave."

Chloe didn't budge. She clutched his wrist, her fingernails

pressing white then red into his skin. Her words wavered as they fell off her lip. "He can do things, you know."

I jumped and gripped the railing on the bed for stability. *Jonah, are you working her right now?* I screamed in his brain. *How could you be so careless?*

He groaned. Maybe my yelling inside his skull hurt all that much more because of his concussion courtesy of Marty's foot. He looked like he was about to puke, and he deserved it, no matter how painful it would be on his cracked ribs. His forehead knotted. *Mind hurts. I swear to Christ, I don't know what's wrong with her.*

Chloe kneaded his hand, but her face twisted while thin tears rolled down her cheeks. "I can't leave you, Jonah, but I don't want to be with you when my head's clear. You make my thoughts trick me."

She wouldn't let go of him.

He spoke softly. "Chloe, I never tricked you."

Every hair on the back of my neck stood on end.

Let go of her, I said. A Mind Game was in the room. He had to be playing one. *Stop yourself.*

God's honest truth, I'm not working her. Not when my head's so jacked up.

Truth, when spoken or thought, felt like dipping my hands into clear water. Jonah told the truth. The Mind Game he began with Chloe had grown too big for him to manage. His energy moved in disorganized trails. It came and went from him, veering off so fast even my feelers couldn't get a grasp. He'd built the bridge linking her mind to his, and now he didn't know how to burn it? He damaged her, beyond damaged. Ruined. All because he couldn't help himself.

Spit wet her lips, and she cried out, "Make him stop!"

This had gone on long enough. My thoughts pushed at Jonah. *This is wrong. She's hurting.*

A wail withered in her throat. The sound seized my hands, flooding them with fiery energy. Too much, too quick. A cooling reaction came off my fingers and grabbed on to Jonah's energy.

Bang!

The door to the hospital room slammed hard enough to jangle the hinges, and the cheap blinds over the window fell where they snapped closed. Chloe yelped, but her squeeze on my brother tightened.

Despite the heaviness of his head, Jonah sighed. "Good show. And you yell at me for showing off what I can do."

He wiggled his fingers free from Chloe's hand. Her aura brightened, though still wide and terrified.

"Freaks!" she screamed.

Freaks. The word carried as much hurt as "gypsy." Both words together pelted my mother when the handcuffs clamped on her wrists. The crowd shouted them as Dad and Rain flanked her when she fled the courthouse in Hemlock. Layered so thickly in paint on Fire Sales' brick exterior that the outline remained.

My mouth fell open. Chloe did it. She broke that window, branded us, and Jonah didn't know it. How lucid was she when Jonah was in her head? She could take our lives, the way he had hers, and drive us out of Black Orchard. I had to sit. The walls slanted too close, and the floor shook as it begged to give away beneath me. I didn't know if the shaking streamed out of me or only in my mind.

She rocked back and forth. "What the hell are you two? Evil?"

Jonah snorted. I felt his anger scalding my fingertips, his fear chilling my blood. "It's not nice to call people names."

With a lurch, Chloe repeated, "What *are* you?"

I gulped, a sound too loud in my head. Jonah kept scowling, and the anger inside him culled together. He polished it until it was smooth and hard, and then he shoved at me.

I needed it.

His push swallowed me and held me tight, forcing me to focus. Fear and hurt couldn't help me cope. "We're ordinary people, Chloe."

"We have unordinary abilities," Jonah completed.

She chewed on her pinky nail. Her eyes, so wide a

moment before, narrowed. She would talk at her first chance. She already made sure everyone knew what I'd said to her at the coffee house. She'd whisper to everybody in the hall of St. Anthony's, pointing toward Jonah and me, and as she'd promised, they would believe her.

Despite the banging in his head, Jonah sank into my mind. *We gotta do something. You can make her forget she was here, Sis.*

You want me to do your dirty work? Did you leave every shred of decency in your soul in Georgia? I shook my head. *I can't push myself on someone like you can. Even if I could, I wouldn't.*

I'm too weak to do it myself. Another groan parted his lips. His pain was real and sharp. *You can do this, Vayda. What happens if she talks?*

We would leave Wisconsin. I didn't want to leave in the middle of the night with nothing once again. I didn't want to leave Ward. Jonah didn't want to go either. Black Orchard had become his home as well. We'd both grown to love the cold. While I might not know how to keep Marty quiet, maybe I could stop Chloe, at least long enough to come up with a better plan.

I'd close the doors he left ajar in Chloe's mind. It wouldn't be manipulating her, it'd be freeing her.

The hand poking out of Jonah's sling touched mine. *I'll try to help.*

I joined my hand to his and then cupped Chloe's shoulder with the promise, "I'll make you safe."

Chloe's sight flicked to mine, wide open and beautiful, a pond where I could dive.

I stole that glance as my chance.

Her pupils dilated until her irises were nearly full black like a hole at the bottom of a well. The light in the room hurt. Jonah's hand was in mine as we moved through the dark, blind as the depth swallowed all light, until we crawled out in the hallway of Chloe's thoughts.

Something had wrecked the inside of her mind. My

brother. Every mind had rooms of memory, and while the hallway of Chloe's mind was sculpted from marble, the doors were nothing more than brittle, smoking wood. Jonah hung his head.

What do we do? I asked.

He gestured to a doorway emitting the amber glow of fire. A fire he started. *Go there.*

I lagged, hesitant because of the paint blistering on the door, so many cracks. *By all rights, Jonah, you ignited this blaze. You should be the one to overpower the flames, not me.*

Curse me all you want later, but get this fire out now before it spreads.

He needed me. He couldn't do it himself.

I sucked in a cold breath. My fingers stroked the fragile doorways, and the firelight shaded Jonah's and my skin. As I breathed, ice rose up my stomach, through my chest, and swirled in my mouth. A draft pushed the hair back from my shoulders. If my brother was heat, I was the cold.

I felt calm. I felt like my mother.

Protecting our family comes before all else. Our family is our clan. We only have each other, I intoned in my head, in the place where Jonah would hear me loudest. *Remember that.*

My breath expanded in my lungs, and I exhaled over the fire in Chloe's memories. The flames sputtered. Then they were nothing. Where the fire had been was a soot-smeared room with ashes powdering the floor. Stepping out from Jonah's hold, I scooped the ashes and again breathed over them until they scattered.

Fire out.

There. I've done everything you wanted.

I flung off my brother's hold, severing my connection to Chloe's mind, but an ashy taste coated my mouth. God, I prayed this worked.

Jonah's head lolled against his pillow, heavy, drained. Yet Chloe's energy had a boost. Not gluey and oozy but still denser than she used to be. What more could I do? I didn't know how taking out her memory would work, if it were successful, but

I had to believe she couldn't sweep up every fleck of ash to make a solid memory.

She blinked. "How long have you been here, Vayda?"

"She just got here," Jonah lied. "You were leaving, remember?"

"Oh. I guess I'll be going." She picked up her purse and lingered by the door when she peeked over her shoulder, shuddered, then exited. Something morally bereft happened between my brother and her, something that went well beyond any mere disapproval of his relationship with her. Maybe I hadn't understood why he'd want that *gadji* back after she'd humiliated him, but he cared for her. His care was broken, and I'd been too enamored with Ward to notice the decay eating at Jonah and his powers. They spoiled. He spoiled that girl's mind.

I sat on the edge of Jonah's bed and twisted the ends of my hair around my fingers. *I swear on my soul. Never again.*

He extended his good arm to me. "Come here, Sis."

"No."

Gritting his teeth, he held his ribs and inched to the side of the bed. "I need you."

I stepped back. It'd always been the two of us, no distance, no misgivings. Why did he have to ruin that?

"Vayda," he begged. "I only wanted her to care about me again. When I was with her, it didn't matter that we're freaks. She made things easier, and I wanted more of that. More of her."

I could have spoken those same words about Ward.

"I didn't know that would happen to her," he confessed.

His voice. He wasn't working me. He couldn't.

I scooted close to the edge of his bed. His hand, pierced with IVs and wrapped with tape, took mine. We could've been seven years old, standing together to watch the black shapes of birds flock to the cottonwood tree outside our ranch in Montana. So many of them, endless with their wings and the cacophony of their screeches, they were mesmerizing. I couldn't turn away then. I couldn't turn away from Jonah now.

"I love you, Vayda," he whispered. "You know that. You and *Dati* are the only people I love. I'm sorry I put you in a bad spot."

"No, you're not."

"Something went wrong with Chloe. As soon as I'm at full strength, I'll fix it. I'll make up for everything."

"Sure you will."

My head ached, but whether the pain was my own or Jonah's...

I promise to God, he vowed. *I'll make this right.*

He sent out the thought to my mind, but before he could get in further, I blocked him with a wall, stacked brick by brick.

Chapter Sixteen

Vayda

For Mom, Christmas began the moment she fastened the backs on her holly earrings before Mass and culminated in the candlelight singing of "Silent Night" in the Catholic parish where Jonah served as an acolyte. Before I fell asleep, she'd stop in my room with hugs and hopes for blessings on her scarlet lips. Then she'd join Dad in the hall, laugh as he unpinned her black hair, swallowing her metal hair comb in his palm, kissed behind her ear, and close my door with a click. I'd listen to their footfalls, the murmur of their voices as they went off together, and then the whole house would sigh.

My father loved my mother. He loved her to death.

A month after Mom's murder, our first Christmas in Wisconsin was buried under fourteen inches of snow. Jonah and I took in a marathon of "A Christmas Story" and ate Frosted Flakes because it was the only thing in the house. Rain called every few hours, saying he didn't like the feeling he was getting, that Dad was squirreling himself away and desperate. Rain swore he'd keep an eye on all of us and help us through the bleak days and night terrors. He gave us the house. He gave us a chance at a life beyond Mom, but sometimes I wondered if Dad would have kept going if it hadn't been for Jonah and me.

It had taken a while, but Dad eventually came out of his study once, hair unkempt and shirt rumpled. I'd followed him as he raided Rain's wine collection and headed upstairs. He didn't know I'd spied him while he unclasped his Archangel Michael medallion strung with a cross, a wedding gift from Mom, and dropped it inside the dresser where it'd since stayed.

This Christmas Eve, I strummed the acoustic guitar Ward loaned me. I felt along the frets and placed my fingers where his had pressed down on the metal strings. I could sense him, pouring himself into his playing, into his art. All Ward wanted was escape. Underneath him, there was someone else, someone so drugged he felt like sliding lower and lower in a warm bath.

Drake.

He was a ghost in the guitar, one that haunted Ward and knew him. His energy lingered in the strings. Seeking the emotion lodged in objects was to find the strongest attachment, and what Drake attached was numbness. I could see his skeletal fingers forming chords on the strings, his other holding a green pick, cigarette in mouth and ratty auburn hair, so tangled like dreadlocks, hanging near his shoulders. He played while Ward begged him to look at a sculpture he'd built, but Drake didn't move. Nothing moved him. Not even his son.

I put down the guitar and rubbed my temples. Jonah rolled over on the couch.

"You get a hit?"

"I don't want to talk about it," I answered.

He nodded, and I believed, at least this time, he wouldn't invade my mind. He couldn't. In the nine days since the beating and two since his hospital release, my brother's pain was overwhelming. Too weak to work Mind Games, the energy crashed inside him then glommed onto me as its outlet. He smelled of sweat and pressed his hand to his ribs. A cough, and the bulb in the lamp popped.

Such a sorry sight, reduced to misguided flares of energy.

I didn't feel bad for him.

I brought him a blanket and, after helping to steady him as he sat up, I began combing through his hair. From my angle, he appeared wary as he took in the walls, running from one end of the floor to the other. As I slicked his hair, I knew his paranoia. Perhaps after his attack in Fire Sales, he'd finally wised up. We weren't safe anywhere.

"Why do you take care of me?" he asked.

"You're my twin. I don't like that you're hurt." The answer was simple, yet I couldn't pretend things were okay. The half-hearted apologies—no more. "Jonah, don't ever do this again."

He lay back, exhausted already. Through the curtains, I could make out the glow of headlights on the driveway. Not moving. Parked and waiting. They'd been there almost every day since Jonah's release from the hospital.

"She's out there again," he murmured. "*Dati* doesn't want me talking to her. He's afraid it would make things worse."

"She won't listen," I replied and pulled back the curtain to spy Chloe's car. "Last night, *Dati* was out there trying to reason with her. He had to call her mom to come and get her."

Try, Vayda. Please.

How could I argue with him? We wanted the same thing, albeit for different reasons, I was sure. I slipped on my coat and made my way down the snow-covered steps and across the driveway. Through the car's windows, I could make out Chloe staring at the house. She clutched the steering wheel with both hands, eyes darting and watchful. I tapped on the driver's window. She only focused ahead.

Time for a different approach.

I walked around to the passenger side. The door was unlocked. If she would listen to me at all, I had to get into the car.

"Chloe, what are you doing here?" I asked as I sat beside her.

"I don't know." She blew a long piece of hair from her face. Not the neat, icy blond I knew, her hair was clipped in a ratty topknot, her matchy-matchy uniform of sweater and skirt replaced with an oversized sweatshirt. "I don't know why I come here, but I have to." She angled her face, and a million questions gleamed in her pupils. "I don't like you very much, do I?"

"Not anymore," I replied.

"I really don't like your brother."

"No, you don't."

"But I did. Once. I liked both of you. Why won't he talk to me? He doesn't come outside when I'm here. He won't answer if I call. I thought he cared."

"He did like you. He still does, but it's not healthy for you two to be together."

"Vayda, what'd I do wrong?"

She had no clue what'd happened, and the guilt churned in my gut because I was relieved she didn't know.

"Chloe, you didn't do anything. I wish you knew that. Is this what you want? To be outside some guy's house waiting for him?" I opened the passenger door and eased out of the car. "Go home."

After a moment or two of waiting on the front step, I finally let out my breath as Chloe put her car into reverse and drove away. Her car slithered down the driveway. The woods crowded around it until the dark devoured even the red glow of the taillights.

I prayed she'd recover with time away from Jonah. Her mind needed healing from the heat, to develop a layer of scar tissue. Not all her memories of Jonah and me were wiped clean but enough that she wasn't a threat, only a sad, bewildered shell.

A shadow moved along the perimeter of the woods. I recognized that gait. He'd come.

Ward's tracks sank into the snow as he cut across the property, and he joined me on the step. I reached for his cold-reddened hand. He didn't take it.

"You should come inside and warm up, *gadjo*," I said. "You want me to make some hot chocolate?"

"Hot chocolate, the obvious beverage for people wandering the Wisconsin woods. I might need something stronger." His teeth gritted and voice tight.

Inside, he stomped the snow off his boots. I reached for his coat, fingers brushing each other, the only touch he was willing to tolerate. He coughed into the crook of his elbow.

Jonah limply waved only to lob a pair of auction catalogs from the coffee table.

Ward ducked the magazines flying through the air. "Throwing shit at me now? Creepy bastard. Can't work any of that voodoo on me—I came from the Christmas Mass. Guess even hellions can get blessed."

Jonah snickered. "Ow. It hurts to laugh."

I went into the kitchen to fetch his pain pills as well as the hot chocolate I'd offered. Sweetened condensed milk, regular milk, real chocolate, I mixed it all together in a saucepan with some vanilla, making enough for three cups. Hushed voices murmured over the rattle of metal spoons against ceramic mugs, and I peered around the doorway. Anything Jonah might tell Ward was a hundred times more honest than what he'd voice aloud around me.

Ward crouched on the floor. "How'd you get so messed up? Vayda said you detect people's energy or something. If that were true, wouldn't you have sensed Marty?"

"You'd think," Jonah answered, frowning. "I was at *Dati*'s desk, tracking shipments and wearing headphones. My guard was down. My mind was on something else, so I wasn't paying attention."

I leaned against the wall, a thick knot in my throat. Jonah misused his abilities with Chloe, no doubt, but they failed him the one time he needed them.

"Danny, the guy Marty hangs out with, came up behind me," Jonah continued in a hoarse voice. "He told me Vayda got in a fight with Chloe. Then he said us Silvers need to be taught a lesson."

My neck and shoulders cramped. Marty attacked Jonah because of *me*.

Because I couldn't stop him from using me to lash out at Chloe.

Because I made Marty into a fool.

Because I couldn't get a grip on the Mind Games.

I wiped my nose with my wrist. *Jonah, I didn't know.*

Another sense crept in, one that refused to accept my guilt.

He knew I was listening. "I laughed at Danny. I didn't know Marty was around, and he cracked me in the head with a table. That son-of-a-bitch got me."

I edged out of the kitchen and noticed his glass of water on the coffee table. The water bubbled, and steam condensed inside the glass.

"It gets sort of sketchy after that," he went on. "At one point, Danny got nervous, wanted Marty to be done with me. My arm got twisted, hurt something fierce, and I pushed what energy I could on Marty. I moved him. I wanted him to stop. Danny turned tail and ran. I blacked out after that."

I handed over Jonah's pain medication. His dark eyes held mine with silent thanks. For more than merely bringing him a couple of pills.

"Mom watches out for you," I assured him, maybe because it seemed like the right thing to say.

"Mom, God, something." For a moment, his chin wobbled, though not from crying. The water in the glass kept boiling. "Marty's gonna wish he never messed with me."

***

Ward and I hadn't been alone together in over a week. His choice, not mine. Now that we were, I didn't know what to expect.

"What the hell was that with the water?" he asked, closing the door to my room. "How did Jonah do that?"

"He's mad. Anger always finds a way out. Haven't you ever been so mad you wished something would break?"

The question caught Ward unprepared. I held out my hand to him, but he pressed his back against my door and reached for the knob. Too much. Step off.

"Sure. When Drake got strung out," he answered. "I wanted to break things. Sometimes I did."

"Then we're the same," I said.

He gave a sarcastic laugh. "Oh, no, you're different. *Really* different."

I took my scrapbook from my curio cabinet and flopped on my bed, motioning him to sit. He perched near me but still kept a foot between us.

I scooted toward him.

He inched away.

"I won't bite," I told him.

"It's not your bite that I'm afraid of."

"Come here, will you?"

Winding his arm around my shoulders, I sidled up beside him close enough to nuzzle his neck. At first, his body was hard, not as he was the last time we were in his room, but stony. Then he touched his face to the top of my head, and a breath rose up from deep within him. Full of want in spite of himself. I sank against him where it was easy to remain in the lapping waves of our combined energies.

"Funny how we're both here because our parents messed up our lives," I remarked, offering him my scrapbook.

He scanned a few pages. "You're not messed up, Vayda. Troubled, I'll grant you that, but you're not broken. Not like me."

We could get into a pissing contest, to use Ward-speak, over which of us was more damaged. He had secrets, but I had more. The wind listened, my mother used to say. The wind remembered names. Real names, not ones you faked, not ones that made you jittery because it would be all too easy for someone to expose you for what you really were. A fraud in your own flesh. No matter how long I lived as Vayda Silver, I always feared someone was watching.

"Ward."

Maybe he heard the way I said his name, maybe it was a coincidence, but he raised those gray eyes to mine. So serious. So full of questions. He was ready.

"You need to know something about me," I told him.

"Is it that bad?" he whispered.

"Well, for starters, my name's Vayda Murdock."

Chapter Seventeen

Vayda

*D*ad's on the phone to Seattle. The weather's ungodly humid, worse than usual for late August in Hemlock. Doesn't help that the A/C blew, and Dad won't pay the weekend rates for a repairman. The backs of my thighs are sweat-sticky as I read about the madness of Lady Macbeth for class, but I scan the same lines over and over again as Dad's phone conversation grows louder.

"Listen, I'm not bending over when the problem's on your end." Frustration shortens Dad's usual languid twang, and his undershirt is damp down his back, the sleeves rolled up to reveal the nicotine patch on his left bicep. "I'll blacklist your ass in Georgia and the Carolinas—hell, the entire south quadrant of this damn country—if you screw me again. Don't think I won't."

He slams down the phone and cusses a blue streak. Mom murmurs for Jonah to lay out three tarot cards and pads across the pine floor. Her fingers skim the back of Dad's neck.

"There's something yummy about a man who's riled up," she declares.

"Lorna, the twins…" He trails off, but his gaze intensifies on Mom. A heat more sultry than summer nights radiates between them.

Mom busts out giggling and swats his chest. "You're horrible, Em."

After over twenty years with Mom, Dad can open and close

his thoughts. Unfortunately for Jonah and me, that means occasionally overhearing things neither of us wants to know about our parents.

I shut my book with a groan. "Mom's not the only telepath around here, you know."

She bends over and shoos Dad's hands from her hips.

Jonah lays out his last tarot card. "Reversed Queen of Swords. Emotions blocking logic."

"Enough Mind Games, baby." Mom clears the energy from the cards and wraps them in a leather pouch before placing them inside a drawer. She then tucks my hair behind my ears. Her touch is petal-light while she weaves my hair into a braid. Don't squint so much, Vayda girl. You'll get wrinkles. Now give me a hand in the kitchen.

Yes, Ma'am.

Once we cleared the supper dishes from the table, Mom curls up in Dad's lap on the couch while Jonah and I kneel around the coffee table. A table fan churns out cool air that flaps the four Yahtzee scorecards distributed among us. Mom's on her fifth Yahtzee. Dad smiles knowingly and squeezes her bare shoulder as she whoops. With her messy up-do and cut-off Depeche Mode shirt, she looks more like an actress in a magazine than a thirty-eight year old mom.

After Mom's third win, Dad heads to the kitchen to pour a pair of scotch and sodas. Game time dissolves, and I pick up "Macbeth" again and wait until I'm sure Dad won't know I've put my feet on the coffee table. He'd have a conniption fit if a scratch marred the finish.

A car door slams outside. A moment later, a woman bangs on the screen door.

"Where is she?" June Forgette, one of Mom's tarot clients, hollers through a split lip.

Her hair in tangles and her neck blotted with welts, she pushes her way into our home and is stunned. The burled walnut furniture and rugs hand woven by freed slaves, the polished china on display and Antebellum-era drapes. From the exterior, the bungalow with its terra cotta roof is simple.

The inside, bulging with items handpicked by Dad's years in antiques, is worth more than the house itself.

June sets her wild glare on me. "Get that devil's whore you call a mother!"

"That devil's whore is right here," Mom declares behind me. She cracks her knuckles. "I don't work from my house, June. If you need a consult, be at Antiquaria tomorrow by noon, all right? Gotta take my family to Mass first."

My gaze slides from June's grimace to the quirk in Mom's lips. What is that face? Amusement?

As if snatching a balloon's string before it flies away, June yanks Mom's hair and drags her out to the porch. Her hair clip lands on the steps and rattles before coming to a stop.

"Mom!" I scream as the screen door slams in my face.

June hurls Mom down the stoop where she thuds against the clay dirt. Mom scrambles up to her knees and yells, "Get your daddy!"

Before I can move, Dad's already running out of the kitchen. He descends all four steps in a single leap and heaves his lean frame into June. Dust from the struggle tickles my nose, and a fierce wind bends the cypress tree next to the house so much I fear it will snap.

"This is your fault, Lorna!" June shrieks as Dad struggles to tear her off Mom. "I told Brett you consulted your cards and how you said he's cavorting with that woman like a pair of barnyard animals! He came at me with his fists, all 'cause of you!"

Mom claws at June's bony hands. "I didn't tell you anything that you didn't already know! It was in your mind!"

Beside me, Jonah hollers into the cordless phone, "Seventy-one Indigo Hill! Didn't you hear me the first time? We need the cops now, not later!"

My mouth runs dry as the fire pouring off Jonah sucks away any moisture. Even the steamy night has grown arid. Because we live on the outskirts of Hemlock doesn't mean we need help less soon than the townies.

"I know what you do, Lorna. You're not like the rest of

that gypsy clan 'cross town," June hisses. "They don't want you 'cause they know you work with the devil. You were wild growing up, and you're still wild now. We all should've stayed away from you, but it's too damn late."

Mom's hands illuminate with shimmering red. She fires a blast of energy, hurling Dad and June to the ground. Her hair falls in snarls while a sparkle enlivens her.

"Get your ass up, June!" she orders.

June doesn't have a chance to stand before Mom balls her hand into a fist and twists her wrist, snatching June to her feet by an invisible pull. A jerk of Mom's neck sharply left, and the doors of June's ancient Dodge fling open.

I can't believe she's doing this again.

"Lorna, stop!" Dad lumbers to his feet. "Let Brett and June handle their matters. Don't get involved. For God's sake, don't do this!"

Mom pushes June into the passenger seat. Dad reaches for her, but she holds up her palm, which swells with a fiery orb. "I'm gonna be fine, Em. You know how it is. Gotta clean up my mess."

She climbs behind the wheel of June's car. Ten seconds later, the engine rolls over and Mom drives away, leaving Dad to bang his fist on the trunk hard enough to dent the metal. Tears running down my cheeks, I slump on the steps.

Jonah puts his arm around me. Is Mom gonna go too far tonight?

I can't answer. I don't know.

Massaging his bruising hand, Dad takes the phone from Jonah and dials a number. "Rain, you best get out here. I got a problem with Lorna."

With Mom gone, the air is empty, inert. I clean up the abandoned Yahtzee game. No more games tonight. Jonah waits by the window, peeling back the curtains each time he thinks headlights brighten the driveway. The buzz of the coffee grinder breaks the silence. Numb and acutely aware we need to decide where to go next—Vermont sounds promising, I overheard Dad suggest to Mom last week—we wait for something to breathe life into our phantom-state.

"Lorna, what mess are you in now?" Rain calls as he enters through the backdoor.

Dad emerges from the room he and Mom share down the hallway. "She's gone, trying to fix things with June. This won't end well, Rain."

My godfather's tanned skin pales. "You let her leave?"

Dad lowers his head. "You know damn well Lorna does what she wants."

"Only 'cause you let her work you over. You always were whipped by her."

Dad presses his lips together. The last time he and Rain argued about Mom's abilities, they didn't speak for a year. If tonight's bad, how long will it take before they talk again?

"Dati tried to stop Mom," Jonah intervenes.

Rain holds up his hands as if to calm the room. "Your mama's a right handful. Takes a hell of a man to corral her. Old Em tries mighty hard. She'll be fine. A nutter like June can't hurt her."

The words are hollow.

After forty-seven prolonged minutes, Mom's silhouette appears at the end of the unpaved driveway. Slimy oil, an impermeable layer of filth, wrenches my stomach the closer she comes. She pauses outside the screen door, and when she enters, I gag on her energy.

Something has decayed and adhered itself to her.

Her olive skin is freckled with crimson dots. Both her hands crackle with a residue the same shade as rusted iron. Crying out, I run to the bathroom to escape the rot. Jonah chases me and shuts the door. He throws up a barrier around us to stop Mom from eavesdropping. I raise my own wall to reinforce his.

"She's gone mad," I say.

"She needs us. Dati says we never turn our backs on family." I don't answer, and he growls, "If it were you, she'd be out there taking care of you without question."

"There was blood on her."

"Which is more important—the blood on her skin or her

blood in our veins?"

I don't have a response. No matter what she does, she's my mother.

I don't want to go back into the living room, but I do because I must. Mom curls in a ball on the floor. Dad hunches beside her, his forehead resting on her shoulder. The pain flowing off the two of them buckles my knees, profound and shattering.

Rain leans against the sideboard under the front window. "Lorna, I'm your lawyer. The police can't question me. Spousal privilege protects Em, and they ain't gonna call your kids to the stand. You're safe. So what in God's name happened at the Forgettes'?"

Mom puts a hand on each side of Dad's face. "June's dead. Her brains blew out all down the front of me. Brett sent her to bring me to him. He thought I tried to hurt him by telling June to walk away from him, same thing I'd told her for years. Except this time that man had a gun."

Her face crumbles, and she howls like a trapped hound. "He shot her! Right in front of me! Right in front of their boy! Her blood sprayed all over!" She examines her stained hands, tears trailing down her cheeks. "This is June's blood! After that, I had no choice but to save myself. I'm not leaving you and the twins."

Dad removes his glasses and presses the heel of his palm to his forehead. He pulls her into his lap and rocks back and forth, holding her. "Oh, God, Lorna! What'd you do?"

Dad's agony reaches across the heat to thump hollowly against my heart. Mom rubs her knees as she draws them to her chest, her focus on a painting of workers in a Georgia tobacco field. "Brett had the pistol. He was out to kill me. I found his thoughts, turned his gun around."

Jonah slams his fist against the wall. "Mom, you didn't!"

"Baby, that man was gonna kill me. What could I do?" Mom stretches her hand out to Jonah, and he hesitantly takes it. I don't know that I'd be strong enough to touch her if she reached for me. She breathes hard, talks fast. "Brett Forgette has a hole in his thigh and is telling the police I put it there.

I aimed for his head, and I would have put that bullet in his brain and had this mess be done. It's my bad luck that bastard flinched."

There it was, what I always knew about my mother.

She would use her Mind Games to murder if given the chance.

Rain lights a cigarette, puffs slowly, and exhales blue-gray smoke. "Well, the upside of this mess is that no forensic expert will say anybody but Brett pulled the trigger. But people around here—knowing what you are, knowing what you do and what they want to believe *you do—this will be a hell of a witch hunt. Lorna, darlin', you might be wishing you had killed that man by the time the dust settles."*

Chapter Eighteen

Vayda

W ard didn't speak once I finished my story about that night in Hemlock. I'd had over two years to think about what my mother did with her Mind Games, two years to know why I resented my abilities.

Two years to grow more chaotic from not using them.

Despite my mother's bravado, she had good parts, though I had trouble finding them. I lived with the bad things she did. Some good existed in her. She kissed skinned knees. She had stories about caravans with the *vardo*, and all the places her father lived before settling in Georgia. She had my father's adoration. That couldn't make her all terrible.

"No offense," Ward said, "but your mom was a total shit disturber."

How sensitive of him. I draped my legs over his lap. "Well, I'm more inclined to say something colorful like Mom liked her coffee black with two troubles, but go ahead and cut to the quick. Saves time."

He half-smiled. "I call 'em like I see 'em."

Cardinal rule: Honesty was the best policy. Unless you were a Murdock.

"You know, the night Brett Forgette shot himself was hardly the beginning of the problems she caused." It sounded awful to say.

Ward traced his finger along the iron headboard of my bed. "Um, to refresh your memory, I have lived through some bad shit. You're not the only one."

Yes, he'd witnessed awful things. Drake was an addict who neglected him. Not an excuse but a reason, a pathetic, understandable reason. My mom did bad things because she was bored.

I didn't need to him to hold me and tell me everything was okay, but I wanted him close. I couldn't switch off how much I cared about him even though things weren't okay between us. Not yet.

After a minute, he asked, "How long have you worked Mind Games?"

"How long have you found yourself drawn to metal?" I returned. "It's in you. Mind Games are the same way. Jonah and I've worked them longer than we can remember." I raised an eyebrow. "No one could levitate Tonka trucks like my brother."

Ward laughed, but his face swiftly fell. "Will you end up like your mom?"

I couldn't answer. I didn't know. Had Mom known she would end up the way she did? I doubted her cards would've told her.

Ward stood and peeled back the curtain over my window, staring at the forest shrouded with snow. The tendons in his neck flexed as he swallowed, stifling a cough. I moved behind him. "It doesn't take an empath to notice how tense you are. Will you let me relax you?"

His nod granted me permission. My hands gripped his waist and then lowered to his hips. A rush of calm flowed into him. The coolness spread through him, and he trembled as his body gave in and relaxed.

"What was that?" he whispered as the lamp flickered. "How do you do that?"

"Energy. Did you like it?" I asked.

He faced me, took my hands, and guided them down the front of his jeans to press my fingers roughly against his leg. "Do it again."

I freed another frozen breaker into his muscles. Both of us

gasped, him from the chill and me from the surprise flaring off him. Shocks burst against my palm, voltage searching out a channel. He cupped my neck, and the whisk of his breath made my heart run. He hesitated, open-mouthed, over mine.

Please. Make us close again. Show me you still care.

His lips dashed across my impatient mouth, tangling with mine, wet, reckless. With a few stumbled steps back to my bed, I lay down and eased him on top of me. Primal instinct poured out of him. I sensed his want, the hunger in his kisses, and my body hummed in response. His hand clutched the metal bars of my headboard while the other inched along my side under my sweater. A sting of sparks crackled every time his skin met mine.

"Damn it!" He rolled off me.

"Why are you angry?" I asked.

"It's not you," he said. "It's…weird that I touch you and *that* happens."

"It's not like I can change what I am." I dropped my head. "You're the only person that happens with. I don't know why."

He flopped on his back and shoved his fingers through his hair. After a moment, I rested my head upon his chest. This time, when he put his arms around me, he kept his hands on the outside of my clothing. Up and down, his breathing was choppy. He was holding back a cough. "Why is being angry easier than accepting things are different?"

"Different isn't bad." I dimmed the energy balling in my palms.

"Vayda, I didn't expect this when I moved here. Didn't expect you, your family. I didn't expect anything good."

"Am I good?"

His forefinger tipped up my chin. His breath whispered cool against my lips, and a shudder danced up my neck as his fingers curved around the back of my head. He stared at me and pressed his chin to my forehead. "You're good."

As if deciding the sparks weren't so bad, he stroked my back under my sweater, toying with the clasp on my bra. One part of his life shifted, and like the kinetic wind sculptures he built, one movement set off another until all the metal gears were spinning. He lost Drake, fell off the only foothold in his old life. If Drake weren't arrested, Ward wouldn't be in my bedroom with his arms around me now. I wouldn't feed off the blissful, warm glow generated by his legs weaving with mine, his lips locked with mine. All because the wind blew. No, things between us weren't perfect and may never be, but were any relationships perfect? Love wasn't flawed, yet the people who were in love were always flawed. Did it matter as long as the emotion was true?

I was okay with imperfection.

"Magpie, come down!" Dad hollered.

I jumped up from the bed and motioned for Ward to sit up. Dad wasn't supposed to be home. A quick comb through my hair, and I straightened my clothes. "I'll be down in a second!"

"Hurry back. I'm not done with you," Ward promised as I bent down to kiss him before exiting my bedroom.

The wind whistled through the drafts. I caught sight of my reflection in the mirror at the base of the stairs and stopped. Not my mother's face again, but rather a sense of something in the house, some unusual energy that sprang the hairs on my neck. A suitcase rested by the front door, but Dad rescheduled his winter buying trip for April since he didn't want to leave during Jonah's recovery.

"*Dati*?" I called.

"In the kitchen."

Ice cubes clinked against crystal. He wore a green sweater and jeans, nicer than his work attire when he restored furniture, more casual than his buying trips. He mixed two drinks and left them on the counter.

"Work so stressful that you're double-barreling your shots?" I kidded.

"I haven't been at the shop," he said and swirled his drink around his mouth before adding, "but I tell you, I must've gotten more gray hair sitting in traffic at Milwaukee's airport."

Airport?

Dad nodded over my head. I pivoted and came face-to-face with Rain Killian.

***

Rain stood shy of six feet tall, and his sandy hair was cropped much shorter than last I saw him. He smelled familiar, of Stetson and Marlboros, as he hugged me, though underneath I got whiff of Georgia mildew and Spanish moss. A coil of homesickness churned through me. Everything we'd lost and nothing we could ever reclaim.

All because of Mom.

"Em, your girl's the spitting image of Lorna," Rain remarked and winked. "I bet you're as talented as your mama."

My cheeks burned. I couldn't go along with that, not really.

Jonah shuffled into the kitchen before a trace of a smile crossed his mouth. Showing a gentleness for my brother's injuries, Rain patted his shoulder and nodded toward his sling.

"Your daddy told me you were jumped."

Jonah slouched against the counter. "Some jerks from school. We're handling it."

Rain wasn't satisfied. "Is it true the son-of-a-bitch was charged as a minor?"

"It wasn't our decision," Dad cut in. "If Jonah had his way, there wouldn't even be charges. The attention's not good."

I spied Ward hanging out on the bottom step. A ghost of our old selves came to life in the kitchen, and he was there to witness it. He lingered, drumming on the banister, and even though I gave him a little wave to urge him to come forward, he stayed back.

Rain caught sight him of lurking. "So you're the boyfriend. Your pictures made you look taller."

Ward gritted his teeth and edged out of the shadows. "Sorry to disappoint."

"You got a smart mouth." My godfather clapped him on the shoulder. "I like that in a fella. Shows you're quick on your feet. I hear you're working at Fire Sales."

"Emory's teaching me about antiques restoration."

Ward went rigid. Every door into him slammed and locked.

Even if most of what I felt around him was a quiet peace, the slightest change in his mood registered in the air.

"I'll catch up with you in a bit, Rain," I said and took Ward's hand. Getting him out of the house would be the best thing for him.

Outside, we plodded through the snow to the barn. That feeling came back, the one of someone in the shadows. I spun around and scanned the woods when a swooping blackbird caught my sight. It darted under the gutter near the peak of the house's roof and vanished inside.

"What are you watching?" Ward asked.

"A bird. We get them in the attic. They keep me up at night," I answered.

He pushed open the barn door. The last time we were out here, he punched the wood, and I wasn't sure what all was broken. This time, we slipped inside and passed a few shrouded antiques. Ward picked along the wall beneath the hayloft, the place where old farm tools hung or leaned on the brittle wood—rusted shovels, a threshing blade, and a pitchfork. His finger ran along the pitchfork's tines.

"What would you do to make those into art?" I asked.

"They already are," he answered, touching a pair of iron baling hooks. "Did you know that silver is the best conductor for electricity? The cost is so high though. Copper works well. The current moves through it freely. It never gets hung up.

"I mean, think about lightning rods. They draw the strike and carry it to the ground harmlessly. They take in all that energy that would probably burn up anything else. If not for the metal, the lightning strike would pass through whatever it could. Nothing could control it. It wouldn't be safe. The metal is a conductor, but it's also a shield."

He began to cough, a hack he couldn't shake. I rubbed his back and sent out cool currents, my mind conjuring an image of a bellow opening to allow air to pass. Maybe it would help, I didn't know, but there was no harm in trying.

"Have you talked to a doctor, *gadjo*?" I asked. "You've had this cough for as long as I've known you."

"Longer," he managed between ragged breaths.

"Did you get some medicine? I could ask my father what my mom put in the tea she brewed whenever Jonah or I got sick."

He caught his balance against a wood post supporting the hayloft. "I'm trying to get healthy, okay? I didn't take care of myself when I lived with Drake, and I'm paying for it."

"You haven't lived with Drake for a while," I countered. "Shouldn't you be over this by now?"

He wiped his lip with his sleeve. "You haven't lived with your mom for a while, and you're not still over that."

I linked my fingers with his. Veins mapped his hand, winding between the scars. I couldn't ignore the shadow hovering around him. More than being haunted in the mind.

"You're not telling me something," I said.

"Why don't you read my mind to find out?" he asked. It was a challenge, and I wouldn't accept it. "It's gotten better, Vayda. It's nothing."

Nothing didn't hang around. I hadn't paid enough attention to notice if he'd gotten any better.

That was the danger.

You never noticed how bad things were until it was too late.

***

The trick to Mom's prize-winning fried chicken was hot sauce in the buttermilk marinade, made her chicken wings the hit of every picnic. *It's not good unless it's got the devil's bite*, she always said.

Supper was livelier than usual, despite the ghosts of the past lingering around the table as Rain and Dad bantered over how the other had changed. Two years thinned Rain's face and paled the edges of his sandy hair, yet he still talked loud and fast. There was a reason Dad claimed to predict Rain would become a lawyer back when they were teenagers, and we hung on to his every word. We'd forgotten how quiet we'd become in Mom's absence.

Rain dabbed his mouth with a napkin. "I hate bringing this up over supper, Em, but for as cold as Lorna's case is, her name still crops up in the papers down south. It's no real surprise that so does yours."

Dad stopped eating and moved around some peas on his plate. "Rain, I was never one to dabble in people's affairs the way Lorna did. I ran an honest business. People make assumptions 'cause of who I married. I've done my share of unforgivable things, but marrying Lorna wasn't one of them."

Rain twirled the ice in his scotch with the handle of his fork. "Em, you're too hard on yourself. Lorna was trouble before she ever met you—Lord knows I saw that side of her plenty. Mind Games clouded her judgment. She was doing bad before you ever came along. With you, she found her partner-in-crime."

Dad smirked. "Oh, there was no finding. That woman could've made either one of us do anything she wanted. And she did. She did it all the damn time."

I'd never heard Dad speak so candidly about Mom, and my head swam with uneasy waves. Anger that I hadn't known the alluring side of my mother that made my dad and Rain forgive her again and again, anger I hadn't really known her. Then loss because grief wasn't something that happened and was over all nice and neat, it came back, some days worse than others. Jonah squeezed my shoulder. We both felt it, the sorrow of not knowing the people around you.

"Look," Rain interrupted my thoughts. "Whatever the truth is about you and Lorna, there's no use ignoring that the people in Hemlock thought y'all were trouble. Lorna's been gone two years, but the good ol' boy cops still want you real bad, Em."

I couldn't keep quiet any longer. "For what?"

The reflection of my face in Dad's glasses repeated my question. "That fire was set by vigilantes pissed about Lorna's sentence, a sentence *you* haggled."

"They think you know things," Rain replied. "To be honest, you don't leave a burned-out house with a body inside and not break some laws."

"What kind of laws?" Jonah asked.

"Let's say that if your daddy's caught, he'll have a passel of questions to answer."

Dad's mouth was tight. "I don't know a damn thing, and I left Hemlock to protect what was left of my family. I don't much want to discuss the past any more tonight. Let's move on."

My father was in trouble, more than we'd wanted to admit, but he was also a good man. With one storm cloud of a lie thundering over not only him but also my brother and me. Jonah pushed back his seat and sighed. The room was cold from the hollow reality that we couldn't hide forever, especially not if someone in Black Orchard knew Dad was Emory Murdock and all that the name entailed.

Rain shook his head. "I'm sorry I brought it up. It's the lawyer in me, I tell you. I won't let anything happen to this family—any of you." He eyed Jonah and me. "You gotta know I go back with your mama and daddy a long time, long enough to do damn near anything for them. Your mother was special, and she knew how to pick a man."

Dad raised his drink. "And once she did, she left a hell of a mark on him."

***

After supper, Dad vanished into his study as I rinsed the dishes. Dishwashing was Jonah's chore, but he earned some leniency while he recuperated. Rain appeared in the kitchen with Ward's backpack. My godfather hoisted the backpack onto the counter and slid open the zipper.

I set a plate in the dishwasher. "That belongs to Ward."

"If he's involved with my goddaughter, don't you think it's wise to know what kind of boy he is?"

I knew what kind of boy Ward was—one who didn't like anyone snooping around where they didn't belong.

Rain gave me a long look. "Do you know about his history,

about his daddy being a junkie and whatnot?"

I plunged another plate into soapy water. Dad wouldn't have told Rain about Ward's past, which meant Rain did his homework. The lawyer doing what he did best.

"Did he tell you he has quite an arrest record?" Rain went on. "He's not some innocent kid."

I knew this, but having it pointed out was a kick in the back. "He's not in that life anymore. Trust me, will you?"

"Of course."

Rain closed the backpack but kept out a drawing pad. Other than me, Dad was the only person granted permission to review Ward's sketches of metal sculptures. Rain smiled as he paged through the pad. "Might be your daddy sees a shadow of himself in young Mr. Ravenscroft. Once an artist, always an artist."

I finished loading the dishwasher and retrieved the menagerie of cups Jonah accumulated in the living room. The couch was empty, the blanket hanging off the cushions. I touched the couch. The fabric was still warm. His black Chucks were gone from the mat by the front door, too. Where the hell did he go?

I raced to the kitchen. "Where's Jonah?"

Rain plundered the bowl of chicken in the fridge for one more wing. "Right before I came out here, he said he wanted some fresh air. Too cold for me. *Brr*."

I rushed back to the living room and slipped into my coat. Something wasn't right about this. My brother could hardly get off the couch for meals, let alone go for a midnight stroll through the woods.

This was one secret he couldn't keep to himself, barriers or not.

Outside, tracks other than Ward's and mine trampled the ground between the barn and the house. Snow powdering the evergreens gave their only definition. I spread my fingers and sought out Jonah's fire. Wavering puffs of steam rose from the soil under the snow, and a heated, invisible fog illuminated the path around the barn. Pulling my coat tight, I followed Jonah's trail between the trees. The path was deliberate.

He'd walked this way before.

My feet sank inside my brother's tracks. The tip of my nose went cold while I trekked several hundred yards into the woods until the forest cleared. Seven pine trees marked a circle. Jonah knelt in the snow, shirt gone, skin almost glowing under the moonlight. He'd removed his sling, and his left arm dangled at an uncomfortable angle, the shoulder and collarbone still blotchy with bruising. His wild, black hair fell around his chest. With eyes closed, he arched his spine and stretched out his arms. What was that devil up to?

I lurked behind a white pine and gasped as Jonah's chest heaved. One hand thrust into the snow, and a guttural roar tore from his mouth. The noise startled me so that I tumbled back over a slick rock.

His head jerked, and his burning eyes found me. He smiled like our mother.

"Sis, come here."

"Are you nuts?" I staggered into the clearing. "What are you doing?"

"Working with energy. Get down like I am. I want to try something."

"I don't trust you."

"Read me. I won't hurt you."

Ward already tried testing me tonight, and I wouldn't do it then. I wouldn't do it for Jonah now either. He knew I'd feel guilty for not believing him, but why should I go along and blindly do whatever he asked of me?

Because he was my twin.

Because we were born within a minute of one another.

Hesitantly, I knelt before him. With his right hand, he guided my fingers over his chest before placing his palm over mine. The skin, which I expected to be icy and smooth, burned. My fingertips tingled. The heat from his hand moved through my skin, past my bones, and rode a current toward my heart. Within seconds, our pulses matched, mine elevated to meet his.

"Get ready," he ordered.

"For what?"

A scalding surge rampaged through my body, flooding from Jonah's hand to my chest. I doubled over, sick from the blow but also invigorated. Red flashed behind my eyes, and I saw inside his mind, saw myself through his sight, and sensed the crashing of cold and hot between us. Surely, he saw himself, untamed, and felt the fear and awe pumping in my veins. An orb of light the size of a supper plate rose between us. The flare lasted a mere moment and extinguished as I snapped my hand away from my brother's chest and broke the filaments of our threaded energy.

"What in God's name was that?" I asked, sweat trickling down my cheeks and growing cold in the wind.

"I gave you a boost." He grinned while he panted. "Our energy together is like a cold front colliding with warm air. Lightning. This is what happens when we join together."

"We shouldn't mess with this." I stood to wipe the snow from my knees. "I'm freezing my ass off. Let's go."

I helped Jonah into his secondhand T-shirt, hooded sweatshirt, and sling. With his shirts and ratty jeans, he was like any other guy at school. He was something else altogether, a boy who dabbled in dark things.

A twig snapped in the woods. Jonah grabbed my hand, and our backs pressed against each other. As he scanned left, I dispatched my feelers to the right. Nudging, prodding, searching. Someone was out there, hiding in the trees.

Who is it? Can you tell? Jonah asked.

I can't find anything, just the night.

Again, my feelers raced out. A murky energy was nearby, though I couldn't be sure of where it came from. It felt familiar enough. Marty? Sister Tremblay? Maybe. She'd been to Fire Sales and followed me at school. What was to stop her from coming to the house?

"Let's go," I whispered.

I strode away with Jonah from his place in the woods until we came around the barn. Under the lantern-light by the front door, Dad approached the house with a bundle of firewood. I noticed a cloud of smoke where Rain puffed on his cigarette by the porch.

"What are you two doing?" Dad asked.

"Only an evening constitution through the woods," Jonah replied, speaking with the kind of heavy drawl we'd heard on the old timers in Georgia. "*Dati*, I think somebody's hanging around. Someone who doesn't belong."

Dad set down the firewood. "I'll take a gander."

Rain shook his head and held up his cigarette. "I stepped outside not more than thirty seconds ago. Don't tell me y'all are getting paranoid like your daddy."

Dad glanced over his shoulder. "Being paranoid doesn't mean someone's not after you."

Yet nothing was to be found.

By midnight, the fire in the woodstove crackling as flames ran over pinesap was the only noise. Dad and Jonah were asleep, and Rain sat in Dad's recliner as he leafed through my scrapbook. I perched on the couch and propped Jonah's legs on my lap.

"Em said he's undisciplined," Rain said, tilting his head at my brother.

"That's an understatement," I admitted.

"How so?"

How could I tell the man who vowed before God to guide Jonah that his godson trifled with wickedness? What, if anything, had Dad told him about the swell in Jonah's powers? I wasn't certain if Dad was even aware of how Jonah worked over Chloe, only that they'd had a bad break-up, and I didn't want to betray my twin's secrets even if I didn't agree with his actions.

As if understanding, Rain switched subjects. "I guess your daddy made a friend. A woman who works at your school, I guess."

Friend? Not quite. I picked at my skirt and muttered, "She can go to hell."

"Vayda, mind your mouth. Your mama's been gone two

years, and if Em's got himself a lady friend..."

"No!" I held up my hand to silence him. "It's not like that. She's not a friend. There's a nun at my school from Georgia. Hemlock, actually, but she lives here."

His eyes bulged. "Are you fooling me?"

"The name Polly Tremblay mean something?" I asked.

Rain leapt to his feet and banged on the study door where Dad often slept on a chaise. My father opened his door and glowered. Without warning, Rain shoved Dad's chest, knocking him into the doorway, and yelled, "What the hell are you doing? When I set you up here, you swore you'd tell me everything, and I was stupid enough to believe you might keep your word for once!"

Dad massaged his sternum and snapped, "Rain Killian, you got five seconds to tell me what this is about or we're going outside for a talk."

Rain placed his hand on Dad's shoulder, but Dad shook him off. His face read of years of frustration of watching his best friend dragged around by Mom without question, frustration that everything he did for us might not have been enough.

"Em, you gotta use your head." Rain leveled Dad with his gaze. "You know all too well people down south still yap about how Lorna blew out every window in Sully's market with one of her little tricks. A southerner never forgets a soul's earthly relations. Now you're either stupid or you've gotten complacent in these woods 'cause there ain't no reason for you to talk with June Forgette's niece. Are you gonna tell me you forgot it was Polly and her mama that convinced an entire town Lorna was a witch?"

Chapter Nineteen

Ward

"If you're gonna fuck me up, make it count."

The words sputtered from my mouth as my cheek crashed against the lockers in the empty hall. Marty's fingers dug into my shoulders and shoved me into the metal once more. The salty copper of blood wet my mouth. I swallowed, sneering, "Hit me harder than that."

Marty let go. "That's what all the bitches like you say."

"Not surprising. Your dick's so tiny they can't feel it."

From his lookout point, Danny chortled. "Oh-ho, shit!"

I shouldn't have searched for a fight, but anger felt good. Easy. I never thought I'd get this pissed at Heidi, but my hands clenched up at three a.m. when I descended from the attic with a box under my arm and questions in my brain. The rage in my bones was familiar, an old friend I bumped into who wanted to hang out again. It'd been so long since I craved hitting someone for no reason other than to feel better. Unfortunately, nothing got you knocked on your ass faster than hurling a French textbook at a bastard's head.

"You know, I've had that girlfriend of yours," Marty hissed as he pushed my chest into the locker. "Such a tease." His voice rose high. *"Oh, don't...don't stop."*

More anger bled through my mind as he crowed. I backed up and swung at him, catching him in the jaw hard enough to daze him. Nobody talked about her like that, least of all a dickless rat like him.

He shook off the punch and leered. "I still think about the way that one tasted. Sweet, like a peach."

"You leave Vayda out of this." I threw as much of my weight into him as I could. A blow from Marty's fist to my ear rocked me, and I stumbled to the trashcan to puke, but nothing rose from my stomach, drool and blood trickling from my lip.

"Want more?" Marty asked as Danny pulled me away from the trashcan by my collar. "I can tell you all about the rock-n-roll she got from me."

I closed my eyes and waited for another bash.

Nothing.

Opened my left eye, then my right.

Marty froze opposite of Jonah. In three weeks of healing, Jonah still wore a sling as his tendons mended. Didn't matter. He cast a jarring shadow.

"What do you think you're doing?" he asked calmly. Too calm.

Marty's skin paled. "Nothing of your concern, Silver."

"Leave my friend alone."

Danny freed me and I sagged, coughing, against the lockers. I choked down a mouthful of blood, which immediately tried to climb back up. Jonah parted Marty and Danny with a scowl and stood close.

"Get the hell out of here!" he yelled.

Danny was quick to bolt up the stairs, but Marty dawdled at the base of the stairwell, baring his teeth like a pinned badger. "You know, I saw some crazy shit the night I kicked your ass. I kept my mouth shut. So far. You wanna risk people finding out you're a freak?"

"If you were gonna say anything, you would've already," Jonah snapped.

"Not unless there's something I want. Something that'll be too scared to tell me no."

Vayda. Whatever he saw Jonah do in Fire Sales, that jerk thought it gave him some advantage with her. No way in hell could I let him get near her.

Jonah cracked his neck, swift and direct. "You made your point. Go."

Marty followed Danny up the stairs. I pulled away from the lockers, my lungs in a full-on wheeze.

"You're a mess, Ward," Jonah remarked as he followed me into the bathroom. "Why'd you pull that stunt? Marty could pulverize you."

I snorted. "So could you."

I ran some paper towels under cold water and checked out my mouth. My teeth had massacred the inside of my cheek. Jonah readied more paper towels and kicked the trashcan closer to dispose of the bloody ones. I tried to stop him from picking up one that missed the rim, but he raised his eyebrow.

"You gotta be careful around blood," I explained.

"Did your old man have something catching?" he asked, washing his hands.

"In a way." Then I dropped it. Talking about Drake would make me angry all over again.

Jonah watched as I cleaned up, his face revealing nothing. No one could tell by looking at him or Vayda that they had these abilities. Now that I knew, I was more aware of a halo surrounding them. Something was strange about them, but defining it was impossible. It was *there*.

He tore off a dry paper towel, folded it into a paper airplane, and shot it at me. "People chase us off once they know what we can do, Ward. Why haven't you?"

Gee, I loved loaded questions.

I shrugged. "Your family's good to me. I guess I owe you guys."

Jonah opened the restroom door, and we walked down the hall until he froze, slowly spinning around. Sister Tremblay waited behind us. She regarded him with a coolness as though approaching a rare bird while hiding a wire cage behind her. Covetous.

"What are you staring at?" I asked.

"Some students who should be in class," she replied.

Jonah's good hand balled into a fist, and he flexed his jaw. With a moan, the nun scrunched her eyes shut and pressed her fingers to her forehead.

"Might want to visit the nurse for that headache, Sister," Jonah said, his lips curling.

I stopped my mouth from falling open. He didn't... Yeah, he really did.

He inched closer to her. "You might have some deal worked out with my father, but you don't have one with me. Think about that before I catch you skulking around again."

Holding her head, Sister Tremblay steadied herself against a locker. Jonah backed away, leaving me to gawk over my shoulder before he pulled me down the hallway. We slipped into the church sanctuary. The stained-glass windows didn't let in any light, and only cold streamed inside. All the warmth had gone out of the woodwork, and the church felt empty. In Minnesota, I knew churches. Soup kitchens didn't ask questions about why you came; they simply fed you. The nuns cared. The priest ate with Drake and me. Sister Tremblay was the opposite of them, and this sanctuary didn't offer any comfort.

Jonah and I sat near rows of votive candles. Drake used to light candles for his buddies who hadn't made it out alive. I was too furious to light one for him.

"What's the story with Tremblay?" Pulling out a prayer book from the shelf in the pew, I tried to sound nonchalant while I paged through until I returned it, grabbing for his highlighted copy of *Jane Eyre* beside me.

"Sister Tremblay's from Hemlock. That's a problem."

"Does your dad know?"

Jonah rubbed his thumb and middle finger together. "He's known for months, since he had to bail me out of trouble before Halloween. He claims they have an arrangement, but we'd be stupid to trust she's not talking to anyone back home."

"Well, does she know what you can do?"

"As I said, she's a problem."

After how he acted with Marty, I didn't want to know what he'd do if Sister Tremblay tried hurting his family. What stopped her from contacting the Georgia police? What did she want?

As if hearing my questions, a wisp of smoke rose where Jonah rubbed his fingers together.

* * *

Neither Jonah nor I said anything to Vayda about my fight with Marty, though I was sure she'd guessed something from the marks on my face. After the final bell, I walked her and Jonah outside where Emory and the Chevy waited in the pick-up line. I hated seeing her with her head down, the weight of her worry growing heavier every time I saw her, and I didn't want to add to that burden.

As the Chevy pulled away, the tires of a silver car squealed as it lurched out of its parking spot and cut into the pick-up line. I caught sight of the driver steering erratically to try to catch up to the Chevy.

Chloe had been waiting. Stalking. Now following. Jonah swore he hadn't talked to her in weeks. What the hell was going on?

Heidi's minivan made its way through the pick-up line, and I climbed into the car. As Oliver tried to gnaw the ear off a teddy bear, Heidi drove through the streets of Black Orchard. The roads were winding and slick, everything glassy and frozen from a new coating of sleet. Ice cased the black trees, the cracks in the cobblestones, all of it preserved until the spring melt. My head was a mess: fighting with Marty, weirded out by Chloe, still angry from this morning. All I could do was try to remember to stay calm.

"How was your day?" she asked.

I steeled my jaw to avoid snapping. The hours at school should've been enough to clear my head, to give me the cool to be rational, but I want to rip into her. To scream. The anger I felt as I pawed through that box from the attic—how could she have kept such a secret?

As soon as we reached home, Heidi became serious. "We need to talk."

I unbuckled Oliver from his car seat. He tugged on my hair and giggled, but I couldn't even pretend to smile and carried him inside where he could go crazy with a cabinet full of Tupperware. He toddled across the floor and brought me the lid for a skillet and a wooden spoon, and I showed him to the pantry. Maybe I'd let him tear off the labels from all the cans, see how Heidi would like that.

"I got a call from the head nun today, Ward," Heidi said as she refilled Oliver's cup. "What's this about you fighting with Marty Pifkin?"

Now that she was with me, playing dumb, I scrunched my hand into a fist and considered smashing my knuckles through the plaster wall by the table.

"Like you give a fuck about me."

Bernadette scuttled up the stairs after me, her tags tinkling like chimes. Her breath stank of kibble as she snuffled my face while I crouched on the floor by my bed. *Busy, dog.* I waved her away, but she chewed the cuff of my jeans as I dragged the box from under my bed.

Standing in the doorway, Heidi covered her mouth. "Where'd you find that?"

"You know damn well it was in the attic. Guess you thought I'd never snoop there. Don't you know I can't be trusted?"

My nostrils flared, and I shoved the box into her arms. She dropped it to the floor where the lid popped off. "You weren't supposed to find this."

"He was my dad, too! This was my life!" I hollered, inches from her face. "Didn't I deserve to know?"

I plummeted to my knees and chucked the box lid across the room, narrowly missing Heidi's head. Bernadette nested in my lap, but the dog's elderly gentleness did nothing to soothe me. I flipped over the box, dumping paper scraps and photos annotated in Drake's cat-scratch writing. One note dated a year ago caught my attention. I scanned it before wadding it in a ball and whipping it at Heidi.

Angel—Any chance your brother could stay with you? I'm not well, probably the flu. Congrats on your pregnancy! —Drake

A letter from May was clipped to a photograph. I was sitting on a mattress on the floor, wearing several layers to stay warm. The air wasn't frigid, but I was. That apartment always left me cold. The drafts and the rats and sounds of sickness all around, and all I'd ever prayed for was for an escape. A cigarette hung from my lip, and I'd buzzed my hair. I looked like hell, skinny with acne on my cheeks, scowling that Drake had the nerve to take my picture.

Angel—Please write back. I've been a shit, but I love you. Doc says I'm nearing end stage hep C. Puking blood tons. For Christ's sake, take Ward. I'm too sick to deal with him. Don't forget him.—Drake.

I'd known my dad was sick but assumed it was drugs. If I'd known he was dying...I coughed into the crook of my arm. "How come I didn't know about this?"

Heidi squatted beside me. She and I shared more features than I'd first thought. Her hair was lighter red, almost orange, but our faces were identical, foxlike around large, hollowed eyes and a straight nose. Gathering Drake's letters, she stammered, "I'd heard Drake's lies and excuses before. I didn't tell you after he died because what good would it—"

Her voice broke.

"He begged you to take me!" My throat felt like hands had wrung my airway. "I was alone for months after he was arrested! It was a nightmare! I was hungry and dirty and sick! You left me there!"

Heidi wiped tears off her cheeks. "Try to see my side. I hadn't seen you since you were a baby. I didn't know you. I expected you to be a druggie like Drake. You saw the picture he sent. You didn't look clean, and I couldn't have that near my child."

I pulled up the right side of my shirt and displayed a scar below my armpit. The scar had been there for years and hadn't changed, a shiny pink circle no bigger than a dime.

"You see this? Drake left me with some skank who

stubbed out a cigarette on me 'cause I spilled cereal. I was eight years old." Dropping my shirt, I snarled, "Last winter, I had pneumonia, and the old man decided scoring smack was more important than spending four bucks on my antibiotics. My lungs still ain't right, and you damn well know it."

She put out her hand to touch my arm. I swatted her away and stood. No fucking way. She was *not* going to comfort me.

"You left me to rot with that bastard! He was dying, and you ignored it! No one told me a thing! He promised he'd get clean, but it was another lie!"

My muscles cramped, spent from yelling. Like I'd had enough and had nothing more. Same as when I got the news he was gone. Vacant. Blunted.

Heidi lowered her eyes. "I can't change the past, Ward."

Was that all she could say? A new dose of electric venom streamed into my blood. I flung my drawing pad from the top of the dresser. An empty glass I'd forgotten to take out to the dishwasher. Thrown. Smashed. A stack of books. Thrown. Smashed. The pages came loose and fluttered out between Heidi and me. Everything on top of the dresser, from my stolen iPod to a candleholder I'd sculpted, I threw everything until plastic shrapnel, glass shards, and torn papers littered the floor of my room. My breath came in rasps that made a racket high in my throat.

"Get out of my sight," I managed between huffs.

Maybe she knew I couldn't take anymore, not now, but she ducked her head and left my room. I patted Bernadette's head, and she yawned so widely that she nearly unhinged her jaw, her tongue curling like a question mark. I tucked her under my arm and climbed onto my bed. She burrowed between my pillows and touched her moist nose to mine.

Hours disappeared as I slept.

Knocking on my door roused me enough to raise my head. My clock read seven forty-two. I'd missed dinner. Not that I was hungry. The knocking persisted.

"Go away, Chris!" I pulled my pillow over my head.

The door clicked and swung open. I grabbed whatever I

could reach on my nightstand, a coffee mug, and chucked it in the direction of the door. No crashing sound followed.

"You've got a hell of an arm," Vayda remarked.

I threw aside my pillow and sighed at the girl closing my door. She held the coffee mug and avoided the shattered remnants on my floor before sitting on my bed. Her hair was loose and wavy, and her shirt was lacey and tight in the right places. The cold had finally gotten to her so that she'd broken out some dark corduroys instead of her long skirts, slung low on her waist to show off the wide curve of her hips. Even as pissed as I was, I could still appreciate the view.

She handed me a thin rectangle wrapped with brown paper. "Happy birthday a day early."

"It's been a lousy day."

"So Heidi said. She called and asked if I'd talk some sense into you."

I set Bernadette on the floor. The dog snorted at Vayda before flopping onto a towel I left in front of my closet. Vayda consoled her with a chin scratch and took her spot beside me. I mirrored her body with my own. She grazed her fingertips along my forearm, and trembling, I allowed her to draw cool trails over my skin.

My hands traced her backbone under her shirt. Electric shocks. She kissed my neck, arms embracing me, my fingers finding the softness of her thick body and holding her close. I popped open the button of her pants and slid my hand inside.

"Not now, *gadjo*. Another time."

Deflating, I lifted my hands from her. Over the last few weeks, we'd gone plenty further than kissing and handfuls of skin. The places our mouths had discovered on each other, places I hadn't kissed before, we'd treaded the line of sex yet hadn't crossed it. I wanted to. Badly. I wanted to obliterate that line.

"It wouldn't be right when you're hurting so much," she said.

I rolled onto my side with my back to her. "You have no idea."

She wrapped her arm around my hips, her chest to my back. Wave after wave of cool splashed against me.

I closed my eyes. "Take it, Vayda. Please. Can't you make me forget?"

"I could, but you need those memories."

"Then get in my head. I need to know what it's like when you're in there."

The wait for her to respond felt like an hour but was only a few seconds.

"We need someplace private."

"We are in private," I said.

"I mean *really* private, Ward."

I knew where to go and tossed her a sweater. Then I retrieved two blankets from my closet before sliding open the window to heave the blankets onto the roof.

"Are you touched in the head?" she protested. "I said private, not freezing. The roof's slippery from ice. Your ass will fall, and I'll laugh."

"Won't happen," I promised. My fingers clenched her wrist. "Come with me."

Hesitantly, she followed as I balanced one foot on the roof outside my window and the other on the sill. Her legs were coltishly unsteady as she adjusted to the slant. I hoisted myself onto the peak above the dormer window and guided her to my side. We settled with our bodies snuggled under one blanket. The night was bitter cold and clear. The moon was bright. The stars glimmered like grains of sand on a black beach. To the north, shades of green and violet-pink tinted the blue-black sky above the trees.

"Wow, all the colors." She pointed to the spectral fire across the sky.

"The aurora borealis. Northern lights. Pretty, huh?"

She gazed out across the woods, and a loud ripple of pops burst from her hands as she cracked her knuckles. Powerful hands for a short girl. Powerful hands for anyone, really.

"What kind of boy hides out on his rooftop?" she asked.

"The kind who wants to escape," I replied. "I did the same

thing at my old apartment."

She piled a blanket behind me and eased me into lying back. I didn't object or hesitate, especially not when she climbed on top of me to straddle my hips, one hand on my heart.

"Are you ready?" she whispered.

"Always."

She bent forward until our foreheads touched.

Our eyes locked.

A slice of white flame—I yelped as she entered my mind. Flesh pulled taut and prickled with thousands of shivers. The cold filling me was all-encompassing, a good cold, like being five years old and pitching my whole body into a snow bank. Skies rumbled with lightning as storms crashed inside me. The chill of Vayda's mind spread me open, a collision that rocked and groaned.

I had to close my eyes as she slid inside my head. Her feet carried her along a floor in a hallway lined with doorways shrouded by tattered curtains. Her arms stretched out and fingers snagged each curtain, snapping the fabric to the floor. I breathed harder as she plunged further inside and found my sharpest memories.

How my lips pressed against Audrey's. She was my friend Louis's girlfriend. I helped her find the condom tucked in my back pocket and made quick work of unbuckling my belt. She tasted of weed and Sprite. I hoisted her onto the worktable in her dad's shed. In the darkness that smelled of gasoline, I fumbled for her body when a crack of pain in my forehead killed my hard-on. Somehow, I hit my head on a shelf, and she cackled as I lumbered outside into the afternoon sun in her mom's rose garden.

How I held the phone in the kitchen of the apartment. I had dialed the nine and a one but couldn't push the second one. A spray of blood had squirted from Drake's arm, and he curled up beside the fridge devoid of food with foamy vomit dribbling down his chin. I sighed and pushed the one button on the phone. The dispatcher asked my emergency, and I muttered, "My father shot up on smack. Again."

Vayda pulled aside one more torn curtain, but she was already in the room with me. Her eyes crinkled as she sang an old Mickey and Sylvia song, "Love is Strange," the two of us playing guitar together. I kept picking the lead melody but my beat slowed while I watched her, and I wondered if I was weird for wanting to stare at her—

"Stop!" I shouted, gasping as she receded from my mind, and warmth gushed in my skull to fill the void left in her wake. In my head, she restrung the curtains to close the doorways. She never smiled or frowned, only took in the things I'd endured.

My eyes opened.

The roof of Heidi's house felt like an iceberg beneath me, unyielding and frozen, the northern lights dimmed by clouds moving across the moon. Vayda was still astride my hips, but she searched my face, concerned. "Are you okay?"

After several cleansing breaths, I drew her into an embrace, resting my head in the slope of her neck. In-fucking-tense. My body hummed with the flutter of thousands of magpies' wings swarming inside me. She kissed my cheek, feather-light, and I laughed. Unintentional. Embarrassed. Relieved.

"I'm cold," she said. "Time to go inside."

Back in my room, she offered up the gift she'd brought for my birthday. She clapped and urged, "Open it."

My mind remained cottony from letting her into my thoughts. I tore open the paper. A book. *The Little Prince*. I once had a copy and misplaced it when I left Rochester. She probably already knew that.

"It's awesome," I said and set it on my nightstand.

Vayda dragged over the trashcan and picked up some fractured plastic and shredded papers. I sat across from her, and our fingers reached for the same mangled book. We caught each other's eyes, smiled, and kept cleaning up the mess.

Somewhere in the house, the phone rang. Chris entered my room and handed the phone to Vayda. She listened, her brow pinched and fingers twirling her hair.

"What is it?" I asked as she switched off the phone.

She rose to her feet and brushed off her pants. "I need a ride to pick up *Dati* from Fire Sales. His car's tires were slashed."

"Why would someone do that?"

Her expression was frightened yet fatigued. "It's what always happens. Every place we've lived, it's the same story."

My head dizzied. Vayda held my hands and helped me up, and I sensed a distinct electric field building between us, feeding the currents joining us together. "You're honestly afraid someone might hurt you?"

"*Gadjo*, I've looked over my shoulders for two years," she replied solemnly. "It was merely a matter of time before Black Orchard became like Montana and Georgia. We were supposed to move to Vermont, but then Mom died and we ran. Each time we find a new home, the time we can stay grows shorter. And once people find out what we can do, it only gets worse."

Chapter Twenty

Vayda

According to the news, January reigned as the worst winter month Wisconsin endured in a decade. Canadian clouds unloaded thirty-two inches of snow, and the cold was harsh. With the first storm, Rain flew back to Georgia. Over two weeks, the days of cancelled school were endless, and the snow kept coming. I squinted at the piles outside the house. Fresh sleet crusted the mounds with ice. Ward warmed himself by the woodstove, the door open and fire reflecting like hammered bronze in his hair.

I went into the kitchen and set a pan on the stove to warm milk and sugar. A hard-milled flour sifted through my fingers. I added the yeast and some golden eggs, barely thinking as I pulled together challah dough. After a bit, Ward leaned against the doorway separating the kitchen from the living room, eyes focused on my hands working the dough.

"Think your dad wants us at Fire Sales?" he asked.

"*Dati* closed up shop early." I shaped the dough into a ball and set it into an oiled bowl, covering it with a towel to rise. "This sleet's gonna become a wicked blizzard."

He nodded in the direction of the front door. "Speaking of a storm…"

"What?" I washed my hands, dried them fast on my apron, and hurried to the living room where headlights from a car parked outside shone through the windows. I pulled my violet sweater over my hands and noticed Jonah on the stairs, also keeping an eye on the headlights. His sling was gone, and while I knew he was anxious to stretch his limbs again, he wouldn't extend them to Chloe waiting for him outside.

Ward gestured to the car lights in the window. "Isn't there something you can do about that?"

Jonah shook his head. "I could try, but—"

"—that would show you learned nothing from what you did," I muttered.

"Vayda girl, if I wanted, I could already be with someone else, but I'm not. What I did with Chloe, no matter why I did it, was wrong. There's my confession like a good Catholic." He leaned against the banister and ran his hand over the polished wood. The dark flame in his eyes died down, and his voice changed to something more sober. "Maybe it is a confession 'cause only God knows how sorry I really am. I tried making things right with Chloe. It didn't work, and you've made it more than clear that you think anything else I try will make it worse."

No. Absolutely not. He might've been sorry, but he wasn't about to push the responsibility for what Chloe was going through onto me.

"Things are already worse!" I yelled. "You wrecked another human being! You know what happened when Mom messed around in people's heads—Cardinal rule: It always comes back to you, Jonah. Always."

"And how many times do I have to tell you? I've done what I'm *allowed* to do. Maybe if you weren't constantly shaking your finger at me, I could get a handle on this. We'd be golden."

He jerked away from the stairway and stalked toward the front door.

Ward, who'd stayed out of it as Jonah and I argued, cleared his throat. "I wouldn't do that if I were you."

Jonah hung his head and moved back to guard his post by the stairs, pausing before taking the first step. "I didn't know this would happen to Chloe, and I wish you'd let me try to fix it. You're the one who said she'd get better with time, but it's plain as day that nothing's changed."

"Please don't do anything," I begged.

"I gotta do something, Vayda. Don't you agree? Can't you help me?" He waited for me to say something. I lowered my eyes. "Fine. Do nothing. I guess I'm gonna have to figure things out without you, and if it doesn't work, then at least I tried."

The heat from my brother's frustration was unbearable, my skin absorbing rays of scorching power. As he ascended the staircase to head back to his room, his fire freed my barriers, letting my mind uncoil.

"He'll calm down," I muttered.

Ward dusted his fingers over my palm, comparing the bones of his thin fingers and his palm's breadth to mine. "Your skin is hot. Normally, you're cold."

"It's him. Me taking his feelings as mine."

I exhaled. The lamp hummed and shuddered, dark then bright, dark then bright.

Ward reached over to still the lamp's swinging pull chain, and the flickering settled. He lifted my hand and traced the outline of my fingers. I closed my eyes, enjoying the prickle running up my spine from his touch.

"Are you afraid of your Mind Games?"

My eyes blinked open. "Yes. The way people react to them is worse. I told you before we're chased away wherever we lived. Georgia last time. Before that, it was Montana."

The fire in the woodstove blurred as I recalled the Christmas lights twinkling in Dad's junk shop in Montana, always strewn above the front counter. The Cure's doom-and-gloom anthems mixed with the chime of a sale on a vintage cash register.

"*Dati* had an odds-and-ends shop called Baubles," I began. "It didn't make much money, but we got by. In the back of the shop, past a beaded curtain, Mom arranged her tarot table. The walls were painted red, candles everywhere, totems, herb remedies. Every Tuesday night, a line of people went out of the shop and halfway down the street. Nice Mrs. Murdock who knew everyone's underpinnings. The thing is people don't visit a tarot reader to learn tomorrow's weather. Mom meddled with deeper stuff."

Ward's eyes tightened. Sometimes the stillness I felt around him got in the way. I'd made a promise to listen to his thoughts only when he was aware of what I was doing. Right then I wished I knew what he was thinking. That my mother was trouble was obvious, but did he think we enabled her to do bad things? It was easier to project these thoughts as his than admit they could be mine.

I had to tell him everything. No more secrets.

"Like Hemlock, Mom uncovered bad deals. Someone decided the best retaliation was to yap Mom was an occultist. The rumors took on some life. Jonah and I were teased. A lot. Gypsy thieves. 'Witch, witch, Devil's bitch!'" I pushed back the chant in my ears. "Mom lost her temper when we had to leave our church. People made things rough for our priest. Mom was all, 'If they want a witch, I'll give them a witch.' Her Mind Games went public. People painted curses on our house and *Dati*'s shop. We had a black barn cat. Mom wouldn't let it in the house, but *Dati* called it Nyx—"

"I don't want to know," Ward cut me off. "Especially since you don't have any pets now."

Smart boy.

"We left town soon after. Mom was angry with *Dati* for making us go. That much I remember. She thought she could keep everything under control using her Mind Games."

"Sounds familiar."

Jonah was reliving Mom, but at least he guarded his abilities more often than not. As long as he didn't get ahead of himself.

"You see why I keep the Mind Games under wraps," I said. "I mean, how would an entire school react if Danny or Marty talked about that night in Fire Sales? Or if Chloe blabbed about how Jonah messed up her mind? People won't let us be."

Ward squeezed our joined hands, fire-shadows dancing over our faces. "So you flee from one town and stay until you have no choice but to escape to another."

I inched closer to him, my lips barely touching his. "Yeah, but there's one thing in Black Orchard I don't want to leave behind."

"And what's that?"

"You."

***

A scream reverberated off my skull.

I bolted upright in bed. My skin was slippery with sweat, and my braided hair lay damp down my back. I didn't know if it was dream residue or only me, but the house was unsettled, the shadows too long, too wide. Too dark.

I crawled out of bed, the floor creaking, slid a cardigan over my camisole, and crept out from my room. Across the hall, Jonah's door was ajar. He slumbered on his stomach while his iPod dock hummed a harp and string piece. A biography of Mary Shelley was open on his nightstand. I shut his door, said a prayer he would sleep with nothing going on in his mind.

Farther down the hall, a slant of moonlight streamed from Dad's bedroom. My fingers glided over the plaster walls in search of his energy. He hadn't been in the room since morning. The blankets were undisturbed, corners sharp, not even a pair of shoes out of place.

The scream from my nightmare cut me again with its teeth, and despite the cardigan covering my shoulders, I trembled.

The house wanted me awake. My eyes rose to the corners of the hallway, searching the darkness, but I didn't know what I was looking for. Eyes. Something watching. I couldn't shake the sense that I wasn't the only one up and staring down these halls.

"*Dati?*" I edged along the stairway to the living room, lit with the same silver glow as upstairs. The kitchen made no sound but for the droning icebox, and the study was vacant. Yet Dad's chair radiated warmth. Real warmth. He hadn't been gone long. I switched on the lamp and noticed a folder open on his desk, left abruptly.

"What's this?" I wondered.

Real estate listings, commercial and residential, comments like "private schools" and "historic district" jotted in Dad's neat cursive. Listings in Oregon, Colorado, and Maine, were organized and clipped in the pocket. I whapped the folder closed and dropped it on the desk, hands aflame. If he was this far in his search, then a move would come soon and Black Orchard would be behind us.

A car's engine rumbled on the driveway. Chloe? At this time of night? I darted to the window, shrouding myself in the curtain, and watched the headlights gleam against the icy driveway. Sister Tremblay, in a black dress, climbed out of an equally black sedan. Unkempt ringlets of hair spilled around her shoulders and a trail of dried blood near her lip marked her pallid face.

The barn door opened. Dad approached her with the lantern we used when camping and, ever courteous, offered his arm for balance on the ice.

No time to grab my coat, I yanked on my blue Chucks and headed outside. Every crunch of ice beneath my shoes made me flinch as I slinked closer to the barn where I squinted through a knothole. The forest shifted with the wind, but the closer I drew, I overheard Dad and Sister Tremblay. They were arguing

"Do you even know what that boy of yours is up to?" she shouted.

"Polly, you're bleeding. You need to calm yourself," Dad said.

She touched the blood on her lip. "Don't tell me what to do! I can't stand by anymore, Emory!"

Sister Tremblay shook as she spoke, and a new cut split her lip, dribbling fresh red down her chin. I pulled back from my watch point, heart amplified in my head like orchestra drums. Seeing her cuts appear from nowhere, I didn't know whether to be terrified or astonished.

She pointed a finger. "Your boy's working in a bad way. Jonah feeds off fear, lust, and hate. I've seen his handiwork, and we both knew he has his mama's temper!"

I splayed my hands on the weathered wood. Jonah's handiwork? He fought Marty and messed up Chloe's mind, but to feed off it? That made him sound depraved.

Dad's skin paled. "I can't be with him every hour of the day. What am I supposed to do?"

Sister Tremblay wiped her lip and closed her eyes, but the anger in her voice didn't calm. "You need to rein in Jonah or he's gonna kill someone! Unless you bring that boy out here so we can have a word with him—"

"You'll what?" Dad asked. "Go to the Hemlock police? That won't give you what you want."

The nun folded her arms. Months of watching us, gathering evidence of who we were and what we could do, what did she have planned for us? I bit my lip to stop from crying out. From screaming she had no right to hurt us. To stop myself from wheeling out of control.

A drop of red descended from her nostril, and she sniffed it back. Stress might explain the bloody nose, but the cuts that came from nowhere? A sickness crept over me, like flesh rotting from the inside out. How could such a thing happen?

"Polly, you're all riled up," Dad murmured. "It's not good for you, so stop. All this anger isn't very Christian."

"I won't let Jonah destroy lives like Lorna did," she said. "He must be stopped. He needs control. If you won't teach him, then anything he does is on your head, Emory Murdock."

Dad's shoulders widened with tension. "I guess it's not enough that my life's trashed and Lorna's dead all because your mama wanted to avenge a piece of trailer trash like your aunt. Don't threaten me unless you intend to follow through with it."

I wrenched my hands around my braid. *Please, Dati, don't start something with this woman. She's out of her mind.*

Sister Tremblay's irises were like slits in the lantern-light. The angrier she became, the looser her accent grew, dropping all pretense of formality, until there was no mistaking where she was from. "Aunt June raised me for years before my daddy took me to Athens. June had problems, but she was my kin. Her boy lost both his parents the night she died. All June wanted was help, but your wife got her killed and orphaned that boy. Don't forget that I knew Lorna. I knew her well, Emory. I sat through her trial. She never showed remorse, and you stayed by her side as if she'd done no wrong. You're a stupid, stupid man. Everybody knew Lorna and Rain Killian tramped it up when you came back to Hemlock. To put it straight, your wife was a whore."

Dad's rage threw a ball of fire into my core. Mom and Rain? My stomach rolled with vomit, and my toes were soaked inside my Chucks. The ice and snow melted where I stood, heated by the electricity in my palms, so that watery gravel squished beneath my shoes.

I'd seen the looks Mom and Rain shared. She'd sworn they meant nothing.

Dad clenched his hands into fists, trying to appear calm but so irate even my hands quaked with anger. "Polly, I know the truth about my wife, one way or the other. No need to call upon old ghosts."

Why didn't he defend Mom? Had she run around on him? I couldn't tell what went on in Dad's head—he was too pissed. Every thought came out as a flash of red.

"Lorna was beautiful." Sister Tremblay wiped her mouth with the back of her hand and smeared the blood so that it coated her teeth. "She was also malicious, but you were blind to that. You've always chosen to be blind."

Dad glared at her. "First, you come here to tell me how to parent my son! Now *you're* gonna talk to *me* about how I handled my wife? You think anybody could've restrained Lorna? Without me keeping her in line, she would've torn up that town!"

Sister Tremblay reeled back from his shouts and landed against a bale of hay.

Dad didn't stop. "I'd seen Lorna go out of control before, and she promised when we got back to Hemlock things would be different. It took her a while, but it didn't surprise me when she ran with June again. Those two were thick as thieves. It was only a matter of time before they got themselves in deep. Given what damage those two could've done, I'd say we're lucky June's the only one she killed."

My brows knitted together. I knew Mom and June had gone way back, but unlike Rain, June never came around the house. Dad wouldn't let her, and I had no idea why. He sheltered us from June's family. I pressed my eye closer to the hole in the wall. Sister Tremblay pushed herself up from the hay. She pulled some straw from her snaky curls and then wrapped her blood-streaked hand around the cross pendant dangling against her breasts, winking in the lantern light.

"Lorna's gone, but there's no undoing how she cursed your family, Emory," Sister Tremblay declared. "You knew those twins would be like her. You knew how destructive they would be without the right guidance. The least I could've hoped for was that you'd make them learn from Lorna."

Dad retreated to the shadows, pacing away from Sister Tremblay until only the silhouette of the silver in his hair was visible. His squirminess and the forced swallow in his throat became mine. Shields of paternal steel dammed the black flood of her gaze. My knees shook, but I didn't feel the cold night.

Lowly, he seethed, "Polly, you best leave my children out of this."

The nun jutted out her chin. "I came here to get answers about Lorna, but I also came to watch the twins. They aren't innocent. They will hurt people, and then they'll be monsters."

Dad gritted his teeth in a biting grin and laughed. "Monsters, eh? Usually, it's witches or gypsies or freaks."

"You can't tell me your boy isn't friends with the devil! I'm here to warn you, Emory: You're going to wake up to another fire one of these nights."

"You're threatening me again. We both know Jonah isn't harmless. Absolutely, he's manipulative, but his abilities didn't make him that way. He's not only his mother's child, you know. I've done my wrongs and repented, and I imagine Jonah will as well. With time. If you're worried about power and Mind Games, you're better off keeping your distance from Vayda. She's the one to worry about."

Orbs of energy in my palms sparked with lightning. What had I ever done to make Dad say that about me? Through the knothole, I watched the lantern, and the currents raced from my hands to the only light in the barn, which shattered in a blast of metal and glass.

Over Sister Tremblay's scared yelp, Dad hollered, "Vayda!"

I sprinted for the woods. Pulse compressing and releasing, blood sloshing as loose and wild.

"Vayda, stop!"

I wouldn't go back.

I was a monster, a girl to fear.

I plunged into the snowy thicket. More arduous than wading through knee-deep water, I shambled past the pines snagging my cardigan and hair. With each passing tree, wood snapped as limbs broke in response to the force purging from my being. Ice cracked and dropped into the snow, gouging the mounds.

All this time being wary of Jonah, fretting what he would do, but *I* was the one to fear?

I leaned against a tree and tasted saltwater from tears collecting on my lips. The bark under my hands grew hot until the wood smoked, and with a scream, I fell back. Emotion as energy, energy as heat.

Mom didn't teach me as she had Jonah. I wouldn't learn. I was hurt. I burned. The shocks, electric glitches, and the breaking lights happened more frequently.

Before I was always cold, but there was now a heat in me. A bit of Jonah. I couldn't be like him. I couldn't be like Mom.

I could hurt someone.

I could kill.

It was only a matter of time.

Chapter Twenty-One

Vayda

*A*fter midnight, Mom's gait paces the stuffy hallway of the bungalow. I lie with my pillow over my head, covering my ears, but hope for sleep is lost as Dad murmurs, "Lorna, you're carving a path in the floor. Come on to bed."

"I can't help it, Em," she confesses. "I ain't got any life in my hands."

"Honey, please. Nothing's worth getting yourself this riled up."

"You don't understand. I need to feel."

Mom clambers into my room and rattles my shoulders. Yawning, I follow her to the hall where Jonah rubs sleeping sands from his face. Dad lowers his head and lags behind on the porch as Mom drags my brother and me into the dirt yard with the air thick with heat lightning and humidity.

"Can you feel it?" she asks, frenzied. "All that energy coming up from the earth, streaming toward our hands, and it's ours!"

She clasps our fingers, a three-person circle, and a blast blinds me.

***

Emerging from the woods, I clomped through the snow toward Ward's home. My face was numb despite the electricity crackling in my fingers. Ward's window was too high, and ringing the doorbell so late would wake the whole house. I inhaled, filling my lungs, and pointed to the window.

Open!

The window remained still.

"Come on, Ward." I wiped my nose on my sleeve. *Hear me.* "I need your help."

The nightly train blew its whistle. Snowflakes waltzed on the wind. After a minute, Ward appeared by the glass. Barely awake, he noticed me below and opened the window.

"Vayda, what the hell are you doing?"

The words didn't come, though I ached to scream. I collapsed to my knees in the snow. A wail built from my belly up—a primal howl. Behind me, a tree branch cracked and landed with a whoosh of falling show. The headlights in the Jaguar gleamed bright though the car was off, so garish and blinding until they cracked.

It was me. All me.

Overloaded, overburdened. Exploding.

No wonder Ward avoided me after finding out about the Mind Games. I horrified everyone, including my own father.

Clad in a much-loved Pixies shirt and sweatpants, his boots hastily pulled on and unlaced, Ward was beside me and dragged me out of the snow. "Come inside. It's too cold out here."

Sobbing, shocking his hands as he guided me, I trudged toward his porch. The cries ripped from my chest and pushed me down to my knees on the steps. Ward held me close, ignoring the growing puddle of melted snow around us.

"What happened?" he asked.

My voice wouldn't cooperate. Even if he were telepathic, my thoughts weren't coherent enough to understand. My mom, who I thought was the most beautiful person in the world... How much had she hid? And Dad, strong and unwavering and yet broken with grief, thought I was a time bomb. He hid things as well, too many things.

With my forehead against the curve of Ward's neck, the

story of what I saw between Sister Tremblay and Dad—what
I'd learned about Jonah and me, the possibility of Mom's
affair with Rain—all spilled out as messy as milk oozing from
a broken glass.

The door behind us creaked. Heidi bundled her robe around
her shoulders and pushed aside her strawberry curls. "What's
going on? It's after midnight."

"Bad night," Ward replied. "Heidi, I can't send her home
like this."

If she judged me, she didn't let on and held open the door.
"I'll put on some lavender tea."

My legs wavered. Ward shouldered most of my weight
while escorting me to the couch and mouthed thanks to his half-
sister. She put her hand between his shoulders and ushered him
into the kitchen, leaving me alone with the ghosts whispering
against my neck.

Jonah abused his powers. He was sorry about what
happened to Chloe, but he was also adamant that his power
could fix her. He didn't think it was wrong to try. I knew that.
My parents were in love. I knew that, too. What if Jonah's
ego ruined the good in him? What if my parents' love wasn't
enough to stop Mom from having an affair? She smiled at
Rain, let him take her hand, and kept him in her life. They
shared something, and Dad never objected. It wasn't normal.
What even was normal?

Heidi entered the living room. I raised my barriers to block
all confusion and hesitance streaming off her. No more currents
tonight. I didn't want to feel. I wanted numbness.

She offered a pair of dry socks. "Why don't you take off
those wet shoes and put these on?

The rubber of my shoes squawked as I kicked them off.
Heidi picked up my sneakers and disappeared. A moment later,
thuds and clunks rang through the quiet house, shoes spinning
through the clothes dryer, and she wordlessly headed upstairs.

The phone rang. With Bernadette following close behind,
Ward held out a mug of tea while on the phone. "Yeah, Emory,
she's here...I don't think she wants to talk." I shook my head,

and he said, "Yeah, I'll take care of her." He clicked off the phone and set it on the coffee table. "Your dad wanted to make sure you're safe. He said he's sorry."

I sipped the tea sweetened with milk and honey, my raw throat coated with healing warmth. Bernadette lay across my feet. Her body was a heating pad and thrummed with gentleness. Ward eased the mug from my hands and didn't bother to use a coaster as he set it on the table. "I can't make you any better, but I'll listen. All night, if you want."

"Give me the phone."

My heart hiccupped as I dialed Rain's number, digits I'd had memorized since I was tiny. The grandfather clock read one a.m. In Georgia, the time was an hour later. Rain picked up on the second ring.

"We need to talk," I told him.

He yawned. "Vayda girl, unless someone's dead, it can wait."

I didn't give him a chance to hang up. "Were you screwing my mom? I know something happened."

Quiet. The clenching in my chest spread to my muscles. I couldn't get in his mind. He was too far away to try.

"Darlin', your mama was special. I knew her all my life, but she loved your daddy like no other," he answered. "That was plain as day back when I was seventeen, and it still holds true now. Call me after the sun comes up, and we'll talk more if you like."

As I clicked off the phone, my mouth tasted like I was sucking metal, but the kind of sickness I had was in my soul. Ward and I said nothing. He hugged me, occasionally swiping his lips or his fingers over my cheek. Lots of slow exhalations as I let the energy out of my body, not feeling hot or cold.

Feeling nothing.

For once.

***

Ward leaned over from the driver's seat and kissed me, hungry and apologetic and not giving a damn for who saw. As much as I wanted, I couldn't let go, not even for him.

"No matter what, Vayda," he promised as I unbuckled my seatbelt.

"I know."

"I mean it. I don't care what anybody says."

The front door of the stone house opened, and Dad waited on the step. The warmth of my shoes from the dryer cooled far too fast, and I couldn't tell how much was the winter and how much was simply me.

"I'll call you in the morning," I told Ward.

"First thing?"

"Always."

One last kiss from Ward's warm lips, and I climbed out of the car, keeping my head down as I staggered up the front steps. Dad stretched out his arm.

"Vayda."

I brushed him off, shocking him with electricity, and entered the house. "Don't you dare touch me."

Dad closed the door behind us and locked it from top to bottom, deadbolts, chains, and sliding locks. I cracked my knuckles and huddled away in the kitchen where the dishwasher needed unpacking.

Jonah stood by with a towel. "Need a hand with the dishes?"

He didn't want to make me better—we both knew he was horrible at calming me down. I set a coffee mug in the towel. It was two in the morning, but what else would we do? Sleep wasn't an option.

"Both of you need some rest," Dad said behind me as I aligned the cups in the cabinet. "Get on up to bed."

"You want me out of your sight, is that it?" My chin wiggled, raging. I couldn't hold back. *"You'd be better off keeping your distance from Vayda. She's the one to worry about. Real nice, Dati."*

"That wasn't a conversation for you. You don't know the context."

I thought his glasses made him seem old, but it wasn't his glasses. It was him. The years had worn on him like a constant gale. Me? I looked like Mom, and I hated it because people expected me to be the same as her.

I scoffed and tried not to sound as unstable as I felt. "How could you say that about me? I keep the house in order and care for you and Jonah 'cause you sulk around all the damn time and he's out doing God knows what! I take care of everything! I keep my shit together!"

"Magpie…" Dad stepped toward me.

The cups in the open cabinet rattled.

"Don't 'Magpie' me!" I shrieked. "When you should've defended us to that woman, you stabbed us in the back."

I rushed out of the kitchen. A succession of pops and breaking glass exploded from the cabinets. I didn't dare turn back, didn't care to clean up the mess, but before I could charge the stairs, Jonah grabbed my arm. The shocks crackling under our skin barely stung. "Get out of my way."

"Sis, let *Dati* talk," Jonah argued.

I caught sight of my strained jaw in the wall-length mirror by the stairs. "I'm sick to death of apologies that mean nothing. All the times you've said you're sorry—you don't mean it. If *Dati* apologizes, it's another lie. I heard his true feelings about us, how you—*you* who's been messing around with people's thoughts—are fine and I'm destructive. He can't take that back."

Jonah released my arm and sat on the steps, burying his face in his arms. Nothing could undo tonight. Nothing could make me un-hear the words.

I tore up the stairs, ignoring the sizzle of the electric wall sconces behind me, and hurled myself onto my bed, onto the vintage quilt where I curled into a ball. My eyes didn't run or swell with tears. I'd cried too much. I had nothing left. In the attic, the sound of wings flapped as birds banged into the rafters, still trapped. If only there was some way to free them.

After several minutes, Dad knocked on my door. "I'm coming in."

He sat on my bed, angled so I couldn't see his face. Yet his need for atonement was palpable. He spoke softly as if reciting the same rhymes I'd learned as a child, the ones about blackbirds in pies and blind mice.

"I'm sorry you overheard what you did."

"Don't try to apologize," I muttered.

He fidgeted with a paper scrap from his pocket. "Give me a chance. I worry about you. I've watched you torment yourself 'cause you hate your abilities." He nodded to Jonah leaning against my doorway. "Maybe you like what you can do too much."

Jonah sighed. "Probably."

He narrowed his eyes, ignoring my brother's flippancy, and continued, "If you'd both learn to control your Mind Games, I wouldn't worry as much. You're both pendulums stuck swinging one way without ever coming back to center. If you could even out…"

Didn't he know that a hug and some talk wouldn't gloss over that he betrayed my trust? He called me destructive. I *was* destructive. I could blow the house apart. I could explode everything.

"The last two years haven't been easy," Dad admitted. "I know you're scared the same thing as what happened to your mama will happen to you."

"It always goes back to her," I said. "Why'd she have to be such trouble?"

"She wasn't with everyone she met. She and June went far back, enough so to have one hell of a feud, but June kept coming 'round, so I thought they were mending fences." Dad arched an eyebrow and shook his head. "Those two, like a couple of mad, feral cats."

"And Sister Tremblay is June's niece?" Jonah asked.

Dad nodded. "She knows too much about us, but it's best to keep her close."

"So is it Sister Tremblay that you're worried about or…" I didn't finish. I didn't like the idea that my parents had that many enemies.

"Polly's here 'cause she needs to be. She's June's kin and that brings problems, but there's no telling what hell Brett's crazy family would unleash if they got wind of where little Polly, who ran off and joined a convent, was now. It's why I tell you mind yourselves. The problem with hiding is that you don't know who knows what. Cardinal rule: You never know who's watching, and I promise you someone is *always* watching."

Chapter Twenty-Two

Vayda

U sually weekends brought in business to Fire Sales, yet today was dead but for the occasional slice of Dad's southern twang as he sorted out an order gone wrong on the phone. I passed through the storeroom for a bucket of soap solution to clean a few wood pieces in need of attention. Still on the phone, Dad caught sight of me, popped some nicotine gum, and strangled the air.

Back in the showroom, I began cleaning off years of grime from an apothecary chest, only barely noticing the chime of the entry bells. Ward leaned on a Louis the XVI chair, no greeting but for a grin that curled up his lips while his eyes roamed over the way I filled out a shirt of his I'd snatched for myself. Stains from oil soap and wet dust covered the fabric, and I'd paired it with a ratty pair of jeans I kept for days when I dealt with furniture.

"As much as I like the show you're giving me, pay attention to what you're doing, Vayda," he said.

Damn it. A piece of wood from a carved cherub snapped.

Ward took the broken wing from my hand. "I'll fix it."

"Look at you, *gadjo*, thinking you can repair that naked baby angel," I teased and dropped my rag back into the warm, soapy water.

"I've learned a lot from your dad." He examined the wing's feathers. Soft wood, white walnut, not at all like the black birds in my memories. "I'm thinking of breaking something in

Heidi's house to try to fix it."

I giggled. "And if you can't?"

"Then I'll beg for help from Fire Sales' restoration guru."

Wiping my hands on the back of my jeans, I laughed again. The sound was foreign in the still shop, foreign to me period. Ward put his arms around me and pulled me close to feel him both soft and hard. He took my chin between his thumb and forefinger, and I wondered if my exhaustion showed in my face.

"I've done a lot of reading up on the Romani. I know about how trades are passed down in families," he said. "Your dad's woodworking wasn't passed down to him, but your mom read the tarot cards. She taught you how to read palms."

As Ward let go of me, I sat again beside the apothecary chest and inspected the crevices I'd been scrubbing moments before. He tried to make me better, but there were too many sore wounds carved in my mother's name. Palm reading, it was a parlor trick. It wasn't her *real* trick. That was something I'd have to learn on my own. Her way of doing it, Jonah's way, they weren't my way.

I picked up the soapy rag and wrenched out the extra water. "You know, maybe what they say about people like me is true. We don't know how to be honest. My mom was close to Rain. She knew him before she knew *Dati*. He used to ask Mom to sit in court and listen to the jury's thoughts, let him know if he needed to tweak his case to snag them."

Ward knelt behind me, wrapped his arm at my waist, and rested his chin on my shoulder. "Is this supposed to shock me?"

"Maybe." I ran my cloth over the apothecary chest again. Scrub, scrub, scrub. "My mom messed up things for a lot people, not just *Dati*. Not just Jonah and me. Her own father couldn't be seen talking to her, Ward. That doesn't happen because of some piddly offense. Rain told Dad that being so close to my parents hurt his law career."

I swiveled to face Ward, his lips tuck together in thought, but all he did was tip back his head to the fluorescent lights. "Drake gave me two pieces of advice that have stuck with me.

The first was to head to the free clinic if my prick burned." I gave an unexpected laugh, and he waited until I was finished to add, "The second was if you make a bed, you damn well better be ready to lie in it."

That advice applied to my parents, obviously, but did he know how it applied to himself? Did he know what he'd gotten himself into by being with me? My dad made a promise to keep my mother safe, and he couldn't keep that promise. I wanted to believe I could make my bed with Ward, that he could with me, but too many watchers, too many horrible things could go wrong.

The shop's door chimed again. Marty maneuvered past a row of dressers and dragged his finger along a fireplace mantle carved with laurel branches, sticking out his tongue at the dust.

I rose to my feet and hollered, "*Dati*! We got a problem!"

"Pifkin, you aren't welcome here." Jonah emerged from behind a china cabinet, dusting his hands on his dark cargo pants. He'd had so many barriers up while doing his own cleaning, I'd lost track of my twin. "Besides school, you can't come within a hundred feet of me. You want your bail revoked?"

Marty glanced over at my brother and straightened his back. "I'm not here for you." He walked around to my side of the counter. "What's up, Vayda?"

"You got five seconds before I call the cops to get your ass hauled out of here. That's what's up," I snapped.

His hand slapped my backside hard enough to sting. A light bulb overhead popped and sprinkled glass on the floor. Even my brother and Ward were too stunned to speak.

"Don't you ever touch me again!" I shouted.

"Or you'll do what? Push me? Shove me? Don't tell me the only Silver with magic fingers is Jonah." His chest swelled, smug as he leaned over a counter, level with my breasts. I hoped he saw the poisonous glare I gave him. "I want to make a deal."

"What type of deal?" Jonah asked.

"I'm in trouble after whooping your ass. My court date's

coming up next month, and I'm gonna be convicted and sent to juvie."

Ward snickered. "You'll be eaten alive. There's always some kid in juvie wanting to prove himself by taking out the biggest guy in the cafeteria, which will be you."

The edge came off Marty's ego. His sneer faltered, but he recovered quickly. "Yeah, obviously, I can fight, and I've got nothing to lose." He looked from Jonah to me. "But you two have everything to lose. What could be making you Silvers squirm? Maybe you've got something you need kept quiet, a secret that could flip your world inside-out."

A defensive kick tried to find its way to my voice, but Jonah stayed me by raising his hand. "What makes you think anybody'll believe a dumbass like you?"

Marty grinned, scavenger-like. "My mom gets together with her friends. I hear the way they talk. Your last name comes up all the time. Black Orchard is small enough that, if you weren't born here, you don't belong. For a couple of years, people have wondered about you. They *want* to believe you have a secret, and they'd make sure everybody finds out what you're hiding. How long do you think you could stand having the whole town breathing down your neck?"

Ward wedged between Marty and me. The tightening of his hand into a fist, the urge to clock Marty in the jaw, I felt it coming off him, unguarded and unasked for, and I retaliated by stroking his neck with my fingers and a wave of calm.

All it took to create a panic was one person igniting a fire.

I asked Marty, "What's stopping you from blathering to everybody? You've had plenty of time to run your mouth, but you haven't yet. Why now?"

He gave a perverted curl of his lip. "Vayda, how far will you go to keep your little secret?" He glanced at Ward. "Is that how you got her? 'Cause you found out and the only way she shuts you up is to get on her knees and beg?"

Ward's fist moved quickly, but not as fast as Jonah's arms reaching to pull him back. I shouted at Marty, cussing him out in my mother's tongue. The commotion caused enough noise to draw my father out of the storeroom. "Boy, get outta my shop. If I catch you hassling these kids again, forget the police. I'll deal with you myself. You understand?"

A bluish shadow tainted Marty's skin as Dad tugged on his bicep and towed him to the entrance, but Marty pulled back, hollering, "If you thought what happened to Jonah was bad—"

Dad heaved him outside. "Shut your mouth and get out!" He whipped around to face us, composed on the outside, but his voice gave enough of a quake to give him away. "Listen to me, all three of you. I want y'all to stay away from him. That Pifkin boy is nothing but smoke. No fire. But even smoke can do you in if there's enough of it."

***

A snowball sailed past my head and wetly thumped against the barn. I smiled at Ward drying his hands on his jeans. Jonah buttoned a thrift-store trench coat and stood close enough for his hot breath to skim the crown of my head. "You don't have to do this, Sis."

I chucked a snowball, watching it splat beside the remnants of Ward's, and wrapped tighter in my own coat. "I can't live like this. Marty's scared. Animals attack when scared. This stops tonight."

The energy balling in my fingertips intensified, supplemented by my every shiver, and I clenched my hands to dim the electricity sneaking out. A spark and snuff like flint steel striking against itself to procure a flame.

Save the energy for later, Jonah intoned in my mind.

I'll be fine.

I thought the dark mornings and darker nights of winter couldn't get any blacker, but the cold and storms had been unrelenting. Hills of snow and ice buried Black Orchard. Ward pitched another snowball, this time into the woods.

"I know you're pissed, *gadjo*. We've been over this. It's the only way Marty will let us be," I said.

He didn't believe me. Hell, I didn't believe myself, believe

I'd gone back on a promise I'd made to myself. After last spring, I swore I'd never let myself be alone with Marty, but what else could I try? He wouldn't leave us alone. Even if he wound up serving time, in the meantime he could set a hundred tiny fires that would become an inferno.

"Why's Marty after you?" Ward asked. "Even before he knew what Jonah can do, he's sniffed around you. He said he went out with you. Was he messing with me?"

I kicked at a discarded snowball near my feet. "After we came here, we didn't know anybody. Marty knew Chloe, and when Jonah and Chloe dated last year, Marty asked me out."

"You really went out with him?" Ward's nose wrinkled in disgust, and he coughed.

"No one had ever taken the time to get to know me. I didn't know any better. I get tired of being alone. We were hanging out with Jonah and Chloe at a park, and they went off. I was alone with Marty."

I blinked several times, cracked my knuckles poking through my fingerless gloves as my shoulders went tight. "He was nice, but I wasn't into him. He knew it, and we were waiting for Jonah and Chloe. But it was taking a while so Marty made a move. He kept putting his hands on me. When I told him to stop, he didn't listen and it wasn't okay."

"Did he hurt you?" Ward asked. The tightness had worsened, making my muscles feel like stretched bands ready to snap. I didn't answer him, and he took my hand. "Did he hurt you?"

I didn't want to tell him what Marty did, how he'd gripped the back of my neck when I told him no, how he twisted my wrist hard enough to leave a bruise. Jonah had never explained to Chloe how he knew to come running after me, but they'd found Marty dragging me toward a wooded walking trail as I struggled against him. A bulb in a lamp post exploded. It was the first time I shattered a light. I'd been hurt. I'd been scared. I was hurt and I was scared again—but not of Marty, rather what he could do to my family, my life.

"Don't put yourself through this," Ward pleaded.

"I know how to handle him."

"Vayda…"

"I have to do this."

Marty's SUV snaked along the snowy drive, following the tracks etched by Dad's Chevy when Jonah came home from taking him to work. The SUV came to halt in front of the stone house with an exhaust cloud from its tailpipe as Marty stepped out of the car. He checked over me, as if assessing my value. I buttoned my coat.

"Ready to go?" he asked.

My pulse tom-tommed between my ears. Get in, get out, and hopefully, I'd have a palm full of Marty's memories stuffed in my pocket when I returned home.

"Come on, Vayda." He sounded irritated as he reached for my hand.

I didn't let him touch me as I opened the passenger door.

"Wait." Ward put his arms around me. His lips were beside my ear, his voice a whisper. "You can walk away right now."

"I can't, *gadjo*. He'll always be there. He hurt me. He hurt my brother. He threatened us. I can't let him get away with that. Not anymore."

Ward gave a low growl. As he pulled back, his fingers lingered on my wrist and elicited a spark before he trudged toward the barn.

Jonah tipped his face to the sky. "Pifkin, you've got no chance with Vayda. Give it up."

What was he doing? Trying to give me an out? No. I was tired of always being afraid.

Marty ran his hands over his hair. "This isn't about trying to get with Vayda. I wanna make her squirm. I'm gonna have a hell of a lot of fun doing it. You might have some kind of power, but I'm the one calling the shots."

"Don't even try to play me," I said through the ache of my jaw, molars grinding together.

Easy, Sis. Jonah rubbed his feverish hands on my arms. The heat sank through my coat, underneath my flesh, and into my bloodstream. *I'll be right behind you. Everything's golden.*

Time to go. From the car, I stared out the window, first at my brother and then Ward as Marty drove the gravel path to the street. I was alone with him. My fingers dug into the leather of my seat, and my back was stiff.

I kept my face on the evergreen corridor. "Where are we heading?"

"Someplace to talk. We have a score to settle."

For ten minutes, we wound through Black Orchard, not saying much over the hip-hop music on the stereo. It was heavy on the bass and shook my seat. He parked at a playground near our school. During the summer, the lot teemed with my classmates making out. That night, the park was still. Shadows whisked over the snow, ghosts and memories of the last time I was alone with Marty in this park.

He dropped his hand from the steering wheel. "So are you actually wet for that Ravenscroft punk?"

"Crude, much?" I asked.

"So aren't you gonna ask what I want?"

I rolled my eyes. "You're so subtle."

"I understand why you were scared off before. I'm a big guy, but maybe Ravenscroft's broken you in by now."

I recoiled and leaned against the passenger door. "Oh, my God, Marty. Shut up."

He reached over to the glove box and withdrew a flask, offering me a swig of whatever was inside. No way. I didn't trust him not to have spiked it with something, even if he did uncap it and take a long slug. His hazel eyes surveyed the park, his lips shiny as he ran his tongue across the lower one. I checked for headlights. All the tightness in my neck and shoulders writhed down my veins to my fingers, but I sat on my hands. I had to store up that energy. Just in case.

The park was empty, but the park rangers wouldn't begin patrols until ten. A car, hard to tell the color in the faint lights of the playground, was parked at the other end of the lot. Snow covered the slides and swings and blanketed the ground. Jonah and Ward should pull in shortly.

"Let's do this." Marty sighed and unclipped his seatbelt

before popping the lock on mine.

I exhaled as he pulled me near. I had to let him get close, closer than I'd ever want him. His lips, slick and cold from the rim of his flask, found my neck. I didn't move, didn't push him away. Ward's face, hurt and jealous, lodged in my brain. Though he and I talked the plan over, we both hated the idea. I felt ill and guilty, and my pulse rose in my ear, beating hard and fast like frantic wings. Energy looming and threading, faster, mounting. Filling me until it swam under my skin.

Still, I was patient. All I needed was for Marty to peer into my eyes.

His lips snaked up the side of my neck, his tongue slipping across my ear. I writhed away from him. "Stop!" Writhing under his anger, I muttered, "I'm not into that."

He moved his face to my neck once again but didn't kiss me. Instead, his breath, which smelled bitter—bourbon—blew against my cheek. "So what is your brother, some kind of mutant?"

"Marty Pifkin, your wits have been damaged by too many comic books."

Glowering, he drew a lighter from his pocket. The flint scratched. A flame stretched up from the lighter only for Marty to let it die out. Again, a scratch of the flint and hiss of butane as the flame wavered between us. Then darkness. Without warning, he stepped out of the car, stalked around to my side, and yanked open my door. "We're taking a walk."

Marty's hand extended to me, but I wouldn't let him touch me if I could avoid it. His energy was awful enough; I didn't want another physical touch to overwhelm what I already had stored inside and kept a foot of distance between us as we strolled along the icy walkway toward the playground. I needed to stay calm, but edginess needled me. Headlights illuminated the street leading to the park, and my stomach sank: not the Chevy, but a minivan rolling toward the subdivision beyond the park.

"You see the cuts on Sister Tremblay's face? Jonah jacked her up, didn't he?" Marty asked.

"He didn't do it. My brother's got a temper, but he's not a psychopath," I snapped, wetness from the snow permeating my jeans. "Why do you hate him so much? All he did was stop you when you were out of control."

"He thinks he's better than everyone." Marty glimpsed over his shoulder. I glanced around, only the shadows of the playground looming across the streetlamp-lit snow. "He told me I'm not good enough for you."

His energy hopped, one moment bogged down with spite and the next a blip of excitement. This wasn't right. His thoughts weren't clear or easy to track—could have been the booze—and my feelers instead extended toward my brother but only found frustration. Something messed up Jonah's plan. If I kept Marty distracted, I'd find my opening to his memories, a vulnerable blink.

A breeze blew loose snow in my face, and I asked, "Why would I be too good for you? If it's because I'm *Rom*, well, I'm with Ward and he's not like me."

Marty snorted. "It's because Jonah thinks he's special. He moves things without touching them. I can guess why Chloe fell for him, but he's one twisted bastard. You're like him, right? Show me how you do it."

Nausea battled my stomach. He roosted on a park bench and motioned me to sit, though I stayed at the opposite end. The streetlamp cast dark slashes across his face, the angles of cheekbones and the cleft in his chin turning to black gouges.

"So, Vayda"—his voice was a raspy scrape in the night—"did your mom scream as she burned alive?"

I launched to my feet. My eyes bulged, heart pounding. I ran, but Marty's meaty fingers snatched my wrist and wheeled me around against his body.

"Yeah, I know about it." He backed me toward the bench, his feet clumsily crushing mine. "Maybe with this little game changer, I will have more than tonight with you."

"H-h-how'd you find out about my mom?" I fought against his grip, and the more I struggled, the more energy leaked out of me in small shocks, heat that melted the snow around our feet. He knew not only about the Mind Games. He knew about our past. How long had he known?

He bent forward to touch his nose to mine. "Sister Tremblay left your file wide open on her desk. I'm not much of a reader, but that was interesting. Your family has lots to hide, more than I imagined."

He shoved me, and I fell against the bench. For a moment, all I saw were flashes of red and white, pain blinding me. Marty stood over me with his legs spread wide to block my escape, and he reached into his pocket, flicking on his lighter. The flame quavered in the wind. "Scared of fire?"

I couldn't show weakness. He'd pounce if given an opportunity. I blew out the flame. He had to try harder to make me flinch.

A sickness, something twisted, oozed out from the playground. Marty's energy had a far reach, and this gripped me so hard and close that I wanted to puke.

Suddenly, the left side of my head banged against the bench. Blood gushed from my scalp as I dropped to my hands and knees. I touched my head and tried to stand, but I was too dizzy to hold myself up. "Mother of God, that hurts."

Marty squatted beside me, though I couldn't see his face. My forehead ached, my brain ached. I had to get into his head to take his memories, of all that he knew about us.

Jonah, where are you?

Another slap to my face, and I screamed. "Stop!"

A whimper accented each breath I released as his hands blocked my floundering arms.

"Everyone's gonna find out you're freaks," Marty hissed and pried my legs apart.

"Do it, Marty!" a girl shouted.

Blood streaming down my forehead, I made out Chloe's silhouette sauntering from underneath the playground slide. The wind blew her blond hair, and her blue coat shielded her from the coming storm. Her plaid skirt revealed bare, cold-red legs, but she didn't even seem to notice that she could get frostbite. Her hands pumped in and out of fists, and I couldn't help but recall Jonah and the way he shook out the energy from his hands. Her energy, black and sour like burnt molasses, clung to her. It was identical to Marty's.

Danny lagged behind Chloe, his tan skin greenish under the lights. The urge to flee from the pack pounded off him. "She's scared enough! Can we go?"

"No!" Chloe screeched. "This bitch needs to know what it's like to be used."

Marty nodded at Chloe and forced his body over mine. He ripped at my coat, fingers fumbling with the buttons on my pants. A fingernail scratched my hip as his hand stretched below the waistband of my jeans.

"Get off me!" I wailed.

"This is going too far!" Danny yelled. "Marty, come on! You're done, right?"

Yet he didn't sound so sure.

Marty pushed a bloody strand of hair from my face. He lowered his mouth, his lips against my bared teeth, his moan swallowing my sobs.

"Your brother has to be stopped," Chloe snarled behind him. "You think I didn't know Jonah was to blame for what you said at the coffee shop? I told Marty to find him at Fire Sales. He had a good time working Jonah over. Vayda, you let Jonah hurt me. You even tried to bail him out, but, whatever you did to me, the memories came back. It's your time to be hurt."

Tears on my cheeks, my hands surged with cold fire. Energy. Rising.

Marty lowered his hard chest to mine. A shock erupted from my palms. Airborne, he sailed off me, landing far away on his back.

Motionless. Dead?

Did I care if he was?

"Oh, my God!" Chloe screamed and ran to Marty's fallen form.

Lying on my back and crying, I saw Marty's chest rise and fall. I swiveled my head in the powdery snow smeared with blood. A car's headlights burned my sight as the vehicle careened through the parking lot. An engine idled, the chug of the Chevy. The heaps of snow beneath me began to melt from Jonah's fire flowing toward me and soaking my clothing. He was here. Thank God.

Danny reached his hand to me. "Are you hurt?"

I couldn't answer. My head throbbed, and the energy riding my palms battered my being—blood, bones, sinew, spirit, all electrified.

"Get away from her!"

Ward shoved Danny before moving to where Chloe knelt with Marty. She shrieked and retreated while Ward kicked Marty.

"I will break you!" Every word Ward yelled emphasized a blow to Marty's back. "I will fuck you up!"

"Ward, stop!" I shouted, crouching on my knees. Jonah hoisted me to my feet under my arms. I caught his dark eyes as he forced my fingers between his, collecting the energy bailing from me between our hands.

"Hang on, Vayda."

Our hands interlocked. A whorl of fire smashed against glacier-cold. Waves of energy streamed out, and a breaker of light thrust across the snow. Sightless, all I could sense was an ice-burn slipping under my flesh. My back collided with the earth as the force fell out across the playground. In time to see Chloe flung onto her chest, my vision returned and shifted to Ward landing on his side, both taken out by the expanding blast.

For sixty seconds, a paralysis deadened the playground. Tender and pummeled, I crawled through the snow to Ward. He sat up to rub his shoulder. We helped each other stand and leaned into one another's bodies as the blast's residue dissipated like a shot of Novocain wearing off. A nudge each to Danny, Marty, and Chloe roused them enough to know they were unhurt. Jonah balanced against the bench and caught his breath before walking back toward the Chevy. He opened the trunk and removed the blankets Rain gave us to keep warm during our trip from Hemlock. I wrapped a blanket around my wet clothing. Ward climbed in the backseat beside me and covered me with his jacket.

"We should call the police," he said.

"No," Jonah and I both said at once. "No cops."

"What are you gonna tell your dad? Vayda, your face is all banged up."

I anchored my back to the seat. Every inch of me throbbed. "I'll tell him I fell on the ice. I don't want *Dati* going after Marty." I hugged myself, forcing myself not to feel the hurt where Marty held me down. "I...I want to go home."

Behind the steering wheel, Jonah examined the park, watching while Chloe and Marty made an effort to stand. His shoulders vibrated. He had to be so infuriated to sit and shake, but a tear slipped down his cheek.

"I'm so sorry, Sis. I should've known it was coming, but I never thought—"

"Stop it!" Ward yelled. "It's done. A train stopped us. It was a shitty plan. It's done, and thank God, we got here."

Jonah clubbed the steering wheel with his palm. "I should've handled Marty. There's no way word of this won't get around. I'm sorry because you love my sister, but we can't stay."

Love? The word neither Ward nor I had chanced saying yet it was the only word that would do. He held his sleeve to the cut on my forehead. That was love.

Jonah turned the key in the ignition and drove away. Evergreens lined the streets, and the ground was white, the sky was black. No stars, no moon, no clouds.

"They might not talk," I said as Jonah steered into our driveway.

"Sis, you know that's not true. They'll talk, and, inevitably, we'll run."

Chapter Twenty-Three

Ward

A dozen or so students gathered near Vayda's locker scratched with bubbly letters: WITCH.

"Real nice!"

I pivoted in time to see Vayda's creased forehead, still yellow and green with bruises, before she darted into the restroom. A witch's cackle rose above the rumble of too many people talking.

Jonah's fist thwacked his locker. More tittering. Two weeks of relentless ridicule had unwound him, and he held out his arms, offering himself up for a fight. Or a pie in the face. "You want a freak show? Fine!"

Every open locker in the hall slammed shut in banging succession like falling dominos.

Then stunned silence. The other students backed away as Jonah shoved past me toward the physics lab but not before whipping a trash bin across the hall upside-down, scattering papers.

"Go ahead! Give them something to talk about, dumbass!" I called after him. He didn't swivel back around but stuck up his middle finger. I could get pissed, but honestly, I'd be tempted to use Mind Games to shut up people if I could.

The crowd dispersed once the show ended, but Chloe hung close by. Her lips were a self-satisfied smile as she traced Vayda's scratched locker.

"Who the hell let you out of your cage?" I hissed and

coughed. Damn thing still wouldn't go away.

She eyed me curiously. "Aren't you afraid Vayda's playing you like Jonah did me?"

"No."

I could make some comment on how I had a brain and, thusly, was harder to manipulate, but Chloe wasn't worth it. Jonah messed with her. She was angry. What he did was inexcusable, and it still surprised me that he'd ever thought it would be okay to "free" her mind. What she and Marty planned for Vayda—that was a different level of demented.

Leaving Chloe to admire the graffiti on Vayda's locker, I spied Jonah and Vayda outside the lab. Vayda's cheeks flushed, and she tugged at her hip-length hair. Drawing closer, the scent of pine knocked me back. Her hair was stuck to her hands with some kind of glue.

"What the hell?" I asked. "What's in your hair?"

"Sap left over from the physics class's viscosity experiment last week." Jonah plucked at a knot in his sister's hair. "Some kid ganked it from the supply cabinet with the other sticky gunk they tested, thought it'd be funny to pour it over Vayda."

"How will I get this out?" she groaned. A rope of hair tore, adhered to her skin in a tacky mess.

Chloe edged close, though keeping her distance by walking by the lockers on the other side of the hallway. "Wow, Vayda. Shame about the rat's nest in your hair, or maybe a bat got tangled up in it."

Vayda's mouth dropped, and a silent cry was on her breath. With a strange laugh, Chloe let herself into one of the classrooms, and Vayda wept at the torn hair stuck to her hands.

"It'll wash out." I reached toward her, but she waved me off and charged down the hall.

I took a step after her when Jonah stopped me. "Let her be."

"She needs help," I protested.

He rubbed his face with his arm. "You don't have a clue what it's like for us. No one's written slurs about you or filled your gas tank with sugar. Dad's lost three clients this week. That paper I wrote on *Jane Eyre*? I got a D. I've never gotten a D, but Sister Hillary Lauren gets away with it 'cause Monsignor hates us. Now my sister's got a scalp of pine sap, and *you're* gonna tell her everything will be okay? Fuck that."

He took off after Vayda.

She told me before there was a pattern to the harassment—began with jokes, became vandalism, and eventually someone took it too far. I had to wonder if "too far" had come.

I skipped class. During the final bell of the day, I washed my hands. Paint dust peppered my hands. Chipping the paint was arduous, but Vayda's locker now read ITCH with a scribbled blob over the W. Small victory.

That morning, I'd left a note for Heidi to pick me up an hour late, explaining I needed to do research in the library. So what if it was a lie? Within forty minutes of dismissal, the school was pretty well empty. Fifteen minutes left until Heidi arrived. This shouldn't be hard.

The whispered pace of my stride carried down the cavernous hall of the language arts wing and through the arched doors into the church. I slipped past the open doors of the sanctuary until I reached the main office where Monsignor and Sister Tremblay worked. I peeked around the corner and spied the secretary. She hummed the Beatles' "Yesterday" and sipped tea, thankfully distracted by the phone, and I slipped unnoticed past the doorway. The paperclips in my pocket easily straightened. I found Sister Tremblay's door, shadowed in the corner of a hall within the office, and crouched beside it. Privacy was important for a nun specializing in counseling. How fortuitous for a delinquent with lock-picking skills.

The lock was simple, a cylinder mechanism. Line up the pins, and that was it. Despite my shaking fingers, the paperclips finagled into the keyhole. I chewed the inside of my cheek as the pins' weight shifted against the paperclips. Three, two, one—got it. I glanced at my watch. One minute-seventeen seconds. Not shabby at all for being rusty.

The file cabinet in Sister Tremblay's unlit office had a lock I barely needed to manipulate before it opened. Manila folders contained transcripts, notes, information on every student. Flip, flip, flip. Q, R, S—Silver, Vayda. Her file rustled with papers, and my fingers snagged Jonah's folder as well. Dozens of pages of handwritten notes, each stating a time, place, and one sentence description of "incidents." Mind Games. No time to read much detail, not then, and not much in the way of school papers other than vaccination notes and a homeschooling transcript, which Vayda already explained was a forgery Rain concocted to smooth away any bumps from the lack of official records. For good measure, I read over my own file. Only transcripts from Rochester and a medical report clearing me for public school. Flipping through more random folders, none of the other students had personal notes quite like those in Vayda and Jonah's files.

The secretary's chair squeaked.

I shoved the files in my backpack. My hearing sharpened, breath still. More Beatles' humming.

With a phantom's stealth, I ducked into the hallway, slid past the sanctuary, and then ran toward my locker, my boots thundering on the floor. As I rounded the corner, a cough ripped from my lungs. Heidi had taken me to urgent care last weekend when I'd come back from Fire Sales unable to stop coughing enough to work on my own metal sculptures. In spite of x-rays and breathing tests, my cough was still a mystery, the doctor called it chronic. Maybe even psychosomatic. It wasn't in my head. The tightness in my lungs was real and had gotten worse.

"In a hurry, Mr. Ravenscroft?" Sister Tremblay asked as she stepped around a corner.

"I'm trying out for track."

My chest gave a final cough, and I glared at her face, stoic as a statue in an abandoned cathedral. Untouched. A chill climbed my spine.

"Do you know what you're doing with the Murdocks?" she asked.

I half-smiled. "I don't know any Murdocks. Do you?"

"If you're smart, you won't fall in with them. People with

uncontrolled *talents* such as Vayda and Jonah ruin others."

I tightened my hold on my backpack and glanced at my scar-covered knuckles. Maybe staying with Vayda would leave me broken, but I was fractured before I ever met her.

"Why are you so hung up on them?" I asked, spinning the focus toward her.

Sister Tremblay cocked her head. "A person's past is inescapable. Cycles repeat. Like mother, like child. They need control, and a promise must be kept."

"What promise? To who?"

She didn't listen, continuing, "Instead of forcing them to be trained, Emory excuses them. This can't be allowed to go on."

I moved closer to her. Even though she was taller than I was, she backed up. "What are you gonna do?"

"Like I said, I have a promise to keep."

Sister Tremblay glided down the hall. I should've called Emory. He knew how to handle her whereas my first instinct was to trip her.

I checked my watch. Heidi should have arrived five minutes ago and had to be wondering what the hold-up was. I headed outside to my half-sister's car. My reflection in the side mirror appeared spooked, but Heidi didn't notice as she switched the stereo from bouncy kids' tunes to the Carole King album I gave her for Christmas. Anything was better than "I'm a Little Teapot" set to a reggae beat.

"Want some coffee? Black, right?" Heidi asked and pulled into a drive-thru. She placed our order, and we waited. She peered at Oliver sleeping in his car seat. Sunlight streamed through the van's windows, glinting off Heidi's red hair. There weren't too many bright days in Black Orchard, not during the barren winter.

"Emory called this morning," she declared, "and I have to say I was taken aback. He said you approached him about doing an apprenticeship. I had no idea."

I wanted to work for Emory, but if things got worse for them in Black Orchard, I didn't know what I'd do. Giving me an extra second to prepare an answer, Heidi passed my drink to me, and I sipped the bitter coffee. "Did you know Emory was on the news and written about in magazines? That stuff doesn't matter to me, but I'm telling you 'cause he's that good at his work." Heidi's lips pursed. Time to flip her to my side. I said, "Heidi, I can do this. Emory said he'd show me. He's been training me since I began working for him."

She traced a fingernail along the steering wheel and shifted to flicking the pine tree-shaped air freshener dangling from the mirror. "I've been getting calls about the Silvers, Ward."

"Whatever you've heard—"

"Are they in trouble?"

I stopped my knee from bouncing. "Nobody's perfect."

She quieted and focused on the road. At a red light, she put her hand on my shoulder. "I care about you. Starting over was part of why we let you live with us."

Starting over was why the Silvers might have to leave Black Orchard. Was I willing to give up everything Heidi and Chris gave me to run with Vayda's family? Was that even an option? I'd been a runaway before...

"I know what I'm doing with the Silvers," I said.

"Are you sure?" she asked.

God, I hoped so.

At the house, Bernadette waited by the door and headed for her special spot under a spruce tree. Her wagging tail thanked me for letting her out, and I tied her collar to a lead attached to the porch. Bernie moaned as I massaged the stiff fur on her back. The dog needed a bath. Badly. I pushed her brows from her face, and she panted, happily dazed enough to make me snicker. She liked to watch the ravens from her basket even on cold days, though she usually whined to come inside after ten minutes. Time enough for me to clean up the mess of scrap metal I'd promised Heidi I'd sort last night.

The corner of the driveway I'd high-jacked for metal sculpture had grown to taking up the bulk of the driveway, leaving only a narrow crevice to squeeze the cars through to get to the garage. The cold had done nothing to distract me from sculpture. Looming in sharp-edged curves and spires, I'd crafted trees from refurbished copper. A forest of dangerous metal. Scars twisting on my hands from all the times I'd cut myself, the roots of these trees were in me. Maybe that was why I didn't bend once I'd made up my mind.

The door leading from the open garage into the kitchen clattered. As Heidi carried out a bag of papers for recycling, a shrillness in her voice caught my ear as the wind lifted her words.

"Kate, do you hear yourself? That's nuts...I don't care what people say. Ward's around them all the time. The Silvers are decent people." Her face darkened as she listened then hit the disconnect button, standing with one hand to her forehead and the other pressed into the small of her back.

I placed a sheet of copper onto a stack by one of the sculptures. "Who was that?"

"Kate Halvorsen, Chloe's mom," Heidi replied. "She's the fifth person to call today about the Silvers. There's an informal concerned citizens meeting tomorrow night. What is this about, Ward? Emory said they're Romani, but Kate said Vayda's a witch. An actual witch."

I crossed my arms. What did it say about me that the first response in my mind was the canned one I'd learned from Jonah and Vayda? "People don't like anything out of the ordinary."

Heidi nodded. I knew she believed in giving people the benefit of a doubt.

"Why don't you get Bernadette and give me a hand with dinner?" she asked. "Before all these phone calls, I'd invited the Silvers over. They need someone in this town on their side."

The way she rested her hand on my shoulder, my half-sister and I weren't close, but she could be trusted. I split off from her and walked around the house to the front porch.

Bernadette's wicker basket was empty.

"Come here, Dog!" I whistled. The end of her tie-out coiled like a frozen cobra in the snow. No sign of her. I jogged an oblong circle around the house, searching the woods marking the property line. Nothing, just some paw prints by the usual tracks left by the cars' tires and footprints on the snow.

My hand yanked open the front door and I called into the house as Chris' Jaguar pulled into the driveway. "Bernadette's gone!"

Retracing her tie-out and doddering trail, the only prints I saw were within the length of the leash. If she'd gotten off her lead, she'd have left a sign.

Chris waited with Heidi on the front porch. "You didn't find her yet? She never goes beyond that pine tree."

"She's missing," I said, again scanning the woods. The sun was lowering. Occasionally, coyotes and even a badger crept along the trees since I moved to Black Orchard, but what if something else stalked those woods, waiting until nightfall to emerge from its den?

Heidi nudged her husband's arm. "You go out, Chris. Emory and the twins will be here for dinner soon. I'm sure they'll help us. We'll find her."

Chris took a flashlight since a gray dog blended in all too easily with the snow at dusk. He walked along the evergreens, called her name, and then headed out in his Jaguar. I slumped on the front steps. I shouldn't have left her alone. She was old. She was mostly blind and didn't hear well. No wonder Drake didn't trust me with a pet. I couldn't care for anything. On nights when my insomnia was bad and I paced the house, I wasn't alone. Bernadette paced with me.

Headlights on the driveway. The Chevy's tires ground to a halt and the Silvers approached the house, a trio of black hair and shadowy faces, but Heidi got to them first, out of my earshot. Vayda's expression fell, and she slipped away from her family. Her hair was more than a foot shorter than it'd been when she came to school that morning.

"You cut it off," I remarked, pointing to the waves falling at her chest. "Looks nice. Kind of weird." Jonah's hair was also shorter, barely below his ears.

"Your dog's missing and you want to talk about my hair?"

she asked.

"Well, it's better than worrying about what could've happened to Bernadette."

Emory squeezed my shoulder before he followed Heidi inside. I stayed in the cold dusk with Jonah, Vayda, and a strange weight in the air between us. I should've been out finding Bernadette. My legs moved with speed over the snow. One more sweep around the border of the woods. Nothing. Nothing at all but for a weird glimpse between Jonah and Vayda. They were talking and didn't even open their mouths.

"What?" I asked. "Do you guys know something?"

Vayda reached for the ends of her hair to twirl them on her fingers but missed, still not used to the new length. She backed off from the porch and walked the driveway, pausing alongside each of the metal trees I'd hammered together.

"I told you about Nyx, the cat in Montana," she murmured.

"Sis," Jonah said, "you don't think—"

Her eyes shimmered with tears. "Can't you feel the energy they left behind?"

He dropped his head. "Yes."

Something cold and wet opened up inside my gut. They knew what happened to my dog. Bernadette was gone because of them? Because I wouldn't give up on Vayda? My hands began to shake, the cold inside me surging with a tingling that boiled.

"Where's my dog?" I placed my hands on Vayda's shoulder, turning her toward me. "Was it Marty?"

"Chloe," she whispered.

My chin shuddered. Fury. The prickling shocks of electricity between my palms and her shoulders felt like hundreds of needles piercing the same spots on my flesh.

"I left Bernadette alone for ten minutes, maybe fifteen, and that girl came and took her?" My voice cracked with the question, didn't even sound like me but someone more fragile.

"This isn't your fault, *gadjo*," Vayda assured me, dropping her stare to the ground. "I'm so sorry. If I'd known you could be hurt because of me—"

"Stop! Just stop!"

My lungs began to close up the longer I kept my hands on Vayda. Her palms glowed pale blue-white. I lowered my head, my cheek pressing against Vayda's. All I could think was how that dog was the first thing in Black Orchard to like me and I let her down.

More fury. Now guilt. Now sadness.

A tornado of emotion blowing me apart.

"Ward, let go of me," Vayda whispered, begged. "You're going to get hurt if you hang on."

Her hands crackled with electricity, and a fever-red blush colored her skin. She stepped back, staggering, and fell to her knees. Jonah and I were on either side of her, but he blocked my hands from taking hold of his sister.

Words from a night in December, the night of Jonah's assault in Fire Sales, reechoed in my skull. *People's emotions emit energy. There's something in me pulling that energy. I shut it down as best I can unless someone reaches to me.* She hadn't been able to shut me down this time. I'd overloaded her. Jonah held Vayda's hand and lifted his free one, eyes scrunched shut.

In a sudden gust, the forest of metal trees upended, a storm of edges and spikes that could slice and spear. They lay against the snowy ground like deadly playthings, and then Jonah made a beckoning gesture with his fingers. The sculptured trees righted themselves again.

Somehow, someway, Jonah and Vayda worked together, sucking and expelling energy.

If Jonah was a gun and could fire off, then Vayda gave him the ammo.

"I have to go," Jonah said as he rose to his feet. "I promise, Ward. I'll make this right."

I crouched on the ground beside Vayda, not taking my sight off Jonah. "You've done enough damage."

"I'm gonna get your dog back. I swear to it."

Jonah disappeared into the dusky trails of sunset growing longer across the driveway. The Chevy's engine sputtered as Jonah drove away.

"Where's your brother?" Emory asked as he came onto the porch to investigate the noise.

"Looking for Bernadette," Vayda replied. It wasn't a lie.

"It's too dark to find her tonight. Call the boy and tell him to come back, Magpie."

Vayda furrowed her brow. "He doesn't have his cell phone."

Emory reached for the screen door. "Like either of you needs a phone."

Vayda and I waited on the front step, her hand in mine. My lungs ached, wheezing with each breath, but she hugged me close. The tighter her hold, the stronger the calm she poured into me, making me numb so time meant nothing. The sky blackened and night birds squawked as they swooped around the trees. Chris returned from his hunt for Bernadette, dog-less since he didn't have the lead Jonah did, but Vayda and I remained on the porch.

"It's stupid to get this worked up over a dog," I muttered.

"No, it's not." Vayda brought my hand up to her mouth and kissed my knuckles. "You have no idea how sorry I am. This is what it's like to be with someone like me, Ward."

I knew that.

Knowing and living were different though.

"I'm not going back to school," she said. "At least not for a while."

"Because of the bullshit with Chloe and—"

"I've been suspended." Her voice was hoarse. "Jonah's out, too. Monsignor came to the physics lab after you skipped. Jonah got into it with Marty, shoving each other. Monsignor believed it when some girls said I started it. There'd been too many problems with my brother and me. Marty, Chloe, they did it. They got rid of us."

"What?" I didn't believe it. "But that's not fair. It's not true."

"Cardinal rule: It doesn't matter what's true; all that matters is what people want to believe. They want to believe we come from the devil."

It was so unfair. No one would listen to her and Jonah. I held her closer and said a silent prayer.

After a while, two pairs of headlights crept up the driveway. The Chevy followed a car I didn't recognize. Jonah hopped out of his dad's car and charged over to the driver's door of a blue sedan, practically pulling Danny out of his seat.

"Hand her over," Jonah ordered.

"I'm getting there," Danny croaked from behind a puffy lower lip. Had Jonah done that to him? Something told me that was hardly the worst Jonah's fists saw while he was gone.

Danny pulled open the door to the backseat and hunched inside to retrieve a bundled up blanket. He kept his eyes on the ground as he trudged to where I waited on the front step, arms offering up the blanket. I hesitated to take it. What if I unwrapped it and Bernadette was—

The jingle of tags and a snort flooded my veins with relief. I uncovered Bernadette's head and felt the warmth of her tongue licking my hand.

"My dog," I choked.

"Tell him what you did," Jonah barked.

Danny didn't delay. The words tumbled out of him like rocks sliding down an avalanche. "Be careful of Chloe. Marty's bad enough, but that girl's full-on psycho. Marty called to brag that he and Chloe had your dog, and I heard her saying what she planned to do." He shuddered. "She's lost her mind. I couldn't let them do that and was gonna bring the dog back, but..."

Jonah smacked the back of his head. "You fucking liar. You denied having her. Don't you know it's impossible to lie to me?"

"I was gonna bring her back, I swear!" Danny rubbed his head and backed away. "I couldn't let Chloe and Marty do what they said they wanted to."

The front door opened. Chris stepped outside and exhaled as he saw me cradling the old schnauzer in my arms. He eyed Jonah. "You found her?"

"Something told me where to go, who to talk to," Jonah

replied and elbowed Danny. "Isn't that right?"

"Sure," Danny blurted. "I gotta go."

He hustled his ass back to his car and sped away so fast the wheels shot an arc of snow across the driveway as he fishtailed toward the street. I really didn't care where he went. My dog was back, and after a quick check over from her ears to the toenails that clicked on the floor behind me hundreds of times, she seemed to be okay. Before Vayda ushered me inside the house, I ran my fingers over Bernadette's ears and her chin.

Good dog. Damn good dog.

After dinner, upstairs, I lay on my bed in the darkness, Bernadette on my chest and Vayda curled up against my shoulder. We didn't talk or kiss, simply held one another, and let our minds grow heavy. My thoughts were heavier.

I awakened after one in the morning. The room was hushed. Vayda was gone, and Bernadette had taken her place. Soft snoring. Legs wiggly with dog dreams. I got up to brush my teeth then wandered downstairs to the kitchen for some water. In the living room, Chris watched television and muted the stand-up comedian.

"You're up late," I said.

"Long night. Lots on my mind," he replied. "It could've ended badly tonight, Ward."

An angry nail hammered into my mind, sinking through my brain. Anyone could tell Bernadette was feeble. To take her away from what she knew, to terrify her—that person was soulless. Chloe had every right to be furious with Jonah, but what she'd plotted for Vayda, for Bernadette, was dangerous. It was more than revenge. It was murderous.

"Emory said you kids are having problems. Heidi's gotten calls about them. About you." Chris didn't sound angry but worried. "What do you know, Ward?"

I sat beside him on the couch and stared at the hushed television. "Oh, I know something."

I knew Chloe and Marty were going down.

Chapter Twenty-Four

Vayda

Jonah brought me a slice of red velvet cake and perched on the sales counter. "Happy birthday, Sis."

As we'd watched the sun move above the horizon this morning, gold and silver rays streamed over our faces and anointed our seventeenth year. We were strangers in these bodies. He hadn't needed to cut his hair, too. All that black hair lying on the barn floor as if a dark bird was ripped apart, feather by feather.

I produced two books from below the register and dropped them with a thud. Amy Lowell's two-volume biography of John Keats, 1925 first edition, signed.

"Awesome," he whispered while the book's spine cracked upon opening. "This'll occupy me for a spell."

"You need something to keep you out of trouble," I teased. "You and your writers. Aren't our own lives enough?"

His hand hovered over the pages. "Writers get inside people's heads. Get into thoughts and feelings." His voice was somber, face forlorn. "You think there are more people like us?"

"Somewhere," I ventured. "Can't imagine we're the only ones."

My brother grabbed his coat and tucked his books under his arm. "I'm heading out. We won't get any customers. Ostracism at its finest, right?"

The showroom had been empty for days. Since our

suspension, spending time at Fire Sales was safest, but the idea of people tracking our every move intensified no matter how cordoned off we were from the rest of Black Orchard. The only people in town who spoke to us were Ward's family. At the market, I couldn't choose which box of speckled eggs from the farm or select winter squashes without meeting someone's scowl. Dad said to hold up our heads, but the weight of angry stares curved my spine.

At home, the currents should have abated, and yet they were worse. If I walked past the mirror, it watched. If I walked down the wall, it was too quiet and the darkness breathed behind me. Sometimes, at night, I lay awake in bed, listening to the wind shift in the attic like footsteps, and in a half-dream, I'd hear my mother's voice whispering, *They're coming, Vayda. Soon.*

Last night, Heidi and Chris brought Ward over for supper. It didn't take long before Heidi admitted she attended the "concerned citizens" meeting. Funny, we never knew half the town didn't trust us ever since Dad opened up Fire Sales. Maybe I should've been shocked a mob with pitchforks and torches hadn't shown up at our house. Dad was in scramble-mode. Banishment moved faster here than down south, probably since the people were so cold they did their duty and hurried back inside.

Since Bernadette's disappearance and return two nights ago, Ward fox-holed himself in the shop after school, keeping his dog close by in the storeroom. He should have never aligned himself with us. No apology would suffice.

Dad lugged out a rosewood cabinet with an iron door. Busy work for my *gadjo*. I prepped my barriers to take the full strength of his emotions, yet for the first time in two days, he wasn't blitzed by rage but blunted, anesthetized. It was a relief to slide through without any hang-ups once again. Dad crouched down and patted Bernadette's back before focusing his attention on Ward, who scraped the rusted iron with a sanding cloth.

"Not quite." Dad pointed to a clean spot on the bars. "This

is what you want. Don't scrape any farther or you'll damage the metal. When it comes to the wood, scarcely touch it. Rosewood's naturally oily, so the finish darkens with age. The flaws give it life."

Ward continued sanding the rust, flake by flake. A proud smile poked Dad's mouth, and he offered his student a wire brush to clean between the bars. Ward removed the gloves Dad insisted we use when handling a restoration. "Why are you helping me?"

"'Cause if I don't, you'll do more damage instead of fixing things," Dad replied. "I've made mistakes. They cost me. If I can you teach something I learned by messing up, well, that's worth my time."

Guardedness haunted Ward, and he spied me eavesdropping. His mouth ticked, too much anger still running through him. I inspected his work and gave Dad a thumbs-up before he headed back to his desk. For several minutes, I observed Ward while he scraped and brushed, checking his progress between passes. He was heavy with thought if I sought his energy, but I wanted the slide and dive we used to have. I wanted us back before we hurt.

"*Dati*'s trying to wait until the end of the school year to move, give us time to properly relocate his store and transfer our records," I told him. "But it might be sooner."

"How soon?" he asked.

"Spring break. If we can hold out that long."

He didn't break away from the cabinet. "Where are you going?"

"Mom got anxiety attacks in big cities, too much energy, so *Dati* won't move to one. He's found some property near Lily Dale—some spiritualist community in New York. Real big into séances. Jonah and I won't be so extraordinary there. Being a vessel through which the dead speak trumps empaths, hands down."

A wry arc tilted his lips as he imitated my accent. "Why, Vayda, were you being funny?"

"Your sense of humor's rubbed off on me."

"Hell, *I* want to rub on you."

I tensed, shutting my eyes to beat back the memory of Marty holding me down in the snow. Not the same as Ward. Not the same at all, I reminded myself. Because what Ward wanted wasn't to take, to overpower, demand. What he wanted was to share. Together.

"You'll get your chance," I promised, running my fingers up his spine.

We had plans for my birthday that night. Coffee. Movie. Time alone. In the dark. Every time Ward kissed me, time and trouble pressed in on us so that I felt his hunger as if it were our last chance.

I tugged my hand away from Ward's back as Dad walked past, carrying the mail, much of it documents for his wares. Strange how precise his furniture's history was while he muddled his past. Everything, his family's disownment, his clan's abandonment, the miscarriage Mom had before us, his identity as Emory Silver, all of it bricked up behind his personal barrier. Even before Mom died, he was a man of secrets.

Ward hid things, too. A painful history, ideas about what he planned to do, he was private. Which was why I trusted him.

"Son-of-a-bitch." Dad held up a piece of paper. "Magpie, where's your brother?"

"He's not here." I gestured to the paper. "What's that?"

"A letter from Polly Tremblay. She must've dropped it in the mail slot overnight and Jonah found it. I suppose this here letter made him take off." Anger steeled his voice as he read aloud, "'Emory, I'm afraid my files on Jonah and Vayda have been stolen. You know how delicate that information is and if it falls into the wrong hands—'"

"I have them," Ward interrupted.

The cold filtering through me halted. He what?

Dad snapped up from reading the letter. "And what in God's name do you think you're doing with them?"

"She's been hanging around so much. I wanted to know what she knew. She's been making threats."

Darkness spread through the green of Dad's eyes. "Boy,

you stuck your nose where it didn't belong. What do you mean by making threats?"

"She said that Jonah and Vayda needed to be controlled, that they ruin people. And she said she needed to keep a promise."

"Jesus." Dad pushed his fingers through his hair and motioned for Ward and me to sit on the same fainting couch where I'd become Ward's girlfriend months ago. Bernadette whined and Dad lifted her into Ward's lap. "Polly didn't threaten anyone. She's on our side."

What? I popped my knuckles and released some of the uncertainty building in me. Months of being afraid of what she knew about us, of not feeling safe when she was around, and she meant us no harm?

"We don't agree, never have and never will," Dad went on. "You know that saying of keeping your friends close and your enemies closer? That's Polly. Because of the hell that fired up when Lorna got June killed, I always feared someone from Hemlock would come. Figured it'd be somebody from Brett's side since he took the fall."

"But she's not *Rom*, right?" I asked, and as much as I hated Sister Tremblay, I almost was hopeful to have another Romani nearby, even one who seemed to hate us.

"No. Southern bred and born, far as I know. Polly's intimidating as all get out, but if anything ever happened to me, she'd be there for you."

A million questions swam through my mind. Faster and faster. I felt like I was spinning and had reached the point of vertigo.

"Why Sister Tremblay?" I asked. "Rain was so mad when he found out she was here."

"I couldn't tell Rain 'cause I knew he'd get his fingers in the pie. I wanted them separate 'cause he never liked Polly's kin. He grew up with June, and there was bad blood. When we came here, I needed someone else who knew your mama well. Polly and your mama were friends of a kind. Lorna babysat Polly as a little girl. Back in the day we returned to Hemlock

SARAH BROMLEY

after Montana, she and Polly caught up. Lorna saw Polly has some *affinity* for emotions. Polly joined the convent in hopes of getting rid of it."

"Another empath?" Ward wondered.

Dad held up his fingers, indicating a little bit. "Let's call her sensitive."

"Then in the barn that night and the cuts on her face appeared," I ventured.

"She was angry with me. Rather than force emotion and energy outward, she clamps down on it so it can't hurt other people, only herself. She also picked up your emotions. It was too much for her."

So it *was* me who'd hurt Sister Tremblay. Me who'd caused gashes to open on her face and bleed. Another whoosh of dizziness coursed through me. Dad put his hand on my shoulder. I needed his steadiness to stop my mind's reeling.

"Polly's afraid you'll be like Lorna. All kinds of power, be it too much prosperity or love or the kinds of things you can do, corrupts if not guided. Lorna wanted you and Jonah to be so great that nothing could touch you, and that kind of thinking is how your mama wound up dead. Polly and I agreed it'd be best if you and Jonah had another empath close, and she wasn't to interfere. Telling you to mind yourselves doesn't teach you anything. That's where I fell short." He scoffed and shook his head. "All this time, I'd worried about protecting you two from others and didn't think to protect you from yourselves."

I didn't know what to say. If he had told me in October Polly Tremblay wasn't someone to be concerned about...But again, Dad's secrets created more damage than good, brought up more questions than answers.

"Why can't you be straight about anything?" I balled my hands. "About Mom? About Sister Tremblay? You don't lie, but you don't exactly tell the truth. You let us be wrong about people, to think they'd hurt us, when you know what they're really like. And if Jonah's gone after Sister Tremblay because he thinks the wrong thing about her—"

I cut myself off but still held Dad's eyes with mine.

He lowered his head. "I always figured it was safer to admit to the minimum than give away too much and regret it later."

I reached over to scratch Bernadette's ear. Dogs trusted people. Even if they'd been hurt by them, dogs defended their masters. Dad hurt us by not being up front with Jonah and me, but he did it with his heart in the right place. Everything I'd thought about Sister Tremblay, everything I'd witnessed since she'd come to Black Orchard, how could I know what was true? "Rain said Sister Tremblay's family turned Hemlock against Mom."

"Hemlock already didn't like her." Dad took off his glasses and slouched in a wingback chair. "What happened with the Forgettes only gave people an excuse to be open about how much they didn't care for your mama. Polly and I made peace enough over that. When we left Hemlock, she and Rain were the only people to know where we went. She came here because I called her last summer. I told her I needed someone who knew what your mama could do and would keep watch over you kids without getting emotional. The job at school came up, like it was fate."

Dad unfolded the letter from the nun and passed it over to me to read from where he'd left off.

It's too dangerous for you to stay in Black Orchard. Someone breached my files, and I've had threats left at my home. Someone here knows about you. They will use the information from my files as proof. Last night, I received a phone call from the Hemlock police. They're getting close, Emory. Now that you know they're coming, I expect you to do as you always have. Run.

An Art Deco lamp sizzled, and the light bulb shattered, throwing the lamp to the floor in a mosaic of rainbow glass and oiled bronze. Ward searched for a broom. I wound my hands together, pulse rising. Ward had her files, but she was right—someone had gone through them before.

Marty. He'd read about Jonah and me. He'd told me about it the night he took me to the park. Could he have now decided to turn in Dad to the police?

Jonah rushed into the storeroom. Breathless, cheeks flushed, his skin glistened with sweat. Heat swelled off him and spit like drops of water in a fire.

"Where have you been?" Dad demanded.

Jonah stammered, "I was gonna talk some sense into her or wipe her mind—"

"You didn't!" I shouted.

"No! I couldn't. I didn't." He went pale. "Sister Tremblay wasn't in her quarters at the church. I can't find her, can't even track her energy."

My father receded into a shaded corner and stared into a smoked-glass mirror. His reflection sagged—an overtired, underprepared ghost of a man. He pulled his hand into a fist and smashed the two-century-old mirror.

"*Dati!*" My body froze with a cascading cold. Static. Cool. Static. Cool.

"Get your coats," Dad ordered.

Ward bit his lip and tucked Bernadette under his arm, and then he followed me into the showroom where I shut off the lights and set the alarm. "It's the last time you'll lock up Fire Sales, isn't it?"

"Yes," I answered. "Trouble finds us and we run. It's our way."

His hand was in mine, then his arm around me, and a breathy whine escaped my mouth. Bernadette licked the tears winding down toward my chin before I wiped them away. There would be a painful talk with Dad tonight, something along the lines of how fast we can pack our suitcases. I didn't want to go.

I entered the storeroom where Jonah's heat spread like blood seeping under glass. "I could've stopped this. I could've fixed her memory."

"You wouldn't know what you're doing," Dad argued. "Now I need to tell you some things about that nun, but you leave people's minds alone. Got it? I don't want you being like your mama. She interfered with the natural order, and you're that woman all over again. Stop meddling."

Jonah stormed outside. That Dad adored Mom had always been obvious. It was clear now how disturbed he was by her abilities. All he ever asked was that we learned from her mistakes.

We hadn't.

During the drive, Dad hummed to a song that Ward's fingers tapped along with on his knee. No one attempted to talk, the air stifled by the unknown. We parked outside St. Anthony's of Padua, near the entrance. The steeple stretched high, the bell in the tower hushed but for a flutter of black wings that roosted within its archway. Jonah led us down a path that curved behind the columbarium through a courtyard of skeletal rosebushes. An apartment-like building was the convent where all the sisters lived. Dad already knew which unit was hers, but as we approached, a police sticker marked EVIDENCE sealed the door.

"That wasn't here earlier," Jonah declared. "I swear, *Dati*. I didn't do anything."

Dad withdrew a Swiss army knife from his pocket and cut the tape.

I grabbed his wrist. "What are you doing? You can't go in there."

"What's anyone going to do? Breaking and entering charges are the least of what I have to worry about right now," he muttered. He tilted his head at Jonah. "Do your thing. Open the door."

"Are you sure?" Jonah asked.

Dad nudged him forward. My brother laid his hand near the lock. I sensed his fingers burning, and the lock clicked, undone. Swinging the door open, we let ourselves into Sister Tremblay's cloister.

A cyclone spinning through her apartment would've done less damage. Barebones furniture lay turned over, busted. As a nun, she didn't have many possessions, but everything she owned was broken. Glass from a picture frame and a torn photo of the mountains in northern Georgia rested on the floor. The cross on the wall hung askew. Dried red blots splattered across the white paint on the walls and neutral carpet.

Blood.

More than the upheaval of the furniture and the stains, an echo of something far worse buried itself in my gut. Sheer rage.

Jonah covered his mouth as he gaped at the blood smeared on the wall and a vaguely woman-shaped break in the plaster. "I didn't do this. You have to believe me."

Dad steered him back to the front door. "I believe you."

Had this been Marty? I couldn't tell from the energy leaking out of the apartment's walls into my hands, the hate was too great and my own fear was too loud to make sense of what I felt.

"Hello?" a man called from the entrance. Monsignor. Waves of suspicion rode off him. It was strange to see him out of his cassock, his pants hitched up to his chest as he approached us. "You shouldn't be here."

"Monsignor, I'm friends with Polly, Sister Tremblay," Dad corrected himself. "What happened?"

"Get out or I call the police, Mr. Silver," Monsignor growled. "If you were her friend, you'd know she's in the hospital. Someone beat her this afternoon."

"My God," Dad whispered.

"Who did this?" Ward asked.

Monsignor stuck out his lower lip. "Can you account for your whereabouts today, Emory?"

Dad's spine stiffened. "I was at work. There are cameras at my shop that'll show I was there all day."

"All of you? Even your delinquents?" Monsignor asked, his attention falling on Jonah. "Whoever hurt her must've had the devil's rage to leave her in such a state."

I pushed past Monsignor, my legs wobbly as I hurried down the path through the courtyard and came to rest against the hood of the Chevy. People were hurt because of Jonah and me.

Ward and his dog. Now Sister Tremblay. We hadn't touched her, but someone had because of us. How was I supposed to live with that on my conscience? I twisted my wrists, and one of the Chevy's headlights cracked.

Freak.

As I scooted into the backseat, Bernadette lifted her head from where she lounged on the seat. I stroked her head, running my hands down her bristly fur when Ward slid in beside me and took my hand. "Guess you've had a lousy birthday."

I snorted. Talking about birthdays was trite.

Dad and Jonah came back to the car, Dad's hands shaking so badly he dropped his keys. As my brother handed them over, he asked, "Now what?"

"Monsignor's blowing smoke. I hope. Either way, we go home and pack," Dad replied.

Ward's hand squeezed mine. "Do I have time to get my stuff?"

"You're not coming, son. Maybe over summer, you'll get in touch with us, but…"

My throat closed on itself, and I leaned against Ward. He asked, "How will I know where to find you? Will you even let Vayda call me?"

Dad opened his pack of nicotine gum and clenched a piece between his teeth. "Are you sure you want this life? Even if I wasn't under investigation, the Mind Games cause enough problems that we leave wherever we settle. That's the reality."

Ward's hands pushed against his forehead. My feelers sank into my mind to avoid any of his thoughts. He nodded and sighed. "I've only been to Minnesota and Wisconsin. I wouldn't mind traveling more of the country."

Dad chuckled, a surprising sound amid the sadness as we rode through the streets of Black Orchard. Past the business district and neighborhoods, we traveled outside of town to the woods. As Dad turned onto our driveway, a vile trail of energy plugged my mouth with bitterness. Jonah dug his fingers into his armrest. That energy…evil. So similar to what was in Sister Tremblay's apartment.

Fresh tire tracks swerved from the driveway, ending with a Toyota parked by the barn.

"That's Chloe's car," Jonah said.

He didn't wait for the car's engine to sputter out before throwing open his door. Ward jumped out after him and rushed toward the barn, leaving Bernadette behind in the Chevy. As Dad and I climbed out of the car, an odor like rubbing alcohol but more incendiary clung to my nostrils and mixed with the evergreens.

"What's that smell?" I covered my nose.

"Gasoline." Dad pushed me toward the house. "Go call for help!"

"Are you crazy?" Help meant firemen and police would swarm our property. We'd have no chance to get away.

"Vayda, do as I say!"

Dad raced after Ward and Jonah into the barn, and I hurried behind, ignoring his order. Jonah was on the ground with Marty. Dust and hay stuck to their backs. Dad grabbed my brother under his arms, but Jonah flung him off, intent on keeping Marty down. A splash like water dumped onto the stone floor. Above in the hayloft, Chloe edged along the railing in her blue winter coat. The fumes burned my eyes as she poured out a red gas can.

"Get down from there!" I screamed, choking on the vapors.

Ward scrambled up the ladder to the loft and charged at Chloe. "What the hell are you doing?"

"They have to burn!" She swung the gas can, spraying Ward's feet with fuel before grabbing a second one. He jumped, and she doused the old wood and hay with gas that dripped from the loft to the ground below, close to where Jonah and Marty threw their knuckles into each other's bloodied mouths. As she balanced against the railing, the weak wood shifted from her weight.

"Come down! It's dangerous!" I climbed halfway up the ladder, but the rungs were brittle, one swinging loosely. The others wouldn't hold my weight. "Chloe, stop! This is insane!"

Ward closed in, beckoning her to hand over the gas can.

"You can't be this stupid. If you set this place on fire, it'll explode."

He took another step, and her eyes widened as she brought the gas can to her chest. Chloe tossed the gas can at him and stumbled only to slam against the railing. The rotted wood splintered behind her. She struggled to keep her balance. Ward grabbed her wrist, but gravity already had her. They plunged from the loft, falling twelve feet, thumping against the ground.

"Ward!" I yelped, scuttling over to their jumbled bodies

Chloe took the brunt of the fall as Ward landed on top of her. She angled her neck and groaned. He pushed himself up to sitting and held his head.

"Are you hurt?" I asked.

"Dizzy. Chloe broke my fall."

She rolled to her side, tried to sit, and slumped as she gasped for breath. "Don't think for a second that I'm done with you!"

She attempted to stand, but her ankle rolled, refusing to support her weight. She stretched a hand with broken fingernails to me. "You're dead, Vayda."

Her ankle gave, and she landed on her chest in the gasoline-wet dirt. It was almost sad to see her so far from the girl who'd invited me to scrapbook at her house.

"Take her outside," I said.

Ward scooped Chloe into his arms and carried her into the winter night.

God help her if she came near us again.

She wanted us to burn. Like my mother. She'd murder us if she could.

My attention was on Ward settling Chloe on the driveway when something hard and tall slammed into me. I hit the ground, my palms sinking into dirt wet with fuel. Adrenaline saturated my blood, energy bristling in my fingertips for an outlet. Marty recovered from plowing into me and moved to stampede Dad who doubled over and held his side.

"You sure you want to do that?" Jonah shouted, positioning himself between Marty and my dad. His fingers outstretched.

Gleaming amber light shimmered around his hands.

Shit!

Hot energy and gasoline was everywhere!

"*Dati*, get out of here!" I seized Marty with both my hands. A rush of coolness flowed into him, pushing him down the same way he shoved me into the snow in the park. He smacked the ground, stunned.

I'd blown nearly all the energy my body could handle. My head throbbed from the gasoline and currents coursing through me. Jonah reached to me with his burning hands, but I crawled back. "I can't touch you. This place will go up like a firetrap if we set off any sparks."

Panting, he gave an understanding nod and nudged Marty, muttering, "Get up, asshole."

Jonah and I escorted Marty out of the barn. As we walked out under the night sky, Dad shut off his cell phone. Sirens grew louder as they approached the house. I stared at my father, but he kicked a rock on the ground.

Everything moved too fast. Police cars and a fire truck barreled through the forest and parked wherever they pleased, and the air was thick with the odor of fuel.

At the sight of the lights, Chloe screamed. "You're done, Jonah! You'll never hurt anyone ever again! You'll never touch me again! All you'll do is burn!"

She struggled away from Ward's hold on her, limped past Marty and me, and shoved her hand into her pocket, producing a lighter.

A flick.

A plume of yellow and red flame burst in the dark.

Fire coursed up and down her legs. No one moved, too shocked perhaps, to understand what happened. So much fuel for the fire devouring Chloe's jeans. Even she stood spellbound, lips twisted, as she burned.

"Chloe!" Jonah ripped off his coat and plowed into her, forcing her to the ground.

"Get away from me!" Her voice was a ragged shriek and tears forged trails down the dirt on her cheeks. "I don't need you! I don't want what you made me become!"

Struggling against Chloe's flailing arms, Jonah wrapped his coat around her and eased her to the ground, patting down the flames. A paramedic pulled Jonah off Chloe. I overheard my brother tell them she did it to herself, but they shoved him away. No one listened. No one would believe we hadn't hurt other people.

Quickly, policemen sequestered each of us for statements. They placed Marty in a cruiser and paramedics strapped Chloe onto a stretcher in an ambulance. I didn't find Dad again until I noticed him standing before the stone house passing Bernadette over to Ward and studying the copper awnings and slate roof, the crumbling walls and creaking weathervane atop the barn.

"For a while, I forgot this isn't ours," he admitted.

"It might not be ours, but it's home," I told him. "I found some happiness here."

Dad nodded at the red and blue police lights. His hands, rough from all the work he'd done, cupped my face.

"Magpie, you and Jonah deserve better than always fearing that we'll be found." His voice broke as kissed my forehead. "You need to call Rain."

"*Dati*, don't." I slumped against the Chevy that brought us here from Georgia. The night burned with raw, cold wind.

"Officer," Dad said to a policeman, "my name is Emory Murdock. I'm wanted by the police in Hemlock, Georgia."

Chapter Twenty-Five

Vayda

I couldn't sleep.
When I eventually drifted off, the dream in my mind was hot.
Full of fire.

***

A glowing ember wanders through the darkness and spirals skyward, a solitary spark that snuffs out.

The shriek sears my mind, yanking me up from bed.

"Mom?" I call and clutch my blanket to my chest.

Silence.

A stirring at my neck freezes the baby-fine wisps at my hairline. My heart drums in my ears, and I hold my breath while my sight digs through the darkness for light.

"A nightmare," I whisper and sink back into the comfort of my pillow and burrow under my blanket.

"Vayda!"

Go away, Jonah! I cast the thought like a fishing lure toward his mind.

Reaching over to switch on my clock radio, the screen for the digital numbers is black. In the blue-black of night, my fingers track the cord still plugged into the wall. No power? Had a fuse blown? Happened all the time in such an old house.

"Sis, come on!" The oak door rattles on its hinges as

Jonah's fists batter the wood. "Wake up!"

I kick off the blanket and climb out of bed, feet on the cool pine floor. You'd best have a good reason—

Under the doorway, a curious red glow leaches into my room. I stop short. The knob on my door, normally smooth and cool, gives off a molten-iron heat. I wind my hand in my nightgown, pull open the door, and fall back.

The walls are swathed in amber, gold, and soot as flames whirl in my parents' room down the hall. I scream into a plume of smoke, "Jonah!"

I can't track him through the blaze. My fingers stretch in search of his energy. Heat and fire everywhere and none of it Jonah's natural warmth.

"Where are you?"

Through the smoke, Dad's shadow towers above a second bowed body—Jonah, thank God—and hoists him onto his shoulder, a hunter claiming the limp carcass of a stag.

"Vayda, come on!" he yells.

Flames snake along the floorboards. I'm numb and can't move, my mind stupid with one question. How can the house be on fire?

Fingers clutching hard onto my wrist jolt me from my trance.

"Stay low! Get down! Below the smoke!" Dad orders and I drop to my knees. Harsh coughs scrape my throat as I finger along the plaster wall. My eyes ache, nose stings, and I cover my mouth with the collar of my nightgown.

"We're near the door!" Dad's voice cuts through the crackle of burning wood.

Cool wind strips the sweat from my skin as the backdoor opens wide to the November night. Air! I can breathe! As I stumble to the side yard, my hands knead my eyelids to clear away the charred grit of sleep. Panting, I catch up with Dad and Jonah, spin toward the house, and scream from behind my smoky hands.

The night above the bungalow glimmers with auburn light. Flames sprint from the windows to the roof, and black grunge smears the white stucco. Moss smolders, cascading from the twisted cypress near the house, begging to ignite.

"Magpie, get back!" Dad bellows, his drawl a violent rolling.

Hacking grains of ash, I drop beside Dad and Jonah in the peach grove. I smell charcoal and singed hair.

The smell comes from me.

Jonah coughs as he kneels on the chilly ground. Dad places his hand on my brother's shoulder. "Deep breaths."

"Look!" I point to a crowd on the gravel road fifty yards from where we cower in the dark.

Neighbors, people we know from around town, mill together and gesture to the burning scaffold. More bodies zombie-trudge toward the house in bathrobes and ratty slippers.

"What happened?" someone calls, no more concerned than if asking whether anyone brought marshmallows for s'mores to the beach bonfire. "What started it?"

"How about divine intervention?" a man snorts.

My vision races from one flat face to the next. I send out a probing nudge, my feelers sifting through their thoughts. No pebbles of fear, no worry. Divine intervention? That would mean God was against us.

A fire truck lazes in the street, its siren unheard, lights swirling. A young fireman hops from the truck and eagerly unwinds the hose, nearly losing his helmet, but his superior stops him with a shake of his head.

"Why won't anyone help us?" I ask, gawking back over my shoulder at Dad. "What's wrong with them?"

"Shh." He covers his lips with his finger and pulls Jonah and me farther into the trees, whispering, "Don't move."

I twist away from Dad and again search the crowd. Only three of us, not four, are huddled away from the fire-crackled wood and plaster.

Where's Mom? Why isn't she with us?

I shake Dad's arm. "Mom made it out, right?"

Dad lowers his head. "I couldn't get to her. The fire..."

A keening whimper rises from my throat. Dad's callused

palm clamps over my mouth. His skin tastes of burnt wood and smoke. Our knees hit the unyielding Georgia clay, and my fingernails rake his skin. Tears drop from my face to Dad's hand, washing off the filth of the fire where they land.

Jonah's breathing wetly rattles, and his voice cracks. "Dati?"

Our father rises to his feet, his glasses reflecting the blaze. "Let's get to Rain's house. He'll know what to do."

I take in a view of the crowd. The young fireman, the only one compelled to help us, crosses himself.

"Burn in hell, Lorna! You thieving gypsy!" a woman damns my mother as two firemen laugh.

The word crudely whittles into my spine, slashed onto my bones, and forever marking me.

Gypsy.

***

Snow fell before dawn on Saturday, the day after my birthday. The wind blew so hard snowflakes stuck to the windows. Ward and I lay in my bed with the sky creeping toward sunrise.

He curled up behind me, his chest clammy against my bare back. I relaxed as he cradled me in his arms. His breath wheezy, he asked, "Are you okay?"

"Yeah." I was, at least right then. I wrapped my arms around his at my waist. I didn't want him to let go.

The house had been still, and his mouth gentle, shy, when we climbed into bed. My skin pulled taut, my heart whirring. I'd loosened his belt while the humming between my legs intensified.

"I want you, *gadjo*," I'd told him. My voice had been hushed, the words breathless between kisses. He'd held his breath, shaking as I unzipped his jeans. A spike of arousal had shot off him as his tongue flicked my lip. I'd pushed away my barriers, both those as an empath and those that claimed it wasn't right to be with a boy like him. I knew what I wanted, and this was my choice.

Our shirts flung to the floor, mouths hungry and hands in search of skin. He'd guided my touch where he wanted, but mostly, his fingers tread down my arms, across my bare abdomen, until they snuck lower on my hips.

The lamp by my bed had dimmed as I drew in curiosity and need, energy rising. I'd listened to my skirt fluff out on the floor and the chime of his belt when his jeans followed. His hands slid over my body, my eyelids flickering against the waves crashing over me. He'd taken his time to kiss me everywhere, my neck, the side of my ribs, my hips. It wasn't fair that I loved him. I hated him for making me love someone who could never be like me, yet I held him tight.

"I don't want to let go," I'd murmured.

He'd kissed my cheek and smoothed the hair on my forehead. "I'm staying, Vayda."

He'd reached over to my nightstand to the condom he'd laid beside my clock. Another smoldering ember sparked to life in my blood. Neither of us had breathed as he tore open the wrapper. As much as I wanted him, I'd been scared. Of his history because I knew I wasn't the only girl he'd been with, so what, if anything, did that mean? Of being "spoiled" or even too uptight. Of the change that would inevitably be felt between us.

I'd been scared because nothing in my life was certain—except that I craved closeness, and closeness was what I found when I lay beneath him. I'd felt him against me, then inside me.

I'd been used to touching everything, *feeling*, but it had been all my other senses that heightened. The sweat of our bodies against cold sheets, the creak of the bed's frame. How my room smelled of ghosts and lace and when the first ray of dawn bled through the curtain to glance off the steel ring in Ward's ear. A strange, new energy radiated through my body. I'd noticed it first when Ward's arms wavered, and at once, all my being escalated to drown the ache in me as he kissed me deeply, kissed me from the inside out.

Watching the snowfall as the sun crested the horizon, I felt his breath on my neck and his sweat on my skin.

He painted a lazy circle on my hip. His face was unlike any expression I'd seen from him before. No sorrow pinching his eyes. Content. Peaceful.

"I wonder when it happened," he murmured.

"When what happened?" I asked.

"When I realized I love you. There wasn't an exact time. It's all the moments of being with you and your weird Mind Games and your fucked up family and how I wouldn't take any of it back. Not one second."

I rolled over to lay my head against his chest. His arms around me were cool, the energy between us dreamy, sleepwalking. "I love you, too, Ward."

"Not calling me *gadjo* this time?"

"Not this time."

The phone rang. For a half-second, I hoped Jonah would answer, but he was sleeping hard in Dad's study last I'd checked. Annoyed and slipping into my clothes, I moved slowly as I retrieved the phone from the hall. The caller ID read Rain's cell phone.

"Darlin', I hope you weren't asleep," he said. "I'm in Milwaukee and heading straight to the police station, gotta stop at a bank first if I need bond money for your daddy."

Ward drew in his sketchbook as I sat on my bed. "Thanks, Rain. We owe you."

I hung up the phone and noticed Ward was still smiling dreamily. I kissed his cheek before heading into the bathroom, locking the door behind me. Too much to do today. Too much filling up my mind.

There was something more.

Energy loomed not in my hands but in my core, the bony nest of my ribs. It hurt. I grasped the sink's edge. Cold shocks of energy pinged off every metal surface, the light fixtures, the faucet, the towel bar.

My head ached as the muted thuds of Ward's thoughts from the other room battered my barriers like birds colliding with a window. My energy overflowed in a chilly gust, freezing the water dripping from the leaky faucet. "Get out of my damn head!"

Footfalls pounded the stairs, ascending the steps two, three, at a time. The door unlocked itself and flew open, and Jonah stood in the hall. Ward appeared beside my brother with his jeans hastily pulled on and hair disheveled. "Vayda, what's wrong?"

Jonah barely registered that Ward was beside him. The wariness on his face faded. Even as flares of energy zoomed from my fingers, my brother was calm. "Give us a minute."

Hesitantly, Ward backed away, and Jonah shut the door. On my knees, I couldn't control how fast my breath came. The axis of the room shifted and tilted to the right, woozy and shaking.

"You'll be okay, Sis," he promised.

My forehead rested on the tile floor. The grout cracked beneath my skin. Too much energy.

"Let it out." Jonah's voice was a chant, low and steady. "Don't try to hold back. Move it out of you."

A white-hot flare sprang from my fingers and cracked the plaster ceiling while the light fixtures burst with fire and smoke that quickly evaporated. I rolled to my side and held my stomach, crying out.

Empty. My hands were empty. My body was empty. No more energy.

"What was that?" Ward shouted. He opened the bathroom door and gaped at the cracked ceiling, the fractured tiles in the floor, and smoldering lights. "The hell did you do? Set off an atom bomb?"

"Of a kind." My brother sparked an orb in his palm and snuffed it in his fist. "Empaths feed on emotion. Mom told me some events involve so much emotion our Mind Games kind of flake out. Our energy surges. Fights. Injuries." He cocked his brow. "Anything intense."

My stomach dropped. I covered my face with my hair. "Is this what you and Mom talked about all those times?"

"Nah. I wanted to command my abilities like Mom.

Problem is I don't have much empathy. If I move something with my mind, I release my own feelings. I push energy. Vayda, you pull. It's why you care so much, why you calm people down and I rile them up."

So this was why such a blast ignited when Jonah and I joined.

"Why didn't Mom tell me?" I asked.

He shrugged. "Because she didn't know what to do with you. You're a magnet for emotions. I'm not. I don't have it in me. Mom created and released, and she was volatile. All you need is the right catalyst to push as much energy as you pull. Because you can do both, you are way more like Mom than I could ever dream to be."

Chapter Twenty-Six

Ward

U ntil I met Vayda, I'd never been serious about anyone. Hell, anything. For once in my life, someone wanted me around.

I was losing her.

The kitchen phone rang, distracting me from the caramel popcorn Vayda had mixed up a while ago, right in time to be hot after I dropped off Bernadette at Heidi's home. Vayda listened to the phone, and her voice was snowflake-fragile after the call ended. "Rain said they're stuck deciding charges for *Dati*. He mentioned fraud, arson. It's a mess. He's getting *Dati* released until he's formally arrested."

"*Dati* went off the radar for years," Jonah grunted as he popped the tab on a can of Coke. "The cops won't let him go."

I raised my brows, silently agreeing with Jonah. Why should Emory be trusted? I doubted he'd run again, but who knew what a guy would do for his family when cornered?

Vayda touched Jonah's shoulder. "Rain's good at what he does. He'll get *Dati* out."

After what she'd endured, she still trusted people. I wished I could be like that.

If Drake taught me much of anything, it was, "Don't fuck up." Easy to do when my only model was one mistake after another. Emory? He wasn't my dad, but he'd shown me a lot. Yeah, he'd fucked up, but he made the effort my own father never did.

I closed my sketchpad and unzipped my backpack when I noticed the manila folders I'd stolen from Sister Tremblay's office. I'd forgotten to hand over the files before we left Fire Sales.

"I should've given this to you sooner," I said and showed the file to Vayda.

She took a seat. "How'd you get it?"

"I told you I was a delinquent." I opened her folder. Several newspaper clippings and photos fluttered in the house's persistent draft. "But this isn't really a school file."

A picture was clipped to one newspaper article. A family, two teens with braces and a mother with dark hair grinned at Emory as he put his arm around her. They sat on the grass during a backyard barbeque. I kept the picture in my hand and scanned the smudged newspaper clipping.

Riot Breaks Out After Forgette Sentencing

Hemlock, GA—Police broke up rioters after a judge announced Lorna Murdock's sentence in the Forgette homicide trial. Judge King threw out the conspiracy charge in the death of June Forgette, citing lack of evidence. King also railed against the prosecution for "buying into archaic superstitions and rumors of witchcraft," regarding the assertion Murdock used psychic powers to force Brett Forgette to shoot himself. King told the court she would have dismissed the assault charge but agreed that Murdock was involved in a skirmish with Forgette and sentenced her to forty-eight hours in jail and a small fine. Murdock's sentence will begin after the Thanksgiving holiday.

A decided victory for defense lawyer Rain Killian turned into chaos as the gallery erupted into shouts defaming Murdock as a witch and threw chairs. Killian and Murdock's husband Emory, owner of Antiquaria on Poplar Street, shielded her from the crowd as they left the courthouse. No arrests were made.

Vayda shoved the article across the table and snapped, "Rain's a good lawyer if nothing else. She'd been charged with felonies and, because of him, got off scot-free."

"Scot-free. Yeah, right," Jonah muttered and sulked out of the kitchen, the slam of the door to Emory's office shaking the bones of the house.

Vayda took a deep breath and fanned herself. "Whenever he's mad, all this heat pours out of him."

So I'd noticed.

She flipped through the rest of the articles in the folder, an obsessive collection of every mention of the Murdocks in print—Emory's articles in antiques magazines, published lists with her and Jonah's names for their school's honor roll, tons of articles about Lorna's trial.

She closed the folder. "Thanks. For standing with us."

I touched her cheek. "I don't scare easily."

I kissed her before she had the chance to speak. The last say was mine this time.

***

Sister Tremblay's hospital room was one floor below the one where Jonah had stayed after Marty attacked him. Second time Marty Pifkin had put someone in the ICU. At least now he was in lock-up.

I stood in the doorway of Sister Tremblay's room. Coils of dark hair spread out on her pillow. Her upper lip stitched together, and the skin on her cheek was a mess of shiny purple, handprints visible on her neck. I passed the Shirley Jackson book I'd grabbed in the gift shop from one hand to the other. Maybe I should leave, let her recover before asking questions. By the time she was released, Vayda could be gone, Emory locked away.

"Go away, Ward," her voice rasped.

"I brought you this," I said and set the book on a table by her bed. "I need to talk to you about the Silvers."

"You mean the Murdocks."

I pulled up a chair by her bed and counted the mountains on the screen of the heart monitor. Nothing changed her pulse. Nothing surprised her even in her battered state.

"The Murdocks," I repeated. "Yeah."

Sister Tremblay licked her cracked lips. "Stay away from them. It's for the best."

I coughed, the rattling in my chest refusing to let go of its grip on me, and Sister Tremblay lifted a weak hand toward the pitcher of ice water and two cups on her bedside table. I poured myself a drink and waited until my cough eased up. "You know I can't stay away. Vayda needs help, Sister. I know you're here to help. I want to help, too."

"Then be prepared for the consequences. How long have you had that cough, Ward?"

"A long time," I answered. "It's not contagious if that's what you're worried about."

"The doctors don't know why you have it, do they? Has Vayda ever said why she enjoys being around you?"

Clearly, it was my sparkling personality.

"Do you give her peace?" Sister Tremblay pressed on. She waited, and when I didn't answer, she asked, "Do nearly all your thoughts and feelings stay your own and not invade hers unless you want her to know?"

"It's how we are together," I said. "And I'm not going to talk with you about why I'm with Vayda."

She studied my face with sad eyes. "You need to know there's more than you think. There's a word for people like you. Conduits. You have the ability to safely let the energy inside her come out."

"A lightning rod," I said.

She gave a slow nod. "Lightning rods are nearly impenetrable, but if they're not properly grounded, they'll corrode with time. They fail. The more you are with her, Ward, the worse the effects of all that energy passing through you will become."

The hair on the back of my neck stood on end, and this time Vayda hadn't caused it. My mouth went dry. When I was with her, my cough was worse. My lungs were tighter.

"Every empath eventually wills someone into becoming a conduit to make their lives more bearable. It sounds selfish, but most of the time, they don't even realize they've done it. They only know they need that person. For the conduit, the repeated exposure to energy and emotion finds a weakness and feeds on it. It is a danger of being a conduit. Wherever you are weakest, that's where the damage will have the greatest impact. For some, it preys on the mind or heart. Mental illness. Blocking arteries. For you, it is your breathing."

Vayda damaged me. She had no idea what she'd done, how destructive she was.

There had to be a way to lessen the toll. If there wasn't, was it possible I'd die?

"Wait a second," I argued. "I'm not the only person who can block Vayda. Her dad—"

"—isn't a conduit," Sister Tremblay interrupted. "Emory has merely become very skilled at deflecting anyone who pries into his mind or emotions. He had lots of practice, considering his wife. Lorna had another conduit."

My limbs felt heavy, the weight of everything Sister Tremblay had said slogging through my veins. I slouched in the chair. Muted. Stunned. How could I tell Vayda about my being a conduit? She already didn't accept what she was. She'd never forgive herself.

She would destroy me if I stayed with her.

I could take it. Or I prayed I could.

"You want to help Vayda and Jonah learn to control their abilities," I said. "Can't you help us figure out this conduit shit?"

The spikes in her pulse quickened. "I can't. Getting involved with them anymore...I can't."

"Sister, please." I was begging, didn't care that she was scared. "With Emory being questioned by the police, they need help. You promised him."

She backed into her pillow, but there was no place to hide. "That was before. Helping them can get people killed. I'm sorry, Ward."

"So what changed your mind?" I demanded. "I know Marty attacked you, but you're the only person in Black Orchard who knows what they are, who could help them. Please!"

"Marty?" Her forehead puzzled, and she drew her hand up to the bruises on her throat. "He didn't do this."

If it wasn't Marty…I had to take a deep breath. "Who did?"

She shuddered, and then a strange cry leaked between her lips, one sick, wounded, and terrified. "Like I said, Lorna had a different conduit. Someone close to her. Someone who loved her but couldn't be with her. Someone whose mind she wrecked."

I rose to my feet, the name already in my mind as I backed toward the door.

"Rain Killian."

***

I parked the Chevy in front of the Silvers' house and fished a cough drop from my coat pocket.

How could I tell Vayda? She'd never trust in anything, anyone again.

I didn't want her to be like me, broken beyond repair.

I spat the cough drop back into its wrapper, and despite the heaviness in my shoulders, I charged up the front steps of the house in the woods and flung open the front door. Neither she nor Jonah was in the living room or the study. They weren't in the kitchen, and it wasn't until I went up the stairs and found the attic ladder pulled down that I guessed where they were. Moving so fast my chest heaved, I climbed the stairs to the attic, intent on getting out what Sister Tremblay had told me, but I froze once I pulled my body up through the opening.

A bare light bulb glimmered too brightly against the sharp angles of the roof. Most of the room was unfinished wood coated with dust. Some old trunks, a couch that had to be at least two decades old, and a dressmaker's mannequin were all neatly tucked against one side. Vayda held an electrical cord. Identical wires ran up and down the length of the attic, feeding into the corners. Jonah had barely enough room to stand without ducking his head.

"What are you guys doing?" I asked.

"I've been hearing sounds for a while," Vayda admitted. "I thought it was birds and came up here to check it out."

I took some of the electrical cord, following the odd map where it tacked to the floor until I reached the corner. With a bit of fidgeting, I unearthed a camera set to peer down into the upstairs hallway. Other cameras were situated along the bedrooms, the stairway, and if I had to guess, most of the house was rigged.

"That's one hell of a security system on the house," I remarked. "Isn't it a little overkill to have cameras inside?"

"We don't have a security system," Jonah answered.

There were footprints in the dust, fresh footprints where the tread didn't match my boots or the soles of Jonah and Vayda's sneakers. Someone had been in the attic recently. "Vayda, how'd you guys wind up with this house?"

"It was Rain's," she answered. "He's owned it for years and said we'd be safe here after Mom died."

Oh, God. My chest ached. I threw down the electrical cord. "How many times have you told me you always feel like you're being watched? If you don't have a security system, who sees the feed from these cameras? Who could? Last night, when your dad said to call Rain, did you call him at home or on a cell phone?"

"What? Why? That doesn't make any difference. I called his cell phone because no one answered at his number in Hemlock. What's going on? You're freaking out."

Panic rose up my gut. I wanted nothing more than to get her and Jonah out of that house, get them somewhere safe, but they had to understand why. "No one answered in Hemlock because Rain was already here. How do you think he got to town so quickly? Marty had nothing to do with what happened to Sister Tremblay. It was Rain."

"That's insane," Jonah retorted. "He wouldn't do that. He's

our godfather."

I put Vayda's hands on the sides of my face. She was scared, and I hated being the person frightening her. I wasn't losing it. I knew exactly what was going on, but how to get her and Jonah to believe me? "Sister Tremblay told me everything. Read me. Get in my head. See if I'm making this up."

Shaking as our eyes locked, I felt mine dilate, opening wider to let her into my mind when a car door slammed outside. All three of us rushed to an octagon-shaped window where sunlight streamed into attic, lighting up every particle of dust in the air.

In the sharp light of the sunset, Emory climbed out of a green Buick and climbed the front steps with Rain right behind him.

Chapter Twenty-Seven

Vayda

The front door squealed as it opened. Dad moved slowly, an arthritic gait, the same that plagued him after moving furniture. The smell of furniture polish and coffee came off his shirt as he put his arms around me, and I listened to his heart's thudding. Jonah and Ward had hidden the attic ladder, and while Dad was good at keeping secrets, I wasn't so much.

Before my godfather entered the house, I blurted, "*Dati*, I think Rain's—"

"Shh." My father held the back of my head. "I know, Magpie."

I scanned his thoughts. He didn't think of Rain or Mom. Instead, I saw the jail cell with an unforgiving metal bench. Jonah cracked his knuckles, and his hands sparked and died, sparked and died, until Dad reached to hug him.

"Makes a mighty nice picture, don't it?" Rain lugged in his suitcase. He wore khakis and a red sweater. Good enough to negotiate his client's release from police custody on a Saturday evening. He moved to shake my brother's hand, but Jonah recoiled and bumped into Ward.

"You got a green face, boy," Rain remarked, pointing to Ward. "You okay?"

"I smelled something rotten, thought maybe it was coming from inside the attic."

Rain's mouth pursed. "Vayda, be a dear and wrestle up some coffee. Gonna be a long evening."

I steadied my hands enough to concoct a potent brew of coffee beans and water. As I brought out his mug, his fingers brushed mine and transferred a hate as black and sticky as tar.

"What happens next?" Jonah asked.

"Well, old Em's in a heap of trouble." Rain withdrew his cigarettes from his pocket, tapped one on his hand, and lit it. "He's been slow to learn you never trust the man whose girl you stole to make your own."

My hands cramped, currents stunted. To hear the words spoken hurt more than merely knowing. Dad's face rippled between anger and despair. "Lorna's dead, Rain. I lost her, too."

"You took her from me," Rain corrected him. "By all rights, your life should've been mine."

Jonah stepped forward, but Ward barricaded the path, shaking his head. Not a good idea to rush a demented man.

Dad massaged his temples and asked, "If you've held a grudge for twenty-odd years, why didn't you leave my ass to rot in jail?"

"'Cause, frankly, jail's too good for you." Rain propped one foot on the coffee table. "You did good enough by Lorna, but after y'all returned to Georgia, I'd had enough. You had a wife, kids, everything I wanted, and you rubbed it in my face. Lorna and I were close, but she'd never leave you."

I locked eyes with Dad who glanced to my brother, thoughts fast. *Jonah, get your sister out of here. Take Ward with you.*

I wanted to scream that we weren't leaving without him, but my father couldn't hear me.

As if sensing my reluctance, he ordered, *Do what I say!*

Jonah drew his finger along the side of a lamp on an end table. With a flick of his wrist, the lamp careened off the table, shattering. His fist met the side of Rain's face, forcing him back, head bobbing, but Rain reached into his waistband. A glint of metal. The butt of a pistol caught Jonah in the temple. He dropped to the floor, cradling his head.

I dove to help him, but Dad pulled me back. "I have to get to Jonah!"

Against my struggling, Dad tightened his grip. "Vayda, don't think for a second he wouldn't shoot you!"

I stopped squirming and yet I wanted to break out of his arms to take care of my brother. My twin.

Ward crouched beside Jonah and raised his hands in defense as the safety on the gun clicked. Rain stood over them, aiming. "Are you sure your Mind Games are faster than a bullet?"

Dad angled himself between Rain and the boys. I leaned against my father and yelled, "Rain, are you out of your head? Mom wouldn't want you to hurt anyone."

"Doesn't matter." Rain cracked his neck. "As your daddy said, Lorna's dead."

He shoved Ward, and his shoe drove into Jonah's left side. My brother howled, and my ribs reacted to the crunch of his bones still healing from Marty's attack two months before. My lungs fought to suck in breath. Rain whipped around with the gun and aimed at Dad.

A putrid fog came off my godfather, spoiled like a corpse in a marsh under the July sun. I retched and grabbed the wall for support. Breathing in through my nose, out through my mouth.

Ward put his arm around me. "She's sick. Let me take her to the restroom."

Rain considered the clamminess of my brow. "Hurry on up. We've got important matters to discuss."

In the bathroom, I could breathe. My skin was cool, and my mouth tasted of metal, though my head was clear. Ward shut the door and climbed on the sink to work on the lock on the half-sized window above.

"I'll open this window, and you'll go for help," he whispered. He exaggerated his cough as he banged against the corners of the window. The heel of his palm slammed the lock, and he muttered, "I hate old houses. Between the ghosts and the bad plumbing, nothing works."

A fist thumped on the door.

Ward scuttled off the sink. "Vayda's still sick."

"Too bad," Rain's voice came through the door. "Wash up

and come out."

Again on the sink, Ward jimmied the window while I mocked the sounds of cleaning up. Time. We needed more time. Another bang on the door, the old hinges yielded to the force of my godfather's shoulder, and Rain rushed into the bathroom. He yanked Ward's shirt, toppling him from the sink.

"Leave him alone!" I chased after them as Rain nudged the gun into Ward's spine and marched him down the hall.

"Boy, you're a hassle!" he scolded and shoved Ward beside my father on the couch.

Queasy again, my head lolled. Too many people in the room, too much emotion sliding from their minds. I sensed Jonah probing my thoughts as he lay on the floor, but neither of us could focus. Between Dad's concern and Ward's leapfrogging from escape plan, discard, escape plan, all I had was hissing static in my brain.

If only I could bear down and heave away the energy barreling over me.

"I'm done messing around." Rain grabbed Dad and steered him toward the front door, stopping to pull up Ward from the couch. "Everybody outside."

Energy scorched my palms as I touched Jonah's back. He coddled his ribs while I helped him stand. The pain he was in—overwhelming and brain-blinding. He couldn't be much help.

"My ribs are broken." He cringed. A sputtered groan. "I can't breathe."

Rain opened the front door. "Come on now, darlin'. I'm waiting on you."

I scowled as my shoulders took as much of Jonah's weight as I could. We lurched down the steps onto the gravel drive. Winter's dusk shaded our faces. The snow had begun to blue. Rain cursed below his breath and hauled Ward by the arm, prodding Dad's shoulder with the barrel of the gun. "Woods. Now."

Dad set a long glance on Jonah and me and lumbered around the barn into the woods. The snow was over two feet deep even fifty yards in the trees. The cuffs of my jeans and shoes were soaked, and the cold burned my skin. There had to be a way out.

Ward abruptly threw his entire weight into Rain, knocking him to the ground. I darted toward them, but Jonah snagged my sweater. His teeth ground tight as he fought against pain.

"Let go!" I slapped my hands against his, but he wouldn't release me.

Ward and Rain wrestled in the snow until a sharp echo of gunfire cracked against the sky. I screamed, and everything sounded muffled. No one moved. I wasn't sure if my heart even beat. Rain climbed off Ward, who was on his hands and knees in the snow. My godfather's hand shook as he aimed the pistol at Ward. "Next time you take me on, you're dead."

Ward wiped blood from the corner of his mouth, and Dad held out his hand to help him stand. My ears were still ringing from gunfire.

Tracking Dad through the woods, Rain mused, "Lorna made trouble for herself as I reckoned she would. I whittled down those charges against her and wanted y'all good and relaxed."

Dad stepped over a fallen branch. "Then you succeeded. We honestly thought we'd go to Vermont and start over again."

Rain paused as he waited for Jonah and me to catch up, his face warmed by the pink lemonade-tones of the lowering sun, and gold rays reflected off his hair.

"Lorna confided in me that your marriage was in a thorny patch and she'd been sleeping on the veranda." He tilted his head from side to side. "Easy enough to start a fire in your bedroom. Pour in some gas around that window that never locked too well. You know, the one you were supposed to fix but never got around to since you worked all the time. I lit a match, walked away, and waited. My only fault was that you, Em, were supposed to be in that bed."

Dad staggered. "You hated me that much? My wife is dead because of you. My children lost their mother because you messed up. You've already hurt me worse than if you'd killed me."

I stumbled on a tree branch. The nerves in my hands were

filaments waiting for an electrical arc. All this time we'd been so afraid of someone exposing us, and yet the one person we trusted most to keep our identities hidden was our greatest threat.

Jonah stopped to catch his breath. "You could've killed us all."

Rain released Ward and approached my brother. He slipped the hand not holding the gun under Jonah's arm to give me a break from holding up my brother's bones and said, "Son, losing you was fairer than seeing your mama with your daddy. Still, should've been your mama with you kids on my porch."

My brain blinked, thoughts muted, followed by the crushing of my heart. He was right. Mom never would have ruined her marriage, but Rain knew her secrets. For good and bad, we were comfortable with him.

An owl circled overhead, and the wind picked up as the sun skulked lower. Rain leered at Dad, rambling, "Watching your face when I sent that newspaper with Lorna's photo your way was priceless. Oh, how you squirmed."

Dad trudged twenty more feet into the woods and rested in a clearing. "If this is about you and me, why don't you let the kids go? They aren't part of this."

Rain licked his lip. I didn't like that crooked gleam in his eye.

"Here's the deal, Em. I've got nothing to lose. We'll say it was questionable ethics but I'm banned from practicing law down south. Something needs to change, and I've got unfinished business." He appraised me from head to toe. "Vayda, I saw you and your brother out in the woods. You could work Mind Games in my favor like your mama did." He half-smiled. "Maybe you can pass for your mama in other ways, too."

"Stay away from my daughter!" Dad roared.

Ward peeled away from walking with Dad, fist ready, and Rain slapped him. "Boy, you gonna stop me? I've reviewed your past, how your daddy preferred drugs to you. You got a criminal record that'll fuck up your life. No one would give a shit if you disappeared."

Rain aimed the gun at Ward's chest and backed him up near Dad. Ward shut his eyes and his mouth moved in a voiceless prayer.

"On your knees, Em!" Rain shouted.

I fell on my knees.

Dad knelt, his voice vibrating as he begged, "Rain, these kids have no one without me. They need me."

Rain twisted Ward's arm and held the back of his shirt, forcing the gun into his hand and focused it on Dad's chest. "Too late, Em. You're already dead."

I grabbed my head, peeking through my splayed fingers as I waited for gunfire. Dad shared a glance with Ward, his chin trembling. My hands tingled with sorrow seeping from broken hearts, broken souls. Ward struggled to balk even with Rain pushing the gun in his hand to Dad's head.

The wind froze the tears streaming down my cheeks. There had to be some way to stop more death, more destruction.

"Come on, Rain," Jonah yelled, holding his ribs. "Haven't you done enough?"

Rain shook his head, intoning behind Ward's ear. "Kid, you're gonna shoot this man and never know daylight again."

I whipped around to stop the sickness rising in my gullet. My eyes drew skyward to the peaks of the evergreens. The hair on my arms and back of my neck prickled as new static snaked around my body. I rotated in a circle, bouncing from one treetop to the next.

A clearing marked by seven pine trees.

Jonah's spot.

I checked with Dad who almost imperceptibly nodded. Somehow, he knew Jonah had been here before.

"Come on, boy," Rain urged. His hand squeezed Ward's over the gun.

"I can't," Ward protested and jerked backward, the gun wobbling in his grasp.

"Sometimes you gotta put an animal outta its misery," Rain muttered. He shoved Ward and set his finger on the trigger.

"No!" I howled over the blast of gunfire.

Ward hit the ground. I dashed toward him through the snowdrifts. Scarlet drops speckled the snow. He grasped his left arm around the bicep, and dark blood seeped through the cracks between his fingers.

"How bad is it?" I asked.

He couldn't answer, whimper-breathing through his teeth. Frantic, I shredded apart his flannel sleeve. A deep gouge traced his muscle's curve where the bullet carved his skin. Dad broke away from Rain and clasped Ward's arm in his hands, putting on pressure to stop the blood loss.

Jonah yelled, spilling out the pain of his fractured ribs. His hand pushed through the snow, sinking to touch the earth. My hands were red with Ward's blood. Tears stung my eyes, and numbness, burning and frozen, zipped through my fingers and hands, into my wrists and to my elbows. The lines in my palms, my fingerprints, all quivered as a storm brewed. I took a breath and rested my hands on Ward's shoulders, my back arching as the current moving through him collided with my cold.

Pulled it inside me.

"Vayda, what the hell?" he cried as a spasm shook every muscle on my skeleton.

Hundreds, thousands of static pops crackled from his body to my hands and condensed in my core. A fire kit in my gut.

Loaded with energy and shuddering, I staggered toward Jonah, falling to my knees. He steeled himself against the ground. His breath heaved as he found clean strokes of heat trapped beneath the earth's surface. He lifted his face, the black light in his eyes glittering while his body trembled.

The electricity in my hands nudged my fingertips. One way or another, the energy I'd accumulated, more than I'd ever before drawn into my cells, had to dispel.

Is this safe? Jonah asked.

Does it matter?

God, please don't let us kill ourselves.

"Get down!" I yelled to Dad and Ward and laced my fingers with Jonah's.

The electrified ball inside me exploded like a star in its millionth year of dying.

One, two, three strikes of lightning streaked out from our clasped hands.

Dad knocked over Ward and their bodies were sheltered by the snow. My breath came in heated, stuttered gasps, but the awe streaming off Dad and Ward fed the current, trailing over the ground and absorbed by my knees.

Four, five, six more lightning strikes rocketed from the union of my brother's hands with mine.

Jonah's heat and fire, my cold and ice—they stumbled over each other, obstructing the path for release before relenting and coming together as a singular blast of silver light. Branches and icicles plunged from the trees and speared the ground.

Seven, the last bolt of lightning.

The breaker crashed through Rain. He careened through the air and landed in a crumpled ball. Jonah's hand slipped from mine, and he slumped forward. My head was so heavy. Torrents of coolness gushed out of me, unstoppable, a river undammed as I collapsed in the snow.

***

Fingers untangled the knots from my scalp to the ends of my hair. My ears rang. I opened my eyes to the dark sky. Craning my head toward the ambulance's lights wrenched my neck. I sprawled on my back near the barn. Jonah reclined on a blanket beside me. Bandages wrapped his palms, and his cheeks flushed with sunburn as he unwound another knot from my hair.

"What happened to your hands?" I asked.

"Burns, like I held my hand on a hot stove. The paramedics need to bandage your hands, too."

Crimson splashed my palms. Similar burns marked the top of my hands, though these were the same size and shape as Jonah's fingers.

"You were releasing energy before you took my hands."

His voice was hoarse. "I gave you a boost and waited for what you could do."

"*Dati* and Ward?" I asked.

"They're fine. The paramedics want to take Ward to the hospital for his arm, but he refused to go until you were awake. *Dati*'s bruised but okay."

I leaned against my twin as I sat up. A fire truck, two ambulances, and several police cars parked between the barn and the house. Rain was belted onto a stretcher, unconscious and wearing an oxygen mask as he was loaded into the hull of an ambulance. A paramedic smacked the door, signaling the driver to take the patient to the hospital.

"Is he gonna make it?" I asked.

"Not sure. They think he had a hell of a fall and a coronary." Jonah gave me a one-armed hug then cringed. "The energy release messed him up. We did that to him."

I wasn't sure how to react: corrupted and relieved.

"He would've killed us," I said.

"I don't like knowing we could end someone's life doing what we do. We need to be more careful."

This, coming from Jonah of all people.

"Sis, I…We…" My brother was lost for words. "I'm sorry. I'm so sorry."

I stood and needed a moment to adapt to the tilt my headache gave the earth. Ward waited on the steps as a paramedic finished taping his arm. He limped down the stairs to join me.

"Hey." He coughed and embraced me. "You're up."

"Why are you limping?" I asked.

"My knee got messed up when I hit the ground." He pointed at the sky. "If you wanted a light show, why didn't you come onto the roof with me? The northern lights are beautiful tonight."

Sure enough, magenta and chartreuse trailed across the black sky. Breathtaking even with the lights of the emergency vehicles blinking at the corner of my sight.

Dad edged away from speaking with an officer. He clapped

his hand on Ward's shoulder and then took my hand. "You okay?"

"I think so."

"Magpie, maybe it's time you and Jonah live openly with what you can do. With more eyes on you, you'll be more aware of the consequences. Something to think about."

"Maybe." My head was like a basin full of warm, sudsy water. Relaxed, drowsy. I wasn't ready to think about what tomorrow would bring, let alone beyond.

Ward gestured to the police cruisers. "Do you have to go back to jail?"

Dad shrugged. "I haven't officially been charged with a crime. That could happen Monday. Don't know, don't care tonight. For now, I'm gonna ride with Jonah to the hospital 'cause he needs those ribs checked out. Afterward, I'm bringing home some Thai food, taking a shower, and going to bed. Emory Murdock's a real lively bastard, isn't he?"

I grinned as he called to my brother who waited by the barn, examining his bandaged hands. Frowning, Jonah lowered his hands to his sides. He dragged his feet toward the Chevy, his arm brushing mine as he passed. Nothing. No sparks from our tinder rubbing together. Just a brother clumsily bumping into his sister.

Ward drew me into another hug. He put his hands on my shoulders and moved to kiss me but stopped when a spark flared between us, stinging our lips.

"Ouch!" He touched his mouth. "There you go, shocking me again. What am I gonna do with you?"

My lips hovered over his.

"Get used to me."

Chapter Twenty-Eight

Vayda

Three weeks later

"I always wondered if Lorna's kin was gonna turn up someday. Guess someday's come."

I ran my finger along the top of Mom's gravestone. Underneath a bower of Spanish moss and cypress trees, an elderly woman sat on a marker shaped like a bench and stuck her hand into a bag of birdseed as a flock of pigeons pecked near her shoes. The southern sun caught her eyes, a glossy, piercing blue, and her drawl was kindly.

"You're the Murdock girl, ain't you? You got enough of Lorna's face, but you ain't quite the same." She scattered some more seed for the pigeons. "Plus, I reckoned you're her daughter since it was all over the papers that your daddy has come back to answer some questions about running off like he did. What charges did they get him on?"

None of your damn business, I wanted to say, but instead murmured, "None yet. He'll get in trouble if he leaves the area."

The woman gave a dove-like coo and snickered at two birds squawking. "Some would say the man's already been in prison, all things considered."

If not prison, at the very least the holding cell at the Hemlock police station where he stayed between interrogations. Dad wasn't under arrest, only came down to Hemlock for a voluntary interview with the police. We shouldn't have been here more than a day or two, long enough for Jonah and me to take in what we'd left behind. The days stretched to too many, and I had no idea how much longer it would be before Dad would leave Hemlock.

Again, I reached over the short wrought-iron fence surrounding only Mom's grave and wiped away a clump of clay from the granite etched with her name. The location at the back of the Hemlock cemetery deterred vandals—not well. Her marker was dirty with what appeared to be crusted egg yolk. The rose Dad laid on the stone only two days ago wilted and lost much of its brilliant red.

Something glinted in the sparse sunlight filtering through the cypresses, and I dug through the moss to find a silver coin. And then another.

All around Mom's grave were dozens of coins.

"If people hated my mother so much, why's all this money by her grave?" I wondered aloud.

Though my question wasn't directed at her, the bird woman replied, "'Cause for as much trouble as your mama was, she helped enough folks, and they're still hoping she can do some work on their behalf from the other side."

I reached into my pocket, found four quarters, and laid them out in a row before her headstone. A little string-pulling from Heaven would be nice about now.

The woman nodded toward the footpath in the graveyard. "My guess is that boy ain't here to pay his respects, not with the way he's eyeballing you."

In spite of the sorrow in standing over my mother's grave, I warmed at the sight of Ward ambling down the walkway, Bernadette trotting a few paces ahead of him. My body shuttered back a cry, my arms winding around him. We hadn't talked in days, not until yesterday when I woke up and found myself alone in a motel in Georgia. I shouldn't have been alone. Jonah was eerily quiet since the night Rain would've killed us all, not sleeping, not reading. Staring off blankly with so many barriers blocking my feelers. I'd gone to bed while he stayed awake in a dark motel room with only the lights from the parking lot casting rays through the blackness. He was gone by dawn and so was the Chevy.

Ward hadn't hesitated when I asked if he'd drive down from Wisconsin.

"You were supposed to wait for me at the motel," he reminded me. "But I stopped by the police station and talked to your dad for a bit. He says you need to go home and Hemlock isn't home anymore."

"It's not," I agreed.

"Your dad'll get released soon. Jonah will show up. Promise."

Such a bad liar, Ward couldn't even convince himself. I wanted to believe him. I wanted to believe the mess of the last two years could be wiped away with a few days of answering questions for the police, but no matter where we went—Hemlock or Black Orchard—there were consequences.

"How'd you know where to find me?" I asked.

"Your dad told me where the cemetery is. He figured that's where you'd be. Are you ready to go?"

I held up a finger. "One second."

He watched from the footpath, his hands deep in the pockets of his leather coat protecting him from the breeze. Bernadette lay on the ground, face between her front legs as if bowing her head while I stood over my mother's gravesite. Currents of longing swelled within my hand, and I pressed my fingertips to her headstone. A crackle, a flare of cold fire.

Energy wasn't created or destroyed, only transformed.

***

A few days after coming home from Georgia, I still wasn't ready to go back to school, but I was restless. Sister Tremblay had gotten my suspension lifted and grades restored, but I didn't care. I spent time in the kitchen, kneading dough for bread. Bernadette wagged her tail while I stirred an egg yolk to improve her coat's shine. How Ward didn't succumb to that dog's big eyes was a mystery. Hopefully he'd forgive me for sneaking her a bit of cheese. The kitchen was one of the few rooms not boxed up for the move Dad planned. A Victorian renovation in downtown Black Orchard had come up for sale before we went to Hemlock.

The red light on the answering machine flashed, but I hadn't checked the messages. The only numbers that called were from news stations that had gotten wind of Dad's story. Some producer wanted to film a special for an investigative report show, put it on the air in time for Rain's murder trial right around Halloween. I was all but sure they'd bring up Mom's abilities and her tarot business. At least Ward's family and Sister Tremblay already vowed they wouldn't speak to the media.

Strange when you walked past a phone and it rang.

"Vayda, I wanted to check in," Sister Tremblay's voice came over the answering machine. "If there's anything you need from the food market, let me know."

Another call from Sister Tremblay, Polly, as I still needed to adapt to calling her. She'd been checking on me, even helped pack some boxes since Ward and I returned from Georgia. She kept her distance enough, but Dad was right—she wanted to help. I should've called her back. Maybe I would later. Ward tensed around her. Months of her creeping around had done nothing to help in the trust department, but perhaps both Ward and I needed to work on accepting help. If Dad didn't come back from Georgia soon, I'd need more than help from Polly and Ward's family. The police in Hemlock were taking their time interviewing Dad, but he'd come home again before long. He had to come home.

Ward stood behind me at the counter, sliding his hands up the front of my body, and crossed his arms over my chest. I swiveled my head over my shoulder to kiss him, but he stopped me with his cheek.

"You'll be okay, Vayda," he said in my ear. "I swear."

He coughed hard, and I poured him a glass of water. "What about you? That cough of yours isn't getting any better. Did you ever find out what's causing it?"

With a sip of water, he shook his head. "No idea. Don't really care either. Whatever it is, it's not going away."

I saw something flicker in his eyes, some doubt.

"*Gadjo*, is something wrong?" I asked.

"I'm fine."

Now I had my own doubt, fed by the strange way he regarded me. I opened my mouth to speak, but he laid his finger over my lip. "Shh."

His fingertip slipped beneath my mouth and raised my chin. I held on to him as he kissed me. A kiss so deep it took away his breath.

Afterward, I paged through the mail. More than ever, we had mail addressed to the Silvers. Vayda Silver wasn't me. Neither was Vayda Murdock.

Stuffed between advertisements and interview requests, I held an envelope from Jonah addressed in a script I could mimic as well as he could mine. I sought him out. I wasn't angry with him for leaving me in Georgia. He'd been so quiet since the night Rain tried to kill us, and if Jonah needed to work out something, he'd do it on his own. But, damn it, we'd never gone so long without speaking. He had to be in this world somewhere, and I couldn't believe that I wouldn't be able to find him. My muscles grew warm, and a heavy, iron door forged from a hammer and fire blocked me.

Not yet, Sis.

Where are you?

The unrepentant fire of Jonah's mind dimmed to cold ash.

He needed more time. There was nothing I could do but wait, keep trying, and pray he'd open up to me again.

I opened Jonah's envelope to find a photograph of Mom. The picture was one I saw hundreds of times. Dad kept a framed copy on his desk at our old house in Hemlock. A black-and-white portrait showed Mom's cat-like smile as she peeked out of the corner of her eye. The edges of the picture were soot-stained and charred. Something else was in the envelope. My mother's metal hair clip with red flowers and green stones.

I didn't dare touch it, but I did take out my brother's note, which simply read: *They survived the fire.*

By the middle of the night, the house was too quiet, my bed too cold, and I couldn't get back to sleep. Ward was lying in bed with me when I drifted off, but he was gone. A quick check in Dad and Jonah's rooms, more habit than anything else, proved they were gone as well.

I wasn't ready for this. I didn't want to be alone.

The living room was amber with the light from a single lamp. Ward slept on the couch, a blanket over his legs and a book of crossword puzzles open on his chest. As if sensing me, he stirred.

"What are you doing awake?" he asked.

"Can't sleep, *gadjo*," I said.

He patted Bernadette sleeping at his feet. "God, do I know what that's like."

He climbed off the couch, taking the blanket with him, and together we curled up on the floor in front of the wood stove. Too many shadowed corners and empty rooms. I hung onto him, and his lips grazed my neck before he gathered some kindling. The winters in Black Orchard were long and bleak. The dark months would end, but I was still cold. Terribly cold. Ward and I took turns striking the flint and steel together until the sparks ignited and became a steady fire we couldn't afford to let die out.

ACKNOWLEDGEMENTS

This book came to be with the help of many people. I am so grateful to them.

My agent, Miriam Kriss, whose continued passion and dedication are fierce. I trust my word gremlins to you.

My editor, Courtney Koschel, for her guidance and trust, for pushing me in just the right places. My publisher, Georgia McBride, for taking a chance. The Month9Books crew, especially Lindsay Leggett and Cameron Yeager, for their time in making this book what I always hoped it'd be, and Jaime Arnold, who is such a powerhouse.

I can't write without my elements. Windy Aphayrath, you made the crazy girl crazier. Amanda Bonilla, we held hands and skipped down this road together, and hasn't it been quite a journey? Cole Gibsen, our timeshare in "the Pit" has gone up for sale. Thank you so much for agreeing to meet Shawny and me that day, even if you did sit with your back to the wall in case we were certifiable. Shawntelle Madison, birthday parties can change everything. Hillary Monahan, a kindred spirit, you push to me to be better.

Heather Brewer who took me under her dark cloak.

Heather Reid who is always there with words of wisdom and love.

The YA Scream Queens—Cat Scully, Courtney Alameda, Dawn Kurtagich, Hillary Monahan (again!), Jenn "J.R." Johansson, Lauren Roy, Lindsay N. Currie, and Trisha Leaver—because we need more spooky.

So many people who helped me as I wrote Magpies and in the time getting ready for the book to be shared: Christina Ahn,

Wolf and Gypsi Ballard, Sandra Fenton, Maria Fernandez, Valerie Gerbus, Emily Hall and Main Street Books in St. Charles, Missouri; Shaun David Hutchinson, Antony John and the coffee gab crew, Beth and Gabrielle Jones for more coffee, Sara King, Jackie Morse Kessler for her mentorship, Jamie Krakover, Andrew Lovitt, Jenny McCormick-Friehs, Meredith Maresco, Marie Meyer, LS Murphy, Bebe Nickolai, Rachel Nygren, Kelly Oswald and Mary Beth Pilcher, Rachel Rieckenberg, Dorothy Rush, Judi Tabb, Dawn April Terviel, Dawn Thompson, Dana Waganer, Judy Williams for letting me write in junior year English class instead of taking notes, Melissa Williams, Erich Zwettler, all of Jabber Jaws, the BookYArd, Walter, David, Annika, Gwendolyn, Adrian, and Brendan.

For Jack and Lucille Powell. Lucy, I have known you longer than I knew my own mother, and I am so grateful for all that you do, all you say, and all your love.

For Ericka Zwettler. There is no better big sister. Ever.

And Tim. There was always Tim. Dad was right when he said you're like Superman.

For my parents, Sharon and Richard, and my brother Michael. I love you. See you on the other side.

SARAH BROMLEY

Sarah Bromley lives near St. Louis with her husband, three children, and three dogs. She likes the quiet hours of morning when she can drink coffee in peace, stare into the woods behind her house, and wonder what monsters live there. When she's not writing or wrangling small children, she can be found volunteering at a stable for disabled riders.

OTHER MONTH9BOOKS TITLES YOU MIGHT LIKE

BRANDED

INTO THE FIRE

PREDATOR

CROWN OF ICE

ENDLESS

PRAEFATIO

THE LOOKING GLASS

OF BREAKABLE THINGS

FIRE IN THE WOODS

LIFER

A SHIMMER OF ANGELS and A SLITHER OF HOPE

SCION OF THE SUN

CALL ME GRIM

GEORGIAMCBRIDE.COM

SHE WILL DISCOVER A TRUTH
THAT SHOULD HAVE REMAINED HIDDEN

BONE SEEKER

BRYNN CHAPMAN

KIT FORBES

SHADOWS
FALL AWAY

Falling in love with a proper Victorian girl from
1888 London may be the least of his problems.

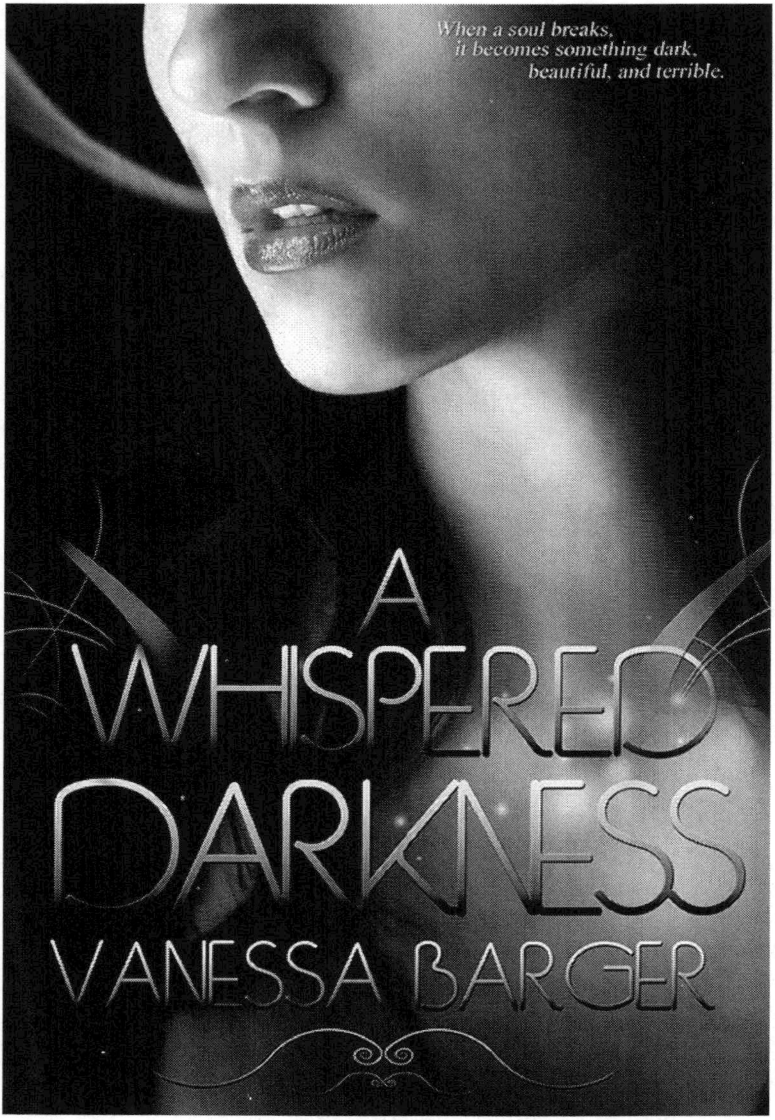
When a soul breaks,
it becomes something dark,
beautiful, and terrible.
A WHISPERED DARKNESS
VANESSA BARGER

ELIZABETH HOLLOWAY

CALL ME
GRIM

Find more awesome Teen books at Month9Books.com

Connect with Month9Books online:

Facebook: www.Facebook.com/Month9Books

Twitter: @Month9Books

You Tube: www.youtube.com/user/Month9Books

Blog: www.month9booksblog.com

Request review copies via publicity@month9books.com